ALONE

Beth Ann's Story of Survival

By:

C. M. Hollerman

Apoc Publishing mass market 1st Edition: December 2016
Updated: February 2017

Published in the United States by:

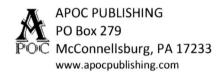 APOC PUBLISHING
PO Box 279
McConnellsburg, PA 17233
www.apocpublishing.com

Cover photo by Ryan Ubry;
Cover design by Jonathan Hollerman and Rob Williams

ISBN: **0692814892**
ISBN 13: **978-0692814895**

Note to Reader:
Although every precaution has been taken to verify the accuracy of the information contained herein, the author and publisher assume no responsibility for any errors or omissions. No liability or responsibility is assumed for damages, losses, or injuries that may result from the use or misuse of information or ideas contained within. This book is published for entertainment purposes only and is not a substitute for specialized instruction with qualified professional consultants.

Dedication

This book is dedicated to my husband, Chad, and our
daughters, Lydia and Madeline, who lost many months of my
time and attention while I worked on this project.
Now let's make up for lost time!
I love you so much more than I say or show.

This book is also dedicated to my extended family members
who encouraged and supported me through the tough spots.
And to my brother Jon, who planted the seed and believed I
could…and I did!

Acknowledgements

I could not have written this book without the professional input of my "little" brother, Jonathan Hollerman. Through his wealth of knowledge and vast resources, I learned a lot about EMPs and survival as I journeyed with the characters through life after an electro-magnetic pulse event. It was a true joy to work with Jonathan.

My beta readers–Leann, Mary Ann, Heidi, Lisa, and Mary–were a great help to me in determining if the story in my head was making sense on the page! I truly appreciate their insight and questions…and especially their criticism when I needed it.

Special thanks to Ryan Ubry for his work on the cover photo, and to Heidi Haney for being our cover model; to the New Castle Public Library, for their dedicated table and electrical outlet; to the Kellygreen Bed & Breakfast in Tionesta, for an inspiring place to get away and write; to the bloggers who work tirelessly to educate about prepping without fear-mongering; and to the editors who help us aspiring writers become better through your online training.

This process has been absolutely amazing, and there is no way to mention every single person who has made an impact on it. Thank you…just thank you.

Prologue

14 years ago…

"Mom! Hold my hand! MOM!" Beth Ann shouted to be heard over the din as she eyeballed the disinterested security guard leaning against the hand-painted "Enter Here" sign.

Her mother gripped Beth Ann's small outstretched hand tightly as she led her family straight into the commotion: the excited voices of hundreds of strangers, vendors shouting, music coming from every direction, children squealing, random bouts of laughter. Even though Beth Ann was practically a fourth grader and shouldn't be seen in public holding her mother's hand, its safe comfort was worth the potential teasing.

Beth Ann loved–really, truly loved–going to the county fair. Every year, after the Fourth-of-July parade, she counted down the days by marking a large "X" on each square of the kitchen calendar, knowing that when the page turned to August, it would be time! And now, after weeks of waiting, the big day had come. But this year…THIS year was a big one for Beth Ann. She squirmed with barely contained excitement as she looked at the blue wristband her dad had just put on her. Blue! Finally! Just like her big brother's band. And that meant one thing–she was finally tall enough to ride the

1

Magic Mania, which for the last three years her brother had ridden with his hands in the air and his face wide open in delight, while she had stood watching with envy.

"Com'on, guys!" Christopher shouted, running ahead. He was eleven this summer...and brave, so he didn't have to hold anyone's hand. Beth Ann looked longingly at the carnival rides to her left while her mom pulled her to the right, following Christopher and her father to the tractors. Christopher climbed into the seat of a shiny green riding lawn mower, and dad stood beside him, pointing to the gauges and levers as he explained what each one did. The salesman headed in their direction, and Beth Ann had to run to keep up with her mom, who instantly accelerated to intercept what could be a potentially expensive conversation.

"Let's keep moving, dear," Betty said to her husband with a smile, placing her hand gently on his back with a little chuckle. Beth Ann loved to hear her mom laugh.

James grinned. "Yes, dear," he said, giving his wife a quick kiss.

"Ewww!" Christopher declared as he scrambled down from his perch, trying to get as far away as possible. Beth Ann didn't understand his aversion; she felt warm inside when her parents showed their love for each other.

As the Dalton family moved slowly down the path from the farm machinery, they entered a section where the majority of the vendor booths were located. There seemed to be an infinite number of tables with jewelry and t-shirts and wood-carvings and beer cozies and airbrushed license plates and hats and...oh, Beth Ann thought it was all wonderful. Her mom stopped to look at some pillows, but Beth Ann spotted colorful rag dolls on the next table. Since her mom had let go of her hand to dig through the bin, Beth Ann stepped slightly away, just to see the dolls a little closer. But, it wasn't close enough, so she took another step around the corner of the table...and a couple more. She could still see her mom, she justified.

The dolls were simple, not like the porcelain doll at home that stayed on her bed; she wasn't allowed to play with that. These ones didn't have actual bodies, just fabric that bunched up at the neck and flowed down to where the bottom of the feet would be. Three tiny buttons at the neck and a satiny thin ribbon tied in a bow gave the neckline the appearance of a dress. The cloth face had hand-drawn features–pretty eyes and eyelashes, a stubby small nose with three freckles on each side, and rosy smiling lips. Fascinated, Beth Ann slowly reached out to touch the doll on top—

"Beth! Beth Ann!" her mom called. "Beth…Ann!" Her dad bolted from across the path, literally parting the crowd with his arms. Christopher trailed reluctantly.

"I'm right here, mom!" Beth Ann called as she started to run toward her mother. But her toe caught on something and she fell headlong, knocking her wrist hard against the edge of the table on her way to the ground. The lights in the booth flickered and went out, and Betty gasped. Beth Ann fell flat on her stomach and started to cry.

"It's okay! It's okay, folks!" the pot-bellied vendor said as he rushed forward to plug the extension cord back into the power strip. He knelt down where Beth Ann had fallen, and she heard him mumbling to himself. "Every year I tell those people they need to cover these here cords with a mat or somethin.' But they don't never listen to me. No-sir-ee. They're just a trippin' hazard, and I say that every doggone year…."

The lights in his booth flashed back on, and that's when the man saw Beth Ann sitting in front of him on the ground, hugging her knees to her chest, eyes round with fear and silent tears flowing. Helping her up, he kindly asked over and over if she was okay, but she could only nod in humiliation and stare down at her feet, her breath coming in little gulps. Her mom scooped her up and carried her to a narrow grassy spot between two booths, off the busy path, to inspect her. She brushed the dirt and grass off her clothes and knees, and picked debris out of her pigtails. Her dad made her wiggle her fingers, declaring, "Good news! You'll live to see another birthday!" She tried not to smile, but half of it came out anyway. She got lots of hugs and kisses to make her feel better, while impatient Christopher reminded them twice to hurry up.

The rest of the evening went pretty much according to their annual ritual, except for the weather. It was always hot and sticky in Western Pennsylvania in August, but this night felt hotter and stickier than ever. Beth Ann's bangs were matted to her forehead and her face was streaked with the smeared mixture of dirt, sweat and tears. As much as she wanted it to rain and cool her off, she willed the clouds to lift so the rides wouldn't be shut down. She just *had* to ride the Magic Mania tonight!

Her dad and Christopher bought their tickets for the demolition derby, while the girls parted to check out the animals: sheep, goats, pigs, and horses–in that order. The rain started when they were in the 4-H tent looking at the rabbits. Beth Ann could hear it coming: first a gust of wind, then a slight patter, and suddenly a rushing sound that drowned out the music and voices and car engines. She and her mom, along with a small handful of other people in the tent, ran to the open flaps to watch it rain.

"Oh, no! It can't rain! I want to ride the RIDES!" Beth Ann whined, stomping her foot in protest and tugging at her blue wristband.

"Let's just wait and see," her mom said with her gift of infinite patience, turning Beth Ann around by the shoulders and pointing her in the direction of the rabbits. "It might clear up. And if it does, half the people will have gone home and the lines for the rides will be short!"

Beth Ann's old "play" tennis shoes scuffed across the hard-packed dirt floor as she made her way back to the shelves stacked with rabbit enclosures. Her mom always had to say something positive, but she just felt like pouting. Now the rabbits didn't seem at all interesting and she was bored.

But her mom was right...as always. The rain fell with a fury that lost momentum quickly and moved on, leaving large pools of water and mud behind. Darkness set in quickly under the cloud-covered sky, and the delayed demolition derby finally ended. Betty and Beth Ann navigated the mess with difficulty, winding through the hundreds of wet people flowing out of the grandstand area. Beth Ann spotted her dad first and then laughed at her brother, pointing at his soaking wet hair and clothes.

"I don't care!" Christopher responded, pushing his sister's arm down. "At least I got cooled off!" He stuck out his tongue at his little sister. She grinned back saucily.

"Who wants to ride the rides?" dad asked, changing the subject.

"Me! Me!" they shouted and jumped, forgetting their tiff.

After slogging their way through the muck to the upper side of the fairgrounds, the kids started with the burlap sack racing slides and worked their way to the Ferris wheel, the carousel, the parachutes and the spinning tea cups. Finally, after years and years and years of waiting, Beth Ann was in line for the Magic Mania. Unfortunately, she was required to share the seat with her brother, because her parents refused to ride this one on account of nausea or some such annoyance of the aged. But, it would be worth it.

Beth Ann glanced over the flimsy metal safety fence surrounding the ride to make sure her parents were still there. They saw her and waved enthusiastically. She didn't wave back because she didn't want to look as dorky as they did. But she did smile. She couldn't help herself.

Christopher yanked her arm. "Come on, Beth Ann! Pay attention!" The line had moved up. They would get on after the next group! Her heart started pounding in her chest and she began to have second thoughts. Standing right in front of it, the ride looked much bigger than she remembered. Did she have enough courage? Was she ready? She gulped down her fear and clenched her hands. She couldn't back down now. Christopher would call her a baby for the rest of her life.

Before she knew it, the music ended and the riders exited. The bored teen-aged ride attendant walked slowly to the entrance and opened it for the next group. Beth Ann's legs felt like jelly as she approached the steps. In front of her, Christopher bolted up the three steps to claim a good seat, even though they were all going the same place...in a circle...over and over.

Beth Ann had just started up the steps when suddenly the Magic Mania went completely dark. She froze, foot in the air, and watched in horror as the lights on each ride went out in succession. People gasped and murmured as it grew darker and darker. Beth Ann turned around to see if her parents were still at the fence, but she forgot that she was on the steps and lost her balance. She fell forward into several people and ended up on the ground for the second time that night.

She tried to push herself up, but someone tripped over her. She yelped in pain. "Mom! Dad! Christopher!" she shouted, but now that everyone else was yelling, she couldn't even hear her own voice. She wanted someone to come rescue her, but she was smart enough to realize that if she stayed down, she would be trampled. With great effort she forced herself to get up. Reaching her hands out in front of her into the darkness, Beth Ann tried to find the fence. It should have been right beside her, but she couldn't find it.

The scene quickly spiraled into pure chaos. Invisible people, people who seemed much larger and stronger than in real life, pushed and jostled her as she tried to find her parents...or anything solid to hold onto or lean against. "Dad!" she tried again. The black hole seemed too big for her; she was drowning in it. "Mom! Where are you?"

One of the loose giants ran squarely into her and down she went again, this time falling against something hard and rough, like the walls in her basement. Standing up, she ran her hands along it as she walked to the corner, turned and kept going. She came to a door, but it was locked. Beth Ann leaned against the door, trying to be brave and thinking what to do next...besides cry. Looking around, she noticed small round lights bouncing haphazardly, and she realized the fairground security guards were running with flashlights. That little glimpse of light gave her hope. "Mom! Mommy!" she tried again...just maybe her mom would hear her.

"I can help you find your mom," a voice spoke.

Beth Ann screamed. She had thought she was alone. She started backing up, but she kept her hands on the wall; she was terrified to lose the one solid thing in the horrid blackness.

"Com'on, sweetie. I can help you. Don't be afraid!" The voice was following her–how could she not be afraid? She rounded the corner and moved faster. She felt something...or someone...brush her arm. With all her might, she punched and kicked and clawed into the thick nothingness. And then she ran. Away from the wall. Away from the voice. Now she was the one running into people. Running and pushing and panting.

Wham. She slammed full-body into the cement block wall. Somehow she had run in a full circle. That's when she gave up. The voice was going to get her and there was nothing she could do about it. Sliding down the wall and burying her head between her knees, she let the pressure out in gulping sobs. She wrapped her arms tightly around her knees and thought maybe if she squeezed hard enough, she could shrink herself away.

It felt like hours, waiting in fear for something to happen. And even though there were hundreds of people yelling all around her, she had never felt the emptiness of being alone like tonight. Where were Mom and Dad? What had become of Christopher? Did he get off the ride? Beth Ann no longer cared about the fair or the Magic Mania. She just wanted to go home!

Suddenly, with a couple of flickers, the lights came back on, flooding Beth Ann with relief. There was no scary man beside her, waiting to snatch her. She stood slowly and looked around for her parents, swiping at her blurry eyes. Glancing at the silent Magic Mania, she shuddered, realizing life would never be the same again. That ten minutes of darkness had left a permanent scar on her young soul.

Chapter 1

Present Day...

"Kenny! Where's my Number Four?" Beth Ann shouted to be heard over the exhaust fans and leaned her head as close to the steel shelf as possible without scorching her hair on the heat lamps. "Mrs. Pascarella has been waiting almost fifteen minutes!"

Without warning, Kenny's red face appeared on the other side of the shelf, startling her into pulling back. "I'll get it when I feel like it! I'm cooking everyone else's orders, too, so gimme a freakin' break!"

Beth Ann squinted her eyes and glared at him.

With an exaggerated huff Kenny turned his back to her and flipped a row of burgers, pressing each one down until it sizzled. An annoying beeping alarm went off and Kenny lunged to the fryers to pull out the fish planks and fries, grumbling under his breath.

As Kenny rushed around the kitchen, "Little Joe" came around the corner struggling with a heavy stack of plates. He loudly plopped them into a shallow box at the end of the prep line counter and arranged them into two stacks. He smiled shyly at Beth Ann and scurried back to the dish room. An awkward, gangly high school Junior, "Little Joe" was skittish and all the cooks picked on him mercilessly. But, he was a hard worker and Beth Ann tried to encourage him whenever possible.

They called him "Little Joe"–which he hated–to differentiate him from "Big Joe," of course. Big Joe was not only bigger on the outside, he was bigger on the inside–aggressive, loud, and sometimes downright mean. Beth Ann thought Big Joe acted belligerent because he was insecure, and she mostly tried to avoid him. Thankfully, he wasn't cooking today.

Kenny turned around and noticed that she was still standing at his window. "Don't you have salt shakers or ketchup bottles to fill? Go check your tables. Get outta here!" he growled, brandishing his spatula at her.

"I'm not going back out there until I have a plate in my hand for Mrs. Pascarella!" She set her tray down with an emphasizing "clang" on the metal counter.

"Good grief! It's comin' right now." She picked out a nice parsley sprig as Kenny tossed a half-warm grilled chicken breast onto a plate along with a scoop of blazing hot steak fries. He slid the plate across the warming shelf with such gusto that she barely caught it before it slid off the other side.

Just then, Sandy, the day's shift manager, strode in from the dining room and clipped a new order to the turnstile. She gave it a little spin to rotate it halfway, announcing the new order to Kenny who scowled in reply. "Hang in there, Kenny," she said in a soothing tone one might use on a frustrated two-year-old. "Matt will be here in about twenty minutes." As she pivoted to head back out, Sandy glanced at Beth Ann and said, "I seated you a two-top; I'll get their drinks." She was gone before Beth Ann could thank her. Placing the garnish precisely as she had been trained, Beth Ann quickly set the plate on the tray and headed out of the kitchen to poor, hungry Mrs. Pascarella.

The early dinner rush was an indicator of a busy evening and before she knew it, they were locking the doors. *Another half-hour to clean up*, she thought, *and I can go enjoy a long, hot shower.* Obviously, the cold front and accumulating snow they were expecting in a couple days had inspired people to get out of their houses to enjoy the last of the dry, mid-40s weather. Sweeping at a record pace under the booths and around the tables, she chuckled to think that all her customers had probably stopped on their way home to strip store shelves bare of milk, bread and bottled water. She shook her head and wondered why it was always those three items…she would definitely buy toilet paper before milk. And maybe ice cream.

She took off her apron, heavy with coins and not-so-thick with bills, and put on her coat before saying goodbye to the crew. Beth Ann liked working at the diner. Her co-workers all had their quirks, but she had met some of her closest friends there and it was fun…sometimes. Even though an early childhood education degree hung on her bedroom wall, Beth Ann didn't mind that she was still working at the diner. After all, there wasn't a teaching job within a 50-mile radius that would pay her more than her tips from the diner. So, here she was…still living with her parents and still waiting tables. It wasn't so bad. She called it contentment; her mom called it a rut.

Approaching her car in the parking lot, Beth Ann shivered in the cool night air and fumbled for the keys in her coat pocket. Suddenly they slipped out of her hands onto the pavement, and she let out a moan of tired frustration. Stooping to pick them up, she froze as a movement caught her eye.

"Need some help?" a voice asked. She screeched as she stood and whirled around to face the man, arms out in front to defend herself.

"Oh, jeez! I didn't mean to scare you, Bethie." Kenny's eyes were wide, and he looked as startled as she felt. She started laughing hysterically as the adrenaline coursing through her body surged, then began to diffuse.

"Kenny! You about gave me a heart attack!" Her heart was indeed attacking her rib cage, pounding to be freed. Her legs threatened to give out, so she leaned her back against the car for support. Kenny bent down to pick up her keys. Good thing, because she didn't think she could move at all.

Handing her the keys, he grinned at her. "Maybe you should walk out with someone when you're a closer. It's dark out here. And you're jumpy." Kenny did blow off steam when he worked, but overall he was a decent guy.

"Yeah...," she nervously giggled, gaining a little more control over her body. "I think you're right. Thanks for...getting my keys...." He turned away, and she somehow managed to get into her car. Letting the engine warm up, she gave herself a few minutes to calm down. In her small town, there were seldom violent crimes, so she usually didn't think twice about walking outside at night, even though she hated the dark.

An ache in her hands indicated that she was gripping the steering wheel a little too tightly. "Missy," her first car, was a dependable 2002 Honda Civic. Even though she had racked up the miles driving to and from college, the little car was still going strong. Giving Missy an encouraging pat on the dashboard, she pulled out of the Table Talk Diner lot.

Home was only a couple short miles away—a small ranch at the outer edge of Tionesta, a rural village bordering the Allegheny National Forest, population of a whopping 453. She loved living in a small town where everyone knew everyone and the days were predictable. "Home of the Wolves," the Native Americans had named it, and it brought a shivery thrill to Beth Ann's shoulders every time she thought of her comfortable hometown in its primitive, untamed beginnings.

The homes on her street had been built near the end of World War II: modest, cookie-cutter ranches and cape cods, built for efficiency and economy. She preferred the older, more ornate Victorian homes; with their fancy turrets and gingerbread trim, they made her think of doll houses and castles. She grimaced at her useless romanticism and wondered when she would outgrow it. It certainly wasn't serving any purpose. But when she pulled in her driveway, she felt a warmth from the golden light pouring out of the windows of a home filled with love. She was one of the lucky ones.

"I'm ho-ome!" she called in a sing-song voice as she entered the house from the garage. Her yellow lab mix, Romeo, was waiting at the door to greet her with his usual exaggerated welcome. Beth Ann knelt down to snuggle him close and rub his back. She had begged for a dog, and finally her parents had relented when she started high school. Instantly she had fallen in love with this one at the shelter and promptly named him the only appropriate name a fourteen-year-old girl could think of. Romeo's whole body wagged with his tail, as if he hadn't seen her in weeks.

Beth Ann found her mom was in the kitchen, unloading the dishwasher. "Hi, Mom. I smell. I'm gettin' in the shower."

Betty smiled as she watched her daughter use the toes of one foot to pull the heel of her black thick-soled shoe off the other foot. "You know, dear, you need to untie your shoes first. You're going to ruin them."

Beth Ann rolled her eyes. "I know, I know! But my feet are killing me! I can't wait to get into my pajamas and sit down. C'mon, Romeo," she called, leaving her shoes where they fell and breezing out of the kitchen.

Betty saw a flashback glimpse of the teenager once again. She sighed and thought, *Yes...time sure flies.* Christopher was already married and farming nearby. Beth Ann was all grown up in a way, but she seemed to be stuck in a revolving door—just putting in her time until someone special came and whisked her away. She went for her degree because she felt like it was the right thing to do, but she didn't seem to have any career motivation or love interest. Turning back to the dishwasher, Betty sighed again. Beth Ann didn't seem too interested in any of the young men in town, so where would she possibly meet her Prince Charming if she stayed here? On the other hand, Betty didn't want her to move away; she sighed once more.

"What's all this sighing I hear, Mrs. Dalton?" James came into the kitchen and wrapped his arms around his wife, high-school sweetheart turned life-long partner. "You should be humming and smiling, dreaming about our romantic 30th anniversary getaway! That's what I've been doing...and I'm just about all packed!"

"That's because you don't do housework, and you just throw random things in your bag...without counting underwear or socks or matching anything." It was an accusation. "And you don't have to accessorize or think about makeup and hair products and...."

James kissed her, just to shut her up. She was always too serious when she had something on her mind. In this case, he knew it had nothing to do with his socks. He pulled back and just waited.

She took a deep breath and started to chuckle. "Sorry, honey. Don't you worry. I'm very much looking forward to sunny beaches, a good book...and handsome pool boys!" she said with a twinkle in her eye. She leaned her cheek against his chest. "I was just thinking about Beth Ann. She seems so stuck here."

"And whose child is she?" James reminded his wife gently. He paused before continuing quietly. "I think God has given her great potential. We've done our best, and now we have to give her some room...and some time...to find her way."

"I know. I just want her to be happy." As if on cue, sounds of "Tomorrow" being belted out in the shower flowed from the hall bathroom. Betty and James laughed. Beth Ann had always liked musicals.

"Let me hurry and finish these dishes, then I'll join you in the bedroom," Betty said, extricating herself from his arms.

"Mmmmm....," James's eyes lit up as he grinned.

"To pack!" Betty emphasized with a snap of the dish towel at his middle-aged belly.

A grey-haired James clutched his heart and turned from the room, smiling.

The next morning, Beth Ann made her parents some coffee for the road as her dad loaded the bags in the car. They rarely left town, so this trip to Florida was a big deal for all concerned. She closed her eyes to appreciate the aroma of the brewing beverage more deeply. Coffee was something she couldn't live without and would never give up for any reason.

Her mom came rushing into the kitchen–she rushed every morning–with both hands held up to her ear. "Here, Beth Ann. Can you help me get this earring in? I don't have time to keep messing with it!" Beth Ann smiled and calmly inserted the earring in a matter of seconds, wondering how much longer it would take them to leave. "Thanks, honey! Now, where did I leave my purse?"

Beth Ann dedicated the next ten minutes to helping her parents get everything together. Her dad came back into the house three times to check for forgotten things. Her mom kept nervously going through her mental checklist out loud: "Did you get the phone chargers? The GPS for the rental car? Your toothbrush? Money?" They repeated household instructions to Beth Ann as if she had forgotten what they told her yesterday…and the day before. Finally they were ready; they had truly just run out of things to fuss over.

Leaning in to hug her over-protective but loving parents, Beth Ann felt a strong wave of emotion rush over her.

"What's wrong, dear?" Her mom looked concerned. "Are you nervous about staying here alone? Don't forget the Howards next door promised to look in on you, and they are expecting you to call if you need anything. Oh, and you could maybe call Meghan or another friend and have them spend a night or two here with you." Romeo barked on cue, as he was obviously following the conversation. "Yes, Romeo! We know you will take good care of her, too." Betty gave him a perfunctory pat on the head. "And we'll be back on Saturday," she said as she reached out and cupped Beth Ann's cheek in her usual motherly way.

"I…I'll be fine. You guys have a good time–you need this. I love you both." A final hug and they were gone. Beth Ann watched them pull out of the driveway onto the road before shutting the garage door. She thought she would be excited to have the place to herself, but standing in the now silent house, she felt all alone. Romeo whined and leaned against her leg. Maybe she just needed more coffee.

Chapter 2

"This is Meghan. Leave a message and I'll call you back." Beth Ann hung up the phone and sulked. Meghan, her best friend since elementary school, was probably working. After graduation, Meghan went to nursing school and managed to get a job at the big hospital in Warren. It was a long commute, but Meghan was still able to live in Tionesta...which made Beth Ann happy. However, she worked so many hours, and had such an unpredictable schedule, that they weren't able to get together very often. Why did things have to change? Beth Ann sent her a text to call when she finished her shift.

She tried Kristen next. She had met Kristen at school as well, which happens when everyone in town attends the same school, and saw her a lot more often because they both waited tables at the diner. Kristen didn't answer, either, and Beth Ann wondered if she was at work. She texted Kristen and checked the time. It was almost 11:00 a.m. Beth Ann didn't realize it had taken her so long to get ready. After her parents left, she had watched the news and fixed her hair and makeup at a leisurely pace. Then she started a load of laundry, specifically to wash her work uniforms. She could probably wait another hour before she would have to make a big decision about whether or not to go shopping by herself.

Hoping to hear from Kristen soon, she logged onto her laptop and navigated to Facebook, then email. Finally, she ended up on Amazon for her daily check of Christmas specials with her favorite holiday playlist running in the background. Beth Ann loved the holiday season, especially the music. Singing full out with Mariah Carey to "All I Want for Christmas," she almost missed hearing the phone ring. She grabbed her cell and muted the music at the same time. "Hello? Kristen?"

"Hey, girl! What's going on?" the bubbly voice on the other end of the line asked.

"Are you working today?"

"No, I needed an oil change and Aaron took me so we could do some window shopping while we waited." Aaron was Kristen's boyfriend. It had been a long, rocky road for them, but it looked like they were finally getting the hang of it.

"Oh. Wait…window shopping? What are you saying?" Beth Ann shrieked into the phone.

"We looked at rings! I'm so excited! I think he's going to propose on Christmas! Ahhh!" Kristen shrieked back, approaching that proverbial glass-shattering pitch.

"O-M-G! I'm so happy for you! This has taken you guys forever!" Beth Ann was happy for her friend, but she also felt a twinge of jealousy—one more friend leaving her behind and crossing into the mystical world of matrimony. Time to change the subject. "So, I was calling earlier to see if you are free for a couple hours…or the rest of the day, actually. I have to finish up my Christmas shopping, and I need someone to go with me."

Kristen laughed. "You 'need' someone, or you just don't want to go alone?"

"Well, isn't it more fun to go with a good, dear, sweet friend?" Beth Ann begged.

"Don't worry! I'm free, and I would love to go with you. Where are we headed?"

"Just to the mall. I will treat you to dinner! When can I pick you up?"

"Whoa, horsey! What's the rush? Can I at least eat some lunch and change my clothes?" Kristen asked, laughing again.

"Well, I have to open tomorrow at the diner, so I don't wanna be late getting home. But you're right–I'll eat, too, and then I'll be over. We'll leave whenever you're ready." They said their good-byes and hung up.

Beth Ann was anxious to get out of the house, but she didn't realize that she was hungry until Kristen mentioned "lunch." She made a sandwich and zapped it in the microwave for twenty seconds; she didn't like cold lunch meat. With a handful of pretzels and a glass of sweet tea, she was set. It didn't take long to lose all five Candy Crush lives on her phone while she ate, so she didn't linger. After brushing her teeth and digging through the store coupons on the kitchen counter for anything that was still current, she grabbed her coat and purse. "Bye, Romeo. Be a good boy!" she said as she ran out the door.

Her friend lived across the river from the diner, and it was nearly 1:00 when they finally left Kristen's house. With a thirty minute drive ahead, Beth Ann calculated her time for the rest of the day. If she wanted to be home by 9:00, she would have to leave Cranberry by 8:15 so that she would have time to drop Kristen off at her house on the way. That meant being at her favorite steakhouse by 6:30, just in case it was busy. They would have almost five hours to shop.

"Girl, you are going to grow some serious wrinkles if you keep thinkin' about whatever you're thinkin' about!" Hearing Kristen's voice in the car startled Beth Ann, and she started to laugh.

"Sorry! I was just trying to figure out our timeframe. We're good. We got plenty of time. I can relax now!" Beth Ann assured Kristen. "Thank you for coming with me."

They chatted the rest of the way and then entered the mall determined to shop with a mission. Beth Ann was a bargain shopper and wanted to go item-by-item down the list, but Kristen liked free-styling, checking out all the top brand names and the latest fashions. So, occasionally they got side-tracked. Passing a jewelry store, Kristen showed Beth Ann bridal sets similar to what she and Aaron had looked at earlier that morning, and Beth Ann offered an appropriate number of "oohs" and "aahs" to support her friend's excitement.

The mall was crowded with holiday shoppers, and the girls enjoyed people-watching from a bench with a mid-afternoon smoothie, or what Beth Ann called a "pick-me-upper." Kristen turned to face Beth Ann and honed in on a forbidden topic. "So, where are we going to find a guy for you? Suzanne is engaged. Lauren and Katie are already married. It's just you and Meghan now. Let's go through the possibilities. David is still available...."

"No! Stop!" Beth Ann began gathering her bags. "We are not going to talk about this. I cannot see myself with any of the guys we already know. Okay? Let's go. We still have a couple more stores to hit." Beth Ann was off the bench and moving diagonally across the wide hall before she finished her last sentence.

Kristen scrambled after her with a grin. She had a new mission in life...to find a good man for her friend.

"Mmm! This is delicious!" Kristen had opted to try the Cajun-style blackened chicken special, while Beth Ann had ordered the same dish as always–petite sirloin, medium well, with baked potato and extra sour cream. "You should be more adventurous. You're missing out on the variety of life!"

"Yeah, yeah," Beth Ann chuckled. "You sound like my dad! But I know that I like this–no, I love it–so if I order something else that's not as good, then it will be a waste of money. I stick with what I know I like."

Kristen laughed and shook her head. Then she slowly leaned forward and sat very still, watching Beth Ann and waiting expectantly.

Beth Ann looked up from heaping spoonfuls of butter and sour cream on her potato. "What? Why are you staring at me?"

Kristen raised one eyebrow. "I'm waiting to see you pour ketchup on that beautiful cut of perfectly seared meat." Beth Ann picked up the ketchup bottle and made a dramatic show of forming a small, red lake beside her meat...being careful not to get it on the potato. She stared back defiantly at Kristen, and after a long pause they burst into laughter. They enjoyed the meal and the friendship, and before long they were leaning back, moaning and rubbing their stomachs. Waiting for the check, they watched the servers rush from table to table. It was nice to be the ones being served for a change.

The moment was short-lived as Beth Ann became aware that her phone was ringing. She jumped into action, digging into her purse for the phone which was singing "Mama Mia," the ringtone assigned uniquely to her mother...obviously. "Hi, Mom," she said.

"Hi, honey!" her mom's voice came through clearly.

"How was the flight?"

"Long. We had a layover in Chicago, but we're in Tampa now. Your dad is doing the paperwork for the rental car and I'm guarding the bags," her mom said with a chuckle.

"Well, that's an important job! Kristen and I went Christmas shopping today and just finished a great dinner at McCulley's. We're heading home in a few," Beth Ann said, figuring she would just offer the information because her mom would be asking what she was doing anyway.

"Oh, good! I'm glad you had a fun day. I was a little worried about you when we left this morning.... Is it snowing yet?"

"Nope, not yet. Supposed to start tomorrow morning, I think."

"Okay, well, be careful. It's always the most slippery when it first starts."

"I know, I know. Dad taught me to drive, remember? I'm pretty sure he covered every possible scenario! I'm just going to work and back, so I think I can handle it."

"Just take it slow. Oh, I think your dad is finishing up now, so I have to go. Don't forget to lock the doors tonight, and if you use the toaster oven in the morning, make sure you unplug it when you're done–I don't trust that thing. Did you turn the heat down when you left today?"

Beth Ann rolled her eyes for Kristen's benefit. "Yes, M-o-m. I am an adult, you know. And you've told me all this four hundred times already! Don't worry about me. Just go have fun and do…whatever old people do when they're on vacation. Okay?"

"Yes, dear. Love you. We'll give you a call tomorrow around dinner time."

"Sure. Gotta go; the waitress is bringing the check. Bye!" She flung the phone back into her purse and complained to Kristen, "I thought I was going to have almost a whole week to myself, but apparently we are doing a daily check-in call to review all the reminders they've already reminded me about." She realized with a small twinge of guilt that she had not told her mom she loved her. Oh, well. She would be sure to tell her tomorrow.

They argued over the bill, which Beth Ann paid in the end, and Kristen left a generous tip for the waitress. In the car, Beth Ann played the radio softly–Christmas songs, of course–all the way home. They were almost too tired for conversation and between good friends, silence is a comfortable thing. After dropping Kristen off, Beth Ann pulled into her garage, noticing that coming home to a dark house felt empty and lonely.

Thankfully, Romeo met her at the door, making her feel instantly better. "What would I do without you, boy?" Beth Ann crooned, dropping her bags and taking him into her arms. She was happy that she had finished everything on her list and that Kristen had been able to go with her. Going to the kitchen to get a glass of water, she noticed her lunch dishes were on the table where she had left them. *It's late*, she thought; *I'll clean up tomorrow.*

She had stuck to her plan to be home by 9:00, and she was glad because she was completely worn out. She set the alarm on her phone and went into the bathroom to complete her nighttime ritual. That's when she suddenly realized that she had not dried her uniforms

"DANG IT!" she shouted to her reflection and then rushed to the laundry room. Now she would have to wait up until they were dry enough to hang. Otherwise, she'd have to iron them in the morning, and she wouldn't have time. "Arrrgh!" she exclaimed. Having a mom around came in handy.

As the dryer started tumbling, she double-checked that all the house doors were locked. Taking her phone to the couch, she browsed through her Facebook feed and turned on the TV for background noise. Romeo curled into a ball near her feet. It was nearly 10:00 when the clothes were finally hung up and she fell into bed. She slept much more soundly than she had expected to on her first night home alone.

At the hospital in Warren, Meghan sank into a chair in the nurse's lounge and sipped at a cold bottle of water. She rubbed the back of her neck and tried not to think about her lower back. These doubles were killing her! She glanced at the clock. Only a couple more hours until midnight, when she could rinse in the shower and collapse into one of the residency beds, with its crackly mattress protector and stiff, flat pillow. Hospital beds certainly weren't made for comfort. But, she should be thankful that they allowed her to stay overnight, otherwise she would have to face a long drive home and a shorter amount of sleep before returning to work.

She checked her phone for messages and saw Beth Ann's text. Part of her wished she could spend more time with friends, but part of her wanted to move on, to find her purpose in life. She had always wanted to be a doctor, a surgeon actually, perhaps even on a foreign mission field. But she couldn't afford medical school. Her parents had divorced years before, and although they supported and encouraged her, they weren't able to help very much financially. So, she had implemented her "back door" plan: get through nursing school fast and find a job as an LPN, then work her butt off to be the best, hopefully finding favor with someone who could open doors for her.

Kristen, the matchmaker of the friends, didn't take Meghan's ambition seriously. She suggested—on multiple occasions—that simply marrying a rich, handsome doctor would accomplish more with less. But Meghan disagreed. She felt called to healing. That passion is what would get her through the muscle aches and the dark circles under her eyes. That and her faith. So, here she was…stuck in this old town, far away from her big dreams.

Replacing the cap on her bottle and putting it in the refrigerator, she took a deep breath and pulled open the heavy door into the hall where the endless needs could not possibly all be met. Sometimes she doubted her plan. Sometimes she wondered if the track she was on formed a loop in which there was no way out. She had no idea that tomorrow her mission field would emerge, and it would be on her own soil.

Chapter 3

W *hose job was it to research and harness the most annoying sound on the planet and then build an alarm around it?* Beth Ann complained as morning came way too early. She forced herself to get up and do all the things required before one can be seen in public. Romeo lifted his head off the bed briefly as she retrieved her hideous, but comfortable, waitressing shoes out of the closet, but he didn't follow her out to the kitchen. Apparently even he knew that it was too early to be awake. She put some food in his dish for later, stuck her phone in her purse, and pulled on her coat. Choosing a strawberry toaster pastry to eat on the way, she glanced out the window. It hadn't started snowing yet, but the stiff wind indicated that it would be coming soon.

She hustled to work, if for no other reason than to drink the free coffee. The opening shift was not Beth Ann's favorite. It was usually slow, she had to bus her own tables, and she would have to prep the salad bar before the lunch crowd arrived. Washing and chopping veggies and lettuce, and filling crocks with lots of things she wouldn't eat, was not something that she enjoyed. Then she would have to haul dozens of buckets of ice from the walk-in freezer to pack around the crocks. Finally, she would have to garnish the ice.

Seriously? Who thought that it looked realistic to see mounds of kale growing out of the ice? She never understood that one.

This morning was no exception. She went through the motions, bantering off and on with a handful of regulars at the coffee counter. They were all retirees without a timecard to punch, discussing current events and sharing pictures and stories of their grandkids. Apparently, one of them had a new phone–the "smart" kind–which seemed to be more frustrating than useful to him. His friends huddled around him as if they'd found a purpose for their day. Beth Ann tried her best to hide her smiles at their attempts to help him. Each time she passed by, she overheard bits and pieces of their conversation:

"What does this button do?"

"Wait…why aren't there any numbers? How are you supposed to make a phone call?"

"Aha! It's one of those touch-the-screen things. Slide your finger across…no, no! Don't leave your finger on it. Now I don't know how to go back."

"I'm never getting one of those. Too complicated."

"You should see my 4-year-old great-granddaughter use her mom's! These kids nowadays, always on their gadgets. Don't even know what 'outside' is!"

"I don't need a blasted phone to tell me how dumb I am." Way too much laughter…and consternation…was happening at that counter.

Beth Ann snuck a peek at her own phone in her apron pocket to check the time just as Kristen showed up for her shift. Beth Ann intercepted her in the break room.

"It is really getting cold out!" Kristen said with a theatrical shiver, hanging her coat on one of the wall hooks. "And the snow is already covering the ground."

"How are the roads?" Beth Ann asked.

"Not bad. They're salted. I didn't have any problems."

"They're calling for four to six inches by tomorrow. I guess winter is here!" She watched as Kristen tied on her apron and checked her hair in the little wall mirror. "Okay. Sally is checking shakers and sugars on all the tables. The salad bar is almost ready. I just have to mix up some more ranch dressing, and Big Joe has to put out the soup and chili. Would you mind changing the seating chart into three zones and putting on a fresh pot of coffee?"

"Sure. Big Joe's here, huh? I keep hopin' he'll get himself fired…."

"Yeah, wouldn't that be nice? He's been fine today, probably because we haven't been that busy. I've just left him alone." Beth Ann felt her apron vibrate and reached into the pocket for her phone. She started laughing and turned the phone to face Kristen. "Look at this! My parents just sent me a picture of their feet in the sand. When I get home later, I'm going to send them a picture of my feet in the snow!" With a good laugh to start them off, the girls headed into the dining room.

Beth Ann seated her third table in five minutes with the hope that a busy lunch would make up for her slow breakfast. She would be done at 1:30, unless they were slammed. While filling beverages at the hostess station, she snuck another look at her phone: almost noon. They really weren't allowed to have their cell phones in the dining room, but the managers let it slide as long as they didn't "see" anything. Carefully carrying the tray filled with drinks to the newest patrons, she noticed that Kristen and Sally were bustling, too.

At that moment, without warning, all the lights went out. Beth Ann instinctively stopped in her tracks. She heard a couple of quiet gasps in the dining room, followed by a crash and a loud curse coming from the kitchen and then…silence. The dining room was dim because of the cloudy sky, but the many windows along the front and one side of the building allowed the wintry cool light in. People gradually went back to their meals and menus, talking in awkward hushed tones. As Beth Ann delivered the last drink on her tray, she couldn't help but overhear her customer's cell phone conversation. "...Hello? Hello? Honey, are you there?" The woman looked up at Beth Ann and said, "That's weird. My phone just died.... Oh, well. I'm ready to order now."

As Beth Ann headed for the kitchen with the new order, she noticed that Sally and Kristen were opening the blinds to maximize the amount of natural light coming in. Turning the corner into the kitchen area, however, she was caught off-guard. It was as dark as night back there. She hadn't thought about it before, but she realized now that they didn't have any windows in the back. She slowly walked forward to where she knew the warming shelf would be, seeing its shadowy form as her eyes adjusted. She could hear shuffling noises and she now noticed a strange, blue glow. "Guys? You okay back here?"

Kenny answered her from somewhere nearby. "Sure, we're okay, other than the fact that this stupid kitchen operating at full steam is not the safest place to be in the dark. And that doesn't count being left alone in the dark with Joe, either." His voice sounded like it was moving around the room. Just then, a narrow vertical rectangle of light invaded the area to the right of the stove; Joe had propped open the delivery door at the end of a short hallway from the kitchen.

Beth Ann could see Kenny's form now. "What crashed back here? We heard it clear out front!"

"I was trying to find the stupid flashlight and I knocked over a stack of chafers. Ah! Here it is." He clicked on the mag light and went to the fryers first to lift out the baskets. Big Joe walked in then, carrying two large candles in glass jars that he had found in the manager's office.

"Here. We can light these. But the girly smell is gonna suck." He placed one on each side of the grill and lit them. One of them had three wicks and seemed unusually bright in the darkness. That's when Beth Ann saw that the blue glow came from the gas flames which were still burning in the grill. She tried to quietly clip the new order onto the turnstile without being seen.

"No new orders, Beth Ann, unless we can grill or broil it," Big Joe said, grabbing the flashlight out of Kenny's hand and leaning across the prep counter to read the ticket. "Or people can eat off the salad bar. That's it until the electricity comes back on." For a change, Big Joe didn't sound mean, just matter-of-fact. During the workweek, the cook with the most seniority was the acting manager until a "real" manager came in mid-afternoon to close. Like it or not, today it was Joe.

She left to give Kristen and Sally the message, and the three of them checked on all their tables, changing orders as needed, and letting people know they would have to pay in cash if the registers weren't up and running by the time they finished eating. The fountain drinks weren't working, so they made pitchers of iced tap water. After about ten more minutes, the three waitresses found themselves huddled at the hostess station.

Sally asked, "Did you notice that no one else has come in since the electricity went out? We were getting slammed…now nothin'. I wonder what's going on?" She abruptly turned and walked out the front door. Beth Ann smiled at Kristen; they both liked working with Sally. A middle-aged single mother who had worked at the diner since it opened, Sally was a hard worker and a good cleaner. She was a quiet type, but she had a quick smile and an empathy that made her a favorite among the patrons.

Sally came back in, shaking the snow out of her hair and stamping the slush off her shoes. "It might be a car accident. There are cars sitting in the middle of the intersection, and some people standing around. If someone hit a pole, the electricity might not come on for a long time."

Kristen shrugged. "Shouldn't the police be here by now? Do you think we should call?"

"I'll call 911," Beth Ann volunteered and the other two went back to doing whatever they could to help their customers through the current mess of lunch. Thankfully, no one seemed too upset.

Heading back to the kitchen to place the call, she heard the cooks arguing over the flame. Joe was accusing Kenny of turning down the flame, but Kenny was denying it. She picked up the phone: no dial tone. *That's weird,* she thought, *landlines are supposed to work when the power is out.* She pulled her phone out of her apron pocket. It was off. She tried to turn it on. Nothing. *Stupid battery; had a full charge this morning.* Turning her attention to the dueling cooks and randomly noticing that the kitchen was cold from the open back door, she asked if one of them could use his cell phone to call the police.

"Sally said there were cars in the intersection down the street, so maybe it was an accident. I can't get a dial tone on the landline and my cell phone battery died," she explained. Kenny said he was too poor to have a cell phone and Big Joe said he had left his at home by accident that morning. They turned back to the grill. *Good grief,* she thought. *Good thing this isn't a real emergency.*

Knowing that Kristen would have her phone with her, Beth Ann went back to the dining room where she noticed several half-frozen stragglers coming in the front door. She asked Kristen to use her own cell phone to call the police, and then quickly darted off to seat the new customers. Beth Ann greeted them cheerfully and explained that they did not have any electricity; they could still eat, but with limitations. They didn't seem surprised, yet no one spoke until she tried to seat them all together at the mega-sized corner booth; then they protested. Since they had come in together, she had assumed they were a group. Apparently there were several "singles" and one couple. She seated the husband and wife in Kristen's section, two of the single tables in her own section, and the last two single tables in Sally's section.

Beth Ann waited semi-patiently while the last person, an elderly woman, very slowly removed an outer scarf, then her heavy wool coat with a long row of buttons, and then a thin inner scarf that must have been wrapped around her neck at least five times. As she slowly spread them neatly across the empty chair…one by one…and

29

awkwardly got herself and her bulky handbag situated, Beth Ann felt compelled to make small talk.

"I noticed that it's still snowing. Are the roads getting bad?" Beth Ann asked, thinking that this poor woman probably shouldn't be driving even in the most ideal weather conditions.

"Oh, deary, they're a bit slippy now." Her brow furrowed. "But my car just quit while I was pulling out from the stop sign. Oh, my. I don't know what I'm going to do. That nice man over there helped push it to the side a little. And now I'm going to miss my doctor's appointment." She truly seemed distraught to have walked away and left her car in the street.

"We thought there was an accident, so we called the police. When they come, I'm sure they can help you. You just stay inside here until they arrive. Maybe you should try some lukewarm soup from the salad bar to warm you up," Beth Ann teased, trying to ease the woman's suffering somewhat.

It didn't help. The lines in the woman's forehead grew deeper, if that was possible. "Well, I think there maybe was a fender-bender, but the big problem is all our cars just up and quit. I can't understand it."

"All of whose cars?" Now Beth Ann's brows furrowed.

The woman waved a gnarled hand towards the entrance of the diner in agitation, as if Beth Ann should already know this. "All of us who came in together. They all tried to help each other, looking under the hoods and what not. But we just got too cold to stand out there any longer."

"Oh. That's weird." Beth Ann wasn't sure what else to say, and she wondered if the woman was just confused…or slightly crazy. Also, she really had to hurry back to her two new customers. "Sally will be your server, and she'll bring you some water, okay?"

As Beth Ann turned, she noticed that the man sitting at the table beside the elderly woman suddenly flipped the corner of his newspaper up. She knew that he had been listening to their conversation, yet now he was trying to hide it. She shook her head to clear the fuzz—what a day this was turning out to be. 1:30 could not possibly come fast enough.

Pouring drinks for her new customers, Beth Ann explained to them what the lunch options were. They both chose the salad bar and Beth Ann led the way, knowing that some of the items would need to be refilled. She made a list of toppings and sides to pull from the cooler on her order pad and swung through the side door into the kitchen slowly, remembering that it would be dark. The candle glow from the cooking area at the far side of the coolers helped a little, but she still had to feel her way to the walk-in door.

As she held the latch and gazed into the pitch-black cooler, she wondered how to identify what she needed without light. For as long as she could remember, she had always hated the dark. She thought she would outgrow it, but in twenty-two years she hadn't. She forced her breathing to slow, knowing that there was nothing to fear in the walk-in.

Suddenly, something gripped her arm. She screamed like the girl that she was.

Instantly a light blinded her and the vice let go, followed by laughter. "See? You're jumpy!" It was Kenny. "I saw you come in, and I thought you could use our flashlight. I was just trying to be kind and thoughtful, Bethie." He was working hard to control his laughter…and not succeeding.

"Okay. First of all, don't call me Bethie. And second, scaring me to death does not fall under either of those categories!" She realized she was raising her voice as her fear turned to anger.

"Stop flirting and get back to work, kids!" Big Joe called from the other side of the long, narrow kitchen.

"We are NOT flirting!" Beth Ann clarified loudly as she grabbed the flashlight out of Kenny's hand and entered the cooler. From inside the cooler, she heard Kenny laugh all the way back to the grill.

Before she could pull the first stack of tubs to refill the crocks at the salad bar, Kristen burst in. "Here you are. I've been looking for you!"

Even in the partial darkness, Beth Ann could see the wild look in Kristen's eyes. "What? Why?"

"Well, I tried to call the police, but my phone isn't working either. I asked around at my tables, but…." She stopped.

"But what?"

"No one's phone works. No one's."

The electricity…the landline…the cars…the cell phones…. What in the world was going on? Beth Ann felt a shadowy dread creep up on her the way it had when her parents left. Something wasn't right.

Chapter 4

Standing in the walk-in cooler, Beth Ann and Kristen forced themselves to calm down and decided that the best way to handle the unknown was not create a panic. They each calmly carried a stack of tubs out to the salad bar. While filling crocks and wiping drips and spills off the shiny steel counter, they were able to keep an eye on most of the tables. Meanwhile, Sally was checking people out and making change, and Beth Ann noticed the line growing.

"I'm going to run up front and help Sally check out. I'll be back," Beth Ann informed Kristen as she wiped her hands on a dish cloth and sped away.

"I can help the next person in line," Beth Ann called out as she took her place at the front counter. She noticed that Sally was scribbling figures on scratch paper to work out tax and change, so she followed suit. It only took a few minutes for the two of them to get most of the people paid and out the door into the snowy afternoon.

"Next!" Beth Ann called, just as her pen slipped out of her fingers. It took a minute to find since she had to feel around the disgusting floor for it, and when she stood back up, a handsome man stood across from her. He was watching her with an intensity that made her feel uncomfortable…as if there wasn't a countertop between them. He smiled broadly when she made eye contact and handed her his ticket.

"Good afternoon, Mr. Andrews," Beth Ann greeted him without a smile. He might be the richest man in town, but she still always felt uncomfortable around him…something about his eyes. She glanced down at the newspaper tucked under his left arm and wondered if he was the person who had been eavesdropping on her conversation with the elderly woman. She handed the man his change.

"Thank you, …Beth Ann," he said in a thick, syrupy voice, obviously having read her name tag. "Are you done with your shift soon?"

"No, not for a while yet," she exaggerated, not wanting to give him any personal details. He was creeping her out. She started circling the totals on the receipts and putting them in order by amount, just to look busy and give her an excuse not to look at him.

"I'm sorry to hear that. I was going to offer you a ride home."

"That's very nice, but I have my own car, thank you." Was he hitting on her? He was so… old! She kept shuffling the receipts.

"Ah! Good for you! I like to see young people being industrious, making their way in this world and taking responsibility for themselves. Like having a job and buying a car." He dipped his head slightly, as if in homage to her. "What year is it?"

"Year?" Beth Ann could not think of a way to get out of this conversation. She was thankful that Sally stayed at the counter nearby, tallying the food slips.

"Your car. What year is the model?"

"Uh…, 2002 or 3, something like that. I'm sorry, but what does that have to do with anything?" She stopped sorting and met his eyes in challenge.

Mr. Andrews started to chuckle very softly, as if what she asked him was an inside joke. He leaned forward and said softly, "Well, honey, let's just say more than you know. Things are going to be a little different around here from now on." He stood up straight, put on his wool fedora and touched the brim with his fingertips like a suave movie star. "You be careful now. Good day."

Stunned into silence, Beth Ann and Sally watched him walk out the door and climb into an old pickup truck. The bed was loaded down with lumpy cargo, covered tightly with a large tarp and a blanket of fresh snow. As he backed out of the parking space and pulled carefully onto the main road, Sally spoke up. "I wonder why he's driving that old beat-up thing? I thought he had some shiny fancy car…."

"Well…, that was the weirdest conversation I ever had…with anyone, " Beth Ann said slowly. She turned to face Sally. "Thank you so much for staying here with me. I never know how to take that guy."

"He doesn't bother me," Sally replied, "but I have noticed that he pays a lot of attention to you younger ladies. I saw him purposely let someone in front of him so that when it was his turn to check out, he would be with you. Just thought I would stick around."

"Sicko. He's old enough to be my father," Beth Ann said with a frown. "Well, Kristen is going to think I abandoned her. I'm going to check my last couple tables and relieve her at the salad bar. I think it's about time for me to clock out and go home!" She left her neatly stacked receipts with Sally to finish the tallying.

The dining room was so quiet that it was spooky. The few customers remaining seemed too self-conscious to speak. All the rest of the tables had been bussed and reset. Some of the salad bar items had been completely finished and the crocks pulled. A mountain of dirty dishes waited in the dish room for an electric current that would make the water hot enough to sanitize them. The cooks had stopped grilling because the flames were too low to cook meat properly, due to the diminishing gas line pressure. Kenny had found batteries and powered up the radio, but he couldn't get any stations to come in. After almost two hours, the electricity was still out. Nothing was as it should be. Beth Ann said her good-byes; she was happy to be leaving.

Big Joe and Beth Ann finished their shifts around the same time and silently walked out to the parking lot together, separating to their respective cars. It took a couple of minutes to clear the fresh snow off her Civic; *close to three inches already*, she estimated. Knocking her shoes against the door threshold, she lowered herself into the driver's seat and turned the key in the ignition...nothing. She tried again. Not a light on the dash, not a click, not a grunt, not a growl: nothing. Suddenly Mr. Andrews' face flashed before her eyes and she remembered the cryptic words. *"...Things are going to be a little different around here from now on."* What in the world did that mean? Why wasn't her car starting? Does he have something to do with what's going on? She struck the steering wheel with her gloved fists and let out a bellow of frustration as she beat the back of her head into the headrest...over and over.

Beth Ann jumped out of the car to see if she could catch Joe. He was still there, several spots over, with his head bent deep under the raised hood of his "monster truck," as she always thought of it. Before Joe knew she was nearby, Beth Ann's ears caught a few colorful words. She almost smiled to know that she wasn't alone in her frustration.

"What's up?" she asked. "My car won't start either."

He lifted his torso part-way up and leaned his weight forward onto his arms, his gloved hands clutching the frame. He exhaled loud and long. "Well, I thought it was the battery, but now I think maybe it's the starter."

Feeling a twinge of panic, she stepped away from the truck. It was eerily quiet; she could actually hear the snow falling. She didn't know that was possible because it had always been drowned out by the noise of everyday life–engines, motors, fans, conversations, people, phones, music. Now, as she looked around, there were no people. Nothing was moving, except the relentless snow, oblivious to the mystifying circumstances. A handful of cars sat in the intersection near the Table Talk, but they had been abandoned. From where she was, Beth Ann could see into the "downtown" area, which was comprised of a whole five blocks. The electricity appeared to be off in the entire area. It looked like an Arctic ghost town.

Eyes wide with alarm, Beth Ann turned back to Big Joe. "Joe, what if it's not the starter? I don't know what's going on, but none of this makes any sense. Our cars don't work. Our cell phones, the landline, the radio…. What if it's more than just the electricity, like some 'end of the world' kind of thing?"

"That's crazy! This is freakin' America!" Joe threw his hands up in the air and let the hood slam down. Then he kicked the tire and turned his back to the truck, his hands curled into fists. Beth Ann backed up slightly so that she wouldn't be in the way of his temper. Suddenly he turned back to her; she could almost see the light bulb glowing over his head. "I'm going to get Kenny's keys. Come on. You can try Kristen's car." His tone was commanding; it was not a suggestion. He headed back to the staff entrance, his long strides leaving Beth Ann behind.

When she reached the door near the back of the building, Joe was already collecting keys from Kenny, Sally and Kristen in the break room. Their eyes were wide and their faces pale. Sally caught his sleeve as he turned, pleading softly, "Let us know if…if you can get them to start…."

Big Joe brushed past Beth Ann without saying a word. She gave her friends a small, worried smile and dutifully followed Joe back out into the cold. When she reached Sally's car, there was no indication of having an engine at all, just like her Civic. She sat there, wondering what to do next, when suddenly she heard an engine roar to life. It was Kenny's old clunker! They had always teased him about his classic muscle car. For years he had talked big about fixing it up, but as of today it still sported several shades of paint, scratches and dents accumulated over three decades.

Beth Ann ran over to the wheezing car. Joe left it idling and jogged through the freshly trampled snow path. She was tired of following Joe back and forth, so she just stood there, noticing how the cold was making her fingers cramp and her feet numb. She just wanted to get home and take a hot shower. She lifted her eyes to the front of the diner and realized that Kristen and Sally were watching from the window. Aha! *The front door is much closer than the back*, she realized with a jolt of relief. Since today was a good day to make exceptions to the rules, and since she technically wasn't on the clock, she decided to enter boldly by the forbidden front door.

Inside, Joe was calling everyone to the break room. Sally and Kristen, now wearing their coats as the temperature fell inside, met Beth Ann at the entrance and together they moved quickly to the back of the building. Kenny was pointing the mag light at the ceiling to provide some light in the room, but it made Beth Ann think of her older cousins torturing her with scary ghost stories. This added a new "bad" feeling to all the other bad feelings she had accumulated during the day.

Big Joe's voice brought her back to the present. "Okay. Here's what we are going to do." Joe seemed too calm, as if he was enjoying taking control of a situation others viewed as a crisis. "I'm taking Beth Ann home in Kenny's car—"

"What?" Kenny started to protest, but Joe forcibly held up his hand and kept going.

"…And then I'll swing by Sandy's place. She should have been here by now, but she lives too far out of town to walk here in this weather, if her car isn't working. If there is phone service at either place, I will call the electric company to see if I can find anything out about when they'll have the power back on. Then I'm coming back. If Sandy decides we're closing for the rest of the day, Kenny can drop the rest of us off before he goes home." He seemed proud of himself for thinking of such a great plan.

Kenny jumped in. "I'm almost on empty! I don't have enough gas to run you guys all over creation!" The light bounced agitatedly around the room as he used his hands to enforce his point.

"Well, then, Beth Ann and I better get going–your car is running right now out in the parking lot!" Joe said with a smile, but in a taunting tone.

"Whatever," Kenny said. Big Joe was the alpha male; what use was it to fight him? He dropped the flashlight onto the small table as he turned and left the room, punching the doorframe on his way out.

"Joe?" Sally called in a small voice as he and Beth Ann made their way to the back door...again.

Joe stopped and turned around, but he didn't try to hide his annoyance. "Sally?"

"I don't know what time it is, but I need to get my son...at the elementary school. Could you drop me off there?"

"I can't give you permission to leave. You know that. After I talk to Sandy...."

"No!" Sally gained confidence as her motherly instincts kicked in. She marched straight into Joe's personal space. "I don't know what's going on and I need to get to my son...now!"

Joe held up his hands as if forced into surrendering. "Fine! I don't care. I won't be the one looking for a new job." He shrugged cockily. "Grab your stuff. I'm not waiting. And, I'm not going past the school; I'll drop you off at the split."

Beth Ann helped Sally's right arm find its matching sleeve as they scrambled across the snowy parking lot after Joe. They knew he would leave without them–he wasn't kidding. Beth Ann pulled the front seat forward so that Sally could climb into the back...a true inconvenience of the two-door car. That's when she noticed Sally's black canvas shoes were already soaking wet.

"Wait!" she called to Joe as she took off running.

"Not waiting!" Joe hollered, reversing out of the parking spot with the passenger door still open.

"Pick me up at my car! Joe, please...!" Beth Ann yelled over her shoulder as she fiddled with the latch of her car trunk. Her father always made a big deal about the smallest things and it drove her crazy. But today, more than ever, she was thankful that he had insisted on her keeping an old pair of snow boots and a blanket in the trunk. She grabbed them quickly and let herself down into the passenger seat of Kenny's car. She was somewhat surprised that Joe actually did stop for her.

She handed the boots and blanket to Sally in the back seat. "They might be a little snug, but at least they'll keep your feet dry. Just in case the buses aren't running…."

"Oh, no…I couldn't take your boots…."

"I have another pair at home. Please just use them."

"Thank you, Beth Ann. You are one of the most thoughtful and generous people I know."

"Aw, jeez! Can we cut the crap? I feel like I'm stuck in a chick flick," Joe interrupted. "And turn around! I'm tryin' to drive here."

Beth Ann smiled at Sally and turned around. Then her jaw dropped. The scene looked even more surreal from the street level. Kenny's car struggled to find traction on the unplowed streets. In addition, Joe had to weave around other cars that were dotted here and there on the road, like toys a toddler had lost interest in.

She pointed out her side street, then her house. Big Joe asked her to check the landline and gesture from the window if she got a dial tone or not. It only took two seconds to confirm what she feared, and she gave him the "no" signal. From the front picture window, her heart sank as she watched him back out of the driveway and fishtail in the direction of the school, tires spinning. With her back against the wall between the window and the front door, Beth Ann slowly lowered herself down onto the floor and pulled her faithful dog into her arms, holding onto him for dear life.

Chapter 5

Beth Ann had no idea how long she sat on the living room floor with her coat still on, but she drew comfort from the closeness of her dog. Suddenly, Romeo leaped out of her arms and released one short bark, startling her. Before she had time to react, she heard a heavy knocking on the front door...directly beside where she was sitting. Romeo stood, alert and staring at the door, but Beth Ann noticed that his tail was wagging ever so slightly.

Quietly rising to see who it was, she could feel her heart pounding. Relieved to see her next door neighbor, she opened the door. "Oh, my gosh! I'm so glad to see you!" she said, impulsively hugging him and inviting him in.

Gary Howard stood stiffly and awkwardly in front of her, shifting his weight from one side to the other as he waited for her to calm herself. "I didn't mean to scare you. Just saw you come home and wanted to check on you," he explained. "Did your car break down or something?"

"I...uh...don't know." When Gary lifted one eyebrow, Beth Ann rushed on. "I was working when the electricity went out and then we couldn't get the phones to work and there were cars all over the street and...."

Gary held up his hand. "Whoa, whoooooa! Okay. Just relax for now. I will take you over to the diner later and look at it."

"How about tomorrow? The roads are terrible and maybe they'll plow at some point…if they can get around all the cars on the roads…." Her voice trailed off. Everything was just…weird.

Gary chuckled. "Okay. Tomorrow it is." He held a small container out in front of him. "Linda sent you over some homemade soup she was making us for lunch, before the power went out. It's cold now, but she wanted you to have some for dinner in case the electricity doesn't come back on by then."

Beth Ann's heart warmed as she took the small plastic storage container. "Please tell her I said 'thank you.' It's so nice of her to think of me."

"Well, with our son living out west now, we need someone to dote on! So you're it!" Gary grinned at her, but Beth Ann thought she caught a passing glimpse of wistfulness in his eyes. Plus, she had a feeling that her parents had put in a request for their neighbors to look in on her.

She smiled back at him compassionately. No wonder her parents were such close friends with the Howards. They were good, old-fashioned, genuinely kind people. "Mr. Howard? Do you have any idea when we'll have the electricity back?" She figured it couldn't hurt to ask.

"Sure don't. Do you want to come over and stay with us for a little while?"

"No, thanks, that's ok. I've got my dinner," she held up the soup container, "and I'm going to catch up on some reading. It'll be a nice change of pace."

"Okay. Well, if the electricity is still out when you go to bed, make sure you dress warm and have extra blankets. In fact, see if your dog will sleep under the covers with you–that will help. If you light any candles, don't leave them burning. I'll come over and check on you in the morning. If you need anything in the meantime, no matter what time it is, just come on over. Got it?"

"Got it!" Beth Ann nodded, realizing how much she missed her parents. She sure would be happy to see them in a few short days.

As Gary turned and stepped out into the cold, Beth Ann noticed that the snow falling was much lighter and the flakes were smaller, a sign that it was either letting up, or getting colder, or both. "Oh, Mr. Howard?" He stopped and turned on the steps to face her. "Not too early tomorrow, okay? I don't have to work till lunchtime." He laughed and assured her that he would let her sleep in.

The day had not been bright at any point, but Beth Ann could definitely tell that now the fading light was due to the invisible sun setting, rather than to the snow clouds that hid it. It must be going on 5:00 or after, she estimated. How many times had she checked her phone since she got home? Even with a dead battery, the habit had persisted! *I guess I'm not going to get a call from mom and dad tonight*, she realized with surprising disappointment. *I hope they don't worry.*

It had been a rough day, but Beth Ann's romantic side decided to make the most of the break in the routine. Humming a tune from *My Fair Lady*, she buttered a slice of bread and added it to a tray with her cold, but lovingly homemade soup and other essential dinner items like a spoon and vase of dried flowers. Working by candlelight, she set up two tray tables side-by-side in the living room and covered them with a floral table cloth that her mom rarely used. Finally, everything was ready. Wrapped in a blanket, her dog lying on her feet, candles glowing and a yellowed copy of *Anne of Green Gables* in her hand, the only thing missing was a fireplace…and a man to share it with.

Beth Ann did not sleep well on her second night home alone. Between feeling cold and hearing every little creak of the house and moan of the wind, she felt as though she woke up at least twice an hour. Meanwhile, the night dragged on until her sleep-deprived brain began to wonder if she would be stuck in darkness and cold forever. At some point, she must have slept deeply enough to allow the sun to rise without her knowledge. She slowly opened her eyes and blinked back painful tears. Her room was so bright that it seemed to glow.

Curiosity drove her to crawl out of the warm cocoon of blankets to look out the window. Quickly slipping her feet into plush slippers and pulling on a fleece robe as she crossed the room, she moved aside the white cotton eyelet panels and involuntarily caught her breath. It looked like a painting: undisturbed, pristine, and too perfect to be real. A cold, white sun blazed in a cloudless, deep blue sky. Snow covered everything–trees and grass, houses and cars–and it shimmered like diamonds. The reflection was almost painful. She squinted and shielded her eyes with her hand. *What is the opposite of yesterday?* she asked herself. *Today!* After the darkest night, this bright day gave her hope that everything would turn out alright.

Beth Ann shuffled to the kitchen to get her morning caffeine fix and found herself gazing at the lifeless coffee maker. *Oh, no...not my coffee.... How am I going to get through my day?* She opened the five-pound coffee can, inhaled the glorious aroma, and closed her eyes. Completely unsatisfied, she turned to Romeo. "Come on boy, I'm freezing. Let's get dressed."

She layered some old thermals under sweatpants and a hoodie, and pulled on a pair of fluffy "spa" socks over cotton athletic socks. She dressed Romeo in his sweater, too; he didn't protest as much as usual. Her fingers were nearly numb with cold, so she cut the tips off an old pair of stretch gloves and wore them all day. That seemed to help, although she laughed out loud when she caught the reflection of a hobo in the mirror.

As she struggled to fix her hair without her accustomed amenities, she wished for any heat source, no matter how small. Remembering that her dad would sometimes run heat in the garage, she wandered into the garage in search of the heater. Unfortunately, it was electric. Rustling through some boxes nearby, she did find a little camping stove with a small propane tank, but she decided to hang onto that for cooking. Truthfully, she wasn't very comfortable using it; her dad or brother had always taken care of that sort of thing while she was off with her friends.

Thinking of her friends made her feel isolated. Even though it had only been a day, she missed being able to call people and wished she could be with Kristen and Meghan right now. Kristen at least lived with her parents, so she would be okay. Meghan had been at work in Warren when the electricity went out in Tionesta; surely everything was fine at the hospital. Remembering the panicked look in Sally's eyes, Beth Ann hoped everything had worked out for her and her son. Then she smiled, envisioning her parents walking hand-in-hand in the warm, foaming surf, completely oblivious to Tionesta's plight. What a story she would have to tell them when they came home!

Since she couldn't call anyone, or go anywhere, or watch TV, or get on the internet, there wasn't much to do around the house. Heck, she couldn't even cook meals or wash clothes to pass the time. She wandered around aimlessly for a while, with expectant Romeo at her heels. "Well, I guess we can wrap Christmas presents while it's daylight," she told him. She loved wrapping Christmas presents, but only if she could watch *White Christmas* at the same time. In this case, she wouldn't even be able to listen to Christmas music; it just wouldn't be fun. Sighing, she went about gathering all the supplies. The never-ending quiet was threatening her sanity.

When Mr. Howard showed up at the front door, Beth Ann was about halfway through her wrapping. She let him in and he got a first-hand glimpse of the hurricane zone on the dining room table.

"Being productive, I see! Very good!" Gary patted her on the shoulder and grinned. Beth Ann forced a laugh and tried to hide her embarrassment over the mess; her mother would have been horrified! He didn't seem to notice her discomfort. "How was your night?"

"I didn't sleep very well, but I didn't have any real problems. Any news from the power company?"

"Not yet. I guess it's hard to get any communication out with phone lines and cell service out on top of the electricity. It seems kind of strange…." His voice faded and he shook his head slowly. "You know, I went out to warm up my car to take you to the diner, and it wouldn't start either. Something doesn't add up." Gary had been a volunteer firefighter for many years when he was younger, and he still seemed to have a sense about things.

Beth Ann knew he was right. She could feel it deep inside.

Gary looked at her then and must have realized that she needed a little encouragement. He smiled. "All we need right now is a plan. I don't know how far-reaching the outage is, so I'm worried about water. If the treatment plant doesn't have electric, we won't have any more running water once the tower is empty…which will be very soon. Gather all the clean pots and pans, plastic and glass containers that you can find and fill them with tap water. Just line them up on the counter or wherever you have room. Then, fill the bathtub as full as you can with cold water; you will be able to use this sparingly for washing and flushing. This is kinda gross, but the toilet rule is now 'If it's yellow, let it mellow; if it's brown, flush it down.'" Gary grinned, as if he took some kind of third-grade pleasure in the potty humor.

Beth Ann grimaced.

He laughed at her anticipated reaction. "And for your meals today, eat anything you can out of the fridge…but not if it smells sour. Keep the fridge and freezer doors shut unless absolutely necessary, and when you do open them, be as fast as possible. If we still don't have power by tonight, you will need to put all the frozen foods outside on the back porch. Just check it tomorrow and make sure it's not in the sunlight. We might have to think about what we can do to save it, since the temperature one of these days will probably come back up above freezing."

Beth Ann just nodded her head slowly, her eyes growing larger. She was starting to understand that the situation was a little more serious than she had thought.

Gary tried to reassure her. "Don't worry. We just plan for the worst-case scenario so we're good no matter what, right? Let's deal with tomorrow as it comes."

She nodded again and mechanically repeated, "Fill containers and bathtub with water. Eat the fridge food. Keep the fridge and freezer doors shut as much as possible. Put the frozen stuff outside tonight."

"Right. That's good! Okay. Don't forget the offer still stands for you to come on over with Linda and me, even to spend the night or to stay. You don't have to be over here alone," he reiterated.

Beth Ann realized she had been staring at the floor, and she lifted her eyes to his face. "You keep forgetting that I'm not alone," she responded with forced bravado, bending down to hug Romeo, who was always nearby. "But, thank you. I'll let you know if it comes to that."

"I may try to walk into town after lunch to see if the mayor is in. We'll see. It's sunny today, and the wind has let up, so it's probably a good day for a walk. I'll let you know what I find out." He smiled and turned to leave. She followed him to the front door. With his hand on the doorknob, he turned and said, "When you're done there," nodding his head toward the mess on the dining room table, "Linda has a boatload of Christmas presents you could wrap."

Beth Ann laughed. She was grateful for this kind man, for someone to look after her. She didn't realize how much she had relied on her parents...for pretty much everything. Locking the door behind him, she noticed other neighbors in the street, talking. She watched as Gary joined the small group and chatted casually, the bulk of the conversation involving mutual head nodding and shrugging.

Turning back to her wrapping, she finished quickly and cleaned up. She knew that she had to work on Gary's recommended jobs, but she was hungry and wanted to eat first. Surely it was well after lunch by now. But then, she didn't know what time it was when she woke up. She let out a moan of frustration; there had to be something in the house that could tell her the time.

She rummaged through her dad's nightstand and a couple of drawers in the bathroom, but couldn't find his watch. It was an awkward feeling to be going through her parents' stuff, but they would understand. Her second thought was to check the hunting and camping bins in the garage. The 18-gallon plastic tub marked "camping" had a wind-up style alarm clock which would be useful...once she knew the current time. She also found a sleeping bag which she would add to her bed for warmth, a battery operated lantern, outdoor cooking pans and utensils, and some hand and feet warmers. Eureka! She opened one of the small orange packs and shook it, relishing the heat soaking into her palms.

Her stomach growled, indicating it was time to eat...right now. She had spent enough time looking through the camping bins; she would look through the hunting stuff later, if it was necessary. Turning on the water in the kitchen sink, she soaped her hands and began to lather. Just then, the water made a short spurting noise, like when there is air in the line, and returned to normal. Her eyebrows lifted and her chest heaved: ...*must...turn...off...water....* In slow motion, she turned off the faucet and leaned against the sink, staring at the rivulets racing for the drain. A light dawned. *I should have listened to Mr. Howard right away!*

Plugging the tub and letting the faucet run, she raced through the house, gathering every pot and bucket she could find, including the hunting and camping bins which she simply emptied onto the garage floor. She filled them all with water from the tap, and covered each container so that Romeo didn't drink out of them with his slobbery muzzle.

A couple hours later, Beth Ann was bored out of her mind. She was supposed to work the afternoon shift today, but just getting to the restaurant was out of the question. She had even lost interest in reading; all the books on her shelves she had read before...many more than once. She had to get out of the house.

Taking Romeo on his leash, Beth Ann paid a visit to the Howards out of pure desperation. Linda opened the door and welcomed Beth Ann in. Handing her the empty container, Beth Ann thanked Linda for the delicious soup and asked if they had the current time. She set the wind-up clock to 4:07 p.m.; it was later than she had estimated. What a relief it would be just to know the time!

Gary had not yet returned from town, so Linda invited her to stay and have some hot tea with her while she waited. Beth Ann forced herself not to roll her eyes...or worse yet, smirk. Tea time? She could think of a thousand things she would rather do...but most of them involved electronics. Coffee was what she craved, but right now anything hot to drink suddenly sounded like a good idea. And she didn't want to be rude, so she accepted.

Beth Ann watched as Linda took a flat metal gadget, unfolded it and set a cube under it. With a match she lit the cube into a blazing flame, like a miniature stove! A small pan of water was boiling in no time.

Linda chuckled as she watched Beth Ann's reaction. "We used to take this thing camping with us. But it's been...I don't know, ten or eleven years since we've been camping. Our son was still in high school. We didn't know if the starters would even light, but they seem to be okay. Now I wish we had stocked up on them!"

It was strange, almost embarrassing and truly comical, to be having a neighborly chat with a woman her mom's age. And to drink tea. It made her feel...older somehow. Yet, it was kind of nice, too. Linda did most of the talking and Beth Ann actually found herself halfway listening.

Gary arrived just as the light began to fade into the western sky. He reported that the town was mostly deserted and quiet, but he did talk with the sheriff and one of the town council members who happened to be in the municipal office at the time. All they knew was that the electrical plant on the outskirts of town was out of commission, as well as the water treatment plant. They cautioned him that the sewer was starting to back up into some of the lower lying homes in town and bubbling from some of the manholes. They were trying to find one of the water department employees to make rounds and manually close each house's shut-off at the road, but as of yet, no one had been located. Only a handful of cars and trucks were running, one of which had been stolen, and another had been commandeered by the sheriff for his use. There were no communication lines open, so the sheriff planned to gather as many council members as he could find to discuss sending a small contingent of Tionestans to Oil City or Warren for assistance, probably tomorrow or the next day…if they still needed it.

Linda looked concerned. "So, you didn't see the mayor?"

Gary shook his head. "No, he wasn't there, and it doesn't seem like anyone really knows how to handle the situation."

"It's very discouraging," Linda said, and Gary agreed.

Beth Ann rose to leave. "Thanks for having me over. I'd like to get home before it's completely dark."

"Are you sure you won't stay the night with us? We have plenty of room for you and Romeo," Linda invited, reaching down to scratch the dog's head.

Beth Ann politely declined. Deep down she held onto the hope that if she was home, things would eventually become normal again.

Beth Ann thought she heard voices…but they were small and far away. She strained to hear them. Who were they? Why were they distressed? Her legs wouldn't move; she struggled. She wanted to find them. Maybe they were cold, too. Wait—now they were shouting. Was it her parents? She had to help them! Why couldn't she move? Why was it so dark?

"Dad!" she shouted. Surrounded by the dreaded dark and cold, Beth Ann gradually realized that she was in her bed and had been dreaming. If only she could tell that to her heart, its deafening rhythm pounding in her eardrums. She took a couple of deep breaths and tried to calm down. "Only a dream…only a dream," she repeated until she believed herself.

Ready to lie back down, she noticed that Romeo wasn't in bed with her. She called his name and was answered by a whine from what sounded like the other side of the small bedroom. "What's the matter, boy?" she crooned. "Come on up here. Up, up!" But Romeo whined more urgently and scratched at the door.

"Aah, really? You have to go out now?" Beth Ann moaned, crawled out of her dad's sleeping bag beneath her bed covers, and stumbled out of bed. She pulled the covers up to the pillow in hopes that it would hold a little of her body heat to come back to. She opened the bedroom door and Romeo ran ahead. When she got to the kitchen door, he wasn't there, but she could still hear him whining and scratching.

"Romeo? Where are you?" she asked gruffly.

He barked urgently, as if she understood universal dog language. For some reason, he was in the living room, at the front door. She carefully made her way there, wishing she had thought to take one of her dad's flashlights to bed with her. When she opened the door, Romeo bolted.

Instantly the panic from her dream came flooding back. Now she could hear the shouts clearly, and she saw dark shadows running down the snowy street. Frantically pulling on her boots and coat, she grabbed a flashlight and Romeo's leash and ran out the door.

When she reached the sidewalk, she stopped, horrified. The glowing sky and the heavy smell of smoke cleared up the mystery. A neighbor's house was fully engulfed in flames, while a small silhouetted crowd stood watching helplessly. She tried to call for Romeo, but a coughing fit overtook her. If anyone was still inside, there was no hope for them.

Chapter 6

Meghan stood with a heavy heart, knowing instinctively that the pulse she was taking would stop in the next few seconds. Holding Hilda's wrist with her right hand, Meghan used her left to smooth the elderly woman's matted hair away from her forehead. Her breathing had a rattle to it, but she didn't seem otherwise distressed. With her eyes closed, Hilda may not have been aware of her surroundings. *Maybe it was better that way*, Meghan thought.

Even with the door to the hall closed, she could hear signs of the chaos: feet shuffling, carts creaking as staff tried to navigate the dim passageways with beds parked on both sides, family members shouting for help with one thing or another, nurses and doctors relaying instructions from room to room, a young child wailing. The electricity had gone off three days earlier, and for some reason the backup generators didn't kick in. Within ten minutes of the power outage, the charge nurse had called a floor meeting with every staff person on duty in West 3rd. She had hurriedly reviewed emergency procedures and delegated specific tasks in patient monitoring and calculating drip rates for patients on IVs. Meghan had been assigned to manually check vitals on all patients on the south side of the hall, and when she finished, to start over, as there were no call lights or alarms.

Rumors had circulated on the first day that the maintenance department found the generators damaged by an electrical surge, and they had been able to get them working again for a while. What a relief it was to hear the sudden beeping of monitors and the whirring of the HVAC system, to have lights and communication systems back on. Cheering came from nearly every hallway and patient room. After ninety minutes without power, they thought the worst was over. The staff scrambled to get everything back to "normal."

However, the backup power only lasted until the second day because they weren't able to get any more diesel fuel delivered. It was supposed to be Meghan's only day off in a nine-day stretch, but when she had tried to leave at the end of her shift the day the power went out, her car wouldn't start. Neither did her co-worker's car, and neither did their phones. None of the businesses in walking distance had electricity, so they were no help. Everyone had questions and no one had answers…except for a man with wild hair standing at the corner of Wayne and Palm, shouting about Jesus and the apocalypse. She was stuck in Warren for the time being, so she decided to make the most of it and help out where she could.

Yesterday the water had stopped flowing, so the hospital staff rummaged through every nook and cranny and closet and storage room to gather hand sanitizers at nurses' stations on every floor. The cafeteria director had stayed around the clock and put together a rationing plan for food and bottled water, since no new deliveries had arrived. Each day there were less and less staff to carry out the workload; nurses and doctors and administrative staff left on foot, one by one, to get home to their families. As staff dwindled and temperatures dropped, any patients that didn't have family members in their rooms with them were moved into the hall to be near the nurse's station.

Among the early deceased were NICU babies, ICU patients and many elderly. The morgue in the lower level was full and the refrigerated compartments were not functioning, so bodies were taken to a large waiting room on the top floor. It was a corner room, the wide open windows inviting in the wintry cold air. With the furniture removed, bodies were tagged and lined up neatly…with room for more to come.

Now here Meghan was, exhausted, cold and hungry, standing at Hilda's bedside. Hilda had been here for over a week, admitted originally with pneumonia. The frail woman's only visitor had been a pastor, who informed Meghan that Hilda had recently lost her husband to cancer and had no family in the area. Each day, Meghan had found little ways to spend extra time with Hilda. When she was awake, they would talk and Hilda would pat Meghan's hand tenderly. The elderly woman spoke with difficulty in tedious, halting phrases, but her eyes lit up any time she saw Meghan. However, with each passing day Hilda seemed to get worse instead of better. The night before the power outage, the doctor had started Hilda on oxygen and ordered blood tests for a suspected infection.

But that was before. Now, in this moment, temporarily separated from all the chaos, Meghan realized with certainty that they wouldn't need the test results, even if the lab could run them. The slow pulse stopped and Meghan waited another couple minutes…just to be sure. Hilda looked so peaceful. The thought of moving her into a long line of unclaimed bodies was almost more than Meghan could bear. She smiled through her tears, knowing that Hilda was happy–happy to be reunited with her husband, to have her young dancing legs back, to be free of this world's restrictions and hardships.

Meghan set Hilda's hand gently down on her chest and brought the other hand to meet it. Readjusting the top sheet, she pulled it up…all the way up, covering Hilda's face. Wiping her eyes quickly and taking a deep breath, she reminded herself that death went hand-in-hand with healing; most of the time we will recover, and at some point we won't. It is part of what she signed up for, but it still broke her heart.

She vigorously rubbed her hands with the dwindling personal supply of hand sanitizer she kept in in her scrubs pocket and then checked on Hilda's roommate. On the other side of the curtain, the roommate had slept through Hilda's quiet passing. Meghan checked her temperature, blood pressure, heart rate and respiration and marked the chart. As she turned to leave, the door from the hall burst open and a young intern jumped nearly out of his shoes when he saw Meghan. He obviously didn't expect to see any staff in the room.

"Patient doors must remain open at all times!" he said more loudly than he needed to. His eyes were wide with fear and his hands moved in awkward, jerky motions.

Meghan shushed him calmly. "Mrs. Hamilton is asleep. Let's not wake her up. But Mrs. Verning has passed. I just wanted to give her some peace in her last few moments in this life. You may go ahead and prop the door open now," she instructed as she brushed past him through the doorway.

She had intended to go to the nurse's station to record Hilda's death and put in a request for removal of the body, but she never made it. After almost being run over by a gurney going faster than it should be in the dim light, she heard her name and turned to see Cindy, a fellow nurse, standing in a patient doorway down the hall.

"Meghan! Quick! Come help us!"

Meghan hurried as best as she could. One of the patients was in cardiac arrest; a young male physical therapist was performing rhythmic compressions. They had already discovered that the defibrillators, although battery powered, were not operational. No time to wonder about the "whys"; they had to move him to emergency, two floors down, where the few remaining doctors were concentrated. The gurney she had seen in the hall was already in place beside the bed. When Cindy counted to "three," they all lifted the sheet and heaved the suffering man onto the gurney. As Meghan stood out of the way and watched the bed on wheels roll out of the room, Cindy yelled, "Come on! We need you! This thing is going down the stairs!"

Meghan suddenly remembered that, of course, the elevators were out of service. She forced her tired legs to move. That's when she heard a little squeak, like that of an animal or small child. Looking around she saw a bedraggled woman shrunken deep into the corner, clutching her handbag to her chest and stuffing a fist into her mouth. Meghan ran to the wide-eyed woman.

"Are you a relation?"

The woman pulled her knuckles out from her teeth far enough to manage, "H…his wife."

"Come with us!" Meghan practically yanked the woman's arm out of the socket, but she didn't care. The woman seemed frozen and there was no time for coddling. Once she got moving, however, she seemed capable of keeping up with Meghan. They caught up with the gurney at the stairwell where it had been decided to keep the wheels down and hope the ride wasn't too bumpy for the patient, who was at least breathing on his own. His wife followed them down the four half-flights to the emergency room, where they all stopped…and stared.

The waiting room had turned into a refugee camp with people spread from wall to wall. Covered with blankets and coats, they huddled together in groups. The receptionist was carefully circling the room with a clipboard, writing down information on forms. Meghan wondered where she found them; the hospital had converted registration systems to electronic several years before she was hired. Even though Meghan was wearing her coat over her scrubs, she could tell it was considerably colder down here than on the third floor.

They wheeled the gurney to the edge of the fray to get the receptionist's attention. Stepping over and around people, she quickly approached them with her clipboard and Cindy handed her the patient's folder. Using a small light attached to her keychain, the woman did a quick once-over and asked, "What's going on with Mr. Powell?"

Steven, the physical therapist, spoke up. "During a therapy session, he began to have chest pains and went into cardiac arrest. I applied CPR and he has stabilized, but he should be checked over before we take him back to his room."

"I'll do what I can. We are triaging manually at this time. There are no tests, no monitoring devices, no surgery, no paging. The doctors are limited to the two rooms that have windows." She made some notes on Mr. Powell's chart and laid it on the foot of his bed. "I can't promise that we'll be able to get to him any time soon. There are a lot of patients here with more urgent needs."

"Yes, I understand. This is his wife," Steven said, gesturing to the silent, panic-stricken woman. "She will stay with him. Someone from West 3rd will be back for him in a couple of hours, or whenever we can spare the extra hands. Where do you want us to park 'im?'"

She pointed to a wide hall entrance and turned back to a young family nearby. Meghan watched her smile as she bent down to talk to a child with red eyes and an ashen face, sitting on his mother's lap. She took a limited amount of information to identify the patient, including "fell down the steps in the dark. Possible broken arm and ribs, possible concussion." As she thumbed through the stack to add the little boy's form into the appropriate order of urgency to see a doctor, she asked the mother to try and keep the whimpering boy awake. Then she was off to start a new patient form. Meghan admired the woman's calm.

"Let's go!" Steven said as he rushed past her after settling the Powells. Behind him, another staff person came into the waiting room, carrying a stack of thin blankets to hand out. Cindy was waiting impatiently at the stairwell door. Meghan hustled to join them; she certainly didn't want to go up the dark stairs alone.

Hearing a sudden commotion, she turned to see a group of people wedged between the "automatic" doors from the outside. The receptionist and another staff member ran to intercept and contain them. Everyone was shouting and no one was listening.

"Com'on," Cindy urged, leading the way. Steven and Meghan took up positions beside the other two staff to reinforce the blockade. With the doors open, Meghan realized it was nearly dark and the wind was merciless. Cindy marched straight through the staff to a disheveled man at the center of the pack. He didn't look evil or mean to Meghan, but desperate. Holding her hands up in the air as a command to be quiet, Cindy waited until they calmed somewhat. Pointing to the man she had already singled out, she asked, "Who in your group is sick or injured?"

"Please, ma'am!" the man's emotion was evident. "We just need shelter! And these women won't let us in!" Other voices in the small crowd echoed his plea.

In a compassionate tone, Cindy asked for confirmation: "But no sick or injured?"

"Well, we're all gonna be sick if you throw us out! How can you do that?" The group grew restless and began fidgeting towards the staff who were trying to hold their ground. Patients in the waiting room watched nervously.

Cindy added some command to her voice. "Sir, sir! Everyone! Listen up! I am sorry. We are not equipped as a shelter, and unless you have a medical condition that needs immediate attention, you cannot stay here. We are overwhelmed as it is!"

The group erupted. The receptionist jumped in, clipboard and all. Waving her arms over her head, she shouted, "I have shelter information! Please...! Calm down!"

"We just walked here all the way from the Baptist church– they're out of food and there are a couple hundred people there! We saw a guy smashin' out the window at the dollar store! It's not safe! Please!" the man begged.

The receptionist started to explain that the hospital didn't have food to spare and the spigots had run dry, but didn't get the chance to finish.

"They have blankets!" one of the younger women in the group cried. There was no way that the staff could hold them back. Like horses bolting from the gate, they broke through the clasped hands and began grabbing blankets from the patients who fought to keep them. A couple men that had been waiting with loved ones rose from their seats, but they were either unsure how to help...or afraid to. Cindy pulled the doors shut to keep out the wind and took charge of the situation, barking out orders. Meghan's job was to find security guards.

Making her way down the dark stairwell to the basement level as quickly and safely as she could, she regretted not having a flashlight. She pulled open the heavy door at the bottom and rushed into the long corridor toward the security office. However, she stopped when she heard the sound of the door shutting behind her. Afraid she would get lost, she stumbled back to the door, opened it and stood in the threshold. With one foot in the stairwell like an anchor, she yelled, "Security! We need help in the ER!" She waited. No answer; no sound of any kind. She tried again, louder. "Is anyone down here?" Still no response or indication of movement. Her eyes and ears were starting to play tricks on her. The hair on the back of her neck stood up on end, and she fled back to the first floor.

The ER was still in chaos. Having failed at finding the security team, Meghan rushed down the hall to the right of the stairs, looking for any staff that might be able to help. These rooms were mostly labs and testing rooms, so they were deserted. She half-ran as much as safety would warrant in the dimness, one hand held out in front of her and the fingertips of her other hand lightly trailing along the wall. On she stumbled as the halls connected and looped back around toward the Emergency entrance, looking for any possible reinforcements. The last area was the pharmacy, and here she found two staff members, who froze in mid-action when Meghan unexpectedly burst through the door.

She groaned an audible sigh of relief. "Thank God! I've been looking everywhere…. Hurry! Come with me!"

"Hey! We're...working here, can't you see?" the first man spoke up. He dropped the small boxes in his hands into something behind the counter that Meghan couldn't see and turned around to face the nearly empty shelves.

"We need help in the ER! We need staff! Com'on!"

"Patients are waiting for us. We're in a huge hurry–get outta here!" the other man joined in loudly, taking Meghan off guard at the ferocity of the command. When she didn't move, he came around the edge of the counter, shining his flashlight in her face.

She backed up a step and lifted a hand to shield her eyes, making one last passionate attempt to persuade them. "Please! We all need to help each other right now. There's a group of people who forced their way through the doors! Someone's going to get hurt!"

The man with the flashlight started to laugh as he closed the distance between them, and Meghan felt a new kind of fear. From somewhere deep down she mustered enough courage to ask forcefully, "Where's Dr. Snyder?"

No response. She braced herself as she randomly thought how too much light was just as problematic as not enough light; she was essentially blind. The man grabbed her arm and pulled her to his side. Her first reaction was to gasp, but her second reaction was to elbow him hard in the solar plexus with her free arm. He recoiled with a groan but managed to hang on to her. Then he flung open the door and lowered the light beam to illuminate the hallway floor just across the threshold.

He whispered hoarsely into her ear, and she leaned away from his terrible breath and unbathed body. "If you know what's good for you, go now...and find help somewhere else." He put his large hand around the back of her neck and slowly pushed her out of the room. As the door shut behind her, she realized that the men weren't clearing the shelves for their patients.

Chapter 7

"Time's running out. Where are we, boys?"

Three scruffy men, sitting in a literal pile of mechanical parts and tools and manuals, glanced up at the imposing middle-aged man filling the doorframe. A force to be reckoned with, Gaylord Royce Andrews III was a former CEO for a multi-billion dollar research and consulting firm that developed advanced weapons systems for the U.S Armed Forces. Along with the hideous name, he had inherited wealth, brilliance, and cunning from a long line of ambitious ivy-league leaders in business and politics. When he left home to make his own way in the world, he dropped the first two names and went by Andrews from that point forward. With a slick, debonair appearance and a physique rightfully earned in a high-end gym, his very presence demanded respect. After years of practice in the company's boardroom, his voice could range from silky smooth to solid steel, but at this moment it came across like a demanding boss. "Well?"

The shortest of the three men, sprouting a long, thin braid down his back, stood without speaking and approached Andrews at the threshold, holding a strange sculpture of metal out in front of him.

Mr. Andrews took the large contraption from him, turning it over in his hands. "Looks good. Will it work?"

Travis Long's leathery face broke into a cocky grin. "Let's go find out." A Gulf War vet in his early fifties who fit every stereotype of the "biker" dude, Travis was cold-hearted and calculating, the perfect hand-picked leader for Andrews' motley security team.

Mr. Andrews pivoted and disappeared into the dark hall with the contraption. Travis quickly grabbed a wrench lying nearby and gestured to Mike and Charlie, who held a replica of what Andrews had taken. The three men jogged to catch up, the beams from their flashlights leading the way. The wide underground passageway had a series of doors on both sides, ending at a stairway that led up into the barn. Mr. Andrews had left the door open at the top of the stairs, and they caught up with him crouching behind his old pickup, moving the gadget back and forth at different angles under the bumper.

"It's not going to fit!" he announced in an irritated tone as they arrived.

Charles "Charlie" Sullivan approached nervously, setting down the one he was carrying. He was the youngest of the three recruits and fairly intimidated by Andrews. He, like Travis, was a U.S. Veteran, having served one short tour in Iraq. On this sole experience he blamed his drinking problem and the inability to build meaningful relationships. However, his niche of confidence was his mechanical talent. Now he had to prove himself to Mr. Andrews. He knelt down and quietly rotated the part into place; it fit like a glove. Custom-designed to use the truck's ball hitch and provide extra stability, it would distribute a large weight over the full width of the truck frame. Charlie made a few adjustments with the wrench Travis handed him and bolted it into place. The other men all watched in silence.

Charlie stepped back and waited. Mr. Andrews rubbed his chin and looked the contraption over thoroughly, even standing on it and bouncing until the rear shocks joined in. Finally he smiled. "Impressive!" The men began to breath. Charlie shifted his weight and looked at his feet to hide a half-smile and the color rising in his cheeks. "Let's not celebrate too soon," Andrews cautioned. He gestured to the large part still lying on the floor. "Get that one fitted, too." Charlie scurried to the next bay to attach the hitch onto a second truck, the one Travis had stolen from a neighbor's driveway to get to Mr. Andrews' retreat. He didn't have the key…but that had never stopped Travis.

Nodding with appreciation, Andrews gave two good knocks on the rusted tailgate with the side of his fist and looked at the men with anticipation evident in his sparkling eyes and perfect veneered teeth. "We're ready. Let's roll out in 30 minutes. You know what to do."

The dark, cloud-laden sky made the cold night feel colder. Travis led with the tractor, pulling the hay wagon at a top speed of 30 miles per hour. Charlie's years of souping up vehicles for tractor pulls at local fairs had come in handy, although Mr. Andrews had made it clear that the modifications in this job were for pulling extra weight, not for speed. Crouching in the back of the hay wagon was a large shape in the form of Mike Peterson, a former bouncer at a local bar who had been a football star in college until a series of concussions scared the pro team scouts off. He was wearing night vision goggles and armed with an AR-15. Beside him were two gas cans filled with extra fuel, a siphon hose for pilfering gas from abandoned vehicles instead of wasting their own, a stack of neatly folded tarps, a tool box, a coil of rope, a burlap sack filled with various sizes of bungee cords, and a small box of fireworks, just in case a diversion was needed.

Following the slow moving tractor was Andrews' old pickup truck, driven by Mr. Andrews, and the other old, ugly pickup, driven by Charlie. It was risky, taking three vehicles with only one lookout, but it had only been four days since the grid had gone down, and Andrews was willing to bet that the smaller towns weren't quite in panic mode yet. Plus, he justified it by saying that he was doing a good deed; he was going to save an entire town.

They were a little over two hours into the trip and almost to their destination, a small town just off Interstate 80. It was after 10:00 pm, and if they were to be back at the retreat by dawn, they would have to hustle. To avoid some curious and ambitious group from setting up an ambush, they would take a different route home. Andrews knew that the loud, slow tractor engine would attract attention, even in the dark. The route home would be more circuitous and would take longer, but it would pass fewer residential areas and therefore be less risky.

All four men had studied the maps and knew the plan, so no one was surprised when Travis pulled off the main road and led them into the business district. So far, Mike hadn't spotted any movement, but he was challenged to watch both sides of the road at once, especially now with so many close-to-the-road places for someone to hide. The men noticed that glass storefronts were still fully intact and the town still looked "normal," a credit to Mr. Andrews' theory.

Within minutes Travis pulled into a car dealership, driving past the shiny, new, useless cars and beyond the showroom to a large lot in the back. Lined up in a perfect row were moving trucks and trailers of various sizes. Andrews was only interested in the largest trailers. He needed two, one for each pickup.

"Damn!" His fist took his frustration out on the steering wheel. The large trailers were not there; that was the risk with one-way rentals. He jumped out of the truck without thinking of who might be watching. Mike stayed in the wagon and continued to scan the 360-degree area; Travis and Charlie met up with Andrews.

"Plan B," Mr. Andrews grunted. "I'm not going to waste my time hooking these small things up; we need more room. Keep your eyes open for larger trailers–anything we can pull. We'll get onto the interstate if we have to! It will be a virtual parking lot of hauling trucks."

"Boss?" Charlie spoke up tentatively.

"Speak your mind, Charles," Andrews answered with forced patience.

"Well, I was thinkin' that maybe there will be trucks at the warehouse…you know, loading or unloading when the grid went down. Why couldn't we use them?"

"Don't you think they'd most likely be semi's with full-length trailers and hydraulic systems locked down tight? Even if we could hitch them, we couldn't pull them. Why didn't you say something when we made our plan?"

Charlie fidgeted and his eyes darted around nervously. "I…uh…was hoping that the outage didn't reach this far…and, um, we would get here and find help."

Travis and Mike raised their eyebrows and watched as Andrews stepped up to Charlie, nose to nose, and quietly said, "This outage goes from coast to coast. How would you like to drive that clunker to California to see if I'm right?"

When Charlie didn't answer, Andrews nailed the boy across the jaw and sent him sprawling. Calmly leaning over the startled fallen figure, he commanded softly, "Don't doubt me again."

"No, Sir!" Charlie was smart enough to respond as he scrambled to his feet.

Turning back to the hay wagon, Andrews barked at the other men. "That goes for you, too. Now, roll out!" Everyone darted back into place and Plan B was underway.

Rubbing his jaw from the safety of the truck cab, Charlie wondered if the million dollars that Mr. Andrews had promised each of them after the grid came back up would be enough.

After striking out at the two other self-moving truck locations that he knew of, Andrews had to decide whether they would head to the warehouse on the outskirts of town or in the opposite direction to the interstate. His men wisely waited while Andrews paced, silently thinking through the scenarios. Finally, his head snapped up and he informed the men that it was too late and too risky to head to the interstate, and the longer they stayed in town, the more time it gave the locals a chance to mobilize against them. "Head straight to the distribution center, but watch for something along the way that we can pull. We need more space for supplies. A lot more. Hopefully, we get lucky."

They pulled out of the lot with Andrews in the lead and the tractor last, allowing Mike to watch their rear. The next fifteen minutes were nerve-wracking for Charlie, Travis, and Mike as their eyes scanned side to side continuously for any sign of life. They were only about half a mile from the warehouse when Andrews pulled into another used car dealership. Even on a cloudy, starless night, Mr. Andrews had excellent vision. Although a variety of models and ages of cars lined the lot, the sign also boasted "custom built trailers."

All four men dismounted and pulled up their guns within seconds without making a sound. Andrews gestured to Mike to sweep the outside of the building, while he pointed Travis and Charlie into the showroom. Travis easily broke in through the side door to the service entrance and cautiously looked around, using their flashlights sparingly. The showroom had a shiny new utility trailer that looked like it could be used for hauling motorcycles or a sports car, but they needed something enclosed, or at least with higher sides. Making their way back through the service bays and into an attached pole building, Travis and Charlie found a very happy boss bent over the hitch attachment of an aluminum eighteen-foot long stock trailer.

Andrews stood and manually opened the bay door, startling Mike who had just reached the back corner of the building. Instructing Mike to pull Andrews' truck around and back it into the bay, Charlie readied the trailer hitch for connection. It didn't take long to make the necessary adjustments with the modified hitch, and Mike made a wide swing out of the bay to clear the corner.

In the back of the large room there were a couple of very small open trailers and pieces of trailers, but nothing else that could haul the amount of supplies they needed. However, Mike took the men outside to show them something he had found when circling the grounds. On one overgrown edge of the fenced-in property he had noticed a very old, deep brown colored, fully-enclosed trailer. Partially concealed by the growth, it was nearly impossible to see in the darkness. "It's a bit rusty, Mr. Andrews, but I think it's still solid. What do you think?"

Even though it was a little smaller than the stock trailer, it was the biggest option available for the second truck. Mr. Andrews waved his hand with impatience toward Travis' pickup truck, and Charlie took off running. The other three tried rocking the trailer back and forth to budge it out of the comfortable ruts it had nestled itself into as the seasons cycled past.

"It's no use," Andrews huffed. "Go find us some leverage!"

Mike and Travis dug through the trailer parts in the shop and found a couple of long metal bars. By then, Charlie had backed the truck up to a good spot nearby. The four men heaved until the trailer was clear of the hard earth and rolled it with great effort the last three feet to the truck. The tires were shot from being weathered and sitting for so many years. It took longer than it should have to change the tires and hitch up the trailer, but finally they were on their way to accomplish their mission: to clean all the food and bottled water out of the distribution center and help the people of Tionesta survive the long winter ahead.

Chapter 8

Beth Ann groaned as she lifted the upper end of the twin-sized mattress she was helping Mr. Howard move into the basement. Her limbs felt weak and she knew that the stress and lack of nutrition were beginning to take a toll. She was trying to keep Gary from bearing all the weight – or being pushed down the stairs – as he was at the lower end. Slowly, one step at a time, they safely reached the bottom of the steps and laid the mattress onto the bed frame. Taking a brief rest, her eyes roamed the dim, open space.

The boxes and containers normally stored in the Howards' basement had been searched for anything usable in a world without electricity, heat, water, communication, light, or transportation. Most of the stuff was not helpful; these items were rearranged into the sturdiest boxes and stacked to make a room divider across the basement. Tools, sheets and blankets, camping equipment, and old books about useful things like gardening and first aid, were kept out.

The stacked box divider was roughly five feet high and stretched most of the way across the basement, leaving an opening in the middle about four feet wide. Behind this divider they put the beds: the larger one for the Howards and their son's twin bed for Beth Ann, with a couple of sheets hung between them for privacy. On the "living" side of the box wall was the small table and three chairs from the kitchen, a hodgepodge seating area, scattered mix-and-match rugs from upstairs to warm the concrete floor, a stack of plastic containers holding useful items like candles, matches, pens, paper, board games, and the non-functioning deep freezer, washer, dryer and washtub. The wood burning furnace, a large pile of logs, and a box of kindling took up a good chunk of space behind the stairs. A door through the block wall on the front side of the house opened into the narrow fruit cellar below the front porch, where neatly stacked jars of Mrs. Howard's locally-famous canned fruit and vegetables lined the shelves. Beth Ann's oil lamp burned bravely on a small side table at the bottom of the stairs. They had a little more work to do, but it was nearly done, and it felt good to be doing something…anything.

As she rested, Beth Ann's thoughts wandered to the events of the past week. After the neighbor's house had burned to the ground in the middle of the night, taking the young family with it, a couple of nearby volunteer firefighters had determined the source to be a kerosene heater. Both adults and a toddler were found in one bedroom, along with the old heater. Whether it was knocked over or simply caught the curtains or bedding on fire, the family had no warning from the useless smoke detectors, and the room would have been engulfed within seconds. The entire neighborhood mourned, not just for the family but for their own lives, for modern conveniences and a bit of normalcy, and for loved ones they couldn't reach.

That's the day hard reality set in for Beth Ann, and the day that the Howards decided to move into the basement where the temperature below ground was more moderate. Their wood burning furnace could still be used for radiant heat, but without the electric blower the ductwork was ineffective and a waste of precious wood. Gary closed and covered all the upstairs registers and ripped holes in the exposed ductwork in the basement with a screwdriver and tin snips to maximize the heat.

Every day that week Gary and Linda had urged Beth Ann to move in with them, but Beth Ann held out, struggling to maintain hope that her parents would return and make it all better. When the first Saturday came and went, then Sunday, she felt like she was sinking into a deep pit. She sobbed herself to sleep Sunday night, curled inside her dad's musty sleeping bag, praying that the dark silence would swallow her and she wouldn't wake. Poor Romeo cried with her, not understanding, but just loving her.

But Monday had come. With complete apathy, Beth Ann lay on her back with her face turned toward the sole window in her room until the cold gray light of a cloudy winter day intruded into her death wish. She did not want to move. She did not want to think. She only wanted her parents and her old life back.

But, lying for so long in that cold, silent vacuum, she did think. It was unavoidable. She thought about Mr. Howard's offer to move in with them; maybe it would help her depression to be around other people. She thought about her parents and hoped they were okay; hoped they were thinking of her and trying to get back to her. She thought about her brother, miles away on his little farm; maybe she could walk there…but maybe she would freeze to death before she reached it. She thought about her friends, where they were and if they were okay. She thought about the dwindling supplies: food, water, toothpaste, toilet paper, dog food, matches. She thought about how much she detested having to relieve herself in a pot and clean it out with leaves and snow, and how she couldn't take a hot shower or wash her clothes or hair. She wondered if it was possible, in modern society, to starve to death…and how long it would take.

While her thoughts grew darker, Romeo decided he must answer nature's call. Beth Ann realized that she would get up…for Romeo. Wrapped in layers, she let Romeo out the back door and shuffled slowly around the house, half-heartedly going through her new morning routine. Romeo didn't linger in the cold, and Beth Ann now noticed that a light snow was beginning to fall. She longed to check the weather report; she hated feeling so isolated and uninformed.

Beth Ann spread a thin layer of peanut butter on the last two slices of hard bread; normally she would throw the heel away, but now she couldn't waste anything. There was one more loaf in the now-thawed freezer because her mom had stocked up on groceries before she left. The Howards had helped her cook the meat from the freezer on her dad's grill over the weekend, to make it safer to keep. She carefully poured Romeo a rationed portion of dog food, which he scarfed down quickly. There was another large bag in the garage, but after that...she didn't want to think about it. What would she do without Romeo?

She was just finishing her bread when a forceful knocking at the front door nearly made her scream. Romeo barked and ran to the door. Beth Ann took a deep breath and a few seconds to compose herself. *Good grief,* she thought, *it's just Mr. Howard.* He came to visit every day. She opened the door without checking to see who it was.

"Joe!" she exclaimed in surprise.

"Hey, Bethie. Just coming by to check on you," Big Joe said with exaggerated cheerfulness.

"Why?" she asked suspiciously. Checking on her was not in his character.

"I'm bored. ...And I wanted to make sure you were okay," he added quickly.

"Well, that's nice, but thanks...I'm fine."

Joe gave a dramatic shudder. "Can I come in? It's cold out here!" Without waiting for a reply, he stepped across the threshold. Romeo backed up slightly, but he stood rigidly at Beth Ann's feet, staring up guardedly at the big man.

Beth Ann hesitated to shut the front door. She would rather be cold than stuck in a conversation with Big Joe. Why the heck was he here? She watched him slowly sweep the living and dining rooms with his eyes as if he was looking for something, until he turned back to her.

"So, did your parents make it home okay from their trip?"

"Now, what do you think?" she snapped.

"I'm sorry…I'm sorry," he shrank back defensively, and then his voice softened. "Wow. I'm really sorry."

That almost undid her, but she would not cry in front of Joe. "So…, do you have any idea what's going on?"

They stood talking awkwardly for a few minutes. Joe bought into the theory that the U.S. had been attacked, otherwise by now people outside the community would have come to check on them and trucks from other states would have been rolling in with supplies. Beth Ann despaired to think that this was bigger than she had assumed. He talked about his neighbors in town; some had left on foot to be with relatives, and the remaining neighbors had pillaged everything they left behind, even fighting over their stuff. He finally confessed that he was almost out of food in his bachelor pad and wondered if she had anything she could share with him.

Beth Ann felt compassion for him and went into the kitchen to put some of her pantry supplies in a plastic bag for him. He followed her, and although he kept his distance, she felt extremely uncomfortable. She glanced sideways at him and saw his eyes sweeping the room intently. It had not occurred to her to keep her food stash private; now he had seen everything. The truth hit her in a blinding flash: he was here to scope out her situation, her supplies. With great effort she tried to keep her panic hidden and carry on the small talk. She had to get him out of the house.

Beth Ann took the bag to the front door and stepped out onto the small covered porch. Joe reluctantly followed her out. Handing the bag out to him, she said, "Here. I wish I could help you more, but…."

Instead of taking the bag, he grasped her hand in both of his. "Then let me help you, Beth Ann. I can move in here with you and keep you safe! You shouldn't be alone! We can pool our resources and be survivors together," he urged with conviction…or desperation.

She yanked her hand from his and tossed the bag into the snow. "You told me ten minutes ago that you don't have any 'resources,' jerk!" She crossed her arms and glared at him until he backed down the steps.

He picked up the bag and paused with his back to her. Then he slowly turned and came back, glancing over his shoulder. "Listen, Beth Ann," he said in a hushed tone. "There's lots of stuff at the diner going to waste. We are going there after dark to get what we can. Come with us."

"Wait…what? You're breaking in? That's a crime! And who's 'we'?" Beth Ann was shocked.

"Shhh! Yes, it's a crime. But an unpunishable one. You're out here in utopia, but in town things are insane. Last night stores on the main drag were raided. The grocery store is stripped clean. There's no way for people to call the police. And most of the owners are rich guys who live out of state. You know Mr. Bell, the pharmacist? Apparently he was living in his store and he was killed trying to defend his property. People are getting desperate, Beth Ann! We–Charlie, Ken, Sandy and I–think that if we have a decent size group, it will be less risky. You know, 'safety in numbers.'"

"Joe! I…I couldn't!" Beth Ann couldn't believe what she was hearing. The fear that crept into her heart made the flesh under all her layers tingle.

"Hey–if we don't get it soon, someone else will. And we deserve it more because we earned it! We worked that place!"

She just shook her head slowly in disbelief.

"OK, well, if you change your mind, meet us in the back, by the dumpster, about an hour after dark. And bring some bags." He stood for a few seconds, looking intently at her. "I'm serious, Beth Ann. Things are gonna get real bad, real soon."

She watched him make his way on foot down the street toward town until she couldn't see him anymore, then she raced through the house, dead-bolting all three of the doors.

"Come on, Romeo," she crooned as she pulled an empty suitcase out from the upper shelf of the hall closet. "We need to pack. We're moving in with the Howards."

For the better part of that day, Gary had helped her go through the house and decide which valuables to move. But her valuables now weren't jewelry and money; they were her remaining food and water stashes, her dad's hunting and camping supplies, a couple of guns, her lamp and candles and wind-up clock. Even the dusty fishing rod from the garage got a second chance at life. They waited until after dark to move the items down a shallow grade and through a line of shrubs to the Howards' house.

Exhausted, later that night the Howards and Beth Ann had put together a mini plan for survival to get through the winter…just in case. They talked about alternative water and food sources…just in case. They talked about security and defending the basement…just in case. Some of Gary's knowledge came from his emergency training and some of it came from doing Boy Scout activities with his son's troop. The next morning, which was now today, she finished helping Mr. Howard with his move to the basement.

A melodic voice from the top of the stairs broke her reflection. "Anybody down there hungry? Lunch is ready!" Mrs. Howard was in her element, delighted to have a "child" in the house to take care of again. Mr. Howard smiled at Beth Ann and held his arm out toward the stairs, indicating that she should go first. And with a sudden stabbing pain that made her catch her breath, she realized this was it—a surreal but true reality…her new family…her new life.

Chapter 9

The days went by very, very slowly as things gradually settled into a routine of sorts. Beth Ann went through the motions mechanically, robotically, like she was programmed to aimlessly keep moving. She felt empty and lost, even though she was grateful for the Howards.

Living in the basement was fairly comfortable, although Beth Ann detested the musty smell and it made her head stuffy. When they woke up, they would add layers to whatever they slept in and take turns using the one upstairs bathroom. Of course, the sink, tub and toilet didn't work, but somehow it still seemed the most appropriate way to take care of private business. They would eat a small amount of something perishable, checking the expiration dates for what to eat first, and saving everything canned for the longer term. Then they worked on "chores" or projects together, inside or outside, depending on the weather. Lunch and dinner were light as well, a hodge-podge of things that didn't normally go together...and the same things they may have eaten for the last several days in a row. They used bowls and cups when needed, but rarely used plates, eating straight from the storage containers with their fingers. There simply was not enough water to spare for washing at this point, and the soap supply would run out eventually. In the afternoon they would continue the work they had started in the morning, although most days Mrs. Howard would lie down to rest instead.

A couple of times Gary took his gun and went hunting. He frequently came across other "hunters," some shooting at anything that moved. It wasn't the safest situation, but he had no choice if they wanted meat. He couldn't go very far on foot and still make it back by daylight's end, so he took whatever he could find: squirrel, rabbit, wild goose. Beth Ann got sick to her stomach when Gary brought home game and showed her how to skin and dress the meat for cooking, but it was a life-saving skill that she was going to have to know and she stuck it out.

The evenings were the best part of the day, although Beth Ann was surprised to admit it. Gary would read by the light of the oil lamp while Linda crocheted or sewed. They would have thought-provoking discussions or work through a riddle book and laugh, which made her feel equally guilty and happy. Sometimes he would bring out his guitar, which he played like a fourth-grade beginner, and the mismatched trio would sing their hearts out. It was a great emotional release. In a bazillion years, Beth Ann would never have dreamed that she could enjoy spending her time this way; she would have been out with friends or on the internet or her phone. It made her feel embarrassed to look back on those days…and those days were only two weeks ago.

Gary read aloud from his Bible every night, and Beth Ann found it comforting, even though she didn't understand everything he read. She had a Bible of her own which her parents had given her when she started youth group in 7th grade. Although she had taken it to church faithfully, she had never really thought about sitting down to read it. It was on a shelf in her "old" room, and she made a mental note to retrieve it one of these days.

Gary had also started reading *The Magician's Nephew*, chronologically the first book in C.S. Lewis's *Narnia* series. He read a little each night, and then they would talk about it. What seemed like such a simple children's adventure story took on much greater meaning with relevance to the new world she found herself in: evil and death, the courage needed to face obstacles, the depravity of human beings, and trust in God despite the circumstances.

Even with the occasional moments of happiness, Beth Ann felt mostly-dead on the inside, and constantly sore and tired on the outside. She was not accustomed to the manual labor that made up a hefty portion of her days. And without the caloric values to support the extra work, her body was essentially using up its own mass to get energy. When Gary had put plans in place for chores and projects relating to their survival through the winter, she knew it was going to be tough. But she was old enough to understand that this was literally a "do or die" situation: if they didn't prepare for sustaining their future over an indefinite period of time, they would be dead within weeks, or more accurately a couple of days after finishing their water.

Finding a water source was one of the most urgent issues. The water in the bathtubs at the Howard's and the Dalton's houses was the only wash source, and Linda added a few drops of chlorine once a week. The containers of potable tap water that they had stored were almost gone, and Romeo would finish the water out of the combined three toilets in a matter of days. Beth Ann had brought a case of bottled water from her house, and the Howards had four cases stored from when it was on sale, but that wouldn't last very long. It was frustrating that the Allegheny River was so close, but the access point was too far away to carry heavy buckets of water by foot, and soon the river would be covered by ice.

On Wednesday the ambient temperature rose above freezing, so Gary decided to harvest as much snow as possible before it melted. What sounded easy to Beth Ann turned out to be a lot of painstaking, exasperating work for a very small amount of water. Gary started a small fire in the side yard, which was the most protected place from the wind. Linda tended to the fire while Gary and Beth Ann started at the far end of the back yard, working their way slowly toward the house in methodical 12" wide strips. Each had a bucket with a small amount of the saved tap water. They would add one or two scoops of snow into the bucket and swirl until it liquefied, then add a scoop or two more. It took over half the backyard to get those two buckets filled three-fourths of the way full! Beth Ann wanted to poke her eyes out in frustration, but she kept going, because she knew how important it was.

They retraced their steps around the exterior of the property to the side yard, so as not to trample any usable snow. The hot coals were ready. They helped Linda filter the water through an old t-shirt into the dutch oven pot. Then, while Gary and Beth Ann started over with the next two buckets, Linda heated the water to boiling and poured it into various food storage containers with lids that sealed to be stacked in the fruit cellar. After lunch they worked on Beth Ann's back yard.

The smoke from Linda's fire had drawn several neighbors over, asking for food, but Gary had deflected them by saying that they weren't cooking. He explained how to get extra water for themselves and recommended that they go work on getting their own before all the snow melted, and there was no trouble.

On Thursday, the snow had melted enough that it was nearing the grass level, making it hard to scoop without getting mud and leaves in it. So they gathered what they could from places where the snow had drifted into higher mounds, and even from the shady side of both rooftops. Since they had more daylight to work with and Gary was already on the roof, he had Beth Ann help him rig a rain and runoff water collection system, laying the "inside" of extra vinyl siding pieces facing upward across the gutters on a slight downward slope from the middle to the corners of the house. He let the ends hang past the edge of the house about eighteen inches, and set a large tarp under each overhang. The tarp was staked up at the four corners and halfway between each of the corners, to make a rough catch-basin. Gary explained that without rain barrels or anything big enough to catch the water and snow, they would have to check the tarps frequently and drain them into pots as needed. He didn't have enough extra siding pieces to rig the back side of Beth Ann's roof, so when they moved to the Dalton house late in the afternoon, he modified the existing gutter downspouts instead.

Gary wanted to rig the water collection only in the back of both houses so that it would not be obvious to the whole neighborhood. Beth Ann had argued with him, feeling that they should be helping their neighbors. But Gary had insisted that at some point the neighbors would turn on them and take everything they had; his first priority was keeping himself, his wife, and Beth Ann alive. She really thought he was being paranoid, but she had few options. She would do whatever he told her to do.

Friday was a beautiful sunny day, and they took advantage of the weather to gather every burnable stick or log in both yards, lining them up on the warm, blacktopped driveway to begin the drying process. At lunch, Gary announced that it was time to walk into town. Beth Ann was anxious to get information–and to just get out of the house–so she opted to go with him.

Gary checked the clip in his handgun and holstered it. Then he handed Beth Ann a little revolver. She just stood looking at it on her open palm.

"Know how to use that?" he asked.

Beth Ann looked at him. "My dad took me to the range a couple times, but it's been years."

Gary took it back, emptied the bullets and checked the chamber, then handed it back to her. "For now just carry it as a deterrent. I don't need you shooting your foot!" She dropped it into her coat pocket like a hot coal and they headed out the door.

Joe had not exaggerated about the looting in town. A pile of wood and ash where the donut shop used to be was still smoldering. The main street through town was deserted, but Beth Ann could sense dozens of eyes watching. As they entered the municipal building, one of the Sheriff's deputies stopped them by blocking their way with his baton.

"State your business," he said in monotone.

"We're here to see the Mayor and find out what the plan is for dealing with this crisis...and how we can help," Gary replied calmly, sending a sideways glance to Beth Ann.

"The mayor is out of the office today," the deputy replied, still holding his baton in front of them.

"What?" Gary half laughed and half choked. "Out of the office?" Realizing that the deputy was serious, he continued. "Okay. How about the council? Or the sheriff? Who the heck is in charge here?"

The man paused, apparently debating his options, and then lowered the baton. "Wait here," he commanded.

Beth Ann watched him climb a wide staircase and disappear into the dark hall. The grand foyer was decorated in colonial blues and reds with brass accents. Several stiff wingback chairs lined one wall like sentries, waiting for visitors to sit in them. It would have been a pretty place if the matted dirt could be cleaned off the hardwood floors and wool area rugs.

Hearing voices, she glanced up to see the officer escorting a disheveled man down the steps.

"And here they are," the deputy said by way of introduction.

Gary stuck out his hand. "I'm Gary. This is my neighbor, Beth Ann."

Hesitant, the man finally shook Gary's hand. "I'm Councilman Otto. Please, won't you have a seat?" He gestured to the chairs.

Mr. Otto seemed quite willing to share any information he had. The mayor was sick and would most likely die within a few days without insulin. The council president, Becky Moorehead, had left the day before when her son came down with the flu; she hadn't been heard from since. He had no news of what was going on, how far it extended, or when the power company would have everything up and running again. The sheriff had his hands full with the jail and trouble in town, and he had set up roadblocks to keep hungry travelers out. Most of the businesses on the main drag had been looted clean. Dead bodies were being taken to a sand trap at the golf course. Many of the city council members had left town, and without leadership the chaos was taking over. Otto's defeat was evident in his sagging shoulders.

Gary and Beth Ann left feeling discouraged. As they silently walked toward home, Gary noticed a woman and baby come out of the Lutheran church, where he and Linda were members.

"Hey, let's stop at the church and see if Pastor Dan is there," Gary said with renewed energy, steering Beth Ann into an alley.

They found Pastor Dan in the fellowship hall on the basement level, where people and children were clustered on cots and mattresses lined up on the floor. Dan looked exhausted, even gaunt, as he led them into the kitchen. He confided that he had thought he was helping when people approached him with their needs; his solution was to have people bring everything they had and live communally. Now he had four families from outside of town, all farms, that had been attacked by looters. They had no supplies to bring, and they had already lost family members. In fact, one family was simply three newly orphaned children, afraid and with nowhere to go. Some needed medical attention beyond the first aid he could provide. He had tried to reach a doctor from his congregation, but Dr. Myers' house was vacant and thoroughly trashed when he showed up on the front porch. He had a couple more people from in town that showed up *after* they had run out of supplies, so that didn't help. All the food stored in the church and soup kitchen had been depleted. The men he had sent hunting couldn't find any game to shoot. They were still able to haul water up from the river, but how much longer could they last without food?

Gary had nothing encouraging to tell his pastor, other than he would pray for the situation that needed a real, modern-day miracle. As Beth Ann listened to the pastor talk, she felt a deep sense of dread take root. The violence would eventually find them and they would need to be ready.

More than ready to leave, they scurried home. Gary kissed Linda when he walked in the door and promised that he would not go back into town; it was simply too dangerous.

For the last couple of daylight hours, Beth Ann helped Gary cut down a larger tree on his lot that was leaning and he had wanted to remove for years. The chainsaw worked well, but he had only a small amount of gas and oil in the garage for refilling. To spare the fuel, he used it on the trunk and larger limbs, while Beth Ann used a hand saw for cutting up the smaller branches. Gary wielded an ax on the larger trunk pieces to split them. It would have to season slowly on the covered patio, but Gary had previously stored enough wood for this winter because of his wood-burning furnace.

As Gary suspected, the sound of the chainsaw attracted neighbors. But he was prepared. Each time a neighbor showed up, he asked him or her to come back at dusk to talk. Then he and Beth Ann finished off the daylight getting the tree cut and stacked on the back patio.

At one point, when Beth Ann stood up to stretch and rub her back, Gary set the ax down and came over to her. She assumed he was going to empathize with her aches and pains, but instead he asked her if she had her house key on her. Puzzled, she pulled it out of her coat pocket.

"Let's take a little break," he said. "I need to look for something." He found a small gray bottle in the Dalton's garage and asked for permission to use it. She shrugged and nodded. He asked her to keep it in her coat pocket for now and they went back to work.

Just as the light started fading, Linda came out to help them gather the sticks and twigs that had been warming on the driveway; they stacked them on the back patio with the rest of the winter's wood to be used as kindling.

As expected, by the time they finished clearing the driveway, nearly a dozen people had gathered around the Howard's front porch. Gary stood on the second step so that everyone could hear him clearly. Linda lit a lantern and hung it from a hook that held her ferns in the summer. Per Gary's prior instructions, Beth Ann stood among the crowd.

Gary began, "Thank you all for coming back so that I could finish my job in the daylight. My neighbor, Beth Ann, was helping me today, and in return I am going to help her family cut some wood. I assume each of you is here because you would like to cut wood for fuel." He watched the heads all nod affirmatively.

"We need food, too!" one of the men spoke up.

"I can't help you with that, I'm sorry," Gary said with compassion. "The only thing I can help with is cutting wood." He paused. "Now, I don't have enough gas and oil to cut more than one or two trees, but I thought that if we all pool together, we might have enough to accomplish the job. Do any of you have another chainsaw?" No one spoke up.

"Okay. Raise your hand if you have gasoline stored in a container or left in your car tank." Everyone raised a hand, including Beth Ann. *Good*, she thought; *he's testing them to see who's being honest.*

"Great. As you know, we've gotta mix it with oil. So who has bottles of two-stroke engine oil?" Beth Ann and three of the men raised their hands, with six bottles between them, including Gary's extra one. Everyone agreed to Gary's terms that each of them would donate one of their own trees and their own gasoline; the oil would be split between them, and all would donate their labor to help each other until each tree was stacked at its respective owner's house. If there was any leftover oil, they would vote at that time on the possibility of cutting more and dividing the wood among them. They would all bring their own hand tools with their names clearly marked on the handles, as well as any teen or adult family members who could help, and they would take one 90-minute break mid-day to go home for lunch and a rest. They agreed on a starting place and time for the next morning.

After everyone left, Gary explained to Beth Ann that he didn't want anyone to know that her house was vacant. He wanted to treat her like any other neighbor to keep from raising suspicions, or giving anyone a reason to go rummaging through her home. She needed to start letting Romeo out the front door occasionally, just to be seen at her house. They would stack the wood at her house, and if anyone asked, she would tell them that her parents were very sick. The plan made her nauseous. It felt like a lie, but for all she knew, it might be the truth.

On Saturday they cut trees and split, carried, and stacked wood. Beth Ann was seriously afraid that her arms would fall off and her back would crack in half. And then she wished they would so that she could collapse into bed and not be disturbed for a long time. Everyone worked together, but not in a cheerful "heigh-ho, heigh-ho" Disney way. There was very little interaction, barely even eye contact. The solemn eyes on the long, drawn faces ranged from sad to anxious to fearful. Without adequate food, even the full grown men grew exhausted too quickly. Gary did not offer a smile of hope or a hand of comfort, as he had for Beth Ann. He seemed tense, like his mind was in another place; he acted like he wanted to get through this job and back to his comfort zone in the cellar. They finished Beth Ann's tree and three others before dark, and they made a plan to resume on Monday. Gary also invited them to join him for a short in-home church service the next morning.

No one came to the "church" service, but Beth Ann was secretly glad. She needed a day to rest. The extra quiet time must have helped Gary, too, because he experienced a grand "aha" moment. Going to the fruit cellar to get some green beans and potatoes for lunch, he stopped in his tracks and realized suddenly that there was a lot of water around him stored in the pipes and the hot water tank. He came up the stairs whistling and swung Linda around in a circle, laughing. Between the Howards and the Daltons, they would have an additional two weeks' worth of drinkable water.

After a small lunch, Gary took Beth Ann and Linda for a long, difficult walk into the national forest. Linda knew how to load and shoot a gun, but Beth Ann had little experience with it. Gary gave her some basic instructions and let her shoot and reload both her dad's hunting rifle and handgun until she was somewhat comfortable with them. She didn't think she would ever, ever be comfortable with it. It made her feel more bold and more fearful at the same time.

Late that afternoon a cold, miserable rain started falling, and by evening it had turned to sleet. There was a short Scripture reading, but no lively evening discussion or singing. When Linda went to bed and Gary picked up his journal, Beth Ann and Romeo retreated to their little private space behind the curtain and snuggled into the darkness. Just as she was drifting to sleep, Romeo lifted his head and Beth Ann heard soft sobbing. Gary spoke low words of comfort to his wife, and Beth Ann's heart broke...again. Her last waking thoughts were formed in prayer for her own parents.

Chapter 10

Meghan concentrated on putting one foot in front of the other. She was barely conscious. Barely aware of the cold or the hunger. She felt nothing beyond the nagging weakness that made her want to lie down and give up. But as she fled the chaos and violence in Warren, she was determined to get home to Tionesta any way she could. After hours of walking the two-lane road, weaving around the abandoned cars and trucks in the mechanical graveyard, her body begged her to stop.

The shadows of spindly-fingered leafless trees had already grown long and were now fading into a murky dusk. Not a pretty dusk, like in the summer when she used to sit on her parents' screened back porch, overlooking the river, with as much to eat and drink as she could possibly ever want. No, it was a deep dusk where scary things lived. Meghan knew her mind was starting to play tricks on her, and she needed to find some kind of shelter soon. She was still too far from Tionesta to make it home tonight.

Meghan wasn't alone on the highway. Occasionally other stragglers and families trudged by. With distrustful gazes they would pass by each other, giving wide berth. When Meghan was certain that no one was ahead or behind her, she stumbled off the road and headed into the woods toward the river. Although she could not see it most of the time through the thick trees and brush, she was close enough to hear it in this surreal, silent world. Her mouth was dry and she felt incredibly thirsty. This dehydration was dangerous, but she also knew that she could get sick from drinking the river water. She might have to take the chance, just until she could get home.

Making her way as quietly as possible through the brush, she continued to keep a vigilant watch for people. Whatever this disaster was that took out everything electrical and computerized, it turned regular people into crazy monsters. She would not have believed it if she had not seen it for herself. Of course, in nursing school they had studied a little about mental health and the effects of malnutrition, but the real life version was much more terrifying than a couple chapters in a textbook.

She walked parallel to the water inside the tree line until she came across a tiny dilapidated fishing hut, probably smaller than her bedroom back home. These shed-like structures dotted the banks of the Allegheny, a well-stocked draw for fishermen. She couldn't approach it without being seen, so she picked up a couple of golf-ball-sized stones. One at a time, she tossed them at the shack while also trying to stay concealed behind a large tree trunk. After several quiet minutes, she hoped no reaction meant that the place was abandoned. She said a quick prayer and forged ahead, carrying a large stick with her. The door hung ajar, lopsided on its rusty hinges, and she wished for a light and a broom. Peeking her head in, she asked quietly, "Hello? Anyone here?" With the exception of her wildly beating heart, nothing in the cabin stirred.

It was almost completely dark now, so she took the chance to creep to the water's edge and scoop a little water into a large leaf. Three weeks ago she would have gagged, but now she was grateful for the teaspoonfuls of moss-flavored water. She just hoped that there weren't any harmful bacteria or parasites since she couldn't purify it. How she wished she had been able to get the chlorine bleach, but she shuddered to remember the events of the last day.

Making her way back to the shack, she was still afraid to know what was living in it, and she certainly didn't want to shut the door and be alone in the dark. So she curled up in a little ball with her back against the wall just inside the door. Wishing she had thought to bring one of the hospital blankets, she drew her hands inside the long coat sleeves and tried to fit her knees up inside the bottom of the coat as far as they could go, but her legs would just have to be cold.

Now that she had a chance to rest her aching feet and body, she could not keep her thoughts from wandering back to the events that had made her desperate enough to walk nearly forty miles through hostile, wintry countryside. The conditions at the hospital had progressed from bad to worse within a matter of days. Most of the medical staff had abandoned their posts by the end of the first week. Meghan was naïve to think that she could make a difference by staying to help, but in her heart she just wanted to care for people and think the best of everyone. She was completely unprepared for an event that was bigger than humanity itself.

The staff who remained at the hospital tried to keep order and maintain protocol for as long as they could, but ultimately it ended up being each man, woman and child for him/herself. The food and water ran out fast. The sewer backed up into the basement drains. The deceased were no longer tagged or even recorded by the second week; there were just too many dead bodies. As the patients were dying, people off the streets were invading–literally invading–to take their places. They took, and they fought, and they had no sense of civilized humanity or compassion left in them. They couldn't be reasoned with. She didn't want to believe it. How could this be happening in the United States? Three centuries of building an advanced culture…reduced to ashes in a couple weeks.

By the beginning of the third week, Meghan had given up hope that the cars would start running and the cell phones would ring and the lights would all come back on. But even if they did, Meghan knew that life would never be the same. Stripped of all the cushy amenities and rich food and technology, Americans had changed. The ones who would survive this crisis would be the strongest and the meanest. Meghan knew she would need to toughen up or she would become an uncounted casualty...and she knew she had to get out of Warren.

At night she had hidden in the janitor's closet to sleep, barring the door with a chair. For the last week, she hadn't even tried to help the patients as there was nothing she could do for them or even say to encourage them. Any patients who were still alive just lay in their beds, starving to death... some moaning for help...others without the energy to make any sound. Meghan was heartbroken at first, but she eventually reached a point where she was unaffected by the cries for help and stench of soiled bedding. This scared her more than anything, feeling like she was being sucked into a void.

She had resisted the idea of walking the long way home, but finally she realized that she would have to walk to Tionesta or die in Warren. It was a simple choice, really. Why hadn't anyone come to help them? Why hadn't someone come up from Tionesta to get her? Wasn't she missed there, after three long weeks? Where was the military and where was FEMA? Why hadn't their plight been broadcast around the country with millions of people donating their time and canned goods like after hurricane Katrina? She had finally come to the conclusion that whatever had happened in Warren must be affecting a much larger area.

In preparation to leave, she went to the makeshift morgue on the fifth floor, where it was usually free of live humans due to the overwhelming stench of decaying bodies. She pinched her nose and breathed through her mouth, but instead of smelling it, she could actually taste it. Doubling over to dry heave, her empty stomach was unable to produce a single drop. Meghan pressed her sleeve into her nose and dry, cracked lips and pressed on, stepping over and around the bloated, lifeless bodies, looking for someone close to her size who was wearing clothes rather than a hospital gown. She removed a pair of leggings from one young woman and a pair of straight-leg jeans from an older teen who looked just slightly larger than Meghan.

These would be useful for layering; she wouldn't make it home in just her scrubs. Then she stripped one woman of her tank camisole and a young man of his turtle neck top. The only person wearing boots was an older man, and his feet were several sizes larger than Meghan's. She pulled off some extra pairs of non-slip socks that the hospital issued to its patients and stuffed them inside the boots. She emptied the trash out of a waste basket in the corner of the room and used the plastic liner to store her new wardrobe.

Looking back over her shoulder, she noticed the morbidity of the whole scene. They didn't need the clothes anymore, she justified. She snuck back to the third floor and hid the bag in the janitor's closet, after dousing the clothes with hospital-grade disinfectant spray. That area was like her home base and she kept going back to it, even though her job was officially over. Somewhere along the way she had become just one of the masses.

Her last order of business was to forage through the hospital for any possible medical supplies or tools or anything that might come in useful during her journey home. She stuffed what little she could find in a backpack left in one of the patient rooms. She had to be careful with people coming and going, and the increasing unrest and desperation, but she lucked out when she found, hanging on the back of a door that had stood open this whole time, a man's hooded parka. She was as ready as she could be and it was time; she would head out at first light the next morning.

Sometime during the night, the idea came to her to check in the laundry for chlorine to purify river water on her journey. So when Meghan peeked out the closet door and noticed a hint of new light appearing in the window at the end of the hall, she quietly made her way down the back stairs to the basement level. It must have been very early because she did not run into anyone on the way down. The stench like an old outhouse that filled the hospital air was stronger here, where the sewer had backed up; it flared her nostrils and churned her empty stomach, but she banked on being able to get in and get out quickly.

She stepped into the basement hall and stood still for a moment, remembering the deep darkness from the night she was looking for the security team. It was unearthly quiet. She had been to the laundry suite enough to know exactly where it was, even if she couldn't see it. Holding her left arm out in front of her and placing her right hand on the wall, she paused to picture the layout in her head. The staff elevator should be first, and then the laundry would be the next entrance on the right, with double doors to allow plenty of room for the large carts. The hall continued beyond the suite, where the Maintenance and Records departments had their offices, and across from the laundry entrance another hall branched off, leading to the morgue, the security offices and the main stairs to the hospital entrance and Emergency Room.

Feeling more confident, she took slow but steady steps forward, her shins painfully finding a couple of chairs that she didn't remember being there. The double doors into the laundry area were locked, which surprised her, and for a minute she debated what to do. Unable to force them open and having no tools, she finally admitted defeat and turned toward the stairwell, anxious to get her journey started.

Suddenly, she heard a door open and close a distance away. She froze and forced herself to breathe. Finally she worked up the courage to shout, "Hello? Is anyone down here?"

A human voice responded. "Yes! I'm a little turned around and can't find my way out!"

Poor guy. He sounded so calm, but Meghan knew she would have been a mess if she was lost down here, potentially for hours…or days. "I'll keep talking. Just follow the sound of my voice!" she instructed loudly. "I know where the stairwell is and we can get out of here! I just came down to find something in the laundry room. Do you happen to have keys? Do you work here? What's your name?" She was still shouting when she felt his rough hand clamp over her mouth and his body crush hers against the wall. In her stunned, delayed reaction, she wondered how he had gotten to her so fast if he was truly lost....

His chuckle sounded low and gritty in her ear. "You can call me anything you want, honey." She tried to move away from him, but he bit her earlobe and the fear exploded into white flashes in front of her eyes. She tried to bite his hand but his clasp was too strong. Her legs were pinned against the wall or she would have kicked him in the groin. Pushing against him made no difference; he felt like he was made of concrete.

She forced herself to stay calm and think. In nursing school she had taken a self-defense class; now she struggled to remember what they had learned. Ears and eyes! It came to her in an instant. She wriggled her arms out from between their bodies and he took advantage of the opportunity with his one free hand. Pushing through the nausea, she tried to envision where his ears were, but he was too close to get the right angle for enough force to "pop" his ears. She brought her elbow down hard on his forearm. He pulled it out and grabbed her wrist, twisting her arm halfway around as he yanked it up over her head. She screamed in pain. He pressed harder against her and laughed again, fearlessly.

If only I could get to one of the chairs, she thought. She was having trouble breathing now with his full weight against her, and it gave her a new idea. She went completely limp.

The man was taken by surprise, and in his reflexive confusion he leaned back just enough that she fell to the floor as if in a dead faint. Meghan knew she would only have a split second to put her plan into action, and it would only work if she was as close to the chair as she thought she was. Having purposely fallen sideways and partially onto her back, she reached her arms above her head as fast as she could, sensing that her life depended on it. She grasped the chair legs and swung it up hard and fast, feeling it connect with the man's flesh. He gave an enraged groan, which gave away his position. Still holding the chair above her, she swung her legs toward his in a swiping motion and he fell hard.

She scrambled to her feet and ran down the hall...down the pitch black hall...with a monster behind her and not much hope in front of her. She dropped the chair, hoping he would trip over it if he was running. Meghan was actually surprised to reach the door to the stairwell without being grabbed from behind. She took the stairs two at a time. She pushed herself to the 3rd floor and kept running blindly, pushing through several people in the dim hallway, until she reached the nurse's station just outside the storage closet. She vomited fresh bile into the trashcan and then collapsed onto the floor and rolled under the desk.

Meghan let ten or fifteen minutes go by, waiting for her breathing to return to normal and to come slowly out of panic mode. She didn't hear anyone else come out of the stairway door, but she didn't want to give the man enough time to find her...if he was looking. Locking herself in the closet, she layered and laced and zipped as fast as she could. The stench of dead bodies permeated through the disinfectant and filled her nostrils as she dressed, but she ignored it. With her hood pulled up as far as it would go to shield her face, she took a different stairwell to get downstairs and outside.

As soon as the fresh air hit her, it was like the sweetest fragrance in the world. But she didn't allow herself to linger and enjoy it because she was afraid that someone would try to stop her from leaving the hospital. That was a ridiculous thought, she knew, but she now lived in fear. The kind that made her look over her shoulder every couple of minutes.

The first part of her plan involved checking on her co-worker, whom she hadn't seen since the day the electricity went out. Amy lived only a few blocks from the hospital; Meghan had visited plenty of times, sometimes even crashing for the night after a late shift. Amy was a young single mom who had bailed on her job in order to get her little girl from daycare and protect her at home until the electricity came back on. Meghan just wanted to make sure she was okay. What she found in Amy's apartment horrified her: the toddler's emaciated body and Amy's beside her. The handgun lying on the carpet beside the dried pool of blood that framed Amy's head told the story. The gun Amy had bought to protect herself and her daughter from her ex-husband had taken her own life. Meghan felt blind as she stumbled down the steps of the old apartment; she started running, completely focused on getting as far away from Warren as possible.

The only way she knew how to get home was by the route she drove to and from work. As she forced herself to a walk to conserve energy, she stared at the unbelievable scene. All of the businesses along this stretch had been vandalized, smashed, some even burned. No one was out on the eerily quiet street, and she felt like a sitting duck. But she prayed and she walked. She kept walking all the way out of Warren, almost to the long point at Tidioute, where finally the road bent south toward Tionesta. She passed houses here and there, but they were dark and quiet, and no one bothered her. Somewhere along the way, the adrenaline had worn off and her energy dropped down to nothing. Finally she had stopped at the little fishing hut. She wouldn't sleep well, but she hoped it would be enough to get her home tomorrow. She just wanted to be home.

At dawn Meghan was awakened by a shuffling sound outside the cabin. It took her several minutes to remember where she was and why, and then she was afraid to move. To make it worse, with her back to the wall, she could not see out the door. While she held her breath and waited, her eyes scanned the tiny shack. She could see violet-colored light coming through cracks between the wall boards and through a large area in the ceiling where the roof was missing. There was a small sagging cot on the side closest to her feet, which looked tufted from little critters helping themselves to its stuffing. There were two wooden chairs straight across from her, but near enough to touch if she reached her arm straight out. The floor was littered with cans and bottles that looked recently emptied; someone had already scavenged the place. Past the chairs she couldn't see without tilting her head up, which would have to wait.

The shuffling noise continued, like something was rooting around in the leaves. Then it stopped. Meghan waited, wishing that she could see. She hoped that the smell of death she wore wouldn't attract the animal. It started again and gradually faded toward the north. She very slowly pressed the floor with her gloved hands and started moving her stiff body into a sitting position when a loud bark made her jump. Her head snapped up and she saw the dog, a mangy German shepherd mix, growling fiercely as he faced up river. Although relieved that he wasn't barking at her, she was too close to leave the cabin without attracting his attention.

The next few minutes were excruciating. It was a dog fight to the death. The growling, the squealing, the terrible sounds...the smaller dog was no match for the bigger, hungry dog. Meghan made herself as small as possible and inched farther from the door. She buried her head in her arms but it didn't block out the horror. Three weeks ago, those dogs were loving, family pets. Now they had to survive like everyone else. She didn't think she could take much more.

The victor finally moved on, dragging its reward with it. Meghan waited for what felt like a very long time and then tentatively stood up. She glanced past the doorway at the small wash tub, with no faucet or spigots, and a small empty cabinet and then slowly leaned her head outside. All was quiet. On her way back to the road she chose a bigger, sturdier stick in case she ran into any more dogs. It would take her the better part of the daylight hours to make it back to Tionesta...if she made it at all.

Chapter 11

Meghan didn't see the couple at first. After several hours of walking, her head hung forward and her eyes glazed at the road in front of her just far enough to avoid the occasional stalled vehicle. The winter sun's intensity had forced her to take off the parka so she wouldn't sweat and get her inner layer wet. Her tired feet made a solid wake as she dragged the large boots through the unplowed slush on the road. So she didn't notice a man and woman walking northbound until they were almost right on top of her. She stopped suddenly and drew up to her full height.

"Hullo, there!" the man called. "How'ya doin'?"

Meghan lifted her hand in greeting and tried to skirt around him. "Where you headed to?" he asked as he intercepted her.

"Home," Meghan hedged.

He laughed. "Ha! Ain't no home left! Everything's gone!"

"Rodger...," the woman with him pleaded groggily, as if in a stupor. "Stop it. You're gonna scare her, poor thing."

"Aw, Cassie. You're too soft. She should be scared. This here's the freakin' zombie apocalypse!"

The woman looked at Meghan but her eyes were lifeless; she lowered them back to her shoes again. The man continued, "That there's a nice backpack." He reached out and grabbed one strap hanging loose. "Whatcha got in it?"

"Hey!" Meghan tried to yank it out of his grasp, but he held firm. "It's just medical supplies. I'm a nurse."

"You WAS a nurse," the man said under his breath while pulling the pack roughly off her shoulders and rummaging through it.

"I'm STILL a nurse and I don't have any food or water. Leave me alone!" She dropped the parka and walking stick so that she could use two hands to grab the backpack. He let go of the bag and picked up the coat, all in one fluid motion.

"No! That's my coat!" she yelled.

"It's not yers–it's a man's coat. And I'm a man!" he explained as he rolled it up and secured it under his arm.

His wife, or whoever she was, seemed to come out of her lifeless state, pounding on his old bomber jacket sleeve and begging. "Rodger! You give that back! She'll freeze to death. She needs a coat!"

"Sure she needs a coat. I'm not a total jerk!" he clarified. Then he took off his jacket and tossed it at Meghan's feet. "I'm giving her the jacket off my very own back!" He laughed again and, steering the lethargic woman by the elbow, he led her away toward the north.

Meghan knew she couldn't fight him for the parka; he outweighed her by at least eighty pounds. With tears stinging her eyes, she picked up the walking stick; next time she would use it to act more aggressively with the stranger at the *beginning* of an encounter. She flung the backpack over her shoulder and slowly picked up the man's jacket, dripping with slush. The stench of body odor and old cigarettes made her cringe and motivated her to get moving; if she could reach Tionesta before the sun went down, she may not have to wear the foul thing. Her good intentions carried her another hour or so, but her body was weak. Apathy was starting to set in.

She crested a hill on Route 62 and recognized a cluster of houses ahead as East Hickory, the last settlement before she would arrive in

Tionesta. A little spark of hope led to a feeling almost like joy…almost. More like relief with an internal smile. When she finally reached the edge of the village, a church bell started to clang. She jumped in her man-sized stolen boots. Somehow she knew it was a warning toll…warning everyone nearby of *her*. She continued, but nervously glanced around as she walked.

By the time she reached the midway point, there were six men following her—four of them carrying hunting rifles. She pretended that she didn't care, even though her heart threatened to give out, and just kept walking. But they stopped her and searched her backpack. She leaned against a car that was halfway off the road on the shoulder for support and watched as they emptied the contents onto the slushy road.

So much for sanitized, she thought. "Please, I'm a nurse. I need to get home. I don't have any food. I promise." *That should do it; now they'll let me go.*

Two of the men looked at each other when she said "nurse." One of them spoke up immediately, a flicker of hope in his tired eyes. "We need a nurse real bad." Although she protested, the men forcibly escorted her to a run-down bungalow not far off the main road. Two of the men went into the house with her; the others had silently disappeared.

In the front room, a woman sat in a rocking chair, holding an obviously sick toddler. Another woman sat at the end of the couch, wrapped in a blanket with her legs curled up underneath, head propped on a pillow. Mismatched blankets were piled up in one corner of the room. A very small fire barely burned in the fireplace, and sheets were nailed up across the openings to the hall and dining room to hold in the miniscule heat. The women looked at her but said nothing.

The older man explained softly to the woman in the rocking chair that Meghan was a nurse and had come to make their suffering baby better. The woman kept rocking, rocking. Meghan wondered if she didn't hear well or if she just didn't understand. The man gently took the child from her arms; his wife looked up at him and released the baby...but kept rocking. The man held the baby out to Meghan.

"Listen," Meghan said, crossing her arms and trying to sound authoritative, "I will only examine the baby if you give me something to eat...and drink."

The two men argued quietly, but the desperate father won. The other man went behind the curtain and came back a few minutes later with a glass half full of semi-clear water and a dirty bowl holding about a teaspoon of uncooked rice. Meghan took the items slowly as she tried to decide if she'd rather die of starvation or food poisoning. She took her chances and threw the rice back first, then gulped the water down. Her whole meal took less than twelve seconds.

As soon as Meghan took the toddler in her arms, she could feel the fever burning through the blanket. The child's eyes were shut, and his breathing was shallow and raspy. Then he coughed a horrible deep, barky cough that Meghan could feel going straight through his weightless frame. He started to cry, but not a lusty cry—a painful, wheezy, high-pitched noise that didn't sound human. Then his little body went limp again from the exertion and she handed him back to his mother. That baby was going to die in her arms very soon and everyone in the room knew it.

For a long time the only sound was the rhythmic squeaking of the rocking chair and the labored breathing of the poor child. Meghan finally spoke up. "How long has he been sick?"

The boy's father spoke with a sigh, running a calloused hand across his matted hair. "Over a week. The flu went around and lotsa people got sick. We lost some neighbors. No doctors, no medicine, no food. My brother here," he glanced at the other man, "and his wife moved in with us to share heat and stuff, but we didn't know Alex was gonna get sick." The man stopped. He looked down at his hands and then glanced at his brother. "The people that's left all moved into the church together, you know, because of the crazies goin' around raiding and killing. But they won't let us in till we're past the contagious part." His face looked like it might crack if his troubles got any deeper.

"I think he may have pneumonia," Meghan said softly. "There's nothing I can do to help. But he could pull through. Kids are pretty resilient." She was trying to comfort the grieving family, but she knew that all the rules she was taught in nursing school only applied in a situation where food and water and medical treatment was readily available. "If none of you get a fever in the next five to seven days, you're in the clear. You can tell your neighbors in the church that a nurse checked you out." She paused, but no one said anything or even looked at her. "Please...I really need to go," she said softly. No one tried to stop her as she inched her way toward the door, picking up her pack, coat and stick on the way. Finally she backed out of the room onto the front porch. Still no one moved, and still the creaking chair rocked on.

Although her legs felt like jelly, Meghan hurried out onto the main road and toward Tionesta once again. She estimated at least three hours to walk the rest of the way, but she wasn't sure that she would beat the sun. She had lost too much time. The sound of the walking stick hitting the pavement under the slush added a rhythmic *shh-thunk...shlop...*, *shh-thunk...shlop* to her journey. As she made slow progress, the sky began to glow a softly golden orange...and then it faded into a brilliant pink and died in deep indigo. The rank coat's service was required. Dehydrated and half delirious, she started softly humming to herself.

A heavy knock on the front door forced Gary to leave his soup and race up the basement steps. There stood a man he recognized from the local hardware store, wearing a shiny deputy badge and a weird green belt.

"Can I help you, Harrison?" Gary asked.

"Good afternoon. I am here on behalf of Mayor Andrews with a message."

"Mayor who?"

Harrison ignored him and continued with his script. "Every capable Tionestan is to meet at noon tomorrow in front of the municipal building for a meeting. Everyone who attends will be given a meal to eat. And effective immediately, a sundown to sunup curfew will be enforced."

"What about...?" Gary was going to ask about his wife, who may not be strong enough to walk that far, but the man had already walked away.

Incredulous, Gary stood watching Harrison go from house to house on their street. The "deputy" talked to neighbors at the next three houses, then stood on the porch of the next one, not getting an answer. Gary knew that the couple who lived there had moved in with other family members in town. Harrison marked the door with a large duct-tape "X" and Gary continued to watch the pattern; the man was marking empty houses. After he was gone, Gary rushed over to the Dalton's house and removed the duct tape from the front door. Since Beth Ann was in his basement eating lunch, she had not been at her house when Harrison came with the new mayor's message.

Locking the front door as he let himself back into his house, Gary slowly made his way down the steps. Something strange was going on...and it didn't sit right with him. After they finished their small meal, Gary had Beth Ann help him dig a trench in the narrow mulch bed behind the house. They went straight down the basement block wall; the ground wasn't frozen there and the trench would be hidden by a row of boxwood shrubs. They buried several shoebox-sized plastic tubs of pressure cooked venison and canned goods and put the dirt and mulch back in place. All the while, Gary hoped his gut was wrong.

Meghan didn't remember much of the last leg of her long journey from Warren, except for the odd roadblock that had never been there. A car had been pushed sideways so that it stretched most of the width of the two-lane country road. One of the sheriff's deputies and another man questioned her until they were satisfied that she was telling the truth, then they let her through.

By the time she reached the center of town, it had grown fully dark. Thankfully, there was just enough moonlight to see where she was going...and to see that Tionesta had also fallen victim to the mysterious blight. Several storefronts were smashed out and she vaguely noticed other signs of chaos juxtaposed against the town's cheerful Christmas decorations, which looked untouched.

Meghan passed the diner and noticed what looked like a sleeping person sitting against the side of the building. For some crazy reason, maybe her compassionate nature, she found her path curving into the parking lot to wake him up before he froze to death. As she got close, she could see that his eyes were open and he was staring down at his hands. He didn't answer her calls, so she tapped him gently on the shoulder. As the young man slowly fell over, she recognized the diner's cook, Kenny, with glazed lifeless eyes and three bullet holes in his chest. Horrified, she ran, or more accurately, stumbled, the last couple blocks to her apartment building. She burst through the main entry door and collapsed onto the steps, panting. She would never make it to her third floor apartment without a rest...but at least she was in her building.

Her chest heaved and she closed her eyes to work on calming herself yet again. That's when she heard the telltale click of a gun being cocked. She almost didn't have the energy to care, but she slowly opened her eyes while she curled her fingers firmly around her stick. Although it was dark in the hall, she could see a person partially silhouetted against the door's window. "Please...I'm not armed. Don't shoot!"

The stillness that followed nearly unnerved her, but she forced herself to wait.

Finally, a raspy voice demanded, "Who are you?"

"I'm Meghan Crawley. I live upstairs in 301."

"Meghan? Where you been?" the voice asked suspiciously.

"I got stuck at the hospital in Warren for almost three weeks because my car wouldn't start, and I just walked for two freakin' days to get here!" Man, she was irritated.

Another long pause. Then the voice released her. "Fine. Git upstairs and stop sneakin' around. It's past curfew."

Meghan started to stand up slowly, painfully. "Wait. It's past what?" she asked into the darkness.

"Curfew. We got new rules here, so git going before you get us both in trouble." The voice was irritated, too. It was so raspy that Meghan couldn't tell if it was the building manager or his wife.

"Okay, okay. I'm going. But I don't know what the heck you're talking about." She started going up the steps, slowly, leaning heavily on the railing. She dragged her backpack and stick behind her.

The voice called up to her, "Then you better be at the town meeting at the municipal building tomorrow at noon. There's a new mayor in town, and you got back just in time."

Meghan took in that information, but it didn't make sense. She made it to the landing and kept climbing the stairs, believing that if she could just get into her apartment, she could eat something, change her clothes, and collapse into bed for a fresh start in the morning.

The happy feeling of finally reaching her apartment was short-lived when she discovered that the door wasn't latched. Pushing the door open with her stick, she held back and waited. Nothing happened. She leaned her head in. "Hello?" she called, making a mental note to get her flashlight from the kitchen junk drawer and keep it on her at all times. She stepped into the living room and was instantly knocked to the ground. The stick bounced off the coffee table and flew into the darkness. Stifling a scream and trying to roll away from her assailant, Meghan quickly ran out of energy and found herself pinned down.

Out of breath, she demanded, "Who...are...you?"

"Who are YOU?" came the snarled reply.

"I LIVE HERE! This is...MY apartment and you...need to get out or...." She realized she didn't know how to finish the threat.

"Or what? You'll call the police??? Ha! I am the police..." He paused. "Jesus, you stink!" He loosened his grip and told her to go sit on the couch, but she wasn't sure what to do in this situation. It was pitch black, and some unknown man was in her home giving her orders. She decided to go along with what he said until she could figure out what her options were.

She felt around for her walking stick with her feet while shuffling the short distance to the couch, but she didn't find it. Either he had it or it rolled the other direction.

"What are you doing in my apartment?" She felt she had the right to know at least that much.

"Name's Dillon. I thought this place was vacant, so apparently I'm your new roommate."

How could this possibly be? "What you mean is that you broke in and just helped yourself. I don't care if the phones don't work; that's still a crime."

He laughed. "Maybe. I'm not sure that there is any such thing as crime if there is no law in place to enforce it." He got quiet then. "I told you. I AM the police. I'm on the new security team."

His low voice was more frightening than when he physically tossed her onto the floor. She had to stay calm.

"Well, now that I'm back, you have to go. You...you can't stay here."

"Yeah, well, since there's a curfew in town I can't leave now. So we're stuck together. Wanna share the bed?" He was laughing again, and she noted that he sounded young, probably close to her age.

"Not a chance," she spat with venom, getting up from the couch. This was still her home. "I haven't eaten in days, so you better stay out of my way." She stomped her way into the kitchen with her arms outstretched, feeling her way in the dark. Dillon didn't say anything, and he didn't follow her. That surprised her, but all she could think about was finding anything to eat.

First she felt around in the junk drawer for her flashlight. There was lots of junk but no flashlight. She reached up onto the shelf above the kitchen sink, where she kept a row of candles in different scents. The only thing on the shelf was a dish scrubby and a little dust. *What the...? Forget the light; get some food.* She opened the squeaky bi-fold door to the narrow pantry shelves and reached inside. The shelves were empty...every single one. She opened the bottom cupboard beside the stove where she had kept cereal and oatmeal. Empty.

Enraged, Meghan flung herself into the darkness with a scream, flailing at the intruder. She wasn't thinking clearly. The more she yelled, the more she gave away her location and he could keep his distance from her. But she didn't care. "You ate all my food? You JERK! I'm going to starve to death and you...you're EVIL and you're going to live because you ate MY food!" She was completely out of her mind.

"Hey, hey, HEY!" Dillon tried to get her attention, but instead he had to pin her body against his and clamp his hand over her mouth to subdue her. "Pipe down! You're going to get us in trouble! Jeez!" he said quietly into her ear. "If you promise to calm down and be quiet, I'll let go. I'm not going to hurt you, okay?"

When she nodded, he released her and she sank to the floor in utter despair. She heard his explanation as if she were under water, where the words were muffled and ran together. Something about everyone's food being confiscated and people being assigned jobs to get one ration of food per day. All she remembers after that is lying on the floor sobbing, and waking up in the same place with a blanket over her and not caring whether she lived another day or died in that very spot.

Chapter 12

Gary and Beth Ann trekked into town on Wednesday to see what the town meeting was about. The weather was decent enough for a December walk–cold, but at least dry. Linda was not feeling up to it, so she stayed home to rest. A couple other neighbors trudged behind them but kept their distance, even when Gary waved to them. It was strange that only a few neighbors were going, unless others had left earlier. Telling time was a real challenge these days.

Beth Ann had been wondering for a while if Linda's health was declining, so while they walked she finally worked up the nerve to ask Gary about it. He sighed before answering her. "It's Graves' Disease. Are you familiar with that?"

She shook her head "no."

"It's an autoimmune disorder, something to do with the thyroid and hormone production. She was diagnosed with it not too long after our son was born. Once they figured out what it was, it was successfully treated and went into remission. However, it has come back a couple of times since; in stressful times she can't seem to fight it off. She has to take thyroid medication every day. I had just called in the refill the day the power went out and, obviously, I never got it. That first day that I walked to town, I tried to get it, but there was nothing left at the pharmacy. So, now she's been out of meds for almost three weeks."

"Gosh. I am so sorry. I had no idea...." Beth Ann didn't know what else to say.

"She doesn't like to advertise it. And that's why I have been forcing her to rest as much as possible," he explained in an apologetic tone. "I'm sorry that makes more work for you, but I really do appreciate your help and I know it takes a huge burden off of Linda."

"I don't feel like I can do enough to help, for all you've done for me." They walked a little while in silence, but Beth Ann simply had to know. "Is it...?" She didn't know what other word to use besides *fatal*.

Gary knew what she was asking. "Yes, it can be life-threatening, especially if untreated. Probably the highest risk for Linda is a 'thyroid storm' that would throw her heart out of whack. I guess maybe that beats dying slowly of starvation...." He forced a grin, but Beth Ann saw moisture in his eyes. Neither of them spoke again until they reached town.

Nearly two hundred haggard-looking people assembled on the street in front of the municipal building. They weren't shaking hands and talking about the weather and the grandkids; they were just standing there...waiting. Looking around, she recognized most of the faces: some from school, some from church, others from waiting tables at the diner. Then she noticed a familiar hat and followed it to the other side of the crowd, leaving Gary on his own. Under the knitted version of Curious George with long ear flaps was Kristen! She threw her arms around her friend and held her tight. Kristen just stood stiffly, a blank look on her face.

"Kristen! I've missed you so much! Are you doing okay?" Beth Ann asked with more enthusiasm than she had felt in weeks.

Kristen stared at her for a minute and finally answered slowly. "I don't know."

Beth Ann was stunned. Where was her perky friend? Why was she acting this way? "Hey, where are your parents?" she asked, looking at all the faces nearby.

Before Kristen could answer, someone came up behind them and pulled them into a bear hug. It was Meghan. She smelled like death and looked even worse, and she was crying.

Beth Ann held her and let her cry while Kristen just stood there and watched them with a blank look on her face. After a couple minutes, she let go. "Hey, girl," she said in a soothing voice. "Hang in there. You ok?"

Meghan looked up then, and Beth Ann noticed she looked sickly, just like the people around them. The deteriorating conditions had aged everyone years already. "You have no idea what I've been through! I'm scared, Bethie. What's going to happen to us?"

Beth Ann didn't have an answer for her. Meghan had always been the steady one, the rock, the one that all the friends turned to for advice or prayer. She hugged her again.

A shuffling in the crowd drew the girls' attention, and just as they turned to see what was going on, Kristen came to life with a sharp gasp. Beth Ann followed Kristen's line of sight to see none other than Mr. Andrews taking a prominent position at the top of the steps. To one side of him stood a motley crew of disheveled, but uniformed and badged, deputies.

"Dillon!" Meghan whispered harshly. Beth Ann turned her head to see Meghan glaring with squinted eyes at the lawmen and realized there was a lot she didn't know.

"Thank you, everyone, for coming out on this cold, wintry day." Mr. Andrews' booming voice was more than adequate for the crowd to hear. "These are very difficult times that we are living in, and I want to help. I CAN help." He paused for effect, like he was giving a campaign speech. "For those of you who don't know me, I am Gaylord Andrews the Third. Do any of you know what's going on here?"

A few people shook their heads, but most just waited, dumbstruck. "No? Well I do. For most of my life I have worked in and around the U.S. government and high-tech weapons systems. I can tell you with confidence that we have suffered an EMP attack. And by 'we' I don't mean Tionesta or Forest County, but most likely the majority of North America. EMP stands for electro-magnetic pulse. It basically fried not only the electric grid, but everything with a chip in it–like cars and phones. No one is coming to save us...and core infrastructure won't be in place, likely, for three years or more."

Heads turned back and forth as people gasped and whispered to each other; a woman near where they stood started quietly sobbing. Beth Ann reached out to link her arm in Meghan's for support. It sounded like something straight out of a science fiction novel. Could it really be true?

"Now, I hate to be the bearer of bad news, but the government is dependent on electricity and chip technology as much as the rest of us. So right now they have no way to effectively communicate or mobilize, and what little the military can do will be focused on the larger cities." Mr. Andrews leaned forward like he was telling a secret, punctuating each word: "No one. Is. Coming. To. Help. You are on your own, and the majority of you will not live through the winter unless you let me help you."

The crowd didn't move, didn't make a sound. Mr. Andrews raised himself up, getting on with business. "I am sorry to report that Mayor Dorland has died from complications with his diabetes. But before he passed on, he appointed me as the new mayor." The people came to life, murmuring. "I know, I know. This is usually an elected position, but under these severe and life-threatening circumstances, the mayor felt that it would take too long to hold elections. He wanted to take care of you, his people, by giving the town the kind of leadership and supplies that I am able to provide." Theatrical pause. "It was his dying wish, and I am humbled to be able to serve you in this capacity."

Beth Ann scanned the crowd, trying to find Gary. She wished she knew what he was thinking. The crowd seemed perfectly fine to go along with Mayor Andrews; in their desperate circumstances, it made perfect sense and who could disagree with him?

"I am also here to inform you that Sheriff MacClelland has left town to be with his aging parents up near Erie. Let's not judge him for this act of bravery and concern for his family. Rather, let's give our respect to Tionesta's new sheriff, Henry Branson. Many of you know him as he was on MacClelland's force. Branson wanted to escort his girlfriend Sarah to her parents' farm, but I convinced him that he was needed here. Because of the trouble you've had in town so far, I asked Branson to pull together some extra men from the community to help his deputies keep the peace and help ensure that everyone is working side-by-side for the common good. These Security Team members won't be uniformed, but can easily be identified by the green sashes that they wear." He gestured to the group of men to his right.

"I'd also like to introduce you to my personal security team: Travis, Mike and Charlie." The three men stood stiffly with their hands clasped behind their backs to Mr. Andrews' left. They didn't move a muscle. "You'll have the chance to get to know my men pretty well, as they will circulate among the work teams in the weeks ahead. If there is anything you need from me, you can let one of them know."

Beth Ann felt confused. Nearly half of the town's entire population stood in the street…completely accepting the fact that an outsider had just single-handedly taken control of their community. Was it really that easy?

"I'm glad to see that our new Security Team members were able to cover so much territory yesterday, as evidenced by how many of you are here today. Let's discuss a couple of housekeeping items very quickly before we get you that meal I promised."

Everyone perked up at the mention of food.

"We have a couple new laws in place, effective as of yesterday. I will write them down and tape them to the inside window of the courthouse door for future reference. We will also have these town meetings on a regular basis; the schedule will be posted on the courthouse door and we will ring the church bell thirty minutes before we start.

"Okay. First, for your own safety, the deputies here will enforce a curfew from sundown to sunup every day until we have a reason to revoke it. Second, to protect ourselves from those raiding parties we've all been hearing about, roadblocks will be enforced at both bridges and the remaining two roads coming into town; no one will leave town without permission, and anyone who lives beyond the roadblock will be relocated into town, either into a vacant house or a shared home. Third, every person age twelve and up will be assigned a job according to his or her interests and abilities for the good of the town. Fourth, every person who participates in the community work will receive one protein snack, one meal and one half-gallon of potable water every day. And finally, in order for us to pull together and stay alive through this dark time, we…need…your…help. These are your friends and neighbors and family!" Andrews held his arms out, wide and dramatic. "The deputies will come around and simply take inventory in case we need to pull in some extra resources. You want to help your loved ones stay alive, right?"

The crowd murmured again. Some people just stared at Andrews and others nodded their heads. Beth Ann wondered, *Does this one man actually have enough food to feed the entire town? And do we have any choice?* Then she realized they did: acknowledge the new mayor's leadership or starve to death. Pretty easy choice for most.

"Now, thank you for being so patient. I know that you're hungry." The men in green sashes and the uniformed security guards sauntered down the steps and formed an intimidating barrier. "The Security Team members will escort each household unit into the courthouse for their meal, and they'll help you fill out a brief survey when you sit down to eat." The crowd started to press toward the line of men. "Please, everyone! No one needs to get hurt! All of you will get to eat. Just be patient, and the Security Team will hustle as fast as they can." He nodded to Branson who gave the cue to his men to start extricating people from the crowd. Branson stood at the top of the steps with Andrews, his hand resting lightly on his holster as he watched the crowd.

Beth Ann grabbed her friends' hands and dragged them toward Gary. "Come on! Stay with me," she encouraged them to keep up with her. When she found him, his face was as white as the snow that kept coming back every few days.

"There you are!" he said with obvious relief. Then he leaned toward her and whispered, "Stick with me, Beth Ann. We have to get out of here."

"What? Why?"

"Shhh! I'm not filling out that form. The problem with one man having that much control is the more they know about us, the more we risk them coming to take everything we own. Com'on, before the crowd thins out…." He started to gradually fade toward the back, pulling her with him.

"But…what about the food?" Beth Ann didn't want to leave her friends, and they were looking at Gary skeptically. With the offer of free food, they would surely be staying. Making a split-second decision, she let Gary lead her out of the crowd and into the shadows of the nearest building. They waited for a minute to see if anyone had noticed them leaving, but the deputies were all busy with crowd control, and Branson and Andrews were engrossed in deep conversation.

They snuck away by sticking to the alleys and staying concealed behind buildings, making their way down to the river's edge and following it toward home. It was probably double the distance of going by road. The farther they got from a meal, the more irritated Beth Ann became.

When they passed a narrow dirt lane leading uphill, Beth Ann stopped. "Hold on. Why couldn't we just eat first and then leave? I don't understand!"

"It's control, don't you see?" Gary's eyes were blazing with passion. "Once you take the first bite of his food, you BELONG to him! There won't be any turning back!"

Beth Ann shook her head; maybe Gary was going a little crazy. She still didn't understand. "Well, at least can't we take the road now? I'm freezing!" Beth Ann said, gazing at the path longingly.

"No, I need you to keep your eyes peeled for a boat," he answered and she resisted rolling her eyes. He went on to explain his plan. They needed to find a boat that was close enough to pull to the river and also be able to row or guide with a pole. When they got home, they would immediately pack their dwindling food and water reserves, matches and candles, flashlights, extra clothes, guns and ammunition, his own and James's camping supplies, fishing rods, cooking pots & utensils – anything they would need to survive in the wild. Then they would use the dark to their advantage and make several trips to the closest access point, camouflaging their supplies among low branches. On their last trip, they would head straight to the boat, work their way to the supplies and load them, then get the heck out of dodge before they're caught.

"What if we go to my brother's farm? We could stay with him. He must have crops and animals and plenty to eat," Beth Ann suggested.

"Can't do it. It's way too risky to travel that way and they would look for us there."

"What? Why would they look for us? Why would they even care?" Now Beth Ann knew Gary was really losing it.

"I have a feeling they will be scavenging the local farms soon anyway. Besides, we don't even know if your brother is alive. We can't risk dragging all our supplies there only to have to lug them all back to the river." Beth Ann's jaw dropped open. She hadn't thought about the possibility that her brother might be dead. Gary shifted his weight and looked off into the distance. "I'm sorry Beth Ann. The only way out is to be down river before they realize we're gone."

Beth Ann was flabbergasted…and terrified. Now they would be fugitives? And that was the best case scenario. If they got caught…she didn't want to guess what that would mean.

Meghan watched Beth Ann slink away with her neighbor. Were they crazy? Why didn't they want a meal? She heard her name being called and turned to see Dillon walking toward her. He instructed her to follow him up the walk into the courthouse. Inside the large entry hall, an oil lamp burned and an armed guard handed Dillon one MRE and a bottle of water from a large box as they walked past. A set of wide steps led to a long meeting room set up with rows of tables and chairs. The room was bright from the midday light streaming in the long, multi-paned windows. Like the lobby, it was decorated in a dignified colonial style, mocking their now abject poverty. Other townsfolk were spread out among the tables, some stuffing the food into their mouths and others eating in slow motion, dragging it out as long as they could. Meghan had guzzled the entire bottle of water on the way up the stairs and now desperately wanted to eat.

Dillon sat beside her with a clipboard and pen as she tried to tear into the first food pouch. Frustrated, she tried a different pouch. Her hands weren't strong enough to rip them. Tears sprang to her eyes and she hung her head, but Dillon reached over with his little pocket knife and slit all three pouches for her.

Without a word of thanks, she squeezed the first pouch into her mouth, gulping it down painfully. She didn't even care what it was. Dillon placed his hand on her wrist gently. "Word of advice? Take very small bites, and chew every bite until it is liquid in your mouth before swallowing. That will help. Your stomach has probably started shrinking a little, and you don't want to get sick." He handed her his personal water bottle. "Same thing with the water–just sips."

As a nurse, she recognized the wisdom in his words, and she forced herself to follow his suggestions. While she ate, he pulled out a handwritten sheet with questions on it and set it on the table above the clipboard. On a blank piece of lined notebook paper he wrote the question numbers for reference and her answers. He asked her full name, address, date of birth, gender, if she had any special skills, interests, or training, what kind of job or recreational or domestic experience she had, if she had children, and if any of her household members were sick or deceased in the last three weeks.

Meghan noticed that he had skipped one of the questions, but he had written an answer anyway. She glanced at the list and saw "Other members in household." He had put his own name down. She tried to protest, but he explained it would be better for her, because Andrews meant what he said about bringing everyone from the outskirts into town; some people would be sharing space regardless. If she was already sharing her apartment, he could vouch for that arrangement and they wouldn't move anyone else in.

It seemed like she was stuck, and she didn't have the energy to push the subject any further. She went back to work squeezing the remaining peanut butter onto her crackers. Dillon instructed her to stay in the room until her name was called, and then he stood to go fetch the next person. "Wait!" she reached out and grabbed his sleeve. He stopped and looked down at her. "So, tell me again where all the food in my house went?"

"Yeah, you were a little nuts last night. Okay. Yesterday morning I was recruited for Sheriff Branson's team. He gave each of us a map with a specific area to canvass with Mayor Andrews' message. We were also instructed to mark any house that appeared deserted. Then, for as long as the light of day remained, we were to start going through those vacant apartments and homes for any edible food or water, and any other supplies that would be of use, such as your flashlight and candles. Some of the places had already been ransacked....totally surreal. And since I live outside the roadblock, I was told to pick one to move into. I honestly thought your place was vacant. It's not personal, it's just that we will all have to pitch in to save the town...and ourselves."

Meghan watched him walk away. Not personal? So while she was trying to help save sick patients in Warren, this man was stealing her personal belongings? Yes, it was personal. She noticed Kristen sitting by herself and moved to the seat beside her. The two old friends sat silently side by side, slowly sipping the last of their water. They watched the Security Team members bring in a couple more people and then a young family. They watched the hungry people tear into their meals. They watched the papers being filled out.

Kristen spoke first. "They're dead."

Meghan's head jerked up. "What? Who's dead?"

Kristen was staring down at the empty food pouches and wrappers on the table. She slowly met Meghan's eye. "My parents. They're dead."

"Oh, Kristen...," Meghan leaned her head against Kristen's. "I'm so, so sorry." Her heart couldn't bear much more suffering. She knew she probably shouldn't ask and wouldn't want to know the answer anyway, but her curiosity won. "What happened?"

"Aaron came over. He...he was acting...crazy. I don't know...he just wasn't himself. He demanded food and my father—" She closed her eyes, and Meghan knew that she was seeing a picture in her head that she would never be able to erase. "My father refused. He said that he didn't have enough to feed his own family...and he begged Aaron to go. And then they fought. It was terrible...my mom was screaming...and all I could do was stand there." Her voice faded. Then she looked up at Meghan, and her eyes were troubled, fearful. "Aaron pulled out a gun, I think as a threat, but...then everything just happened so fast.... He shot my dad. Mom lunged for him and he shot her, too. I...I don't think he meant to.... His face, that look on his face...God help me! I just kept hearing the 'bang,' 'bang,' 'bang'...." Kristen closed her eyes and her face crinkled.

Meghan felt like she was in a nightmare. This could not be real. "Oh my gosh, Kristen! How did you get away?"

The flicker of light in Kristen's eyes went out, like she didn't see Meghan sitting in front of her. "I had to make it stop. It wouldn't stop."

"Did he leave? With you just standing there?"

"Leave?" Kristen was still in a daze. She spoke so softly now that Meghan could barely hear her. "No. I...I...don't remember what happened, but when it finally got quiet, they were all dead...on the floor, and I was the one standing with the gun. I don't know how...I can't remember...." Her eyes came back into focus and her face twisted. "My parents are dead, Meg. I killed my boyfriend. And now I'm all alone. I don't know what to do!" She broke down and buried her face in Meghan's lap. Meghan let the tears simply trail down her cheeks while she rubbed her friend's back. There was nothing she could say or do to restore Kristen's life.

"Meghan Crawley?" Her name was called by a deep booming voice in uniform. She lifted Kristen up gently and kissed her wet cheek. She met the officer at the door and was told that she was being assigned to the Medical Team. Her new job would start immediately and he would escort her there.

Gary and Beth Ann were exhausted and chilled when they reached home. But they had found a good candidate for a boat and were anxious to start packing...as soon as they ate a little something and warmed up by the wood burner. They came into the house through the back patio door and immediately noticed that a jar of preserves lay shattered on the floor.

Gary sighed. "The trembling in Linda's hands must be getting bad again," he said to Beth Ann. "I hate to lose a couple days' worth of food, but she really doesn't have any control over it. While I clean this up, go ahead and pull out something for us to eat. I'll be right down. But be quiet–Linda's probably fallen asleep or she would have cleaned up already."

Beth Ann tiptoed the best she could down the creaky wooden steps, but she found a bigger mess in the basement. Not broken glass, but everything was disheveled. It was unusual, because Linda always kept things neat and fussed at them for leaving anything out of place. Even stranger, Romeo should have heard them enter the house and met them at the top of the stairs.

"Romeo," she called softly as she picked up a pillow off the floor and tossed it on the chair. Opening the curtain to the fruit cellar, she froze. It was gone–all of it. The shelves were empty. Before she could even react, a sound came from the bedroom area behind the stacked boxes. When she realized it was Linda trying to vomit, Beth Ann raced to the curtain crying out, "Mr. Howard! Gary! Get down here, quick!"

Mrs. Howard was on the bed with her head hanging off the side over a small trash can. Beth Ann bent over to touch her shoulder and scared the poor woman. She rolled onto her back and held her hands out in front of her. "Don't hurt me! Please, don't hurt me!"

Beth Ann backed up a step and tried to calm her down, but Linda didn't seem to recognize her. Gary rushed past her to help Linda sit up. "She's burning up! Run and get me a wet wash cloth!" he commanded. Linda tried to push Gary away, but he cupped her face in his hands and looked her in the eye. "Honey, it's me, Gary…your husband. I had to go into town with Beth Ann. What happened?"

She narrowed her eyes at him at first, but then seemed to understand what he was saying. "People came. People came into the house." She wrapped her arms around herself and started rocking forward and back.

"People…like who? What people?"

She thought for a moment. "Joey, Susan, James, Betty, Rosie…." She kept naming people who lived on their street. Beth Ann held out the washcloth to Gary in confusion; her parents weren't here.

"Neighbors?" Gary asked her to clarify. "You mean, our neighbors came into the house?"

She nodded.

Gary looked over his shoulder at Beth Ann and clenched his jaw. Her eyes grew wide in sudden understanding. That's why only a couple neighbors went to town; the rest had planned to rob them while they were gone.

Linda continued rocking and explained in a shaky voice. "They asked me to get something and then when I turned around, the women held me tight while the men...the men...they took all of my good jars and...everything!" It was as though by saying it out loud, she was just realizing it for the first time. Then she got angry. "You have to get it back! They took it! They took it all! My jars...I need them!"

"Shhh," Gary soothed as he held the cool cloth to her forehead. "You're okay. Rest, honey. I love you. I'll take care of it." He bent over and kissed her on the lips.

Beth Ann left them alone and called softly for Romeo, fearing the worst. But a faint whine gave away his hiding place behind an overstuffed chair. He limped out slowly. She drew him carefully into her arms and sat down. He yelped and then licked her hand before dropping his head down onto his paws. Beth Ann didn't know if she was more distressed or angry. Their neighbors had taken their food and hurt her dog. She felt like *she* could hurt somebody, given the chance.

Gary walked slowly out from behind the curtain. He sank down into the chair, a man defeated, and raked his hand through his hair. Then he sat and stared at the flames dancing in the wood burner for a long time. Finally he looked up at Beth Ann.

"New plan. Linda's too sick to travel and we have no food." He paused, as if he didn't want to say it. "We do whatever they say."

Chapter 13

The morning after the Howards were robbed, Gary woke up angry. As intimidating as he was, Beth Ann thought she liked the angry Gary better than the defeated, silent Gary. Within an hour after dawn he left the house on a mission, slamming the front door behind him in a show of force. He intended to confront several of the neighbors but found they weren't home...or willing to answer his knock; he wasn't sure. It just made him angrier. He was tempted to break in and take his stuff back, but common sense told him that was a pretty good way to get shot.

Instead, he marched his way into town to make his case known to the new sheriff. He wanted his food back–he and his wife had bought it, grown it, canned it; it was rightfully theirs. He wanted his wife's health back too, but that was a more unrealistic demand. With seemingly great interest, Sheriff Branson wrote down every detail and asked lots of questions. He assured Gary that he would take care of the situation and would send a Medical Team member to look in on his wife.

In the meantime, Gary must be assigned to a Team and work in order to get food and water each day. When he protested that his wife was too weak to work, the sheriff shook his head–there would be no shared meals. You work, you eat; you don't work…there wasn't enough to just give away. Branson assigned Linda to the Childcare Team, when she got better; it was the lightest duty he could offer. Resigned to comply, Gary informed him about his neighbor, Beth Ann, and she was assigned to work in the greenhouses.

On his way home to get Beth Ann and escort her to town for her first day of "work," Gary's burden felt heavier than when he had left that morning. While he walked, he brainstormed options, but none of them seemed feasible. He tried to pray, but it didn't help. Bitterness began to take root…and he let it. It felt justified and satisfying.

The root grew deeper that evening. While Beth Ann was sharing the day's events on the Greenhouse Team, they heard loud knocking on the front door, followed by a deep shout. "Security Team! Open up!" Gary told Beth Ann to take Romeo and stay behind the "bedroom" curtain with Linda as he rushed up the basement steps two at a time.

A deputy by the name of Wyatt, according to his badge, claimed to be investigating their theft for Sheriff Branson. Without giving Gary a choice in the matter, Officer Wyatt went through every nook and cranny in the house—main level and basement—taking notes and asking questions. When he left, Gary watched in bewilderment as other deputies congregated in the street. Three of his neighbors, handcuffed, were being forcibly escorted from their homes, and a large lawn cart filled to overflowing with bags was being pulled by two more deputies.

When the cart passed his driveway, Gary ran down the porch steps and sidewalk without taking the time to put on a coat. "Wait! Is that my food? Hey! HEY! What's going on?"

The parade kept moving, but two rifles pointed at his chest forced Gary to stop and stand quietly. Sheriff Branson and a young deputy did their best to address his concern by thanking him for bringing the theft to their attention. "In these troubled times,"

Branson said, "crime has to be stopped immediately or it will be uncontrollable. And the contribution of food will help the town."

"But I'm NOT contributing it! It's mine! And my sick wife's! You assured me you would get it back for me!"

Branson dropped his head and shook it calmly. "No, no, Mr. Howard. I'm sorry if you misunderstood. I told you that I would get your food back, but I never said *back to you*. You have to understand that if we are to survive, the entire community must contribute what they can. You have to think beyond yourself." He made an attempt to look compassionate, but his eyes were cold.

Gary clenched his hands. Bright white sparks of light exploded in his line of vision as he felt his body temperature rise. In a low voice he managed to growl, "Get off my lawn, you fascist!"

Unaffected, Branson raised one eyebrow and held Gary's glare. "Be careful, Mr. Howard. You'll need to choose your enemies carefully from now on." After a long, challenging pause, he nodded his head to the fidgety young deputy beside him and they left to rejoin the others on their way back toward town. A blood-curdling scream caught Gary's attention, and he saw the wife of one of the men being escorted away crumple to the ground. He didn't feel a thing as he turned and walked back inside.

The next day, Tionesta's work Teams were called by the church bell to the town square to witness their first execution. Gary's three neighbors stood on the platform, accused of stealing from the town's food supply. Without a trial or jury, Andrews drew a name out of a hat and the noose was placed around the unlucky man's neck. The other two men, handcuffed and forced to watch from mere inches away, were returned to their homes without food for that day.

Beth Ann covered her face with her hands and didn't watch. Some people cried openly, others gasped in horror, and the rest stood shock-still until they were forced to move. Gary was deeply saddened at the extreme consequence, but Andrews and Branson had made their point. If inspiration wouldn't work, they would rule by fear. And now everyone knew they weren't bluffing.

Linda held on for a couple days after the invasion. Gary stayed home with his wife while she was sick, but he was not allowed to have any food rations on the days he didn't "work." Beth Ann wished that she could share her food with Gary, but they were guarded while they ate at the town hall and were not allowed to take food out of the building. Sheriff Branson claimed it was for everyone's safety...which was probably the truth. At least Gary had the little bit of food he had buried; it would keep him alive for the short term.

Meghan visited the day after the hanging, and a male nurse came to the Howard's home on the second day; there was nothing they could do except work on bringing the fever down and keep the older woman as comfortable as possible. When a young lady showed up the third day, Gary turned her away. He would spend the day digging a grave. It took all day because he had to light a shallow fire at the back of the property first to thaw the surface ground and then dig the deep hole by shovel. It was excruciating work, even more so for his heart than his back; it was his last labor of love for his wife of thirty-two years.

When Beth Ann arrived home in the evening, she helped to wrap Linda in a soft blanket and pull her body out to the gravesite on a tarp. After they lowered her gently, Gary recited Psalm 23 and said a prayer, his voice low and quavering. Beth Ann helped to move the dirt back into the grave, and Gary set a crude cross marker made of two sticks bound with twine into the ground. He recorded the day on the family tree page in the front of his Bible and went to bed, all without saying another word or even acknowledging Beth Ann's presence. Beth Ann felt Linda's loss, too; grieving her passing drove the wedge of sorrow for her own parents and brother even deeper.

The weeks passed in a slow-motion blur; it was like living behind an unfocused lens. Beth Ann did what she was told; everyone did what they were told. For that they got to eat enough to keep them alive...and to keep them doing what they were told. Christmas had come and gone. A new year had started without anyone paying attention. No one sang about old acquaintances and times from the past. No one feasted or made toasts. Well, maybe Mayor Andrews and Sheriff Branson did. But no one else.

Beth Ann learned a lot during that time about setting up a winter growing system. The Greenhouse Team manager, Mr. Eckley, had run a small nursery on his property just north of town. He and his family had been relocated into town to use one floor of the Historical Society's mansion, sharing the three-story home with the families of the Water Team Manager and the Childcare Team Manager.

The Greenhouse Team spent the first few days moving as many supplies from the Eckley property as could be used or repurposed, and then another day to identify buildings that had brick or stone walls that faced southward, or were at least exposed to the scarce winter sun for the majority of the daylight hours. This would help to attract and hold in heat for the polycarbonate plastic-covered structures. After Mr. Eckley received approval from Andrews for the recommended sites, he had to oversee the greenhouse construction by an inexperienced team with varying shades of green thumbs.

They not only built and assembled the greenhouses, but they dug wide trenches under the shelving on both sides for manure that would be mixed with straw and soil to compost. This would also provide additional heat. Beth Ann wondered where the manure would come from, but she found out later that a Livestock Team of two nearby farmers relocated into town had been set up to care for the handful of horses, cows and chickens that had come in with them. Doors were built into both ends so that they could be opened in summer for ventilation. Gutter-like troughs were attached to the frame at the base of the sloped roof to catch rainwater, and barrels magically appeared one day to catch it. On days when it snowed, they would form snow bricks if it was wet enough to pack. Gradually a snow wall was built partway up the outside of each structure for insulation.

Their team was large because Mr. Andrews wanted the greenhouses ready to go as soon as possible; it would be split into two groups in the spring, when a small number would stay with the greenhouses and a larger number would form a Gardening Team. Beth Ann liked her boss and her Teammates, even though the work culture was solemn. Several of her teachers from the elementary and high school worked with her, as well as Tionesta's head librarian, Gary's Lutheran pastor, and a few people that she recognized from serving at the restaurant. She also met some interesting new people: a young lady who was being homeschooled and her mom, a grumpy older man who could fix anything, and the owner of the new pizza store that had moved into town only a couple years earlier. She thought it was a pity that she had missed out on building these relationships when times were good and she could have enjoyed them; now no one had the energy for friendship and community. Their lives were literally reduced to work and basic survival.

When it was time to start the seeds, Mr. Eckley showed them how to germinate them in a little dish and when to transplant them. She learned that they had to use what he called "heirloom seeds," which weren't genetically modified, so they would keep reproducing for future growing seasons. Since food was so scarce, they planted all the non-GMO seeds, too; they just confined them to the smallest greenhouse so they wouldn't cross-pollinate with the heirloom plants. The delicate seedlings had to be watered from the bottom, to prevent disease and fungus. The Team had to track specific data in handwritten journals: the temperature inside and outside the greenhouses at certain times of the day and night, which seeds were planted, how long it took them to germinate, when they were watered, the attrition rate, and so forth.

Occasionally she found herself enjoying the work and could momentarily forget about the fragile strand their lives dangled from, but she would never find a way to cope with the pungent manure. Even worse than the manure was the unannounced visits by Mr. Andrews or his henchmen. One man in particular made her feel uncomfortable, the one with the thin, gray braid called "Travis." There were days he would lean his back against the door frame and watch her work. On other days he would stand uncomfortably close to her and ask completely irrelevant questions about the plants.

One day Travis came up behind her and leaned fully against her as he reached for a watering can hanging above her head, pinning her against the planters. She clutched the edge of the wooden box and stood stiffly, just hoping that if he didn't get a rise out of her he would go away. At that moment Pastor Dan walked in and asked for the watering can in a way that actually meant Travis should move on. Beth Ann couldn't find the words to thank him; she hoped the good reverend could see the gratefulness and relief in her face.

Beth Ann's way of life only two months earlier was hard to remember; when she thought back to the days before the lights went out, they were fuzzy, as if she had read about them in a book. Except for the hole in her heart from missing her parents. And the keen memory of coffee; she would give almost anything for a pot of hot coffee. And she wouldn't worry about the caffeine or the sugar or whether it was healthy or not; she would just drink the whole pot.

It seemed that her only real pleasure now was reading. On rare days when the Greenhouse Team was done early and the weather was dry, she would sneak through the forest to a spot that had been a favorite of hers since she was a little girl. It was a small rocky ledge in a heavily wooded area; the river flowed not far below the overlook and its gentle sound brought peace to her troubled heart. She could see glimpses of the water now, but in the summer it would be hidden by dense foliage. A narrow deer path led down the shallow ravine to the water's edge. It was a solid twenty-minute walk from home when she and her parents could freely go there with a picnic lunch; now it took much longer because it was outside the secured town perimeter and she had to make sure she was not seen or followed. But it felt good to defy the rules, like she still had a tiny bit of control over her life.

Beth Ann would escape to the ledge with a small blanket and lose herself in stories about better times. Of course, the handgun that Mr. Howard had taught her to shoot and insisted that she keep with her at all times sitting on the ledge beside her was a constant reminder that she, indeed, was not living in those times any more.

While Beth Ann was learning winter gardening, Gary went out with the Hunting Team every day. He was a different person after Linda passed away. Although he was still paternal toward Beth Ann, his will to fight the establishment and to live life fully was gone. They didn't light candles after dark to read or sing. They didn't work on projects around the house. He read to himself rather than aloud, and spent long periods of time writing in his journal. He rarely spoke, and when he did, it was mere phrases of a practical nature. He was grieving, and Beth Ann understood that she needed to let him have the time and space to get through it his own way.

The Hunting Team had an increasingly hard time finding game of any size. As they went deeper into the Allegheny National Forest, their day trips turned into overnight trips. Mr. Andrews supplied some gear, and other cold weather camping gear was "donated" by the men and women of Tionesta "who were devoted to the good of the community." At least that is how Andrews gushed over the supplies at one of the town hall meetings, as people came to refer to them. In reality, the Security Team simply looked through the town's "inventory" list to identify households with the supplies they were looking for, escorted the chosen people home at day's end, and simply took it. Of course they said, "Thank you very much."

While some of the Hunting Team members were gone on overnight trips, others stayed home to skin, butcher and can or smoke any of the game from the previous day, or to supplement physical labor on the Fishing Team or Water Team. Beth Ann hated the nights when Gary was gone–she was lonely, frightened, and didn't sleep well. Since the hanging, the neighbors who had robbed them had not caused them any trouble; in fact, they had not even spoken to Gary. But Beth Ann still didn't trust anyone.

One crisp and sunny day near the end of February, the church bell rang to call a town hall meeting. Beth Ann quickly finished marking her calculation and hung up the clipboard; it swayed back and forth on its designated nail long after the greenhouse door slammed shut. The meeting was just starting as Beth Ann found Kristen and Meghan. They huddled together half listening and half thinking of the food that would follow the meeting, until the unthinkable happened. Mr. Andrews announced that all pets must be released since the food rations were limited and were for human consumption only. Apparently, several people had approached his deputies inquiring about options for feeding their pets, and although he claimed to be genuinely sympathetic, Andrews forbade using any portion of the town's rations for a pet. The only exception was for animals being raised to be slaughtered or to provide a by-product like milk or eggs. He urged citizens to release their pets into the wild with a hopeful attitude, as some would thrive in their new-found freedom; in addition, pet owners would avoid the inevitable heart-breaking scenario of watching their beloved Fifi slowly starve to death.

Beth Ann could not believe what she was hearing. For the first time in months, she didn't feel cold. In fact, even though she was standing outside on a wintry street, she felt scalding hot bile rising in her throat. With great effort she remained outwardly calm so as not to call any attention to herself, hoping that her face wasn't turning any telltale shade of red. She wished that Gary was there, but his hunting party was not expected back until late the next day. She desperately needed his support, and she would keep her dog hidden until she could talk with Gary about her options. There was not a chance in the world that she was going to send Romeo off into the wilderness to die.

Meghan reached out to hug Beth Ann compassionately. She knew how much Beth Ann loved Romeo and sensed her rising emotions. And she had seen firsthand what became of pets released into the wild; but she would never share that story with Beth Ann.

Meghan was doing well on the Medical Team, essentially taking the role of a visiting nurse. Mr. Andrews had provided basic medical supplies to help with contusions, burns, fever, frost-bite, simple fractures, and that sort of thing. For viral infections and contagious illness, an in-home quarantine policy was in place. An infirmary had been set up in the former Visitor's Center in the middle of town, and it was there that people would sign up to receive treatment on the spot or request a visit to their home.

The part Meghan didn't like was the intense record keeping she was required to do on her home visits; it felt like spying. In addition, she felt like she had to constantly fight for sustenance for her "patients"; she argued that they couldn't get better if they didn't eat, but they weren't allowed to eat if they didn't work. The Medical Team leader, Mr. Thorpe, finally convinced Mr. Andrews to release broth to the people who were receiving medical care. Thorpe wasn't a doctor, but as a veteran paramedic he was the closest thing left in town; heart surgeon Dr. Nejeli and his wife had been shot and their house burned to the ground, while Dr. Sorenson, Dr. Myers and two pediatricians were nowhere to be found.

Her roommate situation with Dillon had worked out as well as could be expected so far; he was not around much and he treated her respectfully when he was. That is to say, he incessantly teased and flirted with her, but so far he had kept his hands to himself and Meghan mostly ignored him.

Above all, she worried about Kristen. As Meghan held her arm around Beth Ann's shoulders and Mr. Andrews droned on, she watched the void in Kristen's eyes grow deeper, if that was possible. They were like black holes, a vacuum into which her friend's spunk and fun-lovingness had been sucked after watching her parents and boyfriend die violent deaths. Now considered a "single" household, as well as in a home outside the roadblock area, Kristen had been moved in with a family. Luke, the dad, and two oldest children, Abby and Ben, were assigned to the Water Team like she was. The wife, Allison, and youngest son, Brian, went to the Childcare Team. Their baby had died early when the food ran out and Allison's milk had dried up; they had scars of their own to match Kristen's.

As Kristen grew thinner, she grew weaker. Meghan knew from her training that without a resolve to live, people willingly succumb to depression and lethargy. At this point Kristen was having trouble keeping up with the physical labor on the Water Team, and the manager had written her up twice in his reports to Mr. Andrews. Meghan and Beth Ann tried to encourage her when they saw her at lunch, but nothing got through the deep, dark hollow that had eaten her heart and soul. They felt helpless to reach her.

When Mr. Andrews finally finished his grandiose speech, he released everyone for their meal. Beth Ann, Meghan, and Kristen shuffled forward together in the long line. On normal workdays, Teams arrived in a staggered fashion to the municipal building to sign in. But on town meeting days, everyone gathered at the same time and had to wait in a long line to funnel into the building. For some reason, the irritability of the long-suffering mob grew to fisticuffs this day, and Security Team members had to step in. They broke people into smaller groups and created a second line entering through a side door. Dillon stepped in to help the frazzled woman behind the desk to alternate the two lines through the registration process and up the stairs into the cafeteria rooms.

Meghan watched the stress build and resisted the urge to shake her head. The Mayor and Sheriff didn't trust the hungry townspeople with food storage and preparation, so they had originally put the Security Team and Deputy force in charge of meal time. However, the lawmen were stretched far too thin between the 24/7 roadblocks and security, managing the jail, reporting on the work of the Teams, and handling Mr. Andrews' grunt work. So they added a few more sturdy, but not too young, deputies to the force with wives who could help–while guarded, of course. They had to keep meticulous records on meals served, but there was no inventory to keep because Mr. Andrews brought into town whatever was going to be used for each day from some mysterious, outlying location.

Meghan smiled at the woman and thanked her as she signed in, hoping it would make her day better. The woman stopped, holding the pen in mid-air, and stared at Meghan as if she hadn't heard a kind word in years. Before Meghan could respond, a deputy handed her an MRE and pushed her toward the steps, yelling "Move along!" Meghan stumbled, but Beth Ann steadied her and they hustled up the stairway, zombie Kristen trailing behind. As they reached the top, they could still hear the guard berating the woman for being too slow. Meghan glanced at Beth Ann and wondered if she was thinking the same thing: the "green sashers" were becoming increasingly cockier and deserved the sneered nickname.

The next day, Beth Ann anticipated Mr. Howard's return to the point of distraction–tipping the wheelbarrow of manure, spilling the watering can, and shutting the door on her boss. Finally her Team was called to the municipal building for their meal, so she knew that time was moving forward, albeit too slowly for her. As they approached the lawn, she was horrified to see yet another "lesson" taking place. While Travis looked on, hands clasped behind his back, a man wearing a collar and rope leash was being forced to run in circles around one of the Deputies, like a horse being broken. The man was obviously exhausted, barely able to clear the ground with his feet as he stumbled. But each time his knees buckled, Travis would nod and the Deputy would yank him up by collar, practically choking him.

Mr. Andrews' lessons were always public, and the Teams on their way to their meal were required to pass by. Beth Ann kept her head down as she made her way up the walk; she didn't like to see people suffer. Suddenly she ran into the woman in front of her. Travis had stopped them, forcing them to watch. Looking up, Beth

Ann nearly fainted when she recognized the gaunt man as Gary Howard.

"This man ran from an attack on his Hunting party, rather than fight back!" Travis announced. "And as a result, his partner was killed. Since he likes to run so much, now he'll run until he fully understands his error. Next time, it will be his life for another!" Travis then shooed them off in the direction of the municipal building's front steps so that he would be ready to explain the lesson to the next Team.

Beth Ann fought her way out of the line and ran back to Travis. "Let him go! He's learned his lesson, I'm sure!" she demanded, breathless.

Travis lifted his eyebrows and cocked his head. A smile formed slowly on his leathery face, like he had just noticed a spider that needed squashed. "Oh, really, young lady? And how can you be so sure?"

"Because I know him, and he'd never do anything to hurt anyone. There must be more to the story! He's had enough – can't you tell?" Beth Ann cried out as Gary fell again and stayed down, his head bouncing hard against the ground. When the Deputy looked to Travis to see if he could stop, Beth Ann bolted toward Gary. But Travis caught her fast around the waist, lifting her nearly off the ground.

"Hold up, small one," he said, laughing. She started kicking and punching. "Ooh, You're a feisty one!" He pinned her arms behind her back with minimal effort. Leaning into her face he offered her a deal: "Give me a kiss and I'll let you have your man back."

Beth Ann spat in his face and took advantage of his surprise to jerk free of his grasp. "You're SICK!"

He slowly wiped his cheek with the sleeve of his jacket. "Why, yes...yes, I am. We will continue this later; I got work to do. Now get that coward to the infirmary. And no meal for you today!" With a wave of his hand, Travis signaled for the Deputy with the "leash" to escort Gary and Beth Ann away.

She didn't care. She didn't think she could eat anyway, after being harassed by the repulsive man and seeing the way Gary had been treated. She let Gary lean his weight on her while he stumbled down the street to the Medical Clinic under the Deputy's watchful eye.

After a fitful night's sleep at the clinic and some warm broth, he was able to tell Beth Ann his side of the story. Gary had been paired up with Mr. Shannon for the three day hunting trip. They had managed to get a couple small rabbits and a squirrel, so at least they weren't coming back empty handed. But on the morning of the third day, as they headed toward Tionesta, they were ambushed. Gary never saw who was shooting at them or how many there were. Mr. Shannon went down instantly, but Gary was able to get away. There was no way he could have saved his buddy, and there was no way he could have fought off the men who took their meat and camping gear. When he reported back to the Team Leader, he was taken to Mr. Andrews and then turned over to Sheriff Branson and finally to Travis for his punishment. He took Beth Ann's hand and clasped it between his two rough, red hands.

"I wish...," he started, then just closed his eyes. She swallowed the lump rising in her throat and gave him time. He finally looked up at her. "I wish I could protect you. I wish I could make things better. I wish I could tell you God has a plan." He turned his head away. "But we're all on our own now, just marking the days till we die."

Chapter 14

The first March after the EMP attack came gentle as a lamb, and the scent of the coming spring hung in the warming air. On the days that weren't frozen, the earth was pure mud, at least that's what it seemed like to Meghan, and she hated mud. As she walked a good portion of the days when she was assigned to house calls, she prayed for her patients, her out-of-town family and friends, and her own safety. At the same time, it was hard not to worry about the leadership of the town and the future of Tionesta. In a strange way, she felt like she had found her mission field, her calling. In the midst of tragic circumstances all around her and her own physical suffering, she found it liberating to practice gratitude for each day of life granted.

One windy, cold day near the middle of the month, Meghan visited the Taylor's sick child in a home near Lighthouse Island, the home base of the Water Team. When she was finished, she took a short detour, hoping to catch a glimpse of Kristen. Instantly she was amazed by the industry and organization of the large Team. The stronger members were hauling buckets from the river or chopping wood for fuel. Several people were tending fires and carefully boiling the essential resource. Other members worked at filling and securing containers of all shapes and sizes into a low-sided hay wagon pulled by an old tractor. When full, the wagon pulled away and *put-putted* its way to the municipal building for distribution. Empty containers were being re-sanitized and readied for the next batch.

Just as Meghan was taking in the whole scene, she was spotted by a Security Team member. He approached her aggressively, with his bold sash flapping against his thigh and his rifle in the low ready position. She quickly identified herself as a Medical Team member and explained that she was there to report on the Water Team's general condition. The middle-aged man snatched the clipboard out of her hands and scanned the three clipped sheets.

"It's not on your list," he observed, his eyes narrowed at her.

"It's not on today's list, but it's part of my job description to conduct surprise visits on any Team on any day," Meghan said, stretching the truth. She gestured over her left shoulder. "I was just wrapping up with the Taylor Family and thought I would take notes on the Water Team as I was in the area." She paused and looked around, then leaned toward him. "I know you have to make rounds, too, and I bet you've seen people trying to hide things…." She lifted her eyebrows, hoping he would identify with her justification.

The green sasher didn't seem convinced, but he also didn't argue. He handed her clipboard back without commenting one way or the other.

This gave Meghan courage. "I'm surprised you haven't had a visit by one of the other Medical Team members. In a time without hospitals or antibiotics or any advanced medical treatments, don't you think it's important for us to catch viruses and infections before they spread? Or to identify potentially harmful settings where bacteria can grow?" She hoped that by giving her voice a lower tone and a strong quality, it would mask her trembling.

He shrugged. "Fine by me. But you'll have to take it up with the Team Manager." The man escorted her to a three-sided tent with an eight-foot folding table and a couple of chairs set up inside. Two men stood when they entered; the deputy introduced Meghan and left. She recognized the younger man—Mr. Papp had been one of her small church's deacons for as long as she could remember. They shared a smile and the familiarity was comforting.

"Meghan! It's so nice to see you! How have you been holding up?" Mr. Papp asked. She answered him with vagueness and asked about his family. He went on to explain that his job was to track the water supply as it was obtained and distributed, like a business manager of sorts.

She turned to the Water Team Manager. Jared McNight was a tall, large-framed man with graying fringe around his temples and unshaven face. From the sagging skin, Meghan guessed that he had been a food-lover in his former life. His eyes shone with kindness and his smile seemed genuine.

"Mr. McNight," she said with a nod. "It's very nice to meet you." Handshakes were no longer used, due to the risk of spreading germs. But it still seemed weird to meet someone new and not shake his hand. "I will only be a few minutes, but I need to take some notes on the Team's general health and working conditions. I may also need to talk to one or two of your team members. Just standard operating procedure." She gave him her nicest smile and waited, resisting the urge to ramble nervously on.

"Well, Miss Crawley, you go right ahead. And be sure to let me know if you see anything that needs to be addressed. My Team works very hard, I'm proud to say. I wouldn't want anything to jeopardize their chance of survival any more than my own." He paused and glanced around. Then he looked straight into Meghan's eyes and said quietly, "And I would appreciate the chance to fix any issues before they are reported to Mr. Andrews." He lifted his eyebrows in question.

"Absolutely. I understand," Meghan responded, nodding. She had seen Andrews' harsh and public punishments—hanging, dismemberment, imprisonment, caning...even branding.

His relief was apparent in his sigh. "Here, I'll show you around." He gestured to the open side of the tent for Meghan to step out ahead of him.

Mr. McNight led her through the various stations and she made several positive notes about their process for boiling the large quantities of water and the overall health and condition of the workers. Meghan didn't have to explain to the manager how essential having healthy water was for the entire town's survival. It was obvious that he took his job very seriously.

Their last stop was the place where the hay wagon had been loaded. When Meghan stalled, insisting she had to wait for the tractor and final team members to return, McNight went back to his "office." Meghan still hadn't seen Kristen, but she was finished with her notes and could not linger much longer. Plus, she didn't want to be in trouble for checking in back at the infirmary too much later than expected from her rounds.

She paced, waiting for the wagon to appear, while scanning the scene. A commotion caught her attention near one of the fires. A small person, Meghan thought it was a child at first, was lying on the ground, a spilled container telling the story. A man stood over her, yelling about the ruined water. A few people glanced up, but they stayed with their work. When Meghan started running, it caught the deputy's attention and he alerted the Manager. As she suspected, it was Kristen.

"Bring me some water!" she commanded. McNight hesitated. Meghan flung her arms up in frustration. "Tell Mr. Papp to add it to his inventory! This young woman can have my portion for today! Please," she pleaded as she turned back to Kristen.

Within a few minutes, Kristen was able to sit up, though she leaned against Meghan's legs. Meghan made a note on her form and turned to the Manager. "Mr. McNight. This lady is far too weak to be working on the Water Team. She will have to be moved."

"I agree with you, but I've sent two requests to have her transferred to another Team and I haven't received a reply." The man shrugged. "I put her on the lightest duty possible. I'm concerned about her, but I can't babysit her, either. I have a very large Team to manage."

"Well, I want the doctor to take a look at her ankle to make sure nothing's broken. I am recommending that we take her to the Clinic." Meghan frowned. Kristen would never be able to walk that far. Then she remembered the tractor. "Can you please send her on the next water wagon into town and drop her off at the Clinic?" Meghan requested.

"Sure. But it won't be ready to leave for another two hours. It'll be the last load of the day," McNight explained.

"Okay. Well, it can't be helped. Thank you very much. I hear the wagon coming now; I'll check over those men before I go. Please remember to give them a written note of authorization to take this girl."

Mr. McNight nodded and turned away. Meghan stooped to talk quietly with Kristen to make sure she understood the plan, then she helped her move to a nearby tree she could lean against until the wagon was ready to leave. She didn't have ice, but she wrapped and elevated Kristen's foot on some rocks before she left. Jogging back to the infirmary to check in, she felt grateful that Kristen would get some desperately needed help.

Beth Ann let herself in through the front door of her parents' house. At times she was tempted to go straight to the Howard house, but ever since Deputy Wyatt had made his first round three months before, Gary had insisted that she keep up the appearance of living at home. So she would let herself into the front door of her own house, then sneak out the back and enter her neighbor's place by the back patio door. It was habit now, so she honored his advice even when he wasn't home, and even when she was exhausted.

It had been a long night snoozing in a chair by Gary's bed at the Clinic, and an even longer day in the greenhouse. The weather was still cold at night but some days got warm, especially inside the plastic-covered structures, so she decided to raid her old closet and drawers for light layering shirts on her way through the house. She untied her work apron and set it down with the hoodie she was carrying on the kitchen counter.

On her way down the hall, she checked the shelves in the dark hall closet and the bathroom drawers for any kind of moisturizing lotion or salve that hadn't been taken when the Security Teams inventoried the house. Her skin had progressively lost hydration; it started with itchy flaking and was now cracking and bleeding, especially on her hands. The stress and lack of nutrition was affecting her in other ways, too, from fatigue to achy muscles and joints. What she wouldn't give for a hot soak in the tub and a strong pot of coffee…and maybe even some ice cream. Most of all she missed toilet paper. They had run out of that last month.

As she walked from room to room, she felt a deep sadness. There were reminders of her parents everywhere, whom she now assumed she would never see again. In her room, there was evidence of her hopes for a future that would never come to be. There was also an emptiness in the sorrow. Her childhood home had been violated when the Security Team members came to confiscate any supplies that would be useful for the common good: toiletries, medicines, food, camping and hunting gear, guns and ammunition. Even the fuel was siphoned out of her car right in front of her. Each household was allowed to keep only one shotgun, rifle or handgun.

Her eyes were drawn to her wrapped Christmas presents for her parents, her brother and sister-in-law, and her friends. The glittery paper in bright colors was a mockery of the world she lived in. The items inside the paper were completely useless. If only she had known this tragedy was coming. Could she have been prepared enough? Probably not.

Beth Ann felt herself sinking again; she constantly fought for the energy to battle the depression. She forced herself to focus on getting her clothes so that she could get back to the Howard's basement and her Romeo–the only bright spot in her darkness. Gary had agreed to try and hide the dog since the Hunting Team had been instructed privately to kill the released pets for meat. If she had enough food in her stomach to vomit, she would have when Gary told her that. Meanwhile, he would be at the clinic for at least another day.

As she opened the bottom drawer of her dresser, it squeaked oddly, sounding a little like the storm door off the kitchen. But she shrugged it off and began stuffing T-shirts into a bag. Suddenly the hairs on the back of her neck stood up on end and she whirled around to see the creepy man with the braid standing in the doorway of her room.

"Travis!" she yelled. "What the heck are you doing here?" Her heart pounded in her throat, competing with the words.

He just smiled slowly. "I'm sorry, Miss Dalton. I didn't mean to scare you." His squinty eyes didn't look very sorry.

When he didn't say anything else, she stood up and ordered, "Well, then, why are you here? You've already taken everything we have."

"Not everything," he said in a way that made her flesh crawl.

"What is that supposed to mean?" she growled.

He laughed, and she looked desperately around for something to equalize the difference in strength between them. Her pistol was in her work apron on the kitchen counter. Gary had warned her to never be without it.

"Relax. I wanted to discuss the possibility of you joining the new Food Team we're starting," he explained with a smirk.

"I'm perfectly happy on the Greenhouse Team," she said with what she hoped was enough finality to get rid of him.

"But you didn't even hear what the benefits are. Extra food, hot baths—"

"Stop!" Beth Ann stomped her foot. "I don't want to hear about it and I don't want to change jobs. You need to leave!"

"Okay," he shrugged. "That was one option, but there is one more…." He left his post at the door and sauntered over, cornering her.

"Get away from me, you dirty old man!" She shoved him hard and tried to run past.

He caught her hand in a vice grip. "Aww. You've noticed!" He yanked her into his personal space. With her free hand she tried to loose herself, but he was too strong. He backed her onto the bed.

Beth Ann started to cry as she realized what was happening. "Please…please don't…."

His coal black eyes glittered like they were alive, even as the last light of day faded from the room.

Chapter 15

When Gary arrived home from the Clinic the next day, sore and weak, he was surprised to find Beth Ann in her bed instead of at work. Claiming sickness, she sent him away. He used the day to catch up on some maintenance around the place, resting often. He visited his wife's grave, gathered water from the containment system at both houses, scraped the mud off his boots, picked up sticks in the yard, pulled out some of his warmer weather clothes, cleaned his hunting rifle and Beth Ann's handgun, and boiled a little bone broth for her from his buried stash of almost-gone meat. Of course, the neighbors had taken the bouillon and vegetables that he would have included, but now everyone in town would benefit from them. He shook his head in disbelief, wondering which was better: keeping one family alive for a whole winter, or one village alive for a week? It was a difficult question.

When he set the weak, warm liquid on Beth Ann's bedside table, she stirred but didn't sit up. "Oh, you shouldn't have used your propane, Gary. We need to save that!" she protested weakly.

"But if you're too sick to work today, you won't get a meal. I can't let that happen." He reached over to feel her forehead. It didn't feel overly warm, to his great relief.

"Well, thank you for taking care of me," she replied faintly.

He hesitated. "Do you want to go to the clinic? Or I could go get someone—"

"No!" she interrupted, pushing herself into a semi-seated position. "I…just need to rest. I'm fine." She gave him a lopsided attempt at a smile, yet avoided eye contact. "Really. And thank you for making me something to eat." She slowly brought the bowl to her mouth, taking a sip before finally looking up at Gary. "I'm glad you're home."

He left the room, puzzled and worried at the moisture in her eyes.

The next day, Beth Ann did get up and leave for the Greenhouse Team, but she asked Gary to walk into town with her. Gary was on his way back to the Hunting Team, but he was being assigned to stay in town for a week with lighter duty jobs, per Mr. Thorpe's orders. He was glad that he would be home every evening to keep an eye on Beth Ann's health.

Every day seemed the same after that. Beth Ann barely spoke, rarely looked Gary in the eye, and didn't want to go anywhere by herself, but she kept up with everything she was expected to do. In fact, she seemed to have more grit than usual. His ration in the municipal building overlapped with hers twice that week, and he observed that she and her friends barely spoke to each other while they ate.

One night, as Beth Ann settled herself and her aging dog into his son's old bed, Gary forced himself to give her the news that they both knew would come. "Beth Ann?"

Curled into a ball on her side under the covers, both arms around Romeo, Beth Ann opened her eyes. They reflected the single flickering candle flame. She didn't say anything, but he knew that she was listening.

He sighed and looked away. There was no use in sugar coating. "I'm headed out tomorrow. It's a longer hunt this time and we're trying a new area and taking a larger group. Might be three, four days…or more…before we get back."

Her brow furrowed. "You feel up to it?"

"Me? I'm not worried about me. Are you gonna be okay?"

She just nodded her head against the pillow and closed her eyes.

He groaned. "I wish someone could look after you, but I can't trust our neighbors and no one else is close enough. You keep my handgun with you at all times, right?"

She opened her eyes again and tried to reassure him. "Yes, I will," she replied, and Gary noticed a shadow pass over her eyes. He waited until she came back from wherever she went in her mind. "It's okay. I'll be okay. Please be safe and don't worry. Just come home as soon as you can."

"I will," he promised. He knelt down by her bed. "Is it okay with you if I say a prayer for us both?"

Beth Ann tried to feel comforted by his prayer, but somehow she did not. All she could think about was her stupidity for leaving the gun in the kitchen on the night she was raped by Travis. She vowed to never be caught without it again.

Mike, Charlie and Travis had continued to make their random "check-ins" on the work Teams. Beth Ann tried to avoid them and make sure she wasn't alone when they were in the vicinity. It felt as though she looked over her shoulder hundreds of times each day. She thought about confiding in her Team Leader or the pastor, but she feared repercussions and she was embarrassed, even mortified, to even think about saying it out loud. So she did nothing…except work. She poured her heart and soul into her gardening and volunteered to do extra. She could barely put one foot in front of the other to make it home in time for curfew each night, but that's what she wanted.

On the morning of the third day that Gary was gone, Mr. Eckley called an emergency Greenhouse Team meeting. Equally curious and nervous, Beth Ann leaned the rake against the side of the building and hurried out of the largest greenhouse, following several other Team members. She rounded the corner of the tool shed and ran directly into Travis. She froze and he smiled leeringly at her.

"Miss me?" he whispered. Her back was pressed against the wall, the only thing keeping her upright. She willed her feet to move, but they wouldn't. He chuckled quietly as if he was proud of his power and turned away. She forced herself to breathe and ran to catch up with the group gathering in the small parking lot behind the Presbyterian church. She was still trembling when she looked up and noticed Mr. Andrews standing beside Mr. Eckley. This was more serious than she thought.

Eckley explained that he and a couple deputies had gone to his former home the day before to get some larger tools and equipment that they would need when it was time to transfer the plants from greenhouses to gardens. With restrained emotion he shared how he had found a pile of ashes and stone where the house he grew up in had stood. The outbuildings had been ransacked, but not burned. The tools and equipment, including the rototiller, had all been taken. Not a single thing was salvageable.

Andrews gave Eckley's shoulder a compassionate squeeze and stepped in. "I want you to know how deeply saddened I am for Doug's loss. And his property is not the only one. The rumors of raiding parties around us are not just rumors…they are truth. These are not safe times and I hope that you now understand my wisdom in moving everyone into a tight perimeter that my men can defend." The mayor paused until he saw people nodding their heads in agreement.

Beth Ann wondered where this was going.

"Mr. Eckley, here, is a fine and caring leader. He has requested escorts for those of you who live away from the most populated, central part of town. Now, I'm sure that we are all safe if we stay inside the secured perimeter, but to help ease some of the tension, Sheriff Branson has agreed to provide his very busy deputies on a rotating basis to all the Teams, and my own men here will fill in as needed." Beth Ann's eyes grew large and she involuntarily glanced at Travis, who was staring at her with a smug smile. "The Team Leaders will help their Team members form groups that live in the same general areas. The smallest groups, or the members going off in their own direction without a group, will be given an escort. Thank you for your cooperation. And if you ever see anything out of the ordinary, report it to Sheriff Branson or me immediately." He nodded at Eckley and left with his motley entourage.

Eckley sent them all back to their tasks and told them they would work on forming "commuting" groups after the mid-day meal ration. Beth Ann, deep in thought as she worked the compost, jumped straight up when someone came from behind and laid a hand on her upper back. But this hand was gentle, compassionate. She turned around to find the former town librarian, Mary Jo Lowell, staring at her with a startled expression.

"Oh, sorry," Beth Ann said. "I thought...you were someone else."

"You okay, honey?" the still slightly plump, late-middle-aged woman asked. In that moment, Mrs. Lowell reminded Beth Ann of her mother, and she nearly burst into tears. Her bank of denial and fake courage was running out of reserves. Without thinking, she threw her arms around the poor lady and held onto her for dear life, probably startling her even more.

"I don't want any of those...men...escorting me home!" she confessed into the sweaty shoulder of Mrs. Lowell's T-shirt. Mary Jo patted her back sympathetically, as if she was comforting a small child.

"Is there a problem here, girls, or are we slow dancin'?" Jack asked loudly as he came into the greenhouse at the other end, pushing a wheelbarrow of fresh manure. He grunted as he steered it into place. Jack was one of the stronger men assigned to their Team for work that required hefty levels of brawn, and he did his job well. He was also a genius at fixing things. But he complained continuously and spread negativity about every possible little thing. Beth Ann had always tried to give him as much space as she thought he needed, plus a little more. This was definitely not the time to confide in Mary Jo. The women quickly went back to their work while Jack shoveled the pungent organic clumps into the long ditches under the shelves. Pastor Dan came behind him spreading straw over it, and Beth Ann worked herself to exhaustion mixing it all together.

As she already knew and feared, Beth Ann had only one other Teammate going in her direction after work, and not going as far as her street, which was the last one before the roadblock. She protested the escort system with Mr. Eckley, arguing that when Mr. Howard wasn't hunting, he would be escorting her home. But Eckley stuck to his plan, sure that he was providing safety for his Team…and not wanting to go against Mr. Andrews.

It was a great relief, then, to find that a pimple-faced deputy, his dutiful sash cinching in his skinny waist, was assigned to walk her and Lisa home. He kept a vigilant lookout but didn't say anything more than "Good night, Ma'am" to each of them as they reached their respective homes. On their journey they saw a handful of other little escorted huddles, including the neighbors on her street who were assigned to other teams.

There were only four households left on her street, not counting Beth Ann and Gary's "family" unit. Her own parents had gone on vacation and never came home. Then an entire family and house was lost in the kerosene heater fire, followed by an elderly woman whose heart stopped soon after her back-up oxygen tanks ran out. Two families packed up and walked out of town, bound for who knows where and had not been heard from or seen in Tionesta since. Their houses were then stripped clean by the neighbors. Just before Mayor Andrews came onto the scene, two small children had died from the flu, leaving behind a single broken-hearted mother with one teenaged boy. One retired couple opted to move into town with relatives when the opportunity arose in order to avoid the long walks for work and food. Of course, there was the loss of the man who had been hung for stealing the Howard's food; his young wife and toddler still lived at the end of the street and went to work on the Childcare Team every day. The two men who had been arrested with him and then released seemed to be looking out for the woman and child, probably from guilty consciences.

Thinking of all these changes as she absentmindedly let herself into the front door of her childhood home, Beth Ann was taken off guard by a shadowy form waiting just inside. Before she could react, he spun her around, cupped his hand over her mouth, and yanked her close to his body.

"Good evening, Miss Dalton. I wanted to personally make sure that you made it home safely tonight." She tried to scream, but it was too muffled by his hand to be effective. Reaching into her work apron pocket, he pulled out her gun and with one hand emptied all the bullets onto the carpet. Then he tossed the small weapon onto the recliner. He let her struggle until she was worn out, and then he took what he came for.

Beth Ann stayed home the next day, but not to lie in bed and feel sorry for herself this time. She snuck to the overlook with a blanket and a novel…and her reloaded gun. She spent the entire day soaking up the spring sunshine, listening to the river rush southward toward the great Ohio and Mississippi Rivers, and smelling the fresh scent of awakening life. The songbirds were starting to return from the South, yet another mockery of the life-changing disaster being confined to the human world alone. But Gary was right; she did not see one rabbit, squirrel, or turkey as she often had in the past.

She didn't bring her Bible along this time because she just couldn't see how it fit into her circumstances since God hadn't protected her. She didn't necessarily blame Him for the attacks, she was just…confused. Instead, she brought a work of fiction and read the entire book from cover to cover, hoping that by some literary magic she would get sucked into the book and permanently taken away from her reality. It was a self-care day, she rationalized, and one day without food wasn't going to kill her.

She had purposely left the two MREs where Travis had left them on the kitchen counter, beside the two he left the first time; she assumed they were her "payment" and it repulsed her. She didn't think she would be able to eat them even if she was starving, but in this era no one could throw away food for any reason. Now she had four MREs that she should either hide or give to Gary—but then he would need an explanation. She couldn't decide.

As the tree shadows lengthened, she realized she needed to start sneaking back to the house. She wanted to go down to the water's edge first but knew that it was too risky; she would be too exposed. As it was, it would be weeks before the foliage came out to give her adequate cover in the forest. Going from pine to pine, and from outcrop to outcrop, she stopped to listen and watch often as she worked her way back to her street. This was where she needed to be the most careful; this was where people were watching, she knew it.

She refused to go back into her parents' house; that's where Travis always found her. But she didn't want to put Gary in harm's way by leading Travis to the place she was actually living. So she went the long way around, skirting behind the neighborhood, and finally came to the tree line at the rear of the Howard property. In the dusk she could make out the homemade cross standing solemn watch over Linda's grave. She waited as the darkness deepened but did not detect any movement. Beth Ann trotted swiftly across the back yard, heart pounding, eyes darting…until she was safely inside the back door. Sliding her back down the door until she sat on the cold floor, she hugged her knees to her chest. The dam of building pressure finally broke and she wept.

"What's up with you?" Meghan quietly prodded Beth Ann the next day as they devoured their ration. This day it was some kind of weak soup with rice and vegetables in it. It was nice to have a warm meal for a change. "I didn't see you yesterday. And a couple weeks ago you missed a day, too. Everything ok?"

Beth Ann shrugged. "I don't think they care. I just needed some time to myself." She knew if she told Meghan she was "sick," she would start asking all the customary nursing questions and back her into a corner. She wanted to tell her the truth, but she wasn't sure how. Instead, she brought her bowl to her mouth.

"Oh, they care. Well, I don't think they *care*, but they notice. They turn in attendance reports every day to...," Meghan paused and lowered her voice, "you-know-who, I assume for tracking the food." Meghan sipped a little more soup from her bowl and looked at her friend with compassion. "I just don't want you to get in trouble!"

After ten minutes of awkward silence while subdued conversations continued in little groups around the room, Kristen joined them and Beth Ann welcomed the interruption. Kristen gave them a weak smile as she sat down. Beth Ann commented, "Kristen, you are looking better! How are you feeling?"

"Feeling?" Kristen made a noise in her throat that almost sounded like the beginning of laughter, or maybe gagging. She lifted the soup bowl. Meghan and Beth Ann watched Kristen's eyes scan the room twice over the rim of the bowl. She finally set the bowl down and very casually picked a piece of carrot out with her fingers. Without making eye contact with her friends, she stuck the carrot in her mouth and quietly replied, "I can't say."

"Huh?" Meghan responded, a baffled look on her face.

Kristen just shook her head slightly and slumped a little in her seat. "Not here," she whispered as she continued to eat. People didn't talk about things in the wide open room that they didn't want to be overheard. Meghan and Beth Ann followed her lead and finished their meal. They watched other people during the short break, their neighbors, teammates, and in some cases, housemates, scattered around the room in groups of twos and threes. From their clothing and skin to their drawn expressions, everyone had the appearance of being destitute. Of course, there was the ever present deputy just inside the doorway.

"Greenhouse Team!" Mr. Eckley called, and the sound of chair legs scraping the floor around the room responded immediately. The Medical Team didn't come all at once; they took turns. The Childcare Team was usually the first Team to eat. The Water Team would be signing in downstairs as the Greenhouse Team was leaving, and the staggered system continued.

Kristen reached down and pulled Beth Ann's shoe lace. Puzzled, Beth Ann stopped and looked at her. Kristen patted the chair seat and Beth Ann got the message. She placed her foot on the chair and leaned over to re-tie her shoe. She heard Kristen say softly, "Infirmary after work."

"I can't! I have to be escorted home!" Beth Ann whispered back; she couldn't tie her shoe any slower.

Eckley's Team was headed down the stairs and he was standing in the doorway giving her "the look." Kristen & Meghan just nodded at Beth Ann with knowing eyes, and she left. She would have to dust off her high school drama skills and get herself to the clinic by the end of the day…somehow.

"What the heck is going on, you piece of filth? I demand answers! And I want the TRUTH!" Meghan shouted at Dillon as she marched into the apartment, shaking uncontrollably. For emphasis she picked up one of the couch pillows and threw it at him as hard as she could.

"Shhh! Calm down! Jeez, Meghan!" Dillon ran to the door of the apartment Meghan had left wide open and looked to make sure no one was coming up the stairs. He quietly closed and locked it. Meghan had barely made curfew. He turned around and put his hands on his hips. "Now, what are you talking about?"

"You know exactly what I'm talking about, you and your little…boy parts!" She gestured to his pants. She started to pace, hoping to get her tremors under control.

"My...what?" His eyes grew large. He chuckled and sauntered with exaggeration toward her. "I have no idea what you mean, but I'm fascinated...and curious!"

"It's not funny!" She shoved him hard and it took him off guard, knocking him off balance.

"Okay, okay! Why don't you just spill it?" He plopped down and crossed one leg over the other, reaching out to spread his arms across the back of the couch. "See, that's the problem with women. They want to be all dramatic and expect men to read their...OWW!"

In the dim light she had gone behind him, grabbed his arms and twisted them behind his head. With his back arched and his face up, she leaned over him and said in a frozen-solid voice, "See, the problem with MEN is they can't keep their ZIPPERS UP!" She flung his arms with a vengeance. Choking back a sob, she collapsed into the old stuffed chair and curled up into a ball.

"Oh, uh...yeah. I think I know what you're talking about. But I haven't had anything to do with it!" Dillon seemed genuinely uncomfortable, but his tone was defensive.

"Really? You are aware that your Teammates are taking advantage of their position by harassing and assaulting women...even teenagers...and you have 'nothing to do with it'? You have nothing to say? Nobody has the morals or the guts to stand up for what's right?" Meghan stopped herself as her volume rose.

Dillon didn't answer right away. "It's not that simple, Meghan."

"That's not how I see it." She shook her head. "This is unbelievable."

"You need to understand something," Dillon said as he put both feet on the floor and leaned forward. "These people–the people in charge now–are not people you can mess with. They're like, like the mafia in movies. They live by their own set of rules and they have the power and the stomach to do whatever they want to anyone who tries to cross them."

Meghan got up and went to the kitchen to find a small rag to blow her nose into. When she came back, Dillon continued.

"I feel bad, but there's nothing I can do. You know, Sheriff Branson put a stop to a plan to have a designated 'brothel' right here in town. That's good, right? And some of the ladies are actually willing to…do things…for the extra food," he tacked on.

"Oh, and that makes it better?" Meghan asked bitterly. She understood the words he was saying, but she hated the helplessness she felt, knowing that two of her closest friends were victims. And apparently Kristen was now one of the "willing" ones.

"Sorry, Meghan. There's nothing I can do about it." Dillon unrolled his blanket and started to ready the couch for bed. Meghan stood up slowly and managed to drag her heavy heart, one step at a time, to her room. She closed the door and leaned against it, hearing the latch softly click into place. She supposed she should be grateful that Dillon hadn't forced himself on her. But she decided to watch her back more closely in the future.

Chapter 16

True to the old nameless farmer's adage, since March came in as a lamb, it went out like a lion. A late season storm left several inches of wet snow over the landscape as a welcome mat for April. It was this mucky mess that Gary tracked into the house when he finally arrived home from his longest assignment yet. Exhausted, he dropped all his gear on the back patio before stepping into the cold, dark kitchen to take off his boots. Standing in the room where more than two decades of memories had been made, his grief for Linda washed over him again. He squeezed his temples with a filthy, calloused hand, and made his daily wish for a hot shower.

Although he was anxious to catch up with Beth Ann, he was glad she wasn't home from work yet. He carried a burden far heavier than his hunting pack, and he had not made up his mind yet how much he was going to tell her. Was it protecting her more to tell her the changes taking place on the Hunting Team, or to keep the information from her?

It was early evening when a creak on the stairs caused him to snap his head up from where he sat on the basement floor. He froze when he saw the gun aiming for his chest. He had been so caught up in unpacking and cleaning that he hadn't heard anyone come in. A second later, he realized it was Beth Ann creeping down the steps.

"Oh, thank God!" she exclaimed, lowering the handgun and rushing toward him. "It's you! You're home!"

"Yeah. Didn't you see my boots by the door?" he laughed, still jittery from seeing a gun barrel pointing at him.

"No, I forgot to flip on the light switch," she returned, flopping onto the couch. Romeo ambled to her side and she gently lifted him onto her lap. Gary watched how tenderly she stroked him and how they were relaxed and comforted in each other's presence. The poor dog seemed to have aged five years in the last four months; he was thin and weak and his coat was matted. *Maybe Mr. Andrews was right about the pets*, he thought. But he immediately knew that it would have killed Beth Ann to force her companion into a miserable existence…and violent death…in the wild.

They sat in comfortable silence for a few minutes. Gary rubbed oil on the long barrel of his hunting rifle and made sure the inside was dry. Being exposed to the elements for a week was a good way to encourage rust. Keeping his gun in excellent working condition was essential for his personal safety. But the longer he worked, the more puzzled he became. Beth Ann hadn't been herself for weeks, and he needed to get to the bottom of it.

"How did everything go while I was gone? Anything new?" Gary finally asked. He didn't realize that Beth Ann had actually fallen asleep until she jumped at the sound of his voice. He turned his head to look at her and noticed that she was still holding the gun, loosely, beside the dog on her lap. "I'm sorry; I didn't mean to wake you up. If you're tired, why don't you go to bed? I'm almost done here."

Beth Ann just nodded sleepily as she lifted Romeo off the couch and carried him to the bed behind the curtain. A few minutes later, Gary heard her soft "good night" and knew he had missed his chance. He started picking up his mess, his brow furrowed. Maybe he should have been more direct. He decided to question her on the walk into town the next morning.

"What do you mean?" Beth Ann asked with her head down, as if she needed to watch where she put each foot on the paved surface.

Gary mentally worked through several options and finally decided to take the most direct approach. "Why did you come down the stairs yesterday with your gun ready to fire?"

"Just being cautious, that's all. I could see a small ray of light on the wall at the top of the stairs and I knew someone was down there." Beth Ann shrugged, but kept her gaze downward as they continued to walk.

Gary pushed further. "Is there any reason why it would have been someone else besides me in my own basement?"

"Well, you never know, right? Things are all crazy and I don't know who to trust...except you. I just get so freaked out staying alone."

"So that's it? You were just afraid because you were alone?" Gary couldn't explain why, but he knew she was holding back.

She sighed and responded softly, "I never feel...safe anymore. Anywhere." She lifted her head suddenly and looked at him. "Oh, there has been a change while you were away. A biggie. You know my boss, Mr. Eckley? His farmhouse was burned to the ground and the equipment he was storing out there were stolen. Mr. Andrews told us it was one of those looting bands. Now he is requiring escorts home from work for many of us. If you could come by today, I would really rather walk home with you," she pleaded.

He could see the concern on her face, and it stirred something in him. He might have called it paternal instinct, but he didn't try to name it. "Yes, absolutely. You just might have to wait for me because I don't know what my assignment will be yet. They've been rotating the traveling groups since we have to go so far now. I assume I'll be in town for at least this week, but I don't know. There have been a lot of changes lately...."

"I'll wait! It won't be a problem. I can just do extra work until you get there. Thank you. Thank you so much," Beth Ann gushed, her face bright again. Gary watched her to see if she caught any part of his hint, but she appeared to have missed it in her excitement to have him walk her home. It was strange that she was making such a big deal out of such a small thing.

Gary worked out a plan with Mr. Eckley at the Greenhouse, then he headed to the Hunting Team headquarters, a three-car garage on the northern end of town. With the weather heating up, it smelled like roadkill. Deep brown blood stains dotted the concrete floor under the rafters from which deer and a couple cows had been hung earlier in the winter. Now the straps and ropes were empty, hanging loosely around the trusses like jungle vines. The bay doors stood open in the nice weather, lighting the shelves along one wall that held supplies like ammunition and camping gear, compliments of the townspeople of Tionesta. One of Gary's Teammates sat at the workbench area, reloading bullets with the limited remaining supply of brass shells.

Gary set his pack and rifle down and waited on a metal folding chair, puzzling about his conversation with Beth Ann. The rest of the Team members straggled in and finally their Team Leader arrived. The tone in the room was somber as Mr. Groves unfolded a worn map of northwestern Pennsylvania, and Gary wondered where the heck he had found a paper map coming out of a world of GPS and smartphones. The men ambled to the table. Groves looked at each grubby, bearded face around the circle before saying, "Listen up. Today we discuss our shift in assignment."

Trying to conceal his worry, Gary smiled at Beth Ann. She was in the smallest–and hottest–greenhouse when he found her after work. The recent snow had melted and the temperatures had rebounded to above average–just typical western Pennsylvania spring weather. He was later than he had hoped to be. "Ready to go?" he asked.

"Yep!" she answered as she took off her gloves and flung them into a bin. Then she slapped her hands against the sides of her legs to knock off the extra dirt and tugged her clinging shirt away from her sweaty body. "Thank you for escorting me home."

"Sure thing. I don't mind having the company either," he admitted.

Beth Ann waved a hand at Eckley as they exited the greenhouse. "I'm fortunate to have a decent boss," she said quietly to Gary as they walked, fanning her bright pink face with both hands. She glanced sideways at him. "Not like yours."

Gary knew that she was referring to the incident where he was turned into the Sheriff for not fighting a losing fight. "Well, Hank's not that bad. He's a little rough around the edges, maybe, but he's a good outdoorsman and hunter. Unfortunately, he's in a tough position with a lot of pressure coming down from Andrews."

Beth Ann nodded her head. "Everyone's pretty much afraid of Mr. Andrews, huh?"

"Mostly. But we're stuck, because we really couldn't survive without him. He had food when none of us did, and that's the bottom line. That and the fact that our own local leadership fell apart, leaving a gaping hole for him to step right into." Gary grimaced. Even though he and Linda had stored up some food and bottled water and canned a lot of fruit and vegetables, it probably wouldn't have been enough to get them all the way through to a harvest. He had no idea an EMP was possible, or how long the effect would last. He had no idea his provisions would be stolen by his own neighbors, or that he would be taking in a neighbor's kid. He had no idea that he would be living in a communistic society in his lifetime. He had no idea an electrical outage could stop the world from turning...permanently.

Gary arrested the barrage of thoughts and forced himself to head a different direction. "I met the Medical Team Leader, Mr. Thorpe, if you remember," Gary said with a chuckle. "He seemed like he would be a fair boss for your nurse friend."

"Yeah, Meghan says he is pretty reasonable," Beth Ann agreed, "although he has an issue with power. Tried to make everyone call him 'doctor.'"

Gary chuckled. "What about your other friend? She's on the Water Team, right?"

"Kristen? She was on the Water Team, but she was too sick or something, so they moved her." Beth Ann answered him, but her sudden flippant tone and agitated body language gave her away. He decided to press her.

"Oh. So, what is she doing now?"

Beth Ann hesitated. "I think they call it the Food Team. She gets to help with cooking and dividing servings and stuff like that. It's easier work and some days she gets to go home early."

That didn't sound so bad to Gary. But he still felt like he was missing something. "So, how's her boss? Who's the Team Leader?"

Beth Ann kept her eyes straight ahead. "Mr. Andrews," she finally answered.

Gary's surprise nearly knocked him off the road. "Mr. Andrews?" Beth Ann didn't respond but he knew he had heard her correctly. "Wow. Okay. So, how's that working out for her?"

Beth Ann took in an audible breath. "Apparently not so well. On the days she finishes her work early one of the deputies escorts her home and pays her extra food for sex." Her voice was void of any emotion.

"What?" Gary whispered hoarsely as he stopped in his tracks, taking ahold of Beth Ann's shoulders to face him. He couldn't possibly have heard her correctly. "What did you say?"

"It's not just her. There are other ladies who have regular...encounters...and get extra food or cigarettes or scented lotions or whatever they want from the green sashers. But not all of them are...consensual." As he felt his own temperature rise, he searched her eyes but saw nothing. She had apparently found a way to distance herself from it. Meanwhile, he was horrified.

"Come on, we have to get home," she said, nervously turning onto the entrance of their street.

They walked, or rather trotted, the rest of the way to the house in silence. Gary was lost in his thoughts, trying to figure out if there was anything that could be done. He concluded probably not, if the person feels it's worth it to get the extra food and luxuries. *Desperate times call for desperate measures*, he realized in a whole new way.

At the gate to Beth Ann's house, he stopped to wish her "good night" as usual, to make it look like they were parting company. But she kept walking. He paid closer attention then and saw that she was actively observing their surroundings–the houses, the trees, the shrubs, the dead cars in driveways, the house of ashes. He looked around, too, but there was nothing to see. With longer daylight hours, the sun hadn't set yet; there were no deep, dark shadows. The neighbors would have returned home before now, and no one was outside. It was quiet...as usual. He caught up with her at the end of his driveway.

"What are you doing? What are you looking for? I really think it's best if you go to your own house, remember?" he urged gently.

She glanced over her shoulder at the little yellow house she had grown up in. There it was–he caught it, the flash of fear in her eyes. He was getting closer...but to what? "Beth Ann?"

Her face contorted as she turned back to face him. "No! I am never going in that house again and there's nothing you can do to make me!" She ran down the street past his house and disappeared into a vacant lot that was overgrown with trees and brush.

Gary shook his head. He had to figure out what was going on. Turning on his heel, he marched up to the Daltons' property and let himself in through the front door. He stopped just inside to let his eyes adjust and looked around. He was surprised that nothing seemed out of place. Yet what did he expect to see? Just something...anything...to help him understand Beth Ann's change in behavior. He poked his head in each room, but everything seemed fine. He was baffled.

He passed through the kitchen to exit through the back door, and that's when he saw them: four MREs sitting on the counter. *What the...?* His pounding heart made the connection before his brain did. The door slammed behind him as he ran for his rear patio. He had to find Beth Ann. And he had to get transferred off the Hunting Team...immediately.

From her crouched position behind a large stump, Beth Ann saw Gary come flying out of her back door and stop to look around when he reached his patio. Then he went inside. She usually waited until dark to cross the back yard...just in case. In fact, in a little hollow in the back of the stump she kept one of her dad's old wool blankets rolled up in plastic for the cool evening air and days when it rained. Today was different because Gary was home. She walked as nonchalantly as possible through the ankle high grass toward the back door.

Just as she reached for the handle, the door swung open and Gary nearly knocked her off her feet.

"Beth Ann!" he exclaimed as he set his rifle down and wrapped her in a tight hug. "Why didn't you tell me? How long has this been going on? Who is it? I'm gonna kill him! I knew something wasn't right...." His voice broke and he stopped spilling words.

She did feel protected in his fatherly embrace, but since he wasn't her father, she felt more awkward. She pulled away and wrapped her arms around herself. Obviously he had figured it out, which spared her from having to find the words to tell him, but she wasn't sure how to respond to all his questions. Finally she looked up into his eyes; he was clenching and unclenching his jaw and swallowing visibly.

"I wasn't sure how to tell you. I...I tried to fight him off...." She really didn't feel like talking about it.

"You shouldn't feel ashamed, honey. You were violated!" Now he sounded angry, just like the morning after Linda died. He turned and picked up his rifle and a small bag, which he slung over his shoulder. "Stay in the basement and lock the doors."

"Wait! Where are you going? Stay here with me!" Beth Ann felt the panic rising.

"I'm going to give that lunatic a piece of my mind!"

"No! You can't! Remember what happened the last time you went to the Sheriff? No one can do anything about this!" Beth Ann was tired of the violence and living in fear. Her breathing was shallow and rapid.

"Forget Branson. He's just a puppet! I'm going straight to that self-appointed dictator, Andrews!" He started to turn away from her, but she reached out and caught his sleeve.

"Please! You can't! He'll kill you!" Beth Ann pleaded, shaking her head.

"What? And let this continue? I can't do that, Beth Ann. You know, I lost the will to fight when Linda got sick. I thought if I just went along with the new order and did what they said, everything would be fine. But I was wrong! This is a war, and we have to fight for what's right! This starts right here, right now!" Gary's fire was back, reminding Beth Ann of his plan to pack up a stolen boat and head down river.

Beth Ann squeezed her eyes shut and shook her head slowly. "But you don't understand. It's Travis," she said softly.

"What?" Gary leaned his head toward her as if he didn't hear her.

She opened her eyes. "Travis. Mr. Andrews' man with the ponytail. He's not just going to let you walk up to his face and accuse his own inner circle."

Gary's shoulders slumped, but the defeated look did not return. Instead, Beth Ann could have sworn she smelled the gears in his head smoking. She waited, her heart still pounding.

Finally, he looked at her. "Let's go inside. We have to make a plan."

Chapter 17

Meghan sat alone at the table. She was getting tired of the canned and freeze-dried food, and she began to salivate over the thought of fresh vegetables that would hopefully be ready to harvest in a couple months. Finally, Kristen came into the room, towing another young lady behind her. She was pale and thin like most everyone else, but she still had a sense of beauty about her and an almost regal posture. Meghan strained her foggy mind, knowing she had seen the girl around but couldn't come up with a name.

"Hi, Meghan," Kristen said as she sat down, smiling for the first time in months. "Remember Amy Wittenburg?"

They exchanged the usual pleasantries and then Meghan realized that she knew her from school, as Amy had been only two grades behind them. If she remembered right, Amy's mom, a single parent, had died of cancer during Meghan's senior year. She thought back to the huge spaghetti dinner and bingo fundraisers they had held at the school to help raise money for medical expenses. Wow, it made her crave spaghetti and regret the days when they threw away leftovers.

"How are your brothers?" Meghan asked, remembering that they were older and Amy had been able to live with them after her mom's death.

"Johnny's pretty good, I guess," Amy replied as she picked up the peas and rice with her fingers to eat. A small cube of reconstituted chicken went down next. "He's working on the Security Team. But Sam...he's...gone."

"Gone?" Meghan wondered where a body might travel these days.

Kristen cleared her throat and Amy fidgeted, then shot Meghan a sad smile. "Gone...like deceased."

Meghan drew back. "I'm so sorry, Amy. I thought...I mean, never mind." She lifted her bowl to her lips to avoid looking at Amy.

"It's okay. Seems like we should be getting used to losing people these days."

An uncomfortable silence followed until Meghan asked, "He worked at the fish hatchery, right?"

"Yeah." Amy pushed a strand of hair away from her face and pulled more chicken out of her bowl. "He was there when the electricity went out. Lost most of the fry and juveniles in the first few days. He brought some home for us to eat, but.... But then one day he walked up there to get us a few more and he never came home. Johnny and a couple neighbors went looking for him, but he must have been there when it was raided. The place was shot up pretty bad and every last fish was gone. Johnny brought 'im home so we could bury him." She paused. "Just the wrong place at the wrong time, I guess."

Meghan gathered her bowl and water bottle. "Well, let me know if I can help in any way. It was nice to see you again." She stood. "I have to get back to work now. I'm on Medical."

"Hey, wait!" Kristen stopped her. "I've been waiting to tell you my news. I got a promotion!"

"Nice!" Meghan said. "I...don't really know what that means, but congratulations!"

"Well, I'll tell you if you give me two seconds of your attention," Kristen dramatized a hurt look complete with pout and head tilt.

"Okay," Meghan chuckled quietly. "Tell me." She sat back down, perching on the edge of the seat to indicate that she couldn't stay long.

"Mr. Andrews said that I'm doing such a great job on the Food Team that I can be a bigger help at his complex! He wants me to be in charge of inventory and meal planning!" She gestured for them to lean in closer. Kristen whispered, "I heard he has a mansion around here somewhere, and he's all set up to live comfortably. He supposedly even has electricity and running water and all that." She sat back. "Is that awesome, or what? I never thought I'd be in charge of anything!"

Kristen seemed happy, but Meghan felt apprehensive. "Kristen, are you sure you trust him? He has done some terrible things to people around here."

"Well, he does what he has to do in order to keep us all alive. One on one he's pretty nice. And anyhow, I know him from working at the restaurant." Kristen sounded a little defensive, and Meghan felt bad for raining on her parade.

"I'm sorry. If you're happy, I'm happy," Meghan said. "So, I won't get to see you at lunch anymore, I assume?"

"Oh, I don't know. I hadn't thought about that. I guess I thought that I would be coming into town with him in the mornings, but then they wouldn't have me training Amy to do my job here," Kristen said with a frown. "Hmm. Well, I guess we just wait and see. I'll try to get here when I can because I still want to see you guys."

Meghan hugged Kristen quickly and stood up. "Gotta go. Good luck with everything, Kris. You too, Amy. Make sure she trains you right!" she teased.

As Meghan signed out and made her way down the steps to the main entrance, Beth Ann was coming up. They hugged at the midway point.

"I just had the most interesting lunch in recent history!" Meghan winked at Beth Ann's quizzical look. "Go chat with Kristen and you'll see...." The deputy at the top of the stairs cleared his throat

165

and Meghan let Beth Ann go. The whole way to the clinic, she tried to ignore the dark niggling in the back of her brain.

After the meal, Beth Ann walked back to the Greenhouses with Mrs. Lowell. Even though she wasn't alone, she kept a vigilant watch of her surroundings. If Travis ever made his approach, or any other man for that matter, she wanted as much notice and distance as possible.

Mary Jo didn't talk much, so the short walk gave Beth Ann a few minutes to digest the shocking news. Kristen was moving in with Mr. Andrews? And Travis and the other two men? Beth Ann had warned Kristen about Travis. Were there any other women who lived there? Kristen didn't know the answer to that, but she seemed to trust Andrews. She really hadn't been the same since her family and boyfriend had been killed in front of her. And at the clinic when she had told Meghan and Beth Ann about what was happening with the deputies, she seemed emotionally unaffected. A piece of Kristen had died, and in that empty hole is where she put the men. She wasn't a virgin, so the sex didn't matter, she had said.

"I'm going to stop at the shed first and get more flats. See ya over at Presby," Mary Jo said, bringing Beth Ann back to the present with a jolt. She nodded. There were four Greenhouses, and after a little time each one had taken on a nickname to tell them apart. "Presby" was, obviously, the one built against the south-facing river rock wall of the sole Presbyterian Church in town. The biggest one was "Main," and the two smallest ones were "West" and "North." Apparently, literary creativity was not required for working on the Greenhouse Team.

The plants were growing nicely and it was time to separate them. Within the next week or two, Jack, Dan and some of the other Team members would be preparing land in town for planting. The danger of frost wouldn't be over until the end of May, but there were a few hardy vegetables that could be planted early. Beth Ann had volunteered to turn her front yard into a garden, and she felt something close to happy for the first time in months. She would be home in the mornings to weed, water, and whatever else needed done, and Gary would be home, too. The plan they had discussed was for Gary to work out a transfer from the Hunting Team to the Garden Team so they could work together.

Beth Ann was rounding the back corner of the church when suddenly something stung her ankle. She cried out, more in surprise than pain. Stopping to take a look, she bent over but only found a little dirty spot on her lower leg. Rubbing it, she looked around. A piece of limestone bounced in front of her a couple times and rolled to a stop; she froze and drew in a breath. Another rock bounced, this one farther in front of her. She followed the trajectory with her eyes and noticed the basement door into the church slightly ajar. Due to the large stones the wall was made from, the door was inset almost a foot, and so it sat in a deep shadow.

Beth Ann didn't know whether to run or to find out what was going on, but her curiosity won. This wasn't Travis' style, so she felt confident that she didn't have to worry about him. Plus, Mrs. Lowell would arrive any minute. She crept closer to the door, tightly gripping the gun inside her work apron pocket. The door opened a little wider and she saw part of a face; it was Gary. Glancing around to make sure no one saw her, she hurried into the shallow alcove and Gary pulled her inside, shutting the door behind her.

The instant darkness made Beth Ann's heart stop, then start again at double its usual pace. "Gary?" she whispered, hoping that she had correctly identified the partial face in the doorway.

"I'm here. It's okay. Just me," Gary said in a reassuring tone. Beth Ann had confessed her fear of the dark to him when she had moved into his basement. "Give it a minute. There are some block windows down here and your eyes will adjust."

"I don't have a minute. Mary Jo is coming back soon and she is going to expect to find me in the Greenhouse," Beth Ann fretted.

"Listen fast then. I'm supposedly on a bathroom break, and I have already been gone too long," Gary said. He talked as fast as

Beth Ann could listen. "Hank had to take my transfer request to Mr. Andrews, which is why it's taken a couple of days. Andrews approved it, but apparently the groups had already been set for the next Hunting Team assignment and I can't transfer until I get back."

Beth Ann felt the breath go out of her, but she tried to be brave. "How long?"

In the darkness there was no response. Beth Ann could now see the vague silhouette of Gary's scraggly hair and she heard him sigh. "Could be a couple weeks."

"A couple weeks!" Beth Ann shouted, forgetting to be quiet. "Where are you hunting, Canada?"

"Shhh! There's a lot I haven't told you, and I don't have time now. The short version is…there's literally nothing left to hunt and our assignment has changed. We're now mapping the region–who is still alive, which houses are occupied, and…other data. On this trip we're headed up past Warren to the reservoir."

Beth Ann took a deep breath. If she could just make it through the next two weeks…everything would be fine after that. Then a new thought struck her. "What about the bands of raiders?"

His hesitation spoke volumes. There was obviously something he wasn't telling her. Finally, he answered. "Don't worry. Deputies are being assigned to go with us for security. I'll be back as soon as I can. I promise."

"Okay. You better!" Beth Ann said, trying to sound brave.

"There's one more thing," Gary said. "Remember the place where I took you and Linda several times for target practice?"

Beth Ann nodded, even though he couldn't see her in the darkness.

"On the other side of the ridge of shale we were shooting into, head towards the sound of the stream, and you will come across an old iron furnace; it looks like something in between a skinny pyramid and an ancient ruin. Take the tub that the meat was buried in and pack it with anything that might be useful if you had to live there for a couple weeks. Blankets, clothes, the MREs, ammunition, anything you think should be there."

Beth Ann flinched when he said "MRE," but she forced herself to pay attention. He was saying something now about the old fishing rod in her dad's garage that the deputies had left behind.

He continued. "Whatever you think. Cover the stuff with leaves or hide it somehow. Sneak everything out there a little at a time as you are able and don't get caught! Take different routes so you don't wear a noticeable path through the brush. If someone gives you a hard time before I get back, go there and stay. I will look for you there if you're not at home. Got it?"

Beth Ann fought nausea as her heart rate continued to rise. "But why can't we go get that boat we found and escape...down river?" It made perfect sense to her; they needed to run away.

Gary took her by the shoulders. "It's not safe! We can't just float down the middle of the river in plain sight. We don't have any stored food, there's no game left in the woods, and if this little problem we're having involves a larger part of the country like Mr. Andrews says, there's honestly nowhere safe to—"

He stopped when the muffled sound of Mary Jo's calls reached them.

"Please, Beth Ann! You gotta trust me!" Gary begged.

"Yes. I will. Be safe!" Beth Ann gulped down a sob as she broke free from his grasp and turned quickly to leave.

"You, too. And keep praying, Beth Ann. Don't stop praying, no matter what," Gary admonished with a strange urgency in his voice.

She stuck her fingers into the corners of her eyes and squeezed the tear ducts, willing them to plug and stay plugged. Cracking the door open, she waited until Mary Jo's back was turned to step out into the sunlight. She took a deep breath and joined her in the greenhouse.

Gary watched Beth Ann's silhouette slip through the blinding light like it was a door into another dimension. Then it was dark again and he fumbled his way to a side door that was not in sight of the greenhouses. He hadn't lied to Beth Ann, he had just withheld the part about trying to find the bad guys. He felt physically sick, being forced to leave when he wanted to stay. But Beth Ann was going to have to be strong and find out what her womanhood was made of. The luxury of someone else taking care of her while she shopped and talked on the phone with her friends was gone. It was time to grow up…for everyone. And at a dear price.

Hurrying back to the Hunting Team garage, he didn't have to fake the gastric distress. He rubbed his abdomen as he apologized to Mr. Groves for taking so long. With a grunt Hank gestured to Gary's pack and gear lying on the floor and told him to join the group outside and make sure he shut the door on his way out.

Gary was still breathing heavily when he made it to the picnic table where the Team had gathered to take advantage of the late afternoon light. Around the table were five other men: three Hunting Team members and two Deputies. The Deputies had been assigned to help with security, but Gary wasn't sure what two young guys would be able to do against a band of men willing to kill for even just the possibility that they might have food in their packs.

Hank had the area map spread out and was just starting to review the route they would take on this assignment. The Teams were broken up to make a pattern like a search grid, with one Team doing East-West stints, and Gary's Team covering North-South pathways. For this first trip, and Gary hoped his last, they would follow the western perimeter of the forest along the Allegheny River up to the Warren area, then return home on a parallel track slightly to the east. Along the way they would document any sign of life–animal or human. Andrews claimed to be trying to find the looters' home base, but Gary wondered why all the households and communities needed to be documented. They were to stay hidden and observe, not engage unless confronted, but the spying still felt like…spying. He wondered what Andrews was up to now.

Gary sighed, not realizing it was out loud until all the eyes around the table turned to him. He just lifted his eyebrows. Finally, Hank cleared his throat and continued.

"So, while you're here near this bend in the river," Hank said, pinpointing the spot with the tip of his pencil, "you can sneak two men into Warren to check things out there. Don't use any of the bridges; you'll just be sitting ducks if anyone's watchin' them. But here, with this series of small islands breaking up the deeper water, it's shallow enough to wade across and hopefully the 'bad guys' won't know that. Although, with the Kinzua Dam not operational, it may be too deep to cross on foot." Hank looked up from the map. "You gotta watch out, because the closer you get to Warren, the more houses and roads there'll be. Take your time and *don't get killed,*" he admonished in his rough, gravelly voice, emphasizing his point by stabbing the pencil onto the map with each word.

When they finally had the route worked out and the instructions and division of duties agreed upon, the men folded up the map and checked their gear one last time. For this mission they had been given extra guns and food supplies. Evening was approaching and they would leave soon, traveling mostly in the dusk and dawn hours. It wasn't safe to travel in the daytime except in the most remote areas, but since they were scouting, they would need light to see. In addition, they could not travel at night because any light they used at all would be seen.

As they headed into the tree line, the raggle taggle band of "scouts" heard Hank call after them, "If you see my scruffy brother Pete in the city, tell him to give me a damn call sometime!" The phlegmy cough haunted them for miles.

"You all ready, miss?" Travis asked the girl Andrews called 'Kristen.'

"Ah, sure. Not much to get ready, dude," she returned. He felt irritated at first. Here he was, picking her up in one of the only running vehicles in town, and using his good manners to boot. She could at least show some gratitude.

The thin, dark-haired girl with the sad eyes and perfect lips tossed a single bag into the back of the pickup truck, then stood looking at him with her hands on her hips. When he didn't do anything, she said sarcastically, "Hello? Are *you* ready?"

He stifled a smile; he liked a girl with a little sass. Opening the passenger side door, he bowed with a flourish while she climbed into the seat. He walked around the truck and got behind the wheel, turning the key to bring the old engine to life. As the truck lurched forward, he noticed Kristen waving to the family gathered on the porch.

She turned to him then. "Isn't...um...Mr. Andrews coming with us?" She didn't seem quite as cocky now. Maybe she was a little nervous after all.

"He's comin'," Travis replied in his customary drawl. "He had to finish a couple things and we are going to pick him up on our way."

She nodded her head but didn't say anything for a couple of minutes as she looked out the window. Travis, too, watched the blocks of the run-down and overgrown town go by and was glad he didn't have to volley small talk.

Andrews was ready when they arrived at the municipal building, and he greeted Kristen warmly. Travis was impressed by the act, but then Mr. Andrews was a smart and powerful man. And Travis knew that you didn't get to be smart and powerful without developing some acting skills along the way.

Kristen climbed into the small passenger space behind the front seats in the cab, leaning forward on her elbows so she could make conversation. Travis hoped that she would not remember Mike and Charlie; they had been given late assignments in town for a reason. But she didn't. Instead, she pestered Andrews with questions about her new duties and declared her passion and commitment to doing the best possible job that she could. Travis caught Andrews' eye and saw the twinkle in it. She sounded like the perfect candidate.

They stopped briefly at the roadblock for Mr. Andrews to get a quick report from the deputies on watch, then they were moving again...for about three minutes. When they were well out of sight and ear-shot of the road block, Travis put the truck in park and Andrews pulled a burlap sack out from under his seat. He twisted to face Kristen and said in a deeply apologetic tone, "I hate to ask you this, Miss Kyser, but would you mind putting this over your head and lying down back there?"

Travis could see the confused look on Kristen's face in his rear-view mirror.

"It's just that I need to keep the location of my house a secret. Nothing personal." He held the sack out.

"Oh, I won't tell anyone, I promise!" she said quickly. "I'm practically lost already! I can't remember my way around...even in the mall!" Her little chuckle came out unnaturally high-pitched.

"Is that so?" Mr. Andrews queried. "I see. Well, unfortunately, I still need you to put this on."

She hesitated, not making any indication that she was going to take the sack from Andrews' hand. He finally got impatient. "Kristen, would you prefer the easy way or the hard way?"

Travis waited, not sure if he was going to need to intervene. He watched as Kristen narrowed her eyes and slowly took the sack. She huffed and muttered as she put her head in it and lay down out of sight.

"Thank you," Mr. Andrews said. "I do hope you understand." Kristen didn't answer him, and she didn't say another word the entire way to his home.

The truck bounced up the long drive as Travis navigated the steep hill slowly. He passed the entrance to the five-thousand-square-foot log home and drove a little farther to a barn where he parked. Travis jumped out and pulled the carriage-style doors closed while Andrews helped Kristen out of the truck.

Mr. Andrews gently removed the sack from her head and smiled. "We're home. And your training will begin as soon as we show you your new room." Kristen looked back and forth between the two men, the fear in her face evident. Travis nodded at his boss, confident that this girl would catch on quickly.

Chapter 18

The rain didn't help Beth Ann's melancholy, except to draw her deeper into the darkness. It had only been a week since Gary left, and she didn't know how much more she could take. She didn't sleep well. She was always on edge, looking around, suspicious of everyone now. In her mind, people had fangs instead of teeth and their eyes glowed red. Meghan couldn't help her, and Kristen hadn't come to lunch since accepting her "promotion." She missed her parents, she missed Gary, and she worried about poor Romeo who was getting weaker by the day.

She stooped into the partially collapsed entrance of the furnace and dropped to her knees. Feeling around in the darkness of one corner, she moved the leaves aside and unsnapped the lid of the tote. Carefully she opened her rain jacket and extracted the large bulge she was carrying inside. She added the t-shirts, shorts, jeans, underwear, sweatshirts, and several pairs of socks—one set for her and another for Gary—to the bin. That pretty much filled it. She set the lid back on tightly and re-hid it.

Finding a semi-dry spot to sit, she watched it rain in the expiring light. It would be completely dark by the time she reached home, and darker than usual without any moonlight to guide her. Fortunately, as this was her fourth trip to the furnace, she was beginning to know the way pretty well and had found landmarks to help along the way. The triple-trunk tree, the perfectly straight line of evergreens, the stump covered in ivy, the unique outcrops and slopes: these formed a map in her head that she had memorized going both directions.

A few months ago she wouldn't have been caught dead sitting in this bug-infested, dark and dirty place. But now...now she just didn't have the same options as before. She thought about how she had been such a little princess–a picky eater, obsessed with "stuff," whining about helping her parents around the house, not trying very hard to get a teaching job, wanting everything her way. She had changed with the new world; everyone had changed. It made some people meaner and some people kinder. Some people looked for ways to take advantage of the situation; other people looked for ways to help. If she could just get out of her own way and rise above the depression and hopelessness and fear, she wondered what kind of person she could be. What was her potential? Did she really have a purpose and a calling, like the Bible said? Did she have it in her to find out?

The wild scent of mossy earth and the mingling of new life with decay stung her nose and throat. Shivering in the damp air, she pulled her hooded rain jacket tighter around her shoulders. The volume surprised her; she had apparently always tuned the sound of rain out. Beth Ann closed her eyes and listened with intention to the musical cadence of the falling drops as they hit the woody branches and baby leaves and rolled down to splash onto last year's carpet of fallen ones. And she prayed. For the first time in weeks, maybe months, she prayed.

Travis was tired of waiting. Tired and frustrated. It was dark now and she still wasn't home...and he'd missed his ride back to the comfortable mansion. Tonight he'd be soaking wet and have to sleep in the city hall building on some dead politician's fake leather settee. Where was she? Was she staying somewhere else now, trying to avoid him? Probably smart of her, but he would find her just the same. And next time he wouldn't be so nice about it. He slammed the Daltons' back door as he left.

Easter Sunday, April 13. Day 8. The weather is sunny and warm and perfect—not too hot. Last night's rain has given us some trouble with mud. This morning, early, we were surprised to come across a den of new bunnies. Alex shot the mother rabbit before we could talk about the options, and now they're all being cooked for our midday meal. How typical of the days we live in now: to think only of the needs of this moment, to do whatever it takes to stay alive for one day, rather than planning for the future. I guess that's what survival instinct looks like when modernized humans find themselves in desperate circumstances. Other than the little group in West Hickory locked up in the church tower, and one well-fortified, extended farming family, we have not seen another living soul. Even now, camped literally across the river from Warren, every home and business on this side seems deserted. It's an eerie feeling, seeing the cars scattered the length of Route 65, seeing the ruins and ashes, even bodies....

Two mud-crusted boots came into view and Gary shielded his eyes as he looked up to see who they belonged to. It was Joe, one of the two Deputies that had come with them for protection.

"Hi, there, young man. Care to join me?" Gary invited, patting the moss-carpeted ground beside him. He closed his notebook and shoved the pen down snugly inside the spiral binding.

The Team was taking a break, and Gary had found a perfect spot to sit with an old fallen tree as a backrest. Alex, one of the other Hunting Team members, was cooking the rabbits he had slaughtered on a Dakota Hole Fire using only dry hardwood for fuel, which made little to no telltale smoke. Gary hoped nobody was in close enough range to smell it, because the rare scent of meat cooking would now draw any human out of hiding. Alex was in his late thirties, Gary guessed, and a darn good woodsman. The other two Hunting Team members, whom Gary had known previously, were closer to Gary's age, probably in their early fifties. Chuck was resting under a shady pine with his hat pulled down over his eyes and Bob was chatting with Alex, getting cooking tips for free whether he wanted them or not.

The final man along on this mission was the other Deputy, who had introduced himself as "Mad Max." Gary didn't know his real name, but the pseudonym suited him. Claiming post-traumatic stress syndrome from spending years in the Middle East doing contract work, he had definitely developed a crust, both physically and emotionally. The ragged, weathered face had deep lines etched by wind and sun and time, each of which hid stories that would never be retold. The hard-set jaw and the deep-set eyes provided the perfect packaging for the petrified soul living inside. Gary didn't know him well, but on this trip so far he was sure he hadn't seen Max smile once. Still, the man was vigilant and extremely focused…and probably hurting.

Joe sat down with a grunt. "Hey, Gary. What're you doing there?" he asked, gesturing toward the notebook.

"Captain's log," Gary replied with a twinkle in his eye.

Joe smiled back. "Aha. Good one! I thought maybe you had yourself a diary or something."

The two men sat quietly for a few minutes. Joe picked up little dried twigs near his "seat" and methodically broke them into smaller pieces. Gary waited, wondering why Joe was there. A young guy in probably his late twenties, Joe was an enigma. He acted gruff. He grumbled a lot and had choice words in his vocabulary that would make the proverbial sailors proud. He laughed too loud and tried too hard to be macho. Yet there was something solid there, too. Gary couldn't figure him out. He wanted Joe to speak first, but he didn't.

"Who's on watch?" Gary finally asked of the man representing a full half of their security team.

"The Madman Maxter," Joe snorted. "What a guy! We scouted the local area together at the start of break, but he is pretty confident he can handle it on his own now…." He shrugged as his voice trailed off, indicating that he wasn't too happy to be dismissed from his post. "So I'm takin' my break with the mighty Hunters." He made a show of stretching out his legs and lifting his arms to clasp his hands behind his head.

Gary just smiled and shook his head, wondering if he was that cocky when he was young and still thought the world revolved around him.

"Seems to me like he's real good at what he does," Gary finally responded.

Joe kept his eyes closed and didn't change position. "Yep. He's good. Branson made him our official Weapons and Tactics Trainer. So I've been taking lessons with the psycho. It's fun and I've learned a lot."

Gary let the sarcasm go, but took the opportunity to find out a little more about Tionesta's new leadership. "Really? That's cool. What kind of training?" he asked, trying to sound casual.

Joe sat up a little straighter and bent his knees, a more suitable position for conversation. "Yeah, mostly stuff with guns and shooting. A little rescue, a little survival."

The vague answer didn't satisfy Gary and he wondered how much he could push before flags were raised. "Well, now. That's all good 'stuff' for our Security Team to know. Makes me feel more protected!" He paused. "You practice maneuvers, too?"

Joe didn't answer at first, and Gary held his breath. Finally Joe smiled broadly. "Maybe...but that's classified! You military?"

"Maybe...but that's classified." Gary returned the smile, then continued. "Enlisted. Lied about my age to get in." He chuckled at the memory. "I couldn't stand the way people were treating our service men and women after 'Nam and thought I could prove a point by joining." He paused, thinking about that pointless point he had made in his hotheaded youth. "I got straight out as soon as my time was up! You?"

"Nope. Not all that interested," Joe replied. Gary was instantly offended, but forced himself to stay calm. The boy didn't mean it. He was raised in different times.

"Well, it's not the same as playing 'cowboys and Indians' in the backyard, that much I'll tell you. But I did learn a thing or two." Gary turned his attention back to Joe. "So, what *were* you interested in doing?"

Joe's eyes grew large. "Hey, man, I'm sorry. I didn't—"

Gary cut him off with a wave of his hand. "I know. Don't worry." He swallowed with effort. "It's tough, Joe. I love this country. For years I've been watching the apathy and self-centeredness settle in...and I just let it. It's not you; it's me...and your parents and your grandparents. We didn't teach the love of God and country to our kids. We didn't do anything when they voted prayer out of schools. We just sat back and watched it slip through our fingers.... We let it happen; we didn't fight back." His eyes glistened. All he could think about was the application to the current situation at home, and it made his ears ring. He had no desire to let history repeat itself.

Gary realized that Joe was staring at him intently, piercingly. "I'm sorry! You didn't deserve a sermon from my soapbox!" He tried to laugh to lighten up the moment. Joe laughed politely, but his pensive posture didn't change.

Joe looked around, then finally spoke. "I cooked."

Gary was far away in his own thoughts. "What was that?"

"You asked what I was interested in. Only myself and my big truck and girls! But my parents kicked me out of the house and told me to go get a job. So I ran away, sort of, to Tionesta and cooked. At the diner. Not much of an ambition, eh?"

"Nope!" Gary thought of his son and wished he was closer to home. "Wait...you cooked at the Table Talk Diner?"

"The one and only."

"Ahh. You might know my neighbor, Beth Ann."

Joe grimaced. "Oh, yeah. But don't tell her you know me. I don't think she liked me that much."

"Oh, okay. Are you the one who dropped by her house early on? Now I know why you look familiar!" Gary replied.

"Yep, that was me. Seems like a long time ago…." Joe's voice trailed off.

A commotion at the stove caught the men's attention; the men were eagerly pressing in for their chance at some fresh meat. Joe stood and offered a hand to Gary. Gary stood, but continued to hold Joe's hand in a firm grip. Joe's forehead wrinkled as he tried to pull his hand away, while Gary cast a quick glance at the other men to make sure they were out of earshot.

Still gripping Joe's hand, Gary stepped into his personal space and clutched his shoulder with his free hand. In a low voice he took the direct approach he had learned with Beth Ann. "Are you aware that members of your Team are raping innocent young ladies in our very own town?"

Joe must have been shocked by the unexpected question; he stood frozen with his eyes open wide and didn't reply.

"This time I'm not sitting back and doing nothing." Gary released Joe's hand, gave him a smile and a fatherly pat on the back, and walked away to get his food.

Twelve days nearly over, Beth Ann thought with a little spark of hope. *Gary could be home within days!* Then he would stay home and she wouldn't have to be alone anymore. She could hardly wait.

"Whatcha got there, missy?"

Beth Ann screamed in surprise and dropped the bag she was carrying, spilling candles, matches, a couple of towels, some plastic bags, twisty ties, a hammer and nails, and other random items. She spun around to see one of her neighbors standing with his legs apart, pointing a rifle at her chest.

"None of your business!" she hollered, surprising herself. Making a split-second decision to ride the wave of adrenaline, she stooped to pick up her supplies.

"Well, now, I'm pretty sure it is my business. All of our business," he said slowly, without lowering the gun.

From her crouched position, Beth Ann looked up to see two other men and a woman step out from behind a shed at the edge of the tree line and move slowly toward them. Even in the dusk it was easy to see that they were pointing guns at her, too. These people, all of whom lived on her street, had watched her learn to ride a tricycle and bought lemonade from her yard sale table and laughed at her parallel parking practice. Now they were ready to kill her…over a box of matches?

She stood slowly. "Leave me alone! This has nothing to do with any of you!" Beth Ann hoped her voice came across tough, not weak and scared like she felt. She had been stupid and let her guard down; she didn't have her gun in her hand and she had been lost in her thoughts instead of focusing on her surroundings. The foursome now stood shoulder to shoulder.

"You must have a short memory, little girl," the woman said. Beth Ann realized then she was the widow of the man Andrews had hung for stealing the Howards' food. "All of our stuff belongs to the 'community' now." She emphasized "community" with a snarl.

Another man spoke up then. "So the way we see it, you're stealin' from us." He looked to his left and right as the others nodded, affirming his statement. He turned his attention back to Beth Ann. "We've been watching you make these secret little trips into the woods, and we think Mr. Andrews needs to know about it."

"You guys are being completely ridiculous!" Beth Ann forced a laugh. "Here. You want this stuff? You can have it!" She threw the bag straight at the group with all her might and the surprise gave her a three second head start. There was no use trying to bargain with those people and she knew it.

At first she ran in the direction of the furnace, as far as she thought they might have seen her go before; but she didn't want to lead them to the hideout. When she rounded a small rocky crest, she zigzagged sharply to the north, heading towards the back side of town. Behind her she could hear shouts from the neighbors who were still chasing her. She braced herself for the gunshots, but they never came. Her gulping breaths had turned into wheezing; the pain in her side felt like a searing hot knife was carving its way through her guts. In the near darkness it was slower going as she stumbled and skirted obstacles in the unfamiliar part of the forest. By sheer will power she forced herself to keep going.

Finally Beth Ann had to stop. She pulled the small gun out of her pocket and wiggled under a deep ledge. Wrapping one arm around her middle and the other around her face to stifle her heavy breathing, she gripped the gun as if it was a life preserver in this deep sea, wondering if she would be able to actually shoot a person. She waited for a very long time for signs of her pursuers, but the night crept in quietly. Finally, curled up in the tightest possible ball, she fell into a fitful sleep.

Gradually Beth Ann became aware of a faraway noise–a pounding; no, a knocking. Maybe snoring. Was Gary snoring? The knocking became faster, more insistent. She struggled and worked her eyes open slowly, wondering why she felt stiff and groggy. The trees were pink. Why were they pink? Wait…Why were there trees?

She sat up in a panic and cracked her head on the low overhang. The blinding light that followed was bad enough, but when the light faded, a sharp pain set in and brought tears to her eyes. Beth Ann held her head with both hands, squeezing with all her might to compensate for the pressure pushing outward. She tried to breathe calmly and count to one hundred. Ten just wasn't enough.

Eventually she crawled out of her spot and assessed the situation. The woodpecker that woke her up was long gone and it was quiet again. The memory of last night's confrontation had come back fairly quickly when she jarred her marbles loose on the rock. Now she needed to find her way to Meghan's apartment…without getting caught. She definitely couldn't go home.

With the sun rising behind her, she headed in the direction she hoped town to be. Her head pounded each time she placed her foot down, or bent, or stood, or moved. A warm trickle oozed its way through her hair and down the side of her neck. She had nothing with her to use as a compress, so she assumed it was either shallow enough to clot at some point, or she would bleed out in the woods and her body would decay into oneness with nature.

Shortly after mid-day, she came to a shallow creek. She fell to her knees, splashing the cool water on her face and scrubbing her neck. It was torture, fighting the urge to drink it. Forcing herself to continue on, she stepped across the stream. The heat began to get to her as she kept walking and walking without arriving anywhere. Every tree and outcrop began to look the same and she wondered if she was going in circles.

Just when she was ready to give up, the trees began to thin and she saw the rear yards of several homes. She had overshot the main part of town, where she hoped to find Meghan at the clinic. Relieved to at least know where she was, she started to head south when suddenly the sound of voices made her leap for the nearest hiding place—a scrawny young pine.

Two men came around the corner of a cement block building, perhaps a large garage, and made their way to a picnic table. If they looked in her direction, they would surely spot her. She held her breath; she would not be able to move or leave until they went back inside.

The men both wore beards; one was trimmed short and one was bushy and ungroomed. They looked nervous, glancing around frequently and talking in clipped phrases with low voices while their heads moved in different directions, apparently to make it look like they weren't actually talking. One man handed the other a piece of paper, which he quickly stuffed into his back pocket without looking at it. She strained to hear what they were saying, but it was no use.

Suddenly a third man came around the corner, striding toward the men with purpose. He held a large piece of paper which he unfolded and laid on the picnic table. The three men pointed and talked and nodded until a plan was apparently agreed upon. Beth Ann caught a word here and there, such as 'Warren,' 'team,' and 'shallow.' Did this have anything to do with Gary's mission?

"Groves!"

The voice was loud and clear, and it made her shudder. Travis came onto the scene a mere second after his voice. Beth Ann tried to shrink. She just knew he would hear her heart beating loudly against her ribs. She once again forced herself to breathe slower and calm down, while her head pounded with the pulsing blood and nausea threatened to take her down.

The older man who had come out with the map turned around and lifted his hand in greeting, then turned back to the map. Travis joined the trio, appeared to ask some questions and to get answers he didn't like. He threw his hands up in frustration and walked off. The three men watched him go, then just looked at each other. Finally they folded up the map and left together. Beth Ann waited a little while to make sure they were really gone before backing up deeper into the trees and heading south.

Before long the rear of the old visitor's center was in view. Beth Ann heaved a sigh of relief and trudged straight towards it. But the more steps she took, the farther away the building seemed to be. Something was wrong with either her legs or her eyes.

"Hold up, there!" a man shouted.

It was the last straw—the second time in a day that a gun was pointed at her. Too exhausted to even be scared, Beth Ann dropped to her knees and hung her head.

When the young green sasher rushed toward her, she didn't even flinch. Maybe this was how it was going to end...and probably it was for the best.

He stooped behind her, reached his arms under her armpits and lifted her to her feet. "That's a nasty gash you got there. Here, lean on me," he said as he put one arm around her waist. "You need to get that looked at."

Beth Ann was confused. How did he know? What gash? Why was he helping her? She felt herself slipping into a tunnel of darkness.

"Com'on now! Stay with me! What's your name?" His voice came through the fog. He peppered her with questions, which she tried to answer but had no idea what she was saying. They stumbled across the threshold of the clinic as one intertwined body.

"Dillon! Beth Ann! What happened?" The voice was Meghan's, but Beth Ann didn't see a body to go with the voice. She tried to tell her friend that she needed a place to stay, but nobody would listen to her. She fought them, but they were stronger. Somehow she ended up in a bed, and a strange hand held a pungent cloth over her face, smothering her. She wanted to push it away, but her arms wouldn't move. Her final conscious thought was that she could trust Meghan to take care of her, and then she willingly surrendered to the blessed darkness.

Chapter 19

She tried to run, but her legs weren't working. They felt heavy. The ground shook; no, everything was shaking. There was a tree nearby. If she could just...reach...far enough.... The shaking grew harder and she cried out. Then she heard her name being called from far, far away.

"Mom? MOM?" Beth Ann awoke, gasping for air, with sweat beading her forehead and her head throbbing.

"Shhh! It's okay, Beth Ann. It's me, Meghan. Do you remember me?" Meghan's voice was low and soothing.

Beth Ann managed to fling her right hand to her pounding heart in attempt to steady it with a little pressure. She pried her eyes open by sheer will-power. They only opened part way, but it was enough to see half of Meghan's face in the candlelight.

"Hurts," Beth Ann managed to croak through her dry throat.

"Your head?" Meghan asked.

Beth Ann closed her eyes and let her slight nod be the answer.

"You're in luck! We're running out of some supplies, but pain reliever is something we got plenty of. And you need more water too." Meghan lifted Beth Ann to an incline. She helped steady Beth Ann's shaky hands, then gave her two small pills to take.

As Beth Ann lay back down, she asked "What time is it?"

Meghan set the empty water cup on the small side table and tucked the quilt around her friend. "It's the middle of the night still. Go back to sleep."

Beth Ann didn't need to be told again.

A couple of hours later, Meghan woke her up again, but this time Beth Ann was grumpy. "Would you leave me alone? I just want to sleep!" she whined.

"I know, I'm sorry," Meghan cooed. "But you clocked your head pretty hard. We assume you have a concussion and now we need to make sure that it's not something...more. Do you want some more water?"

Beth Ann did feel thirsty, but she didn't have the energy to drink anything. "No! Sleep!" It came out harsher than she thought it would. She would apologize later, if Meghan would just go away.

Meghan place a hand on Beth Ann's forehead, then reached under her head to feel the back of her neck. She must have been satisfied because she left quickly with a warning: "See you in a couple hours!"

Beth Ann's sleep was fitful after that. She drifted in and out, with bits and pieces of yesterday's events coming back to her. The anxiety set in again and made her head hurt worse. She had nightmares about being chased, and she had a strange dream about C.S. Lewis writing a book in code while crying. Where does this stuff come from?

As the sun returned from its deep slumber below the horizon, the room gradually began to take shape. It was narrow and defined on two sides by bedsheets. The wall behind her head, she guessed, was an exterior wall, but without a window. The end of the "room" at the foot of the bed was completely open. She could not see the front door, but she heard it squeak open and shut loudly, followed by low conversation. A deep chest cough coming from behind the curtain to her right startled her. There was no use trying to go back to sleep.

As she shifted position, she realized that she had to find a way to relieve the pressure on her bladder…soon. With difficulty she pushed herself up to a seated position and slowly moved her legs to the edge of the bed. Inching forward until her feet touched the floor, she tested her legs. They appeared to remember how to hold her up, so she tried to take a step. When the floor felt squishy, she realized she wasn't alone in her makeshift cubby. On the floor, curled on her side and wrapped in a blanket cocoon, was Meghan.

Just as Beth Ann was trying to figure out how to skirt around her friend without tripping over her, Meghan woke up. "Beth Ann! What are you doing? You shouldn't be out of bed!" she said as she threw off her blanket and stood quickly. She put an arm around Beth Ann's back to steady her.

"Well, unless you like to hand wash soiled sheets, I need to be out of bed!" Beth Ann replied through gritted teeth.

"Oh, yeah. There is that…," Meghan grinned. "Come on. I'll help you. Do you feel well enough to go outside?"

"I'm fine! Jeez! I mean, my head hurts and my legs feel like they're moving through mud, but other than that, I'm fine," Beth Ann said with a little frustration. What was all the fuss about? After taking a few more steps, Beth Ann said, "Well, you can add nausea to the list now, too."

Meghan smiled in sympathy. "The nausea is probably from putting your meds into an empty stomach. Let me grab you something."

Meghan spoke to Jenny at the front desk who handed her a small packet of two salted crackers. She gave them to Beth Ann and helped her step through the main door. The sun was rising behind the building, so they were stepping into shadow. Yet the light made Beth Ann wince. Meghan must have noticed. "You want some sunglasses? I'm sure we can find a pair somewhere."

Beth Ann shook her head and waved her off, her hands shaking as she tried to open the crackers. "Meghan, I'm fine!"

"You may be extra sensitive to light for a while. That would be normal for concussion, as well as the headache. Oh, and we had to put three stitches in, so those will be pretty sore for a couple days. Then the itching will set in…and that'll drive you nuts!"

Beth Ann reached up to feel the gauze bandage covering the tender spot on her head. "Hmm. Aren't you the bearer of good news today. And you're taking such delight in telling me all this."

Meghan just chuckled and gently side-hugged her friend. They were almost to their destination, and Beth Ann had inhaled the crackers.

"Man, I miss toilets!" Beth Ann said loudly a few minutes later from her spot behind a small storage shed.

"Don't we all?" Meghan agreed. When Beth Ann returned, Meghan asked if she felt strong enough for a little walk. Beth Ann's glare told her all she needed to know.

Before they started, Meghan insisted on wrapping Beth Ann's head with a long, thin strip of cloth, almost completely covering one eye. Beth Ann argued, but Meghan won the battle decisively when she threatened to give Beth Ann a shot to calm her down.

Slightly caddy-corner to the clinic entrance was a two-lane bridge over the Allegheny. They were close enough to see the roadblock on the other side. To the south lay the courthouse and deputy headquarters and the Dalton's street, so they headed north…obviously. Walking at a leisurely pace, Meghan skipped the small talk. "Okay. Time to fill me in on what happened last night and how you ended up in my clinic, girlfriend."

Beth Ann looked around. Houses lined both sides of the road. It didn't look or sound like a soul was nearby, but Beth Ann was still apprehensive. She basically felt like she was always being watched now, unless she was with Gary in his basement.

"It's okay, Beth Ann. Most people have reported to their Teams by now. I don't think anyone will hear us," Meghan said gently.

At the same moment, a door slammed and Beth Ann physically jumped, an instinctive yelp escaping from the back of her throat.

The two women heard clomping feet cross a wooden porch and quickly spotted a ragged woman with two small children in tow, one holding each hand, ahead of them. She was practically dragging them as their little legs ran to keep up with her.

"Good Morning!" Meghan said cheerfully as they passed the trio, who were most likely on their way to the Childcare Team in the former library. The little boy closest to them beamed and pointed at her, but the woman jerked his arm and muttered for him to "hurry up."

"Wow. Yeah, I don't feel safe anywhere, Meghan. How do you stay so calm?" Beth Ann asked when they were alone again.

They walked several yards before Meghan answered. "Well, I could say by praying, or God gives me peace, and they're both true. But honestly? I haven't gone through what you have. I really don't know what that would do to my emotions and thoughts. I do remember how I felt paranoid for days after that guy attacked me at the hospital in Warren. I was really lucky to get out of that situation." Meghan paused. The only sound was their sneakers softly contacting the pavement. "I guess I do feel afraid just about every day, but when I focus on my work and other people's problems, I forget the fear somewhat. It helps me feel better, in a way. The bottom line is I have no other option than to trust God – that He will either protect me or He will get me through whatever circumstances come my way."

Beth Ann didn't say anything. It was hard for her to understand...and even harder to believe.

"None of this is going to make any sense on this side of Paradise," Meghan said with a smile, as if she knew she had just read Beth Ann's mind. "Now, tell me what happened."

Beth Ann filled her in, starting with Gary going away and instructing her to squirrel some things away in the old furnace. "I was just afraid of Travis before this, but now I'm even more afraid that my neighbors will turn me in to Mr. Andrews. Gary told me if I needed to run away, to stay in the furnace and wait for him, but I know they'll find me! I am not going back there, at least until Gary comes home. I was trying to find my way to you because I wanted to ask if I can live at your apartment with you. I'll sleep on the floor—that's no problem. Your place is only a couple blocks from the Greenhouses, so it will be a shorter and safer commute. Please, Meghan," Beth Ann begged.

"Beth Ann, you don't even have to ask! Of course you can stay with me. You remember that Dillon lives there too, right? He has the couch, so you'll have to share my room."

With an audible sigh, Beth Ann thanked her friend. Then she dropped her head. "I...um, have to sneak Romeo out somehow. You know he and I are a package deal. I have an idea how to get him, but I just wanted to make sure you knew that I will be bringing him." Beth Ann held her breath.

Meghan hesitated, but not for long. She responded slowly, "I know you don't have much choice. You can't leave him at Gary's house if you're not going to be there to take care of him. But if he barks, we'll be in huge trouble. And we have to hope that Dillon doesn't feel compelled to turn you in."

"It's only going to be a few days...just until Gary gets home! And Romeo never barks anymore. Honestly, he just doesn't have the energy, poor baby. Thank you so much." Beth Ann struggled with her tears, and the struggle made her head hurt worse.

Meghan gave her arm a little comforting squeeze. "Don't worry. He can stay with you. Now, as far as getting you in and out of the building, if you leave a few minutes early and come home a little late, you might be able to avoid my neighbors seeing you."

Beth Ann stared at Meghan with puzzled eyes. "Your neighbors?" she questioned.

"Yeah. The people in my building. In case Andrews is looking for you...."

"Oh. Oh, my," Beth Ann moaned. "I guess you're right. My neighbors could turn me in without having 'me' with them. Then your neighbors could hand me over as a fugitive." This made the situation worse, for sure. She felt trapped and helpless, like a rat in a maze. "Wait! I'll be putting you in danger just for taking me in!"

"Well, if he really wanted you, he would find you at the Greenhouse or at one of the town meetings. It wouldn't matter where you live," Meghan reasoned.

Beth Ann assumed she was trying to make her feel better, but it simply painted a clearer picture of the hopeless situation she was in. She sniffed back her emotions.

The ever-sensitive Meghan linked arms with her. "One day at a time, hon. For today, I got Mr. Thorpe's signature for you to have a 24-hour observation stay. You'll have a little meal at the clinic this afternoon and can sleep there again tonight if you want. Then you'll have to report back to work tomorrow."

"Fine by me...if you can refrain from waking me up every time I fall asleep!" Beth Ann half-heartedly bantered, blinking back tears. She was more worried now than ever.

Meghan started to laugh, but it ended in a long yawn. Beth Ann realized her friend had had less sleep than she did...on account of her concussion. "Thank you, Meghan, for staying last night. I've been selfish. Here, you worked all day yesterday and then stayed all night and now you have to work again. That's like a...thirty-five hour shift!"

"No worries. They let me stay because I would be the only one you would recognize. Without an MRI or any kind of scan, waking you up every couple hours was the only way to make sure you weren't bleeding on the brain or slipping into a coma. I wasn't even supposed to be there!" Meghan explained. "I had already left for the day and just ran back before curfew because of something I forgot to note in one of my case files...and Dillon was practically dragging you through the door!"

They walked a little longer in silence. Beth Ann was deep in thought, watching her shoe laces flop in rhythm. Suddenly, she heard Meghan say softly, "Just keep walking and let me do all the talking."

"Huh?" Beth Ann said, looking up to see that they were approaching the northern roadblock. Two deputies stood facing them, watching their approach.

"No, look down!" Meghan hissed. "Slump. Look pitiful…or something."

Beth Ann did her best to exaggerate a headache. What the heck was she supposed to do? It was a good thing Meghan had had the foresight to put the large bandage around her head before they left the clinic.

Meghan waved casually to the guards as she took ahold of Beth Ann's shoulders and slowly moved her in a wide, shuffling circle to turn her around. But, of course, the deputies couldn't let them go that easily.

"Hullo, ladies! Stop, please!" the older one said as he jogged toward them. The other man stayed at the abandoned car blocking the road.

Meghan turned back, maneuvering Beth Ann with her. "What can I do for you, sir?" Meghan asked with her sweetest smile.

"Yes, a fine day for a walk. You two on vacation today?" the man with the green sash and receding hairline asked. He was smiling, yet his eyes were narrowed in suspicion.

Meghan held her lanyard identification up in front of her so that the inquisitive deputy could see it clearly. "No sir! I'm a nurse on the Medical Team and this young lady is in our care for 24-hours due to acute intracranial injury and contusions. We must analyze her ambulation to test for any possible temporal damage to her cerebral cortex or meninges. But I must get her back to the clinic; she will tire very easily at this stage."

The man eyed Beth Ann and her neat head-circling bandage. As the silence grew longer, she began to wonder if he would make her take it off to be inspected. Instead, he asked, "What's your name, miss?"

Beth Ann opened her mouth to speak, but Meghan jumped in. "It's Bea. Her name is Bea." Beth Ann closed her mouth, realizing with a jolt that Meghan was trying to protect her identity in case the deputies were already on the lookout for a certain "Beth Ann Dalton."

"Bea what?" the deputy asked, once more scrutinizing Meghan's ID.

"Bea…," Meghan started, then looked at Beth Ann and raised her eyebrows helplessly.

"Lewis. I'm Bea Lewis. It's Beatrice, but I really hate that name," Beth Ann shot a quick look at the innocent Meghan, "so I go by Bea." She smiled, then remembered that she was supposed to look "pitiful," so she dropped her gaze.

"Got your ID?" the guard asked, as he shifted his focus back to Beth Ann. Apparently he was the thorough-type.

Beth Ann looked at Meghan, who was standing beside her, frozen in place with a deer-in-the-headlights look on her face. Beth Ann shifted her gaze back to the guard. She made a show of slowly digging through the pockets of her jean shorts, and finally replied, "No, not with me." She reached her hand up to her head and crinkled her eyes and forehead, hoping it looked like she was having a migraine. She continued, a little more slowly, "Maybe it's back at the clinic. Do want to walk back with us?"

"No, no. I can't leave my post." The guard seemed to lose interest. Beth Ann heaved an invisible sigh on the inside. Her bluff had worked.

Beth Ann looked to the road block and saw the other deputy scanning the perimeter with binoculars. "Thank you for keeping us safe, officer," Beth Ann said with what she hoped was a pathetic smile.

The man tipped his head and spun on his heel to return to his important duty. Meghan was still frozen in place, so Beth Ann tugged on her to turn her around and get her started. After they had walked a good ways in silence, Beth Ann released her nerves in the form of a giggle. "What did you say to him? Am I dying and you haven't gotten around to telling me yet?"

Meghan continued to stare at the road in front of her feet with her eyebrows lifted and eyes wide open. In the voice of daydreams she answered, "I just said you had a head injury and we were going for a walk to make sure you didn't have brain damage. Who's Lewis?"

It took a few seconds for Beth Ann to realize that Meghan had run two separate topics together. "Lewis who?"

Meghan seemed to come to life then. She glanced behind them to make sure that they were out of sight of the roadblock deputies. Then she took ahold of Beth Ann's upper arms and turned her so they were face-to-face. In a barely audible voice, Meghan said, "You told them your last name was Lewis. Do you know someone named Lewis? Where did you come up with that off the top of your head?"

Beth Ann pulled back a little. Meghan's behavior was freaking her out. She shrugged. "I don't know. Gary used to read chapters from one of the Narnia books. Maybe that's why I had a weird dream about C.S. Lewis last night...." Beth Ann's focus faded as she tried to remember.

"A dream?" Meghan pressed.

"Yeah, I think," Beth Ann said, forcing her attention back on Meghan. "It was just the first thing that popped into my head! What's the big deal? Where did you come up with 'Bea'? Now, THAT threw me for a loop!"

"B is your first initial. But listen: We can't talk here," Meghan said, anxiously looking around. "Don't say anything about this to anyone, okay? I will fill you in later."

"Really? How mysterious! I thought you said it was safe here and no one was around. Okay, let's get back. I think I'm ready for some of those surplus painkillers you got now...."

With his heart pounding much too hard for his age bracket, Gary leaned against the tree, pressing his back into its strong, wide trunk. The bark impressed itself harshly into his flesh. He took two deep gulps of air, waiting for the volley of gunshots to pause. When it did, he pivoted and, using the tree as cover, took aim. *Don't think, just shoot*, he told himself. Making as big a show as possible, it gave his comrades ten seconds to run. At the tree slightly behind him and to the left, Chuck started shooting. Gary stooped and ran as fast as he could, holding his breath the whole way. He didn't know which was worse: shooting at human beings, or running for his life while directly in the line of fire.

It had been a beautiful morning until they had stumbled across this little hornets' nest. The house on the formerly picturesque property was a pile of timber and stone and ashes, and it appeared to have been untouched for months, except by the weather and an abundance of insects. The Hunting Team made note of the location and marked it "uninhabited" before continuing across the property on their way southward. However, they missed a small barn tucked into the trees behind an overgrown knoll at the back corner of the property. Unfortunately, this faded, well-camouflaged building was indeed inhabited.

The residents weren't very neighborly. Instead of greeting the small band of six men and inviting them in for tea, they simply started firing their weapons. Thankfully, the Hunting Team and its Security escorts were a good distance away from the shooters, and near enough to options for taking cover, that they survived the initial surprise. Now, in evasive maneuvers that Max and Joe had taught them two weeks earlier, called "bounding," their only objective was to get as far away as possible before the offensive line could surround them and cut off their exit. Were they dealing with two people? Ten? Forty? Adults? Children? They had no idea.

Max signaled to Chuck and Gary to retreat farther while he provided cover fire. Bounding was like playing leap frog…except in this game the loser could actually bleed out and die. When they were well out of sight of the property, the return fire ceased. Forging through the dense brush, they pushed hard to put distance between themselves and the attackers. They reached a country road and stopped to weigh their options in hushed tones.

In the end they decided to cross and head north a ways, in case the people tried to follow them. Gary felt strangely exposed and vulnerable as he ran across the open expanse, even knowing that the other members of his team were scoping both tree lines to the north and south. Would life ever be normal again? Would he ever feel safe, or would he spend the rest of his life assuming every person he came across was out to get him until he or she proved otherwise?

After several hours of zigzagging, they found a good defensible pair of outcrops. The large rock ledges reached out toward each other like cupped hands, forming a cavern-like hollow. Essentially, they would be protected on three sides while they camped for the night, and the watchman would be able to see, or hear, someone approaching for a good distance.

They followed the sound of a small stream to wash and cool off. The light yellow-green haze on the trees was deepening into shades of lush, deep green as every day more leaves unfurled. The rain had helped, but not as much as the sun getting closer to their latitude. The further they got into April, the more intense the midday heat became. The men got riper by the day and Gary wished once again for a hot, soapy shower.

They ate a small, cold meal and then used the remaining daylight to clean their guns and refill magazines. At dark they gathered to revise the plan. Their trip was already running longer than they had estimated, and their supplies were getting low. Of course, their packs were getting lighter, but that was no consolation. Joe was designated to take the first watch, and he stomped off like a teenager told to go clean his room. Gary wondered if he had wanted to stay and be a part of the discussion, but it was the Hunting Team's mission, not the deputies'.

"Obviously we have to go back," Mad Max jumped right in, ignoring Joe's demonstrative exit.

"Go back? Are you crazy?" Alex said incredulously, looking around the circle at the other Hunters for support.

"We need to find out how many there are. If they're just a remnant family or a band of hoodlums; if they just have hunting rifles or if they have more sophisticated weaponry; what kind of food stores they have; anything we can find out," Max explained.

Chuck shook his head. "Now Max, I think we have enough to report on. We know the location. We know there was more than one shooter. We know what kind of weapons they used. If they had ARs or other battle rifles, they would have used them on us today. They have to have a decent amount of food storage because this forest has been cleared out of wild game, and Warren is deserted, as we found out last week."

Bob agreed. "It's not worth losing a man over. Whoever they are, they're gonna be on high alert for the next few days since they know we're around. They might expect us to return."

"Yeah, and we don't have enough rations to extend our trip," Alex said. "We still have a solid four days' walk home…and that's if we don't run into any more trouble."

Max's eyes narrowed. "You think Mr. Andrews is going to accept those excuses? Tionesta's survival depends on finding out who else is out there…what they have…and if they are 'friends' or 'foes.' We have a job to do."

"Ha! That's easy! Put those people down as foes," Bob said, pointing at the ledger Chuck held on his lap. "Thanks, Max. Now we can move on. You said 'we,' but this is a Hunting Team Mission, right?" He stood up to signal the discussion was over, but nobody else moved.

Gary watched Max's face. It looked like chiseled rock, completely expressionless. Was he mad? Irritated? Discouraged? Relieved? By golly, this guy missed his calling in Vegas.

After an awkward silence, Max spoke again. "Okay. We'll compromise. At first light we'll get back to our southward path. Then Joe and I will head back north and gather intel on the barn dwellers during the night. You keep going according to plan and we'll catch up with you by nightfall of the next day."

The guys looked around the circle at each other, concern etched on their faces. "Aren't you and Joe our security detail?" Chuck asked. "Isn't this 'compromise' a bit risky? I don't think it's really necessary...."

"Yes! It's necessary!" Max interrupted with a restrained shout. "There's no one else around; you don't really need security." He stood, hands clenched, and ordered gruffly, "Time to get some shuteye. We leave at dawn." He pivoted and abruptly left the group. In silence they watched him go over to his pack and start to re-arrange it. In silence they slowly got up, one by one, and found a place to set out their sleeping bags.

Gary tried to find a comfortable position on the hard-packed soil. Listening to an owl calling in the distance, he began to wonder if the deputies had a little side mission of their own.

Chapter 20

When the Hunting Team had planned their route with Hank Groves, they had set a series of unofficial "landmarks" known by locals who had hiked, hunted and camped in the forest. At each landmark they left a piece of police caution tape, which Sheriff MacClelland had a bulk supply of for no apparent reason. Gary, Chuck, Bob and Alex were on edge as they forded a wide but shallow stream and found themselves in an area that was more open than forested. Evidence of popular ATV trails still showed in the now high grass. Since their encounter with the hostile natives the day before, every rustle of leaves and cracking stick caught their attention. Their nerves were frayed. It was nearing mid-day, but they couldn't stop until they had a more hidden spot to rest. The sun was somewhere overhead, but the gray clouds hung low, obscuring the light and threatening rain. Alex marked a single tree on a ridge near the middle of the field and the men hurried toward the tree line marking the edge of state game lands.

Gary wondered for the four hundredth time how Max and Joe were doing. It seemed strange that they had such an urgency to go out of their way to "spy" on those people in the barn. For all the missions the Hunting Team had done in the past, they didn't take

Security along; however, now he didn't feel as safe without them. He tried to shake off the nervous fluttering, blaming an aging heart for the palpitations. Would they catch up before dark, according to plan? If anything had happened to Max and Joe, the Hunting Team would never know or find their bodies.

Thighs burning, he leaned forward and pushed himself up the steep incline to Wilson's Mill, a logging operation gone bust with the rest of the country. The men quietly skirted the large equipment, scattered about in their final resting places. It was truly an eerie setting. Bob tried siphoning one of the gas tanks, but it was already empty. Finding that all the tanks had been drained previously, the team made some notes, left their mark on the lifted bucket of a backhoe, and continued on.

After the hilly terrain they had been traveling all morning, it was a relief to reach Lenhard Road because it would lead them to the state road where the area was more level and the slopes more gradual. The thing about roads was that they slowed down progress. The best way to find people was to look for roads, find driveways and follow them to homes. All these homes needed to be checked for signs of life without rousing suspicion or sparking violence. The deputies had insisted that stealth be used and that they stay hidden, working only in the low light. The Hunting Team had wanted to walk straight up to the front doors with a white flag. Their rationale was that in these country homes, any survivors would be families and neighbors, and they might welcome the knowledge that other survivors were out there. The deputies countered that IF there were any survivors, they would be desperate enough for food and supplies to do "crazy shit."

So now, standing at the edge of Lenhard Road, the foursome had to decide if they would continue to follow the deputies' strategy. Since the Team didn't want to wait around until dark, and since the deputies had taken the only pair of night vision binoculars with them anyway, they decided to try things their way. Chuck and Bob stayed hidden while Gary and Alex approached each front door, guns cradled for the appearance of trust and peace. Alex held a long stick with a white t-shirt tied to it by its sleeves–big enough to not be missed unless the person was literally blind.

It was slow going, but no one answered the doors at the rest of the houses on Lenhard. On one front porch they found the bones and shrunken skin of a dog, and a double-wide trailer home smelled so strongly of decay as they approached it that they didn't bother knocking. They started working their way down 305, which had more space between homes, yet still hadn't seen a living soul.

The men took a break in a wooded area off the road and discussed their options. Overall they were happy with their progress and just wanted to get back to Tionesta, whether the deputies caught up with them or not. It still had not rained, but the humidity was building and it was uncomfortable. They hydrated well, Alex made some notes in his log, and they were off.

The trouble came when they reached wide open farmland late in the afternoon. The clouds had finally decided to release their burden in the form of an annoying drizzle, and a good mile or more of the low, oppressive sky greeted them. Gary and Alex could easily take their lives in their own hands and walk down the middle of the road with their white flag, but where would Bob and Chuck defend them from?

Pop! Pop! Pop! At the sound of gunfire, the men hit the ground and each low-crawled to the nearest tree big enough to provide some cover.

"What the hell?" Alex yelled as he rolled his pack off and sat up, pointing his rifle straight up, the stock resting on his thigh.

"Well, now we know the white flag idea doesn't work!" Bob grumbled, panting heavily.

They hustled to get positioned and then just waited. After a few tense and quiet moments, Alex picked up the stick beside him and waved the shirt from side to side, trying to keep his arm behind the tree as much as possible. Gary wished the deputies were with them to give them instruction.

"WE COME IN PEACE!" The surprising sound of Alex shouting made Gary jump. He turned his head to look at Alex in annoyed surprise. Alex just lifted one eyebrow as if asking Gary if he had a better idea. "WE JUST WANT TO TALK!"

Gary closed his eyes, thinking, *Good grief.*

"WE GOT YOU SURROUNDED!" a deep voice finally responded back. It came from nowhere, like the voice of God.

"THERE'S ONLY FOUR OF US! WE'RE NOT A THREAT!" Alex responded, shrugging at Gary. Gary hoped the voice was bluffing.

"PROVE IT!" the invisible man demanded.

Alex, Gary, Bob and Chuck looked back and forth at each other, separated by the distance between the trees. Chuck finally spoke up quietly, "What are our other options right now?" They relayed the message down the line, and Bob and Gary nodded reluctantly in agreement. Alex gave them an encouraging 'thumbs up' sign and an optimistic smile. Gary breathed a quick prayer for "deliverance from evil."

"WE'LL COME OUT IF YOU GUYS COME OUT, TOO! I'M TIRED OF HOLLERIN'!" Alex said.

"YOU FIRST!" came the reply. Alex rolled his eyes.

The four tired men set their rifles carefully on the ground, stood with arms raised, and one by one stepped out from behind his tree. Gary could feel his blood pulsing in his ears, his fingertips, and his temples. After the longest thirty seconds of his life, a short man appeared out of seemingly thin air. In reality, he had climbed out of a trench in which he had been keeping watch over his property. He had the scraggly, unkempt look of the rest of the winter's survivors. His clothes hung loosely and his sleeves were rolled up to his biceps. His graying beard was topped off with a wild mane of deep brown hair, and his one eye was hidden behind the scope of his gun. Gary watched as he pointed the scope at each of his Team members, not liking the feeling one bit.

"Sir, we are unarmed! Please lower your weapon," Gary called out.

The man lowered it slightly, but kept it pointed at the strangers. "State your business!"

"We are from Tionesta, checking for survivors. But do we have to shout across this field or can we sit together and have a civil conversation?" Alex responded.

The man didn't move, and after a couple minutes, Gary began to wonder if he hadn't heard Alex. His arms were aching and his blood was losing its uphill battle to circulate. Chuck and Bob looked nervously at each other and then at Alex and Gary. Finally, the farmer's mouth opened. "Head to the mailbox."

"What?" Alex yelled back.

Slowly, but loudly, the man over-enunciated each word as if they were small children: "Leave... your packs... and guns... and... meet... me... at... the... mailbox! You wanna talk? We talk over here!"

The Hunting Team knew what that meant, and not just that they couldn't dig out their rain gear. It meant that the farmer was pulling them away from any backup they might have hiding in the treeline. It also meant that the man most likely had his own backup...in the house or in other trenches or tree stands, much closer to the mailbox. As they apprehensively crossed the wide, freshly plowed field, Gary identified with the little grinnies and field mice that were afraid of open spaces because the all-seeing hawk could swoop down and grab them. He resisted the urge to look up. But his skin crawled like he was being watched and he came to the conclusion that the Deputies' strategy was probably the better of the two after all.

The farmer reached the mailbox long before they did, and he watched the Hunting Team carefully as they approached the road. Halfway across, he stopped them. "That's close enough!" The rifle was still pointed at them. Gary was close enough to the house now to see both dormer windows cracked open about four inches, and he guessed it wasn't for fresh air. "So, what would you nice people from

Tionesta like to talk about? I don't have any milk or eggs for you to borrow, so I'll spare ya the trouble of asking."

Alex ignored the man's bitter tone. "I'm Alex, and these are my buddies, Gary, Chuck and Bob." The men each nodded at the farmer as Alex said his name. Alex paused, but the man didn't offer his name, so he continued. "As I said, we are from Tionesta and we are just checking to see who in the area is still around and how they're doing. How many do you have here? And do you have neighbors or know of others around who are riding out the storm?"

"Who wants to know?" the man with the wild hair asked, narrowing his eyes to slits.

Alex lifted his eyebrows. "Uh…, I just told you—we do."

The man looked them up and down thoroughly. "I don't trust you. I don't trust nobody!"

"That's fine. I completely understand. You're right that there are a lot of people out there who cannot be trusted these days." Alex said calmly. The man's expression didn't change. "Listen, sir. Just answer my questions and we'll be on our way…and you'll never see us again. We miss our families more than we can say. I'd show you my chart to prove what we're doing, but you made us leave our stuff behind." Alex smiled, trying to ease the man's obvious anxiety.

After another pause, the man surprised them by sharing the information Alex asked for. "Two weeks after the electricity went out, my three closest farming neighbors moved into our place. We combined animals and food stores when we realized how bad the situation was. There was thirteen of us then, includin' the kids. It wasn't like a vacation or nothin' but we were doing just fine until somewhere around the end of March. Bunch of hoodlums attacked us, ran off with our last seven head of cattle. Stole anything they felt like stealing and killed everyone who was outside. Two was just…kids playing in the sandbox." The man looked down at his feet and shifted his weight. "Now there's eight of us to feed with only the little bit those thieves didn't find." He cleared his throat and looked back up at them, his face hard. "You can come back at harvest time and see how many of us are still alive. Unless you got food to spare."

"No, nobody has enough to spare, unfortunately. Thank you for letting us know, and…we're so sorry to hear of your loss," Alex responded in a gentle tone. Gary did feel sorry for the man, but he still keenly felt the loss of his own wife; everyone had suffered in some way. "Can you tell us anything about the attackers? Then I promise we'll go," Alex tacked on quickly. Gary, too, could sense that the farmer had reached the end of his grace period.

"Yeah. There was a whole bunch of them, they were all men, and some of them were wearing bright orange clothes with white lettering, like they was prisoners or somethin.' They had no intention of talking, just blazed in, took what they wanted, firing their guns off every which way, and blazed out. Never saw them again. But someone was snooping around my place last night, outside. Found this snagged on a barbed wire fence just outside the barn." The farmer dug in his pocket and came out with a small torn bit of cloth…kelly green. "We scared 'em off, but we're ready if they come back. This time we aren't gonna be taken by surprise. We're gonna run 'em off or die trying. Now, you people need to go back to Tionesta and stay put." The farmer waved the gun barrel in Route 305's southerly direction and stuffed the cloth deep into the front pocket of his jeans.

"Yes, sir," Alex nodded. The foursome turned to leave, but Alex stopped and looked back. "What did you say your name was?"

"I didn't," the deep voice answered in finality. Alex shrugged and the men headed quickly across the field to get their guns and gear. The rain was light but steady, and the field was already turning into a muddy mess that sucked against their boots at every step. They didn't speak until well after they had passed the farmhouse and were in a wooded area again.

"It would be wise to look for a place now to camp for the night. With the rain and cloud cover, it'll be dark sooner than usual," Bob said. They all knew he was right, and they also knew that he had bad knees and suffered more than all of them on these long treks…and in cold weather…and when it rained or was going to rain….

It took close to an hour to find a semi-dry place to spend the night. Gary wished for the dry heat of a campfire as the temperature started to drop, but he understood the security concerns with lighting one. Instead, he changed into two dry shirts, layering against the chill, and topped them with his waterproof parka. He had already worn those shirts, so they reeked. But it was more important that he get out of the wet clothes than smell good.

"Do you think Max & Joe will find us here?" Chuck asked when they had gathered to have a snack of peanut butter and stale crackers.

"They know our route. So if they're still alive, they'll find us. They're probably closer than we realize!" Alex said with a strange cheerfulness. He was just finishing recording the farmer's location and information, and he shut the book with a dramatic clap. Gary caught his eye and saw something there. He suspected that Alex had connected the dots about the piece of green cloth the farmer pulled out of his pocket. It sure had looked like the fabric of the famous green sashes that the Security Team wore.

"I'll take first watch," Gary offered as he stood and pulled his hood up. He had some thinking to do. The three other men settled into their sacks and soon, after a bit of shifting around, began to make the telltale sleeping grunts and shallow snores. Gary wished for the convenience of night vision as he looked for a good vantage point with cover from which to keep watch. With his eyes and ears alert, he let his thoughts and prayers intermingle. Beth Ann took up most of that space, but he also wondered what Mr. Andrews was up to with their spying reports, what the Deputies' REAL mission was, and what his future would be in a world devoid of rules and respect, honor, trust, and morality, let alone the resources for basic needs like shelter, food and water.

The snapping of a twig caught his immediate attention and drew him back fully to the current situation. He turned his whole body slightly to the left, the direction from which the sound had come. His shallow breathing kept pace with his rapid heartbeat, and he willed his hands to stop trembling as he gazed over the scope of the gun, wishing for those darned night vision binoculars. He listened intently, but all he could hear was the soft rain that had continued to fall all evening.

A familiar coo set Gary instantly at ease; his relief was tangible as his shoulders relaxed. The Hunting Team had practiced the gentle Mourning Dove call early in their journey as a way of signaling to each other, just in case they found themselves in a situation like this. Especially on a dark and rainy night, this simple signal most likely prevented an accidental shooting.

Gary cradled his gun and brought his clasped hands to his mouth to signal back. Within a few seconds, two very soggy Security Team members stumbled out of the brush and into the makeshift camp. Max clapped Gary on the shoulder as he walked past and threw himself onto the driest spot he could find, not even bothering to take out his bedroll. As Joe followed, he reached out to shake Gary's hand. Puzzled at the bygone custom and the strange timing, Gary slowly shook it as Joe mumbled "good night" almost incoherently. Then he paused and drew his face close to Gary's ear. "Don't lose it," he whispered. He, like Max, dropped to the bare ground with his back to the others and curled on his side. Both men were snoring in less than thirty seconds.

Gary turned around and quietly unfolded the small slip of paper Joe had put in his hand. It was too dark to make out any writing, and lights were strictly forbidden. He would have to wait until morning. A tingling sensation in his spine didn't bode well for the days to come. At least he was wide awake now....

Beth Ann was still trying to process and understand everything that she had learned over the last two evenings since she had temporarily moved into Meghan's apartment. What she thought was a dream about C.S. Lewis while she was at the Medical Center turned out to be an overheard conversation in her sleep. According to

Meghan, some of the citizens of Tionesta were beginning to question Mr. Andrews' leadership and methodology. So they were banding together in an underground movement with the clandestine central message center being the Medical Team's facility. For security purposes, Dillon and Meghan didn't reveal the passwords or any names of people involved, but they asked her to pass the message on to Gary when he returned home that they were still recruiting and would welcome him to join their force.

Beth Ann's forehead creased as she worried what it all meant. Meanwhile, Gary should have been home by now....

"Watch what you're doin'!" Jack yelled, interrupting her thoughts.

Beth Ann's head snapped up and she readjusted the rope loop wrapped around her arms. She and Jack were hauling the rototiller to her parents' house on a yard cart, modified to be pulled by humans instead of a tractor. On the flat and going uphill, they pulled from in front. Downhill, they stood behind to resist the gravitational pull. Beth Ann's rope controlled the right wheel, and Jack's controlled the left. In this way they were able to steer the contraption, although with some difficulty since Beth Ann's strength didn't match Jack's.

"Sorry, Jack," she said meekly.

They turned slowly onto her street, grunting as they pulled. Beth Ann's stomach fluttered and she anxiously scanned the area as they walked, even though logic told her that her neighbors should all be working with their Teams at this time of day. Since her concussion, she had been at work every day and eaten lunch in the town hall. And so far no one had yanked her away and carried her off to Branson's jail. It was almost worse, the waiting and not knowing.... But now that she was back on her street, would her neighbors confront her again? Or take her by force to Andrews' office? Or...just shoot her?

"Everything alright there?" Jack interrupted again, a hint of genuine concern in his voice.

Beth Ann realized with some shame that she had basically ignored the man up to this point. Even though he was a little rough around the edges, he wasn't trying to intimidate her. Maybe he really was human and had worries of his own, like they all did. "I guess so. I'm just lost in my thoughts, that's all. And worried about Mr. Howard, my neighbor."

"He sick?"

Suddenly Beth Ann wasn't sure what was safe to say; trust was a thing of the past. She shrugged and tried to act casual. "Oh, I don't think so. He works on the Hunting Team and he's been gone a lot longer than usual this time, that's all."

She saw Jack's eyes narrow. "Hunting Team, my ass. I don't know what Andrews has those people doin', but it ain't HUNTING," he said in a tone that gradually progressed in volume. The cart behind them stopped. Beth Ann waited nervously while Jack rubbed his arms and lower back. "How much farther do we have to drag this blasted thing?" he asked.

Beth Ann pointed two houses farther on the right. "It's right there."

"Thank God," Jack breathed, drawing the tension on the ropes tight, signaling he was ready to go. "Wait. You mean we're gonna have to tear that fence down first?"

"Please, Jack. We'll just break up the land inside. If we need more space, there's a small side yard. But we have to keep the fence, for...for when my parents get home...," she didn't know how to finish her thought. "It just has to stay," she begged quietly. That fence was part of her identity...a symbol of her hope.

She dared to look up at him then and was surprised to see deep sadness in his eyes. He cleared his throat and it vanished, replaced by the usual protective steel. "Fine. You'll just have a smaller garden. I can't get all the way to the edge with a fence in the way. A lot of wasted space...," he grumbled, his voice trailing off as he leaned his weight forward against the ropes to cover the last few yards to the house.

Beth Ann pulled, too. "Well, Mr. Howard said we can use his front yard. I can keep up with both gardens, I know I can."

Jack just grunted. Beth Ann didn't know how to interpret that.

While Jack made steady, slow progress in perfect parallel lines across the yard, Beth Ann followed behind. She picked up rocks, placed them in a bucket, and when the bucket got too heavy to carry, dumped them in a pile in the side yard. These days, one kept everything in case there might be a use for it in the future. She also used a hoe to break up the thick grass clods, tightly matted with roots intertwining for the past six decades. It was hot, dirty labor.

"Water break!" Beth Ann called to Jack as he swore, fighting with the tiller's claws to span the sidewalk that bisected every row. He instantly killed the motor with its rationed gasoline and trudged to the shaded front porch steps to rest. Beth Ann sipped from her jug and waited until Jack relaxed and leaned back against the side of the house with his eyes closed. "I'll be right back, Jack. I just have to…check something in the house," she said, slipping through the front door without waiting for a reply. She ran through the kitchen and out the back door, streaked down the little grade and through the shrubs to Gary's back door and let herself in. Gasping for breath, she waited for her eyes to adjust.

"Romeo!" she called softly, "Romeo! I'm coming!" Carefully she went down the basement steps and found the dog in his typical spot on the couch. She had put a small box in front of the couch to help him get up more easily, since jumping had become painful for him. He lifted his head and seemed to smile at her as she cleared the bottom step. Sitting on the couch, she drew him into her arms and snuggled him close. He felt light and fragile; it was her fault that he was starving to death. Out of her work pocket she pulled the smuggled remnants of yesterday's meal. Slowly he ate the morsels and then licked her palm over and over. She kicked herself for taking the MREs to the furnace hideout. She should have fed them to Romeo. Now she was sure the meals had to be long gone.

"My poor baby," she crooned. She had desperately wanted to sneak him to Meghan's apartment, but the risk of getting caught…or of getting Meghan in trouble…was too high. Putting him gently back in his spot, she promised him she would come back tomorrow and try to bring more food…somehow. She poured a little of her water into his bowl, folded up the top newspaper page with the tiny poo on it and spread out a fresh one. It was too dark in the basement to read the headline, but the picture was definitely Mr. Andrews shaking the hand of a man. The story was old, from the previous September, but Beth Ann remembered it well: the ribbon cutting ceremony at the new high school gymnasium that was built with Andrews' dollars and bore his name. In disgust Beth Ann flipped the sheet over, then sat back quietly on her heels as a thought formed in her mind. She turned it back over so that Andrews' big cheesy grin was facing straight up.

"Poop on him, Romeo. Poop a big one right on that picture," Beth Ann directed sternly just before giving her dog a kiss on the nose and bolting up the stairs.

Reversing her steps back to her house, Beth Ann stopped just inside the front door to take a couple of deep breaths so she wouldn't make Jack suspicious. But when she stepped out onto the porch, Jack wasn't there. The rototiller still sat on the sidewalk where he had left it. Feeling the panicky tightening of her throat at the thought of being alone, she rushed down the sidewalk. Within three steps she froze. There was Jack, in the middle of the street, with a gun trained on one of the men that had almost been hanged for stealing the Howard's food.

Beth Ann slowly reached into her work apron pocket and cocked the hammer of Gary's handgun. The neighbor saw her then, and her hand tightened around the grip as their eyes locked. Finally, the man looked back at Jack, and Jack waved the barrel of his rifle in the direction of the man's house. After what seemed like an unbearably long standoff, the man backed up several steps and sauntered the rest of the way to his front steps. Jack didn't turn around until the man was inside the house with the door shut.

"Wha…what was that about?" Beth Ann asked when Jack safely returned to the partially-dug-up yard. She was completely unable to move, except for the icy shudders that were coursing the full length of her body.

"Just some grumpy guy who claimed to be sick. Said he saw you runnin' off with his property and he was going to turn you in to the authorities," Jack said, looking her square in the eye.

"No! That's not true!" Words started spilling out of Beth Ann's mouth so fast that she couldn't stop them. "I can explain everything! They stole our food and Mr. Andrews wouldn't give it back. He took it for the town and hanged one of our neighbors. But Mrs. Howard died and Mr. Howard went off the deep end and told me to...."

"Whoa, WHOA!" Jack commanded, holding up his hands. "I don't wanna hear the details. Do you want to know what I told him or not?"

"Yes...?" Beth Ann hesitated, feeling very small and very young at that moment.

"I told him to leave you the hell alone because you are workin' on some special projects for Mr. Andrews and you was authorized to move that stuff. AND, if Andrews finds out that his secrets are leaking out, he'll either kill the girl or kill the messenger. I told him to think twice about being the messenger. I don't think he'll bother you anymore," Jack finished. It was the most words at one time she had ever heard him say.

If she wasn't so squeamish about physical contact, she would have rushed at him and thrown her arms around his neck. Instead, she closed her eyes in attempt to control her emotion and relief. Her knees weakened and she crumbled down into a heap.

Jack reached out, but not in time to break her fall. He quickly lifted her up. "Com'on, Beth Ann. You're alright. Show me where we can lock this rototiller up. We gotta run back to town or we're going to miss the meeting and our ration. We'll have to come back and finish this later," he said, motioning to the yard.

"Thank you, Jack," Beth Ann said, blinking back tears. "Thank you."

Jack and Beth Ann reached town just as a crowd was forming on the lawn in front of the municipal building. They separated and Beth Ann easily found Meghan. The people seemed chattier than usual, maybe because of the sunshine and the hope that springtime brings. Even the Childcare Team, which usually just sent two representative adults, all came—some carrying babies and others holding hands with a chain of little people. April was coming to a close; the ornamental trees were in full bloom and the tulips and daffodils had come and gone, making way for the irises. Some trees had leaves, some wore a haze of buds, and others would be late leafers. The danger of frost wasn't over for several more weeks, but each day was closer to summer.

"Ahh, it gladdens my heart to see all of you in such high spirits on this beautiful day!" Mr. Andrews said as he took his usual place on the top step, signaling the time to start. "The town of Tionesta is going to not only survive this global tragedy...but THRIVE! Because of YOUR hard work and YOUR positive attitude! Your WILLINGNESS to give everything you can to BUILD this community!"

Beth Ann refrained from letting her eyes roll around freely in their sockets as he continued. Mr. Andrews sure liked to hear himself talk!

When he finished his dramatic monologue, he turned his excited tone down a couple of notches. "Okay, okay. Now, let's get through this week's business quickly so everyone can get their meal." First he introduced Sam Sawyer, a freckle-faced man in his forties with a curly mass of shocking red hair and a reddish haze of fine stubble along his strong jawline. Mr. Sawyer was being pulled off the Hunting Team to lead a Sanitation Team, specifically to devise and enforce standard operating procedures for dealing with human waste. With the warmer weather, and with pressure from the Medical Team after a small cholera outbreak, it was past time to address this very real concern.

"Over the next day or two, Mr. Sawyer and I will be visiting all the Teams and talking with your Team Leaders," Andrews explained...or warned. "We guess somewhere around eight of you will be re-assigned to the Sanitation Team. If you want to volunteer, tell your Team Leader today and we will consider the request."

Next, each Team Leader gave a very brief report on the status of their assignment and statistics as applicable. Beth Ann waited with great interest as Mr. Groves took his place to report on the Hunting Team. He shared that the East/West mission had returned the day before; they had discovered that very, very few of the families in nearby communities had survived. He said nothing about Gary's North/South mission. Beth Ann's frustration grew to anger inside of her, and she wondered how much longer she could take of standing there and listening to the reports, not knowing what was truth and what was propaganda.

Finally, the sheriff stood beside Mayor Andrews and started his report: a handful of mildly violent roadblock encounters, a house fire, two "domestic" situations, and a missing person.

"Hey Sheriff! Tell us what you're doing to find my niece!" a man's voice hollered from the crowd. Beth Ann couldn't see who it was.

Branson held his hand above his eyes to shield the sun as he surveyed the crowd. "Identify yourself, please! Ah, okay. I see you there. Are you the one who filed the missing person report?"

"Yes! She's only sixteen! The town is locked down! She has to be here somewhere, so why haven't you found her yet?" The man seemed agitated, and the sound of hushed murmuring began to circulate through the crowd.

"My daughter's gone, too! She went for a walk last night before curfew and didn't come back! What is happening?" a woman cried out, her nervous voice rising shakily above the escalating din. Mr. Andrews nodded sharply to Sheriff Branson who took two deputies with him and strode into the fray.

"Calm down, calm down, everyone!" the Mayor raised his arms and used his most soothing voice. "Sheriff Branson will take these two to his office to record their information and every effort will be made to help them." Everyone watched in silence as the man and woman were escorted away. That's when Beth Ann realized the woman was her co-worker with the homeschooled daughter. She struggled to force her foggy brain to think of the last time she had seen Felicia...but couldn't remember.

Chapter 21

Mealtime after the town hall meeting was quieter than usual; perhaps people were feeling apprehensive now that the hushed rumors had been confirmed. Beth Ann barely said "hello" and "goodbye" to Amy, who was manning the sign-in table at the bottom of the broad staircase. She desperately wanted to ask her if she had seen Kristen or heard from her, but with the guard standing at the bottom of the stairs, Beth Ann didn't take the chance.

That afternoon she was glad to be outside and back in her own yard...with Jack there, of course. Breaking up the clods of dirt was achingly hard work, but it was cathartic to the troubled soul. She tried not to think about the missing girls; she tried not to think about the circulating rumors of abuse by the Security Team, which people had started to accept as "part of life" now. She was tired of trying to hide from Travis, and she just wanted Gary to return so she could feel marginally safe again.

Jack finished the yard in a couple of hours, and Beth Ann helped him reload the rototiller onto the trailer and strap it down tightly. They heaved it back into town and reported in with Mr. Eckley. After thanking Jack once again, Beth Ann spent a few minutes in the Main Greenhouse with Mary Jo Lowell, who pointed out her hand-picked plants to Beth Ann. They were the ones that she would be planting in her front yard in the next week or so, once the soil was ready.

Now that Beth Ann was staying in town, temporarily, she didn't have to be "escorted" home. Rather, she joined any small group that was headed in her direction. To end this very long day, she found herself with Mrs. Dean and Mr. Nellis, former teachers whom she still could not bring herself to call by their first names, Zachary Cobb who owned "The Pizza House," and a couple of older women she used to see at the restaurant frequently. Beth Ann tried, without success, to tune them out as they speculated about the two missing girls.

"Well, I thought our young lady, Felicia, was sweet on one of those Green Sashers. I sure saw them together a lot," Eileen chirped. "Maybe *he* has something to do with this." Her eyebrows lifted knowingly, her lips pressed tightly together.

"Oh, Eileen," her sister Alice chided with the same bird-like voice, "you don't know what you're talking about. I never saw her with a Security guard. I hope she wasn't kidnapped, the poor dear!"

"Or maybe she fell into the river!" Eileen suggested with sarcasm, and went back to her Deputy theory. The two continued to argue as if the rest of them weren't there.

Mr. Nellis stifled a smile, but Mrs. Dean's eyes were round with fear. Zachary jumped into the ring. "Maybe she didn't want to be with the man…. Maybe he was harassing her." At this, everyone started talking at once. Meghan's apartment would be the first place they passed, so Beth Ann literally watched her feet and counted the steps until she could excuse herself.

Within minutes, even though it seemed longer, they reached Beth Ann's cutoff. She had just lifted her head and opened her mouth to say good-bye when she caught a flash of movement. Did she imagine it? She walked a few more steps, craning her neck. If it was Travis, he had ducked behind a building and she wouldn't be able to see him until she walked past it…which is probably what he wanted. She walked a few more steps, unsure of what she should do, her heart beating double-time. The others, still in conversation, didn't seem to notice that they had passed Beth Ann's place, so she kept walking with them. After a few minutes more, she quietly stepped out of the group to duck into the Clinic.

"Hey there, Beth Ann," Jenny greeted her from the front desk as she walked in. They had gone to school together, a grade apart. Beth Ann didn't know her well, but she knew that Meghan and Jenny had bonded.

Her eyes not yet adjusted from the bright sunshine, Beth Ann turned her face in the direction of Jenny's voice. "Hey, Jenny. Is Meghan here?"

"No, sorry. She's making rounds right now," Jenny explained, "but she should be back soon."

Beth Ann weighed her options. "Is it alright if I just hang out till she comes back?"

"Sure! Pick a seat and make yourself comfortable." Jenny bent her head down, working diligently on something with a pen and a ruler.

Beth Ann waited for a while, but she got bored and asked if there was anything she could do to help. Jenny escorted her into the storage room with a flashlight to check inventory on a handwritten list attached to a clipboard. It appeared to be a former office, but the desk had been removed; Beth Ann guessed it might be the one Jenny was now using at the clinic entrance. Mix-matched shelving units of various sizes, shapes and colors lined the walls. The shelves were neatly organized but severely depleted of many items.

Beth Ann was hard at work when she heard the front door open. As exciting as it was to count rolls of gauze, she poked her head out of the storage room to see if it was Meghan. Instead, she caught the split-second exchange of a familiar silhouette handing a small, folded slip of paper to Jenny.

"Thank you for your Team report," Jenny said in a voice louder than she would have used if she only wanted the man to hear. She handed him another small piece of paper and, in a lower voice, she continued, "Please give this to Mr. Eckley. It will explain what we need for next time."

Beth Ann caught her breath and pulled her head back into the storage room, flattening herself against the wall even though she didn't think anyone had seen her. It reminded her of seeing the note passed between the two Hunting Team men behind their big garage. So, the pizza store owner was in on the underground movement to oust Mr. Andrews; he must have doubled-back after his coworkers were all safely delivered to their homes. Meghan had told her that messages were passed through the Medical Center and now she had witnessed it for herself.

Beth Ann stood quietly until Mr. Cobb left. She went back to work, but she listened more attentively this time. Jenny shuffled papers around and opened file cabinets a lot. Mr. Thorpe's "bedside" voice spoke on occasion; Beth Ann couldn't make out the actual words but it appeared to be conversation with patients. Another person entered the clinic, an older woman who seemed very upset about a problem with someone in her household. Jenny tried to answer her questions, but her angst was so compelling that Jenny personally escorted her to the doctor's office.

It was the opportunity she had been waiting for. Beth Ann dashed to the front desk, knowing she may only have seconds to find what she was looking for. The muffled sound of the distraught woman, mixed with the voices of the doctor and Jenny trying to calm her down, could be heard from the far corner of the small building. As long as Beth Ann could hear Jenny's voice, she was safe.

Her eyes darting back and forth at the office setup, she wondered where she would hide something if it was secret. Not in the obvious places. She skipped the pencil drawer and instead lifted the file folders lying on the desk to see if anything was underneath. She looked under the desk and peered behind the file cabinets, taking a risk by using her flashlight. *Think, think, think...and HURRY*, she told herself. Closing her eyes, she tried to see the exchange again.

Jenny hadn't opened a file cabinet drawer with Mr. Cobb there; in fact, Jenny hadn't moved from her spot.

Beth Ann suddenly realized that it was quiet, and she took three quick leaps to reach a short half-wall where she could crouch. She watched as Jenny scurried into the waiting room, grabbed a box of tissues from a side table, and rushed back to the woman who was now softly sobbing. Beth Ann ran back to Jenny's chair and sat in it. On a hunch, she reached as far underneath the pencil drawer as she could. Her hand caught on something—a large envelope taped to the bottom of the drawer. Beth Ann pulled out the folded paper inside, stuffed it into her work apron, and slinked toward the storage closet. She had only gone a few strides when Jenny appeared, catching her off-guard.

"Done already?" Jenny asked, giving her a strange look.

"No, no. Potty break!" Beth Ann said, forcing a laugh. She walked straight out the back door, leaving Jenny standing in the waiting room, watching her. Beth Ann took a few minutes to calm herself down. "Holy moly, that was close!" she breathed when she was in the private area behind the shed. Taking the note out of her pocket, she was surprised to see that the two-line message was in code. At least she assumed it was code; it made absolutely no sense to her.

Frustrated, she stuffed the note back into her apron and went back inside. Jenny was at her desk, and Beth Ann wondered how she would put the note back. She hadn't thought about that when she took it.

"Back to work!" she said cheerfully as she passed Jenny.

"You don't have to if you don't want to," Jenny said. "It's not your responsibility, even though I really, really appreciate it...!"

"It's better than just sitting around waiting!" Beth Ann responded as she kept walking, feeling guilty.

Meghan arrived about ten minutes later. Beth Ann could hear her report in and hand over her patient files to Jenny for Mr. Thorpe to check. Halfway through the antacids, Beth Ann hurried to finish counting the bottles and marked the chart with the quantity and date. However, just as she turned to leave, Mr. Thorpe entered the room. Beth Ann jumped, but the Medical Team Leader appeared even more startled than she.

"Hey! Stop! What are you doing?" the man shouted at Beth Ann, their flashlights trained on each other's face.

"I...I...," Beth Ann was too surprised to give a coherent answer; her tongue felt too big and too dry to form actual words. Jenny and Meghan came running.

"Meghan!" Beth Ann exclaimed.

"Beth Ann?" Meghan asked, obviously not expecting to see her friend there.

"Jenny?" Mr. Thorpe demanded, waiting for an explanation.

Jenny rushed forward and took the clipboard from Beth Ann. "Sir, Beth Ann was waiting for Meghan to come back from her rounds and asked if she could help. I thought it would be okay for her to check inventory since we—"

"No, Jenny," Mr. Thorpe interrupted. "It's not okay. Part of our job as the Medical Team is to *guard* these supplies," he said, although not overly harshly–more like he was explaining it to a second grader. He turned back to Beth Ann. "I remember you.... My concussion patient, right?"

Beth Ann smiled and nodded her head, relieved.

"Now, please empty your pockets."

"What?" all three girls asked in unison.

"Actually, hand me your work apron and then empty your pockets," Mr. Thorpe clarified.

Beth Ann looked in Meghan's direction, but with Mr. Thorpe's light shining in her eyes, could not actually see her. At first she had been surprised and scared, but now she was downright mad...and terrified about getting caught with the note. Slowly she untied her apron and held it out for Jenny to take to her boss, saying "You won't find any stolen supplies in there, but you will find my loaded gun. Please make sure you don't shoot any of us by accident." Then

she pulled out the empty pocket liners in the front of her jeans.
"Okay. Are you satisfied now?"

The light left her face and she could see its beam and Mr. Thorpe's hand rooting through the three pockets of her filthy apron. She also saw Meghan's and Jenny's shoes. Beth Ann held her breath, sure that she was going to single-handedly tip off an entire underground organization.

"Almost," Mr. Thorpe said. "But I have to be thorough. Every week, Mr. Andrews stops by for our inventory report and matches it to what we've used in treatments that week. If any of our supplies go missing, he will hold *me* accountable. I need to avoid any kind of scenario like that." He stood back up and pointed his light beam toward Beth Ann once again. "Jenny, pat her down."

"Do what?" Jenny asked with a giggle, incredulous.

"As in, make sure there is nothing stuffed inside any of her clothing articles. It would be less appropriate for a man–like me–to do it, don't you think?"

"I can't believe you're making such a big deal about this! I know her and we can trust her!" Jenny said defiantly. She marched over to Beth Ann who was standing in the pool of incriminating light. "Sorry about this, Beth Ann. I didn't mean to get you in a mess here," she said quietly. "Um…, raise your arms please."

Beth Ann complied, knowing that Jenny felt as humiliated as she did. Finally, Mr. Thorpe handed her back her apron, apologizing for the extreme measures.

"Jeez. I seriously only wanted to help. But don't worry–I won't go back in there again," Beth Ann promised as they all left the room and shut the door. She was still miffed, but mostly she was shocked that Mr. Thorpe hadn't found the note. Probably because he was only looking for boxes and bottles. She also understood his precaution…and his fear of Mr. Andrews. She gave him her most innocent smile. "Now, just out of curiosity, what does a person have to do to get a lip balm?"

224

The front room seemed bright now compared to the windowless storage room. Mr. Thorpe answered, "I have to prescribe it. Step over here by the window." He closely inspected her cracked lips and asked, "You work outside, right?"

"Greenhouse Team," she answered. "But my lips are always dry, no matter the season. And sometimes they burn or bleed. It just really helps if I can put something on them. I have petroleum jelly at home, but I would *love* to have a little balm I could carry with me during the day."

"I think I can help you with that. Give me a minute," he said as he faded into the darkness around the corner.

Beth Ann turned to Meghan. "Oh! My! Gosh! All I wanted was to walk home with you. Are you almost done?" The longer this day went on, the more tiresome it got.

Meghan flinched. "Oh, right. Almost. I got distracted by the sideshow," she said, grinning. Beth Ann rolled her eyes. "Give me five minutes to finish my log."

Meghan disappeared somewhere in the back, and Jenny went back to the other side of her desk and the row of filing cabinets. Waiting once again, Beth Ann rocked back and forth between her feet, careful not to look in Jenny's direction. She paid special attention to the rest of the room, noticing that two of the curtains were pulled shut, presumably housing patients in them. The other two makeshift "rooms" were open with the curtains tied back. Another Medical Team member was in one of the rooms, wiping down all the furniture with a disinfectant wipe and restocking the shelves.

Mr. Thorpe appeared with a clipboard, which he handed to Beth Ann and asked for her signature. It was a handmade appointment form, showing that she was diagnosed with "cheilitis" and was prescribed a lip balm with spf. Beth Ann looked at Mr. Thorpe with an unspoken question appearing between two raised eyebrows. "Fancy medical term for chapped lips," he responded. She signed the paper and handed the clipboard back, which he traded for the lip balm. She dropped it into one of her apron pockets.

"Thank you, Mr Thorpe. I'm...sorry about the whole 'inventory' thing. I didn't mean to cause any trouble, honestly," Beth Ann said.

"Yes, I'm sorry, too. It's just that I cannot trust anyone these days, even the most innocent looking ones!" He left her standing at the front window, waiting for Meghan.

"So, I get an escort home tonight? To what do I owe the pleasure?" Meghan asked with a smile as the two friends walked the short distance from the clinic to her small apartment building.

Glancing around, Beth Ann said quietly, "I think I saw Travis...waiting for me...outside your apartment."

"Travis? Are you sure?" Meghan tipped her head forward as she whispered the words, her smile replaced by a deep frown.

"Yes! I mean, I don't know...I'm not sure! I thought I saw someone, but I couldn't tell who." Beth Ann looked sideways at Meghan. "I was scared...and I panicked. The only thing I could think of was to find you!"

"Okay, well, let's be on the lookout," Meghan said as she linked her arm protectively around Beth Ann's.

When they reached Meghan's cross street, they stopped briefly at the wash-water tub to scrub their arms and faces. Every day of the week, the Water Team delivered large tubs of water to two designated spots in town. It had some kind of detergent added to it and its purpose was primarily for washing hands and clothes as needed, making it gray and disgusting by the next day. When the Water Team replaced the tub with freshly treated river water, they would haul the old one away to the Greenhouse Team for watering plants. They even claimed that the detergent helped keep insect pests away from the plants.

Shaking the water off as they finished, Beth Ann casually said, "I saw someone pass a folded note to Jenny tonight...like a secret message. I—"

"Shhhh!" Meghan practically shouted. Pulling Beth Ann along by the arm, she whispered, "We can't talk about this out in the open!"

In less than two minutes the friends reached Meghan's apartment without incident. Dillon wasn't there yet, as the Security Team's duties took full advantage of the longer daylight hours. Beth Ann collapsed onto the couch, and Meghan perched on the arm beside her. In hushed tones she confirmed that notes were the primary means of communication for the underground movement. Jenny was the only medical receptionist in on it, so if someone else was working the front desk, the messenger would make up an excuse for stopping by. There were also several out-of-the-way places that messages could be hidden, but Meghan didn't know where.

Beth Ann debated whether or not to say something about taking the note, but decided not to get Meghan involved. She could just find a way to give it back to Zachary tomorrow and apologize. For now, it was time to change the subject. "So, what am I going to do about Travis?" she groaned. "I can't live like this much longer!"

Meghan thought for a minute. "I know a few self-defense moves they taught us in nursing school. Want me to teach them to you?"

Beth Ann closed her eyes, wondering if she would have the presence of mind to remember actual "moves" for fending off an attack. But what could it hurt?

The girls worked hard for the next hour, even after the neighbor below their unit came upstairs to ask them to "knock it off." When a very surprised Dillon arrived at the apartment near curfew, they practiced on him. Completely exhausted, Beth Ann thanked Meghan and Dillon for helping her and the threesome sat for a time in comfortable silence in the dark, resting with their backs against the couch.

Without warning, Dillon pushed the girls flat onto the floor and reached for his gun lying on the coffee table in one swift motion. Surprised, Beth Ann looked up to see Dillon's mil-spec AR pointed in the direction of the apartment door; she had not heard a thing. He silently motioned for the girls to get behind the couch. Huddled together, wondering what was happening, they waited. They could hear Dillon creeping toward the door. After a long silence, they jumped and stifled their own screams when Dillon spoke sternly. "State your business!"

"Don't shoot!" a muffled voice said, and the apartment door slowly began to swing open.

"You better give me a reason not to!" Dillon snarled. Beth Ann and Meghan waited in the quiet seconds that followed, sure that their pounding hearts could be heard by the intruder.

Suddenly there was a commotion, a clunk-slide of something hitting the hardwood floor, and a gasp. "Why are you here?" Dillon's voice said, low and menacing. "This is your only chance to give me an answer!"

Though garbled and strained, the voice that answered was definitely female. "Ask...Beth Ann! She knows...why I'm here...," it said.

Startled, Beth Ann peeked over the back of the couch. Dillon was holding a young woman firmly in front of him, one arm pinning her hands behind her and the other arm wrapped tightly around her neck. A large handgun lay on the floor several feet away. Jenny had come for the secret note.

Gary wished for a TV remote, his recliner, and a beer in the cup holder as he stopped to stretch and rub out the spasm in his lower back. The terrain was difficult enough for a two-hour hike, but he and his Team had been walking roughly eight hours every day for nearly a month, spread out as they were now about fifty yards apart each. They weren't following the nice designated paths that the Forest Service had created for visitors; instead they fought thick growth, steep inclines, rocky outcrops, wetlands and limited sightlines. The taxing physical activity in combination with his age, sleeping on the damp ground, humid weather, and taking turns on night watch was all adding up to be a recipe for pain. Though no one complained, Gary could tell that Bob and Chuck were suffering, too.

Gary bent forward, reaching for his toes, and tried to relax. Impossible. "Relax" is what he might have done on a vacation with Linda, not on a spying mission with his life in danger. He forced himself to keep going so that he wouldn't get too far behind. He caught a glimpse of Alex hopping off a short ledge a good distance away to his left. Alex noticed Gary looking in his direction and flashed him an encouraging "thumbs up." Gary smiled to himself and shook his head. That Alex was an incurable optimist. Maybe he was happy because they would reach Tionesta that night, or at the latest the next morning. The happy thought was certainly enough to keep Gary moving forward.

Holding onto sapling trunks as he slid down the next slope, Gary's eyes scoped the area diligently but saw nothing out of the ordinary. The Hunting Team had been instructed to look for any signs of life–human or animal, any useful implements or tools, and potential food resources that could be re-planted near town. They were also taught how to find signs that prior fighting had taken place and how to tell if a large group of people–presumably "bad guys"– had been in the area previously.

Gary's eyes and legs may have been busy, but his mind kept going back to the little piece of paper pinned to the inside of his skivvies:

Do you know Mr. Lewis?

Yes, I know Clive well.

How is he doing?

He is living each endless day in grief.

It was a mystery to him; it held no meaning at all that he could tell. He had never known a person named "Clive Lewis" in town. Joe had made it sound so important when he handed it to Gary, but there had not yet been one chance for them to be alone so that Gary could get a good explanation.

The green fabric that the disgruntled farmer had found on his property was a mystery, too. Gary had asked Mad Max and Joe about it, but they both denied having been near the state highway except the one place they had crossed it, much farther south. As proof, they both presented dirty, but fully intact, sashes. Still Gary was sure that the piece had been from a Security Team member's sash.... He shook his head even now while he was thinking back on it.

The morning after Joe and Max had arrived in camp, they recounted their visit to the barn. They had spent the better part of the night hours lying on their stomachs, taking turns with the night vision. A small group of people appeared to live there: four or five men with at least one woman and at least one child. They did not look well. The men took shifts keeping watch during the night, carrying hunting rifles. It was definitely not a group of violent raiders planning attacks on surrounding towns. Their night was uneventful and they had snuck away after dawn, slept for a couple of daylight hours and then hustled to catch up with the Hunting Team.

Gary reached a span of more even terrain and glanced to his right to see if he could spot the young Deputy Joe, but there was no sign of him. He pushed himself forward, thinking he must be farther behind than he realized. He huffed and puffed up the next hill, the thought of being *home* giving him an extra burst of energy. As he reached the crest, he could hear water. Not just a trickle like the creeks they had been stepping over, but a refreshing rush of water. Looking around he quickly spotted the source: a short waterfall emptying into a wide stream with a decent current.

Suddenly, a commotion behind Gary caused him to turn around, drawing his rifle into place at the same time. Joe was hunched over like a linebacker, running straight toward Gary at full speed.

"What the...!" Gary didn't have time to finish the exclamation or even to process what was happening. Joe tackled him at the same time the gunshots rang out. They rolled down the hill together, hitting rocks and trees all the way down. Gary felt like his body was being pulverized, yet through the pain he was vaguely aware that the gunfire continued, and it seemed to come from all sides. *Battle rifles*, he noted vaguely. *An ambush!*

He rolled to a stop next to the rushing water. Disoriented and groaning, he tried to push himself up so he could find cover. His arm gave out as a shooting pain radiated up into his shoulder; blood trickled into the dirt. Gary didn't realize he had been shot. Boots suddenly appeared, and Joe stood over him with his handgun pointed at Gary's head.

"Play dead!" Joe whispered fast. "They're waiting for you downstream! Remember the password!" Then Joe shot the ground next to Gary's head. The shotgun blast deafened him instantly, followed by an intense, painful high-pitched ringing. Dirt and pebbles flung up like shrapnel, embedding into Gary's face and eye. Pretending to kick the older man, Joe lifted Gary's right hip with his boot, rolling him into the stream's flow. He shot three more times into the water as he backed into the trees.

Play dead, Gary told himself, fighting the instinct to flail and try to get his footing in the rushing stream; he surrendered to the current, holding his breath, not knowing where it would take him. With his ears below water level, he no longer heard gunshots, or much of anything for that matter...just the infernal ringing. *Who's "they"? And password for what?* The ambush had happened so fast, he didn't have time to pray. Now, in a dead man's float and bleeding into the river, he prayed. His last breath was literally in God's hands.

Chapter 22

Every day Beth Ann worked hard at preparing a garden in her parents' front yard, inside the little white fence that represented life as it used to be. The work felt good, even though the soreness never went away. The bugs bugged her, but not as much as they would have annoyed her former self. The birds sang her through the hours and lifted her melancholy for a short while. The earthy scent of the overturned soil filled her nostrils with life and hope. At the end of a tiring day, she could lean on her hoe or rake and see what she had accomplished. It was very satisfying...and it helped keep her mind off darker things.

So far the neighbors hadn't bothered her. She tried to plan it so that someone from the Team was always with her: one day she needed help hauling the fertilizer and manure out to the site; another day she asked for help hauling water (she didn't find it necessary to tell them she had a rainwater collection system and plenty of water stored). She pushed Mr. Eckley until he finally agreed that it was safer for his Team Members to work off-site in pairs.

Soon the garden was ready for planting. Well into the month of May now, they could plant some of the more established and hardy plants, like beets, broccoli, carrots and peas. Until Memorial Day there could still be frost, but these varieties had the best chance of surviving. Also, these vegetables could produce a second harvest if the weather cooperated and if the soil was fertile enough. Mary Lou had explained that not everything would grow successfully in a freshly tilled grass plot, at first.

On planting day, Mary Jo worked with Beth Ann to load the chosen plants on the lawn cart and haul them to the Dalton house. It was unusually warm and humid for this time of year in Tionesta. The two women took water breaks often, standing in the shade at the property line where it felt ten degrees cooler. Even with the frequent stops, they worked efficiently–dig a hole, drop the plant in, build up a dirt mound, water; move eight inches to the left and repeat...over and over. They were happy with their progress when it was time to stop for the midday meal.

Walking back to town as quickly as Mary Jo's arthritic knees would let her, they chit-chatted about little things–what they missed about the "old" life, what comforts they wished they still had, who had died, how the town had changed...how people had changed. Beth Ann was building up the courage to confide in Mary Jo about Travis's attacks when the clanging of the church bell caught their attention. Mr. Andrews was calling an unscheduled town meeting.

"Oh, no!" Beth Ann cried, grabbing ahold of Mary Jo's arm.

Mary Jo patted her hand and tried to hush her. "It's okay, hon. It's okay!"

"No! No, it's not! I can feel it...something bad!" Beth Ann did indeed feel a dread that sank into her feet, weighing down every step.

"Well, I don't like to borrow trouble. Let's wait and see what happens," Mary Jo said, breathing heavily as she walked.

The two women weren't very far from the town center when the bell had been rung, but to Beth Ann it seemed that it took days to get to the meeting spot. She fought the urge to run ahead, but she knew she shouldn't leave Mary Jo alone. Everyone else, because they were coming from a shorter distance, had arrived sooner and the announcement was nearly finished when Beth Ann arrived.

"...and we will let you know more details as they come to light," Mr. Andrews was saying. "There is no need to panic. The perimeter will be strictly enforced and the deputies will be doubled at the roadblocks. Every possible suspicious sign of intruders will need to be brought immediately to my or Sheriff Branson's attention! I will not rest until we find and eliminate these violent attackers!"

Beth Ann looked around, wishing she hadn't missed the beginning of Andrews' speech. *What attackers? What had happened?* But the crowd today was unusually still and quiet, not giving her any clues to overhear.

Mr. Andrews switched on his gameshow host face then and softened his tone. "Now, please line up in orderly fashion for your meal. It may take a few extra minutes since you aren't arriving in staggered groups today. Your patience is greatly appreciated!" He half-bowed and strode with Branson straight into the town hall while the deputies corralled the dazed people.

"Beth Ann!"

Looking around for the voice that had called her name, she spotted Meghan working against the flow of the crowd to get to her. "Beth Ann! God help us–I'm so, so sorry!" Tears welled in her eyes and her cheeks were splotchy red. She enfolded Beth Ann into her arms in a deep hug.

"Meghan! What happened? I missed the announcement!" Beth Ann said, confused. She could feel the dread rising out of her feet as it transformed into hot panic which rose up, up through her throat and into her head, pressing against her skull to be released.

Meghan held both of Beth Ann's shoulders with her hands and bent her face close to Beth Ann's. "The North-South Mission was...ambushed. Several men were shot...and Gary.... Oh, Beth Ann, I'm sorry. Gary didn't make it."

Surprisingly, the hot panicky feeling vanished, and Beth Ann felt hollow...empty...emotionless. As if she was floating. Gazing at Meghan's tear-streaked face, she was suddenly eight years old again at the fair. It was dark, she was alone, and the voice was coming for her.

She was no longer floating; she was falling…free falling. She had to escape.

Beth Ann turned from Meghan and ran for her life.

Travis had all the time in the world. He didn't know where that little brat had been hiding for the last several weeks, but she had done a darn good job of not being alone. Today she would play right into his hands. He smiled. After the big announcement in town, she would naturally gravitate to her home, like a child would.

High-and-mighty "King" Andrews sometimes let Travis play with his little trapped mice, but they were defeated, limp, utterly lifeless. There was something invigorating about conquering a person who was free. He was the hunter and she was the prey, and the wild fear that filled her eyes would spur him on. There had been other girls, but they hadn't fought back as much…so what was the fun of that?

He paced the Dalton's living room in anticipation, occasionally glancing out the large picture window, being careful not to move the sheers. His excitement was building and his release would not take nearly long enough. A flash of movement caught his attention and he watched Beth Ann, running at top speed, pass her own house…and the next house…and run straight into the woods of a vacant lot. Where the hell was she going? He was too close to lose his chance; he would not let her escape this time.

Blazing through the trees and past the blur of Linda's grave, Beth Ann did not stop running until she reached the back door of Gary's house. She slammed the door shut and leaned against it, doubling over and heaving bile onto the floor. Sobbing and hyperventilating simultaneously, she could only breathe in gulps. Her legs shuddered and threatened to collapse under her. The ache in her lungs, like a vice grip, grew tighter and she tried to stand upright to see if it would ease the pain even a little.

"No…NO!" she cried out between gulps. "How could you let this happen?" Her eyes burned as she accused the air, the universe, Gary himself, and especially God, for the death of her only hope of safety.

Leaning against the counter for support, Beth Ann moved weakly forward toward the basement stairway. She needed to hold Romeo. Her poor dog, who loved her and trusted her, would mourn with her. For all intents and purposes, they could mourn their own impending deaths while they were at it. No one else would be there to mourn their passing.

She had only taken a few steps when she heard the door's telltale squeak behind her. In the single slow-motion second that it took Beth Ann to turn around, she had two distinct thoughts. The first was a flash of hope that somehow Gary had survived and found his way home. Snuffing out the joy of that thought was the second one—an unspeakably dark one–that Travis had somehow found her.

With no reaction time, Beth Ann sensed more than saw the blur of the fist. It connected with a *crack* and she fell to the floor, blinded by the explosion in her left eye. She lay where she fell, the despair too heavy to fight against. She surrendered, overcome not only by waves of pain but of sheer hopelessness. *So many ways to die*, she thought. She had never really thought about it before.

Travis didn't move from his spot, but even with her eyes closed Beth Ann could feel his presence. "GET UP!" he shouted at her in his raspy, time-hardened voice.

She didn't move.

Silence. Unbearable silence. She braced herself, waiting for him to make contact with her limp body.

Instead, he laughed. It started low, almost a growl in the back of his throat. And it grew into a maniacal version of dominance. "Look at you, little princess! You've been hiding from me…." The laughter came closer, but still Beth Ann kept her eyes closed and laid still. "Sorry. Game over." The whole side of her face throbbed with heat, and the arm she fell on sent radiating pain through her shoulder and back. No matter what moves Meghan had taught her, she couldn't fight Travis.

She could sense that he was standing over her now. She flinched when the first boot hit the floor, but not the second boot. When she heard him unbuckling his belt, she started to dry heave.

"Oh, ho! She is alive!" Travis declared out loud to himself, with delight.

Beth Ann shuddered. Travis was the embodiment of the voice from the fair, and the sum of everything she had ever been afraid of.

Instinct kicked in and she fought back, which only seemed to spur him on. Just as she reached the point of exhaustion, Beth Ann felt him suddenly stop. She could barely make out Romeo standing behind Travis, hair bristled, ears flat, and teeth bared. Romeo growled deeply, like a trained police dog. Beth Ann had never heard him make any kind of noise like that...ever. He snapped his teeth and growled again. *How did he get up here?* she wondered. He had not been able to climb the steps for two months.

"A dog?" Travis questioned, turning his face slowly toward Beth Ann. "Tsk, tsk, tsk, bad girl!"

"Get 'im, Romeo! Get him!" Beth Ann yelled.

Romeo barked once and lunged. Travis rolled off Beth Ann and she pushed up to her feet, prepared to run for the front door. However, that only gave her a clearer view of the scene as Travis pulled his gun out of its holster and shot twice. The dog's weak body went limp in mid-air and he landed in a heap.

"No!" Beth Ann cried out, scooping Romeo into her arms. "No, no, no, no, no! Romeo? Romeo!" She snuggled his warm, furry face into the curve of her neck and willed him to live. The hyperventilating sobs started again and she whispered, "You're a good boy. Good boy." He whimpered once and was gone with a shallow sigh. "Good boy...don't leave...please don't...."

"It's against the law to have pets, Beth Ann. I did you a favor. You're lucky I don't report you to Mr. Andrews." Travis sauntered toward her, his gun dangling at his side.

Beth Ann inched backwards toward the front door, holding Romeo's body close to her chest. "You're…you're a…MONSTER!" she spat.

The playful look in his eyes went away, replaced by ice. Travis slowly lifted the gun and aimed it at Beth Ann's face. She glared back at him. If he shot her, all her suffering would end, just like Romeo's had. It would be better than living in fear; better than the suffocating darkness; better than running every minute of every day.

"Take one more step and I'll shoot," Travis warned.

"Okay, okay. Don't shoot!" Beth Ann said submissively as she stopped and let Travis close the distance between them. When he got within range, she kicked him as hard as she could. As he doubled over with a yowl, she unlocked the deadbolt and flung open the door. But she wasn't fast enough.

"Enough! You're gonna wish you hadn't made me MAD!"

Chapter 23

The shovel moved mechanically, automatically–*slice, push, lift...slice, push, lift.* The rhythm of moving dirt sounded loud in the still night air, but Beth Ann didn't care who heard it. The crescent moon gave just enough light to do the job and no more, but for once Beth Ann didn't think about the darkness surrounding her. Her body shuddered with every movement, but she pushed through the pain. She had only one option left: make it to her brother's farm, or die trying.

As she dug a final resting place for Romeo beside Linda, her mind stayed busy, too. The hours after the rape were fuzzy for Beth Ann. She had lain on the floor in a fetal position for the rest of the day, wishing to die. Whether she slept or passed out, she eventually awoke to realize it was dark outside. From out of nowhere, she felt a completely senseless desire to fight for life and an unexplainable urge to find her brother. Somehow she was able to sit, and then to stand. As a plan took shape in her mind, her stamina and willpower increased.

Apparently this time Travis hadn't felt it necessary to leave the consolation MREs, so she would have to check the furnace in the forest. The four meals there–if they were still there–should give her enough energy to walk to her brother's farm. The trick would be carrying enough water because of the weight it would add to her backpack.

Slice, push, lift. Beth Ann dropped the shovel and eased herself down onto her knees to reach her arm into the hole. It was almost the depth of her arm and it would have to do; she simply couldn't dig any more. Wearily, she pulled the stiffened body toward the opening and lowered him down, clumsily at best. Romeo didn't quite fit the shape of the hole, so she rotated him several times, grunting with effort at the awkward angle and nearly falling headfirst into the grave. When she was satisfied with the placement, she sat back on her heels and rested, wondering if she should say a prayer...or something. She simply did not feel like praying, and since she was all alone and Romeo couldn't hear her anymore, she opted to just finish and get her long journey started.

Dirt replaced and packed down as much as possible, Beth Ann made a cross out of sticks and marked the grave. Back inside the house, she packed her backpack with only the most necessary items and added extra water from their homemade stash. Unfortunately, the little bit of food Gary had hidden under the shrubs was long gone. She put on a holster to carry her gun and decided to take the shovel as both a walking stick and weapon. The small battery-operated travel clock on the basement table blinked 2:34 a.m. when she was finally ready to leave the house. She pulled paper and pen out of the basket to leave a note, but realized with finality that Gary would not be coming home. No one needed to know that she was leaving, or where she was going. She was completely on her own now.

Her hand lingered on the doorknob as she closed it for the final time. Could she do it? Could she let go of something solid and head into the darkness, the unknown? She closed her eyes, drew a deep breath, and stepped away from the house. Yes, partly because she had to and partly because she was *determined* to. It was past time to stand on her own two feet.

She went as cautiously as possible, skirting the wooded edge of her neighborhood. She knew the way to the furnace well and felt confident that she could find her way in the dark, especially with the sliver of moonlight. At the town meeting, which now seemed like a long time ago instead of yesterday, Mr. Andrews had said that they were tightening the perimeter security, so she took extra caution to be quiet, as her street was closest to the roadblock. Several times she stopped, thinking that she had heard a snapping twig or a moving branch. But when nothing came out of it, she brushed it off as overactive nerves.

After nearly two hours of painstaking stealth, Beth Ann finally saw the angular outline of the furnace tip against the night sky. With a mixture of relief and apprehension, she stooped under the low lintel and immediately tripped over something. Catching herself against the mossy interior stone wall, she gasped and brushed the spider webs out of her hair. She turned around quickly, wondering what she had tripped over. A waft of noxious odor hinted at decay. Normally taboo because of the danger light posed now, she pulled her flashlight out of the side pocket of her backpack and flicked it on.

Beth Ann crammed half of her fist into her mouth to keep herself from screaming. It was a body...a human body. Still clothed, but obviously having been there for several weeks, there was very little flesh left on the blackened remains. Beetles and other insects were still busily feasting, unphased by Beth Ann's light beam. The woman must have fallen through the opposite doorway, with her head and shoulders exposed outside the furnace. Telltale stains on the victim's t-shirt indicated that she had taken two bullets to the chest.

Fighting the urge to run, Beth Ann shone the light around the inside of the little space. The tub was gone, and along with it her only hope of food. A flash of something shiny caught her eye. Looking closer, she saw that it was an MRE wrapper, reflecting her light. With a heavy heart she concluded that her neighbors must have not only found her stash in the furnace after they confronted her, but they must have fought over it.

Beth Ann turned off the flashlight and hurried out of the furnace. It was essential that she put more space between herself and town before dawn. Unfortunately, she only knew the way to her brother's place by road, but now the roads weren't safe. She would have to find the road first, then follow it while staying hidden. Heading southeast, she whispered a belated thanks to her dad for teaching her how to read a compass. The sudden rush of memories, fishing and hiking with her parents, made her want to sit and cry, but she knew that she had to keep going. No one was coming to save her.

The tree canopy obscured most of the subtle moonlight, and given the fact that Beth Ann wasn't familiar with this area, progress was slow. Just as the eastern sky began to blush, she came to a two-lane road with painted lines. This was not the road she needed to follow; she had to cross it. Holding her breath, she hunched over and ran across the opening into the treeline. Finding a large tree and leaning against it to rest and get another drink of water, she listened. All was quiet, except for a couple of birds that had risen early to welcome the dawn. She found the sound comforting, like she had company with her now.

Time moved slowly and her feet carried her forward, the shovel helping to hold her up. The weakness and foggy brain only motivated her to push harder. If she gave up, she might as well choose a spot and dig her own grave; no one would ever find her. Her entire body hurt, and one eye and cheek were swollen with bruises. But somehow, in the daylight, her troubles didn't seem quite as dire as they felt in the darkness. And she felt something new: empowerment.

By late afternoon, she was borderline delirious. Her mind and thoughts didn't seem to be inside of her body any longer. She didn't feel any pain or hunger, just exhaustion. More than anything she wanted to lie down...but the shovel forced her to stay upright. Lying down meant never getting back up. She agreed with the shovel, but still she argued with it.

Suddenly, she stumbled on gravel and realized it was the long lane that led to Christopher's house. It gave her a surge of energy. Had she really done it? Found her way through the dark and wilderness, without food or guide, to safety? She veered off the lane to stay hidden, even though she knew she would come to a large clearing before she reached the house. Out of nowhere, dark thoughts barraged her. What if something had happened to her brother and his wife? What if the house was abandoned and there were no provisions to sustain her? She began to move faster, as if Death itself was pursuing her.

"Freeze!" a deep male voice said. It was definitely not her brother's.

With a yelp, Beth Ann froze. Not just her body, but her heart, her lungs, blood circulation, cell division, electrical synapses—everything stopped.

"This is private property. You will need to turn back now and follow the road away from here, ma'am." The voice was rich like chocolate, but stern like carob.

Beth Ann came out of her shock into a state of confusion and fear. She squeezed her eyes shut, hoping it would force her brain to work. She dropped the shovel and slowly lifted her hands into the air. Now, if she could just make her mouth move. "I...I'm...sorry.... My...brother.... Need to...brother!" she finally managed to say. But she didn't know if she actually said the words out loud or if she just thought them. She opened her eyes slowly to see a soldier standing not far from her...cradling the largest gun she had ever seen.

Oh well, she thought as her strength gave out and her breath followed it; *I tried my best*. She crumbled to the ground, thankful for the comforting arms of darkness.

"Shhhh!" Mike said as he thrust his arm in front of Tony, the sloppy Deputy with him. Tony stopped and hunkered down beside

Mike, looking quizzically at the large, intimidating ex-bouncer who worked for Mr. Andrews. Mike pointed first to his ear, and then in front of them. Looking around, he motioned for Tony to crouch behind a large rotting stump, while Mike backed into a low spot and lay down on his stomach. They readied their rifles, but just waited and listened.

The two men heard a sound like a muffled voice followed by a staticky response. Mike was puzzled; in a different time, he would have thought he was hearing a hand-held radio. There was a long period of silence in which Mike got plenty of amusement watching Tony, the only person in town who still carried an ample girth, change his kneeling leg several times. But just when Mike thought they should move on, a conversation started in the woods ahead of them. Mike and Tony couldn't see anyone, but it sounded like two men. They were speaking so quietly that Mike could only understand bits and pieces.

"...wandered here..."

"...find out who..."

"...medical attention..."

The voices began to fade and Mike stood to follow them, motioning for Tony to stay put. The man nodded and stayed like a puppy waiting for a treat. Mike sighed. Tony Salino was a nice guy, but he wasn't as well-endowed in intelligence as he was in muscles. He didn't need Tony getting them both killed.

Just before dawn, while Mike was covering a walking perimeter shift, he had heard movement and followed it. He had been shocked to see a young woman, all alone, dart across the state road leading out of town. He had quickly checked in at the roadblock, a solid mile to the north, and Sheriff Branson had reassigned Tony, an extra roadblock Deputy, to go with him. His order was to follow the lady, since it could be more important to find out where she was going than simply to catch her and punish her for breaking Andrews' ordinance.

Using the trees as cover, Mike advanced just far enough to see the backs of two men. The one wearing long camouflage shorts and a solid t-shirt with heavy hiking boots was tall and carrying a flat Dark Earth colored AR. He was headed deeper into the woods to Mike's left. The other man was much shorter, but even from behind he looked dangerous. He was dressed in full military-looking camouflage fatigues and black boots with a bolt rifle secured across his back in a scabbard. He was walking down the gravel lane carrying the young lady Mike and Tony had been trailing all day. Judging by her position and the way one arm dangled freely, she was either dead or passed out. Mike recognized that both men carried themselves with a confidence that comes with training and experience.

Squinting, Mike watched the men disappear in different directions while he weighed his options. These men did not appear to be part of a simple farm family waiting out the storm. He sensed that it was a bigger operation and his curiosity urged him to get closer and see what he could find out. However, he was smart enough to know that a fully-trained survivalist camp would have tight security at the perimeter and he wouldn't stand a chance at getting very close. Yet they didn't act like looters, unless they were going to just take the girl and keep her for...entertainment. He shook his head as he quietly made his way back to Tony. He just wanted to get the heck out of there and take this one to Mr. Andrews to handle.

Beth Ann felt like she was floating, but the peace that came along with the sensation was a miracle. It was like swimming...or flying...and yet at the same time, nothing like either one. There was no effort on her part, just "being." She wanted to stay there forever, wherever "there" was. She hadn't felt so calm and relaxed since...since....

A rush of overlapping images suddenly flashed through her mind: saying goodbye to her parents, the electricity going out at the restaurant, moving into the Howard's basement, her neighbor hanging by a rope, burying Linda, Kristen's empty eyes, Meghan, Mr. Andrews, Gary, Travis, Romeo….

The peaceful feeling evaporated, replaced by a free-fall into despair. She moved her head from side to side, trying to make the images stop, trying to escape, but it felt like she was buried in mud. Why wouldn't her arms and legs move? Why couldn't she see anything? Why was she always lost in the dark?

Beth Ann began to hear voices, several different voices that seemed far away at first. They spoke in frantic tones, but she couldn't understand what they were saying. Her heart started to beat faster—she wasn't alone. Was that good…or bad?

Someone touched her hand and she tried to scream, but it got stuck in her dry throat. She felt the person pick up her hand and stroke it gently. Gradually she understood the voice. It was saying over and over, "Shhhh, honey. It's okay. You're okay. Shhhh, relax…." It was a soothing voice, like her mom's.

"M-o-m?" Beth Ann was surprised to hear her own voice, even though it came out like a croak.

"I think she's waking up! Hey! Get Darren!" the voice said, and it seemed very loud in Beth Ann's ear. She cringed, evidence that she was getting control of her body back.

Prying open her eyelids was hard work, but she finally did it. She was in a stranger's living room, lying on an old couch. The room was disheveled and there was something wrong with the walls—a haphazard pattern of marks…holes, maybe? One window was boarded up and the room was dim. On a round side table sat an oil lamp, but it wasn't lit. There were two women and a man on the other side of the room in deep discussion. Beth Ann blinked and tried to focus through her blurry gaze as she continued to scan the room. In one corner, beside an old floor-model television, sat a bag that caught her attention: it was her backpack lying beside her shovel and her gun.

Beth Ann felt a cool hand on her forehead and shifted her gaze to a woman older than her mother sitting in a chair beside her. As soon as their eyes met, the woman took Beth Ann's hand in hers again and leaned forward.

"Hi, honey. I'm Kathy. What's your name?" she asked in a soft voice.

The voice was pleasant and her eyes had that look of crinkled kindness with deep laugh lines. But Beth Ann hesitated. She had no idea where she was or how she got there.

"It's alright, dear. My husband is a doctor. We can help you...don't be afraid!" the woman said soothingly.

"Water?" Beth Ann requested with another croak.

Kathy helped prop Beth Ann into an inclined position and raised a small canteen to her lips. The water wasn't cold, but it was very refreshing. An older man entered the room with a bowl in his hands. The woman introduced him: "This is Darren, Dr. Sorenson, my husband."

Dr. Sorenson smiled at Beth Ann and handed the bowl to his wife. Taking Beth Ann's wrist, he took her pulse and listened to her heart with his stethoscope. "Hi there, young lady," the doctor said in a voice as soothing as his wife's, just deeper. "You gave us a little bit of a scare. We would all love to know who you are and how you came to be here."

Beth Ann opened her mouth to speak, but Darren held up his hand. "Not now. First, you drink this broth and if you need to sleep, you sleep. When you get some of your strength back, we'll talk, okay? And I suspect we need to do a full examination."

Two men approached the couch aggressively. Beth Ann shrank back, but couldn't take her eyes off of them. It was the soldier who had found her and another soldier, enormously tall and featuring a full mountain-man's beard. "Were you travelling with anyone?" the tall soldier demanded. "Are you alone?"

"Not now, Sean. She needs to rest," the doctor said firmly.

The soldier gave him a sharp look and then turned back to Beth Ann, crouching down to her level and softening his voice. "Are you travelling alone, ma'am? If you have people looking for you, see, someone could get hurt. We wouldn't want there to be a misunderstanding with one of your friends, now would we?"

She slowly shook her head, but the man didn't seem to understand.

"Please say 'yes' or 'no'—"

"Sean!" The doctor protested sharply, but the man calmly held his index finger up to the doctor without taking his eyes off Beth Ann's.

He spoke slower, gentler. "Was there anyone else with you? I need you to tell me that first, so no one gets hurt." His voice was insistent. "Then you can rest."

"No," Beth Ann finally worked up the nerve to speak. Her voice was still raspy. "I...I'm alone." She clenched her jaw to quell the threatening emotions.

The tall man stared at her with a frightening intensity for several seconds, then abruptly stood and turned to the shorter soldier. "Do you think she's lying?"

The man rubbed his chin for a moment. "I don't know, Sean. Caleb did a sweep and didn't find anyone. But he found large impressions, like a man's boots." They both stared down at her.

A third man came up behind them. He was handsome, with long hair that looked freshly washed and combed, and dressed in civilian clothes. "Double the watch for now, till we can get more information."

Beth Ann sat frozen, unable to tear her eyes away from the three men towering over her, arms crossed, studying her like a germ...or a prisoner. The doctor patted her hand gently while he sternly banished the men to the other side of the room.

She closed her eyes in relief but could still hear them talking, an anxious tone in their voices.

"That's a good idea, Damian. I'll stay here; maybe I can get some more information out of her once she's eaten and rested."

"After dark, I'll take the NVGs and do a sweep of our perimeter...." Their voices trailed off as they left the room.

When she opened her eyes, Kathy was beside her again with the bowl of chicken broth. It smelled so delicious that Beth Ann instantly felt ravenous. Everyone in the room was lucky that the liquid was hot, otherwise she would have embarrassed them all by guzzling it as if she had been raised by wolves. When she finished every last drop, she closed her eyes and drifted in and out of restless sleep. Meanwhile, Kathy fussed with the pillows and offered her more water and generally hovered close by. At some point, Kathy had pulled down dark blinds and lit the small oil lamp.

Dr. Darren was right; she felt much better after finishing the broth and resting. And now she needed to leave so she could finish her journey. She must be close to her brother's farm. These people didn't need to know anything about her; they could be spies for Mr. Andrews for all she knew. Sitting up, she set her feet on the floor and tested them with a little weight. They felt wobbly, but they would hold her. Kathy caught hold of her arm and forced her back onto the couch.

"Lie down, honey. You're not going anywhere," she said in that deceptively sweet voice.

Panic began to rise in Beth Ann's chest. So she was a prisoner or a hostage or something. She should not have trusted these strangers. What if they had poisoned her? No one else ate the broth! Why was she so weak and stupid? Forcing herself to calm down, she looked for her gun; it was still lying beside her backpack.

Beth Ann did her best to smile at her grandmotherly guard and asked, "Might I have some more water, please?" She held the empty canteen out to Kathy.

"Oh, of course! Now you get comfortable and I'll be right back." The woman seemed genuinely happy to have a patient. *What an actress*, Beth Ann thought.

As soon as she left the room, Beth Ann leapt off the couch and tried to run for her gun, bag and shovel: it was all she had left in the world. If her legs would cooperate, she might have a fighting chance to get out the front door. The soldier might be waiting for her outside, but at least she had to try. She had come this far; she would not quit. Unfortunately, her legs weren't up to running yet and she tumbled to the floor just as Kathy rounded the corner with the refilled canteen.

"Darren! Come quick!" she yelled, her eyes wide. Beth Ann crawled as fast as she could; this would be her only chance. Darren and the other people she had seen earlier came rushing in and intercepted her. While she kicked and bit and screamed, it took all five people to awkwardly manage carrying her back to the couch. They held her arms and legs while she thrashed, all talking at once.

"Enough!" Darren commanded in a loud voice. Everyone stopped moving and yelling, even Beth Ann. Darren bent his head over hers, breathing heavily from the exertion, and said, "Young lady! I know you must be scared out of your mind, but you can trust us. If we let go, will you sit calmly and talk with us?"

Beth Ann looked with her wild eyes at each face above her. They looked scared, too. She looked around for the soldiers who had questioned her earlier. Not seeing them, she took a deep breath and nodded. The others slowly let go and backed a few feet away, and Darren sat down in the chair.

"Please," she started, her voice quavering, "I don't know where I am or who you are, but if you let me go, I promise I won't cause any trouble and I won't tell anyone about you." She blinked rapidly as the tears threatened to flow and her chest burned.

"Where did you come from?" Darren asked.

Beth Ann hesitated again, not knowing how much she should divulge. "Tionesta."

"You walked here from town? And you came all alone?" Darren asked, still confused.

Beth Ann nodded. "Please," she begged again, "I really need to go."

Darren twisted in his chair to look at the others, pointing at them as he introduced them. "You've met my wife, Kathy, and me. This is Peter Gabnor and his wife, Helen, the owners of this farm where you are right now. And this is Maria. She's...," he hesitated as Maria's eyebrows lifted and she barely shook her head, "...a neighbor." He turned back to look at Beth Ann. "If you tell us your name, we won't be strangers anymore."

She looked at the doctor and his wife, at the elderly farmer Peter with his arm protectively around his petite and fragile wife, and finally at Maria who was very, very pregnant and held her gaze with compassion. "I'm Beth Ann," she offered quietly.

"You're not our prisoner, Beth Ann, but you must understand that it's not safe to let you just take off in the dark by yourself. I would never forgive myself. You can spend the night here and we can make a plan in the morning. Where are you headed that's so urgent?"

"To my brother's farm. I need to find him. He...he's all I have left!" Beth Ann drew her knees in and wrapped her arms around them, burying her face like she used to when she was a little girl. Her shoulders shook as she cried–she had lived three lifetimes since yesterday and she was completely worn out.

Just then a rhythmic knock on the side door made everyone jump. Helen rushed to the door with her little shuffling steps and answered with a knocking code of her own. Its reply must have satisfied her because she opened the door.

A man's voice spoke. "Hey, Mrs. Gabnor. Sorry to barge in on you so late. Sean asked me to come over and get—"

"Chris? Christopher?" Beth Ann lifted her head. She would recognize that voice anywhere. "Christopher! O God, thank you! Thank God!" She got to her feet, using Darren and Kathy for support. Her brother stood completely still, eyes wide open in shock.

"Beth Ann?" he whispered. And then he rushed to her and wrapped her in his arms. "What? How did you...?" Christopher didn't even know what to ask. "Wait–*you're* the girl who fainted and made Brody carry her all the way up here?" He held her at arm's length and just looked at her as if he didn't quite believe she was there.

Darren spoke up. "THIS scrawny piece of work is the brother you're looking for?" Everyone chuckled and the tension in the room was dispelled. "Well, we have lots of questions, but why don't we all get a good night's sleep and talk tomorrow?"

They made quick plans for the next day and reviewed the overnight security shift schedule. When Beth Ann left arm in arm with her brother, she clung to him like she would never let go.

Chapter 24

The night she spent on her brother's couch was the best night's sleep Beth Ann had had in months. When she awoke, Christopher was on his security shift, so she caught up with her sister-in-law, Tanya, and helped get their active two-year-old daughter ready for a new day. She was shocked to see Tanya preparing a simple breakfast and was informed that everyone at the "retreat" was rationed for two meals every day. Sitting on the counter beside Tanya was a mug filled with a dark, steaming, fragrant liquid.

"Is that...coffee?" The sides of her tongue twinged at the very thought of the bygone luxury.

Tanya chuckled. "Sort of. One of our neighbors showed us how to make this from chicory root. You know, those plants with the little blue flowers that grow on the side of the road?" She poured some into a mug and handed it to Beth Ann. "It's not too bad...at least, it's the closest thing we have to coffee. I think our neighbors mix the chicory with a little bit of coffee to make their supply last longer, but we ran out in February. We cook the leaves, too, so we transplanted a bunch on Peter's farm."

Beth Ann gripped the mug with both hands and stared into the shimmering surface. She blew off the wisps of steam and sipped. Not coffee...but not bad for a desperate substitute. She smiled at Tanya. "Thanks!" Now her days would start better.

After they ate, Beth Ann played with little Molly while Tanya busied herself with preparations for the day. She felt safe, being with a family. The night before, on the dark walk between Butch's house and Christopher's, Beth Ann had told her brother that their parents had never returned from their trip to Florida. She told him that she had moved in with the Howards and that they were both gone now. But there was so much more to tell.

"Molly! Beth Ann! Time to go!" Tanya called, her voice clearly heard from the next room. Beth Ann wondered where they were going but held Molly's hand as she toddled toward the sound of her mother's voice, chattering all the way.

In the kitchen, Tanya was tying her shoes, a pair of old, ratty sneakers that had seen better days. She tossed a tiny ball of fabric to Beth Ann that turned out to be a pair of Molly-sized socks. Beth Ann set the little girl on the edge of the counter and fought with her wiggly feet to get the socks on.

"So, where are we going?" Beth Ann asked as Tanya took Molly to put dirt-caked lace-up shoes on her. Beth Ann sat on a kitchen chair to put on her own shoes–the only pair she'd brought with her. Then she pulled her hair up into a messy ponytail.

"Garden duty!" Tanya said. "Come on. I'll explain on the way."

The threesome stepped out onto the small front porch and into the bright sunshine. It was going to be another sweaty day. The farmhouse looked pretty much the same as when Beth Ann was there for Thanksgiving, with a few subtle differences. Two footpaths had been worn in the high grass forming a "v" through the yard from the porch steps. Tanya hadn't put out the pretty rattan furniture or filled pots with petunias and ferns. The side door was dented on the outside and bore evidence of suffering, from the hole where the deadbolt lock should be to the two window panes covered with plywood. Overall it gave off a downtrodden, weary vibe.

Tanya, carrying Molly, led them down the left-hand path that disappeared into the woods. Beth Ann was pretty sure that this was the path Christopher had brought her on the night before. On the way, Tanya informed Beth Ann that they had joined with a "retreat" just up the hill, swapping labor and their chickens for food and security. The retreat members had prepared for a long-term disaster, so they had food and supplies and manuals stored to get them, and their families, through this time. Peter's farm was included, as well as a couple of other nearby neighbors. The doctor and his wife had been brought into the mix in December, not long after the power outage, and they had moved in with Peter and Helen. Altogether, there were close to thirty people in the group, including children.

"Are they all soldiers?" Beth Ann asked, remembering her interrogation.

"I'm not sure who they are or what their background is–they're pretty secretive–but I'm positive that several of them have military training or something similar. And some of them do wear camouflage when they're out patrolling. The one who found you is Brody," Tanya explained.

"Well, he scared the crap out of me!" Beth Ann laughed nervously and changed the subject. "So, what's involved with gardening duty? I worked on the Garden Team in town, so I can definitely help with the garden here."

As Tanya explained the retreat members' joint duty on the two-acre garden plot, raised beds, grapevines and large greenhouse, they came into the clearing where Peter's house sat. In the daylight Beth Ann could see that the front of the century old farmhouse was dotted with random black spots, like the ones she had seen in the living room. Tanya saw Beth Ann's quizzical expression and explained that the retreat had been attacked several days earlier by a large group. It had been a terrifying ordeal for everyone, and one of the neighbors had been killed in the watchtower. Since then, they had changed their security strategy a bit and had been running practice drills for different scenarios. They would have to bring Beth Ann up to speed.

Beth Ann heard Tanya's words as she spoke them, but she processed the information more slowly. With fresh anxiety, she realized she had conjured up a false expectation of security, thinking that once she and Christopher were together, everything would be fine. Mr. Andrews hadn't been lying about the raiding and looting forces, apparently, and he *had* provided a safe perimeter for the Tionestans. Maybe she had misjudged him….

"Here we are. Do you want to plant, water or weed?" Tanya asked, breaking Beth Ann's mental wandering.

Beth Ann looked up. At the edge of the large clearing behind Peter's house stood the largest garden Beth Ann had ever seen; she couldn't even see the other side of it. On the edge of the garden nearest to the house stood two long rows of raised beds. The greenhouse was a short distance away, partway up the adjacent hill in a southern-exposed clearing. She counted nine people, including a couple older children, already working in various areas of the garden. A faded red barn stood nearby and on the other side of it, a fenced-in pasture. Closer to the house was a trellis covered in a gnarled, brown vine fringed with new green growth, and a line of rough posts coming off the trellis joined by rows of wire. Between the posts were new plantings; they were obviously expanding their grape crop.

Tanya picked up a hoe and took Molly by the hand. "If you have any questions, just find Peter...or Emily. You haven't met Emily yet, right?" Beth Ann shook her head. Tanya shielded her eyes with one hand to look over the garden workers, while Molly yanked on her other arm. "That's Emily, in the brown tank top. See? She and Peter are basically in charge of making sure this works. Alright, Molly! Go!" Tanya turned her attention to the little one and was dragged away.

Unsure where to start, Beth Ann stood and watched until she noticed a woman approaching with a distinctive waddle and recognized her as the "Maria" Darren had introduced. If she was a retreat member, it now made sense that Darren had hesitated, referring to her as "a neighbor."

"Morning!" Maria said with a broad smile. "You look a bit better than when I saw you last night."

"Yeah...feel better, too!" Beth Ann replied self-consciously, thinking of how ghastly her bruised face must still look. "How can I help?"

"I could use some help planting in the beds," Maria suggested. Beth Ann picked up a spade from a work cart filled with tools and followed her. They passed two other women who appeared to be only a few years older than Beth Ann. Maria stopped and introduced them as Rachel and Rose. Rose smiled and thanked Beth Ann for helping, but Rachel just nodded an acknowledgement and kept working, When Maria and Beth Ann reached their spot, Maria pointed out quietly that Rachel was the widow of the neighbor who had been killed in the attack a few days earlier; she hadn't spoken since, and Rose had been spending a lot of time with her.

Digging her hands into the sun-warmed soil, Beth Ann already felt an attachment to these people who had welcomed her with open arms, but what she really wanted was to get some time with her brother.

Brody and another retreat member, Caleb, were assigned to cart water for the garden and greenhouse, a job which required an abundance of brawn. The Allegheny River was nearly a mile away, but one of its branches cut through both Peter's property and the retreat, making it a closer and safer option for obtaining water. This being their first summer to live entirely off the land, they were hoping that the little crick didn't dry up in the heat. Unfortunately, water always cut through land at its lowest point, Brody complained to himself as he leaned his weight into the cart. No matter where they got the water, they would have to haul it uphill. Caleb grunted as the cart hit a rock in the path, jarring his shoulder.

They stopped at the garden first to fill the assorted buckets and watering cans. Distributing the water into smaller containers made it more portable for the gardeners, especially considering that many of them were children. That would use up over two-thirds of their haul, but it would significantly lighten their load to take farther uphill to the greenhouse. There they would offload the 50-gallon trash can, which had been previously bought for this purpose and never used for trash, with the remaining water and take the empty one in the dolly back down the slope for a refill. Several trips to the stream had to be made on days when it didn't rain, especially with the early unseasonably hot weather. Their very lives hinged on the garden being successful. Damian was researching ways to tap into the wells on the properties without use of the electric pumps, but for now they had to haul the water.

Setting down the last bucket, Brody caught a glimpse of Christopher's sister kneeling beside Sean's wife, Maria, in one of the raised beds, transplanting young vegetables that had been started in the greenhouse. There was something about her that made him want to know who she was and what made her "tick," maybe because she had been so vulnerable when he found her and his protective nature was kicking in. Seeing the deep purple and green marks on her face had made him want to rip someone apart limb by limb. He watched her tuck a stray piece of dark blonde hair behind her ear and wipe her forehead with the back of her hand.

"Take a picture—it lasts longer!" Caleb said quietly into Brody's ear. Then he straightened up to drink some water from his canteen, his laughter ringing out between sips.

Brody punched him in the arm, embarrassed at having been caught. But caught doing what? Curiosity wasn't a crime. He was just making sure the girl he rescued was doing okay. Wouldn't anyone?

Beth Ann was surprised when Tanya came over to her a couple of hours later, carrying her fussing daughter. "Molly's had enough for now, and so have I. Wanna take a break with us?"

"Sure, thanks," Beth Ann said gratefully as she stood. She was hot. While they had been working, the clouds had moved in and gradually thickened. Although it was temporarily a relief from the sun, the humidity had risen and made the air mighty uncomfortable. Peter's sweet wife, who was too frail to do the harder labor, had walked around to all the workers a few times with cool water to drink, but Beth Ann felt she could use a few minutes to lie down in the grass and stretch her aching back.

Beth Ann followed Tanya, but was confused when her sister-in-law sped past the house and into the woods. She jogged to catch up. "Wait! Can we just leave like that? Did you tell Peter?"

Tanya laughed. "What do you mean? We all help out, but we come and go as we please. We have other responsibilities, too."

Beth Ann didn't realize how much she had bought into the regimented, guarded system in Tionesta until she exercised the freedom to walk away from the garden when she needed a break. It blew her mind.

When they reached home, Tanya wiped Molly down, gave her a small snack and put her to bed for a nap. Then she woke Christopher and he joined the two ladies at the kitchen table. Over glasses of cool water and a handful of freeze-dried peaches, Beth Ann told Christopher everything. He and Tanya grieved over her words, but Beth Ann felt cathartic relief.

Christopher reached across the table to clasp Beth Ann's hand. "Oh, Sis. I had no idea. I'm so sorry." His eyes were full of anguish and his voice thick with emotion. "I just kept thinking that the electricity would come back on any day. By Christmas we had run out of food and I walked to town to see if I could get help. The Sheriff—some new guy—had all the roads blocked going into town and his officers wouldn't let me through, even when I told them my parents lived there! It was unbelievable. Then, on my walk back home, some ruffians jumped me, but I had nothing for them to steal so they let me go. I was stupid and hadn't even taken my little Remington."

"I remember that gun!" Beth Ann interrupted. "Dad got it for you as a graduation present, didn't he? And mom was mad because he didn't tell her." They both chuckled softly over the memory, the way people do at funerals. Tanya swiped at her eyes.

259

Beth Ann broke the long silence, her gaze piercing into her brother. "Christopher, what are the chances that mom and dad...might be...might come home?"

He lowered his eyes to their clasped hands and sighed. "I saw Sean briefly during my watch and asked him the same question." He shifted in his seat. "It's his opinion, just opinion, that they would have very little chance." Her tears began to flow down her cheeks in a steady stream, and as he patted her hand in comfort, she could feel his hands shaking. "You see, they were in a crowded tourist area that would have run out of supplies quickly. They're older, so they would be ill-prepared for a difficult journey of a thousand miles without food and proper gear. Then there are bad—"

"Yes! I get it. I understand," Beth Ann cut him off as she dried her face with her sleeve. She didn't want a picture painted in her head of all the possible ways their parents might have died.

Christopher changed the subject. "I didn't know you were all alone, Beth Ann, honestly. If I had known *half* of what was going on in town I would have found a way to get to you. I'm so grateful for the Howards taking you in like that." Christopher ran his hand through his tousled hair. "I...just can't believe they're all...gone."

They sat in silence for a few minutes. Finally, Tanya asked quietly, "Did you talk with Damian?"

"Yes, dear, it's all taken care of," Christopher said, giving his wife a disapproving look.

Beth Ann caught the subtle exchange. "Take care of what? Does this have something to do with me?" She lifted her eyebrows and leaned forward into the table.

Christopher sighed and paused before answering. "The retreat as a whole has limited supplies. We can't just take people in. The retreat members have to vote and I will have to find a way to come up with extra food for you, or re-distribute our rations to include you."

"Vote?" Beth Ann cried. "You mean they could send me back? I won't go! They can't make me! I won't eat much, I promise–we only got one meal a day in town anyhow. And I'll work double-hard! I'll dig holes for people to poop in! I don't care, but I won't—"

"Beth Ann!" Christopher raised his voice to stop her rising panic. "I said it's taken care of. You're staying with us."

Beth Ann hung her head in relief and clasped her hands to stop them from shaking. It had never crossed her mind that seeking her brother's help would cause his family a hardship. Molly fussed and Tanya left the kitchen to get her.

"We do have to introduce you to the retreat members, and they have questions for you about what is happening in Tionesta. Damian asked for us to come just before dark tonight."

Beth Ann nodded meekly. She suddenly felt exhausted...and nervous about being interrogated by a bunch of soldiers.

That evening, Christopher and Beth Ann walked up the hill to the retreat cabin. Along the way he pointed out different things: the path to the river, a watch tower, a "spider" hole. The retreat itself was much bigger than the house they grew up in, but it looked like a regular house. It was sided in a natural brown with a metal roof; the narrow front porch had just enough room for rocking chairs, and the beautiful windows made it look inviting. From one end of the house rose a rock tower that gave the house an older, mountain lodge appearance.

Damian and Brody met them on the porch. While Christopher continued inside with Damian, Brody stopped Beth Ann.

"Hi, I'm Brody," he said, reaching out to shake her hand.

She stared at his hand for several seconds, then finally reached out and timidly shook it. It seemed strange to Beth Ann, now that she was accustomed to the town rules.

"I'm glad to see you're feeling better," he said.

"Yes, yes, I am. Thanks. I'm Beth Ann, but you already know that," she responded with a crooked smile, dropping her gaze to her feet. "Sorry to make you carry me. But...thank you." She dared to look up into his sky blue eyes.

"No problem!" he said with a comfortable laugh. "I'm just glad you didn't hit me with that shovel!"

In spite of feeling a little disconcerted being alone on the porch with the guy, she found herself chuckling at the thought of her swinging a small shovel at all that muscle. She turned toward the front door—she had to find a pocket of air somewhere away from Brody so she could breathe.

Brody held the door open for her. "I just wanted to officially meet you before you got sucked into the madness...," he said with a grin, gesturing inside the house. Beth Ann took a breath and stepped bravely into the din.

Damian was waiting just inside the door. He took Beth Ann's elbow and escorted her through the throng, making introductions as they went. Beth Ann noted that he was very business-like and didn't waste any time. Meanwhile, Christopher never left her side. She was overwhelmed by the sheer number of people congregated there; she knew she would never remember them all. At least they weren't all dressed like soldiers; they seemed like regular people. Everyone treated her kindly and the children seemed fascinated to have an outsider in their home. The group quickly settled into the large, wide open great room for the meeting. Even with nearly twenty people in the room, it didn't seem crowded because of the living, dining and kitchen spaces all flowing together under a cathedral ceiling vaulted with rough-hewn beams.

Beth Ann could tell right away that Damian and Sean, the tall soldier who questioned her at Peter's, mostly ran the show. But the people in the room seemed to respect them, and Damian and Sean respected them back by asking their opinions and ideas and working out solutions together. Brody took the leadership on security items, and two other men—Randy and Andrew—took some of the leadership as well. When it was her turn to speak, Beth Ann gave them the short, edited version of her story and then they threw dozens of questions at her. They had obviously been curious about what was going on in town and had been too isolated to find out.

She had thought it would be best to stay as positive as possible, but it backfired. One of the wives, the Emily of the brown tank top, asked, "If things were good in town and food was being provided, why did you run away?"

Beth Ann shot a panicked look at Christopher and then dropped her gaze to her tightly clasped hands. She couldn't tell these strangers her deepest, darkest secret. Especially with children in the room. And that nice soldier, Brody—what would he think of her? She simply shrugged and Christopher came to her rescue.

"With our parents presumably dead, she wanted to be with me, her only remaining family," he explained. "Is there anything else? Beth Ann needs more rest and I'd like to get her home now." He stood and pulled Beth Ann up to her feet.

They said their goodbyes and walked down the path toward home in the twilight. Beth Ann shivered as the wind picked up. It smelled like rain.

"Thank you, Christopher," Beth Ann said softly. "I've probably never told you before, but I love you."

He pulled her toward him and kissed the top of her head. "I'm going to take care of you from now on. I promise. And believe it or not, I love you, too."

Chapter 25

Over the next few days, Beth Ann was brought up to speed on the ways of the retreat. She worked in the garden every day, received training on her revolver, practiced reloading, and learned where to go if they were attacked. Occasionally, people tried to ask her more in-depth questions about Tionesta, but she brushed them off each time. Eventually they stopped asking.

She helped Tanya in the kitchen and with caring for Molly, assisted with water purification, and read a gardening manual that went into depth on the topic of greenhouse growing in cold climates. When she was first assigned to the Greenhouse Team in town, she had not liked working with the dirt and manure. But she gradually found a passion for growing things. Now, in each seed she saw a miracle, the hope of a chance at life.

Maria worked with Beth Ann every day on the basic operation of her weapon and they became fast friends. Since she was due to have her baby in early June, Maria didn't shoot. Between the noise level and the airborne lead and metal dust, it wasn't safe for the unborn baby. But she did teach Beth Ann proper grip, form, and stance. Beth Ann's handgun was a revolver and Gary had taught her how to reload the chamber. But Maria also had her get familiar with her own

Glock 19a, and they practiced mag changes until Beth Ann could do it almost as quickly as Maria.

"I miss shooting!" she confided in Beth Ann with a twinkle in her eye. "Yearly qualification training was my favorite part of being in the military!" Maria was spunky and fun, but had a hint of intensity that Beth Ann hoped she would never have to see in action. "All the neighbors and retreat members get together weekly to practice essential weapon handling skills like this," she explained. "You'll be able to join the next one and be able to keep up!"

Twice Brody took Beth Ann outside to practice what to do in different scenarios, how to find cover, and various evasive maneuvers. He explained that target practice wasn't safe because it would give away their location and draw attention in the form of hungry neighbors. But since she was new to the retreat, one morning he took her to a makeshift range to practice with a silenced .45 handgun and carbine. It was a short session because they had to conserve ammunition. As intimidated as she had been at first by Brody, the more they saw of each other, the more comfortable...and safe...she felt around him.

One afternoon while Molly was napping, Rose and her youngest daughter stopped by the farmhouse carrying bags. She explained to Beth Ann that she managed the retreat's food inventory, but Beth Ann got the impression that it wasn't her favorite thing. Rose handed Tanya a heavy tote with a large bag of rice, four jars of canned meat and two large cans of freeze-dried fruit. Meanwhile, the little girl set down a much smaller bag on the floor and clutched her mother's leg.

"I'm really sorry. I wish I could give you more, but we have to be very cautious about our food stores until we see what the harvests look like," Rose said as she chewed a hangnail off her ring finger.

Tanya took each item out of the tote and set them on the counter. "Please don't apologize, Rose. You've all done so much for us already. Christopher and I don't mind sharing our food with Beth Ann," she said as she handed back the folded bag.

Beth Ann watched the exchange with a sense of shame. "I didn't mean to put any of you in this position, showing up empty handed," she said to both women. "But I will work my butt off to help in any way I can to earn my keep."

Tanya hugged her. "Don't worry, honey. We're just so glad you're here and you're safe."

Rose smiled. "We understand the strength in family, believe me. And we do appreciate all the ways you're helping out, Beth Ann." Rose turned and picked up the small tote that her daughter had set down just inside the door. "Wish I could stay and visit, but Lexie and I are going to run this pasta down to Rachel, and then I have to get back to the cabin to prep for dinner." At the sound of her name, the little girl peeked up at Beth Ann and smiled shyly.

Tanya opened the door for Rose and Lexie, then she and Beth Ann followed them out to the porch. "How's Rachel? Any better?"

Rose shook her head. "No, not really. She just needs more time." She looked off in the direction of Butch's property. "I wish she would agree to move in with us. It would be safer...for everyone." After a pause, Rose took Lexie's hand and they moved in sync down the three steps. That's when Beth Ann noticed a familiar man standing in the yard, a rifle resting in the crook of his elbow. He held up his hand in greeting to Tanya and Beth Ann. "Stop by anytime for a visit!" Rose said over her shoulder as she reached the man and the trio walked away.

"That's Caleb, Rose's husband," Tanya explained. "Rachel lives beyond the range that the retreat can successfully patrol or see from the watchtowers, so an armed guard has to escort anyone who wants to visit. But she refuses to leave her home." She sighed. "I just feel so bad for her. She was in the watchtower with Butch when…. I can't imagine…." Tanya's voice trailed off. She turned abruptly and went straight into the house. The screen door *skreeeeeked* open, then banged loudly once followed by two softer echoes on its spring.

Beth Ann watched Rose and her family disappear from view, wrapping her arms around herself to ward off a sudden chill. She thought of the incredible stress of providing food, without any stores, for thirty people for a year—literally a matter of life or death. She thought of the children, clinging to their mothers for security. She thought of Maria, facing her first delivery with no medical facilities or emergency backup. Even though the people here were kind and smiled and laughed, underneath they were strong and rugged and determined. They didn't run or hide or lie around in self-pity; they bore their scars bravely and faced fear head-on. They were like pioneers, these survivors. And Rachel was a constant reminder that death could visit on any day without warning.

The next couple of days brought rain—the drenching, miserable kind. It was good for the garden, but apparently not so good for little persons. Molly was a tyrant; she refused to be entertained or cuddled or consoled. Christopher came and went, taking care of business, but he was grumpy from being wet and deprived of a hot shower. Tanya, too, was cranky and tired.

Beth Ann needed to escape. She excused herself and borrowed a raincoat for a walk. Trudging through the backyard, she ducked into a large three-sided shed. On one end was an empty chicken coop; the chickens had been moved up to the retreat as part of the partnership. On the other side was space for goats, which Christopher had not yet invested in before the collapse. Since he had bought the tiny farm three years before, his strategy had been to start small and grow the farm as he learned the ropes.

Other than some tools and small equipment, there was nothing else to see in the shed and Beth Ann's restlessness drove her back out into the rain. She headed aimlessly into the woods, being careful to stay within sight of the path so she could find her way back. A cluster of large rocks caught her attention and she clambered up to a flat spot on the largest one. The wet surface made it slippery and difficult to climb, but it was worth the effort. Hugging her knees to her chest under the raincoat, she looked around. Unlike her favorite outcrop in Tionesta near the river, the view from this spot was tree...tree...tree...pine...thistles...tree...thicket. The sound of the rain was relaxing, and even though the water was starting to find ways to infiltrate the coat, Beth Ann began to feel some of the tension melt away.

A movement caught her eye, and she jerked her head toward the thickest part of the brush. Reaching slowly into her pocket, she gripped her gun and cocked the hammer...just in case it wasn't her imagination.

"Beth Ann?" a voice called out. It sounded far away and nearby at the same time. With the sound of the rainfall amplified on her plastic hood, she couldn't even pinpoint where it came from. Beth Ann slid down the back side of the rock, took cover, and pulled her gun up, just as she had been taught.

"Beth Ann! It's me, Brody. I'm coming out now. I didn't want to scare you, and I sure as heck don't want you to shoot me, either!"

Beth Ann carefully released the hammer and stood up, relieved. "I'm here!"

Brody stepped out from behind a nearby tree. "Hey. You know it's raining out, right?" he asked.

Beth Ann smiled sheepishly and cast her eyes down to her soggy shoes. "Yeah, pretty sure there's more of me that's wet than dry! I just needed to get out of the house. The walls were closing in on me."

He nodded, which marked the beginning of an awkward silence. Beth Ann fidgeted with her hair, trying to push it deeper into the hood of the coat, while Brody tapped the rock methodically with the toe of his boot. The rain pooled on their hoods and drained off as tiny waterfalls.

"You on security detail?" Beth Ann finally asked.

Brody's shoulders relaxed. "Yeah. Actually, I'm in the watchtower." He turned partway around and pointed. "That's how I saw you out here."

"Oh, right," Beth Ann said as she peered around him to see the small box built on old telephone poles and well camouflaged into the surroundings. Even though her brother had pointed it out to her a few days earlier, she had forgotten it was there. When Brody didn't say anything else, she looked up at him. "So, did you need something?"

"No, no, I don't. I…just wanted to make sure you were okay. It makes me nervous to see you…or anyone…wandering around. But if you stay in this general area," he said, gesturing in a circular motion with his arms, "you should be safe."

"Oh, okay. Thanks," Beth Ann replied. "I won't be staying out in this weather too much longer, so don't worry."

She placed her hands on fingerholds and leaned her weight forward to climb back up to her perch when Brody presented another option. "Or, uh…you could come up and help me in the watchtower for a little while, until you're ready to go back…if you want."

"Really? Wouldn't that be… against the rules or something?" Beth Ann asked, her forehead wrinkling.

"The rules?" Brody asked, lifting an eyebrow. "Our only rule around here is everyone be responsible and help out wherever you can. As long as we are watching for possible threats, and as long as we don't make a lot of noise, it will be fine. A little cramped maybe, but fine."

Beth Ann weighed her options and decided she *wanted* to go. But she shrugged casually. "Okay. If there's room."

Brody grinned and led the way. Climbing up the forty-foot, aluminum extension ladder in the rain in her soaking wet sneakers was treacherous, but within a few minutes Beth Ann found herself on watchtower duty, shoulder-to-shoulder with Brody. He looked out an opening facing south, the direction in which the nearest road lay, and she looked out the opposite one with a limited view of the path.

"In an ideal world," he explained, or maybe justified, in a hushed voice, "we would always have two people in each watchtower. But we don't have enough people to go around for two on every shift." At Brody's words, Beth Ann instantly thought of Rachel, who had been in the other watchtower with her husband when he was shot in the head. Suddenly she had a graphic visual of the reality of the daily threat; she tried to shake it off and act "normal."

They talked a little off and on, very quietly, sticking to safe topics. But Beth Ann felt increasingly unnerved at being in the small space with Brody and she knew it was a mistake, accepting his invitation. The last thing on earth that she wanted was for this kind man to think that she could return a romantic interest. She was far too broken.

Heat from the panic began building in her chest; she had to get out of there. "I'm sorry, Brody. I gotta go. I..I...didn't tell Tanya and Christopher that I'd be gone this long and they're going to be worried sick!" Abruptly turning, she descended the long ladder as fast as she could, her shoes slipping on every rung.

"Thanks for keeping me company!" he said. She stopped her descent and looked up, blinking as the rain fell on her face. There was Brody's head, leaning over the window ledge. He gave her a nod with a little-boy smile in the middle. She dropped to her feet and practically ran to her brother's house. This was not good...not good at all.

After a night of fitful sleep, Beth Ann woke to see sunlight streaming through the window. The rain had finally moved on. A chill in the house proved that the front had passed and taken the humidity with it. The household rushed through the morning meal and indoor chores in anticipation of being outside again. Molly ran through the house from room to room, giggling and telling them to "hur-wy" and "go owt-side." It took longer than usual to find layers to wear in the cool morning air, and Beth Ann fought an exhausting battle with her still-soaked tennis shoes just to get her feet into them.

Christopher walked them to the garden, as he was on water duty with Andrew. Molly saw a couple of her mini-sized friends and tugged at her dad's hand to let her run ahead. When they got close enough to the garden, he turned her loose. He laughed along with

Tanya and Beth Ann as they watched Molly's eager little legs carry her to freedom. She announced her arrival dramatically with her arms in the air and was immediately welcomed into the game. Christopher saw Andrew a short distance away and gave his wife a peck on the cheek just before he hurried off.

Beth Ann was used to the routine now and had no trouble jumping in where she thought she was needed. On this day she saw that the weeds were racing to catch up with the vegetables, so she picked up a hoe. Rose and Emily waved to her and she headed in their direction, feeling the warmth of their acceptance fill her like the new day's sunshine.

"Good Morning," Beth Ann greeted the two young women with a smile, and they stood to exchange pleasantries. "I thought I would hoe for a while, unless there's something else you want me to do instead," Beth Ann said, lifting the hoe in front of her as proof.

"Sure! That would be good," Emily agreed. "When Rachel gets here, maybe she can help you. The weeds certainly must have liked that rain," she said as she grimaced and glanced around at the daunting task. Beth Ann and Rose looked at the never-ending garden rows and nodded with exaggerated helpless expressions on their faces.

Beth Ann left Emily and Rose to their transplanting and headed for the tallest plants, the snap peas. In town, Mary Jo had told her that peas liked colder weather, so they were good for planting early and may even give a second yield before fall. This large garden had three separate rows of peas at different heights, so they must have been planted a couple weeks apart to spread out the harvest. The row Beth Ann worked on had a little fence-like structure to support the viney stalks as they grew taller, but the other two rows had sticks and small tree branches sticking up out of the soil. *Creative solution*, Beth Ann thought.

The soil was still muddy from the deluge the day before, making the weeds easy to work out. But it also made it harder to walk as the mud sucked at her shoes and built into a thick layer that would need to be scraped off after it dried. As she worked the hoe methodically, bending occasionally to pull out the longer roots and toss the weeds into a pile that would be picked up later, Beth Ann realized that she hadn't looked over her shoulder recently. She was finally not afraid that Travis would find her and simply materialize at the woods' edge. Smiling to herself, she thanked God for this place of refuge.

When she had nearly reached the end of the first long row, Peter's wife came along with water. Beth Ann had not realized she was so thirsty. The air was refreshing and cool, but the sun was becoming more intense as it rose higher in the picture-perfect blue sky. She took off her sweatshirt and took the small cup from Helen gratefully. They chatted casually while Beth Ann drank her fill, until they were suddenly interrupted by a strange noise in the distance. Instantly everyone in the garden dropped their tools and began to run full speed, scooping up any children in their path.

"Oh! It's...it's the alarm!" Helen said with a start, bringing her hand to her throat. Her eyes opened wide with fear and she stood without moving. Beth Ann had not yet heard the car horn alarm that had been rigged by the retreat leaders, but she quickly put the connection together.

Beth Ann took the heavy jug of water from Helen's hands and helped her move as quickly as possible to the farmhouse. They had practiced drills for a scenario like this, for which Beth Ann was now grateful. Even still, her heart was beating faster than she could run with the elderly woman hanging on her arm.

"Let me go!" came a shout, and Beth Ann glanced up to see Emily and Rose wrestling at the edge of the garden.

"There's no time!" Emily shouted back. "Come on!"

"I need to get to Rachel!" Rose said, her face twisting with emotion.

"No, Rose! It's too late! Damian needs us!" Emily put her arm around the distraught woman and turned her forcibly toward the path. Caleb, who had been delivering a wheelbarrow load of compost, reached the other side of Rose and together the three of them ran up the path toward the retreat.

Beth Ann and Helen, along with the rest of the people and children who had been in the garden, ran to the closest house–the Gabnor's. Just as they had practiced, they filed quickly down the basement stairs. Peter came last, locking the reinforced basement door with a deadbolt that had been installed to lock from the inside.

As Beth Ann's eyes adjusted, she looked around the dark, dank area. Peter crouched in the far corner beside his pale wife with his arm protectively around her. Tanya held Molly tightly on her lap and tried to calm Emily's daughters, Cheyenne and Penelope. Rose's sister, Alicia, pulled a handgun out of its holster and concealed herself behind a storage unit near the stairs. Beth Ann swallowed the bitter fear rising in her throat and followed Alicia's brave lead. She moved behind a stack of boxes and took her gun out of her pocket. Alicia gave her an appreciative nod. Beth Ann realized that if anyone came down the steps, a couple little handguns may not be enough; they would be sitting ducks...trapped, with nowhere to hide.

Then the waiting began. Beth Ann thought it was unbearable– the silence and the anticipation of worst-case scenarios. She worried about Christopher and Andrew: Had they heard the alarm? Were they able to get to safety? The only sound was someone occasionally shifting position. Molly eventually fell asleep. After a long time, Beth Ann thought she heard footfalls above them, but she also thought her ears might be playing tricks on her. She tightened her grip on the revolver and raised it toward the stairs. A firmly knocked code on the basement door confirmed that someone was indeed in the house, and the familiar rhythm brought an instant relief to the people huddled underground. Beth Ann could literally hear everyone start breathing again. Alicia reached the top of the stairs in a flash and knocked back a reply.

Christopher was waiting for them upstairs. Tanya rushed to him with the still sleeping Molly in her arms, and he held them close for a full minute without saying a word. The rest of the group waited respectfully for news of what happened.

Christopher turned to them and spoke in a somber tone. "Everything is alright. We just had some visitors. The unwelcome kind. Sean, Brody and Randy met them at the end of the retreat's driveway. There was no gunfire, but the guys are worried about the situation. So they're calling a meeting in about thirty minutes, or as soon as we can check the perimeter and get everyone up to the retreat. Just be quiet and observant getting up there." Tanya shifted and Christopher took the heavy Molly into his arms, snuggling her close.

"They were from Tionesta, so the retreat leaders are especially interested in getting some insight from you," Christopher said softly, looking directly at Beth Ann. Beth Ann's eyes grew large and she gripped the back of a nearby chair as she felt her knees weaken. They had found her; how had she ever thought that she could find a safe place to hide?

"I'll go tell Rachel," Alicia said, taking hold of her son Aiden's hand.

"No!" Christopher said loudly, making everyone jump. "I mean, it's not necessary, but thank you for offering. Damian and Andrew went to check on her and...uh, let her know about the meeting."

This drew quizzical looks from the adults, but Christopher didn't wait to be asked any more questions. "I'm headed to the southern border," he said to Tanya as he handed the squirming Molly back to her. "I'll see you up at the retreat." A quick kiss on the cheek and he was gone.

An awkward, empty silence filled the room as the screen door slowly shut on its hydraulic hinge, punctuated by Helen's, "Oh! Oh, dear."

Tanya turned to Beth Ann. "Let's go home and change into clean clothes before we head up the hill."

Beth Ann looked down then and noticed the muddy tracks on the hardwood floors and across the plush hall runner. "I'm sorry,

Mrs. Gabnor, about your floor," she said softly. But the poor woman, now seated in a brocade wing-back chair with her eyes closed, didn't respond.

Peter, who was trying to get his wife to sip a little lukewarm water, paused to look at Beth Ann. His sorrowful gaze drifted to the bullet holes in the front wall from just a couple weeks earlier. "It don't matter," he said, shaking his head. He turned back to his wife and everyone filed quietly out of the house.

In Tionesta, Meghan stepped as carefully as possible around the deep puddles left by the previous day's downpour and tugged the strap of her tote up higher on her shoulder. The files of the patients on today's rounds seemed especially heavy to her, although maybe it was simply the heaviness of her spirit adding to the weight. She had not seen Beth Ann for over a week. The spring season had brought a new strain of a stubborn flu, so Meghan had been busy and had received her meals at the clinic with the other staff, working almost around the clock. But she hadn't seen Beth Ann at the apartment, either, and the worry grew each day.

Hoping that Beth Ann had just decided to move back into Mr. Howard's house, Meghan finally had the chance to check on her when her rounds took her to the edge of town near Beth Ann's street. Approaching cautiously, Meghan noticed two women working in the front yard of the Dalton house. The little white fence surrounded the garden in a strange juxtaposition of eras: "Then" and "Now." She waved with a smile and flashed her Medical Team badge.

The women stopped working and met her across the sidewalk gate. The oldest introduced herself. "Hi, there. I'm Mary Jo. What can I help you with?"

"I'm Meghan. Thanks. I...I'm looking for someone who lives here. She's on your Team. Name's Beth Ann Dalton."

The two women looked at each other and back to Meghan. "We haven't seen Beth Ann since...what, early last week?" Mary Jo said, looking at the other woman to confirm it with a head nod. "She had already planted her garden, and we couldn't afford to lose these plants, so Lisa here and I have been tending to it." She shrugged. "I don't know what to tell you. I hope she's okay...."

"Oh, well, that's not what I was hoping you would say, but thank you," Meghan said as she backed away from the women and hurried toward home. Something was definitely wrong. Although she was supposed to report into the Clinic, she went straight to her apartment, hoping to find Dillon there.

She was completely out of breath when she arrived on the third floor and would normally have laughed at Dillon's surprised face when she burst through the door, but she was not in any mood to laugh. She dropped her bag on the floor and tried to speak, but what came out wasn't in word form.

"Whoa, whoa!" Dillon said as he stood from filling out a report in a sunny spot near the window. "Breathe slower...breathe.... Keep breathing and answer my questions with your head, okay?"

Meghan nodded and leaned against the wall, chest heaving with each breath. She gripped her waist with her hands and squeezed.

"Are you hurt?"

She shook her head "no."

"Is someone chasing you?"

She shook her head again.

"Wow. This might take a while," Dillon teased. "Uh...did you see a fantasaical creature, a unicorn or fairy, perhaps?"

Meghan narrowed her eyes and took a step forward. She had enough air in her lungs to talk now. "Dillon," she said, grasping his shoulders with her hands and looking directly into his eyes. "Beth Ann is missing. You know she hasn't been here for over a week, and today I checked her house. There were two women from the Greenhouse Team working her yard garden because she hasn't shown up for work. I think she's one of the missing girls! We have to do something!"

Dillon's gaze dropped while Meghan was talking. He took her hands gently and removed them from his shoulders.

"You know something, don't you?" Meghan asked quietly. Dillon crossed the room and looked out the window. "Don't you?" she asked louder, accusingly. "Tell me!"

He turned to face her but didn't look up. Clearing his throat, he stuffed his hands in his jean pockets. "Beth Ann is on the 'wanted' list."

"The what?" Meghan whispered as the color drained from her face.

Dillon looked up then, the pain evident in his expression. "Andrews has declared her a traitor and a spy. If he finds her, she will be hanged."

Chapter 26

"Mr. Andrews?" Beth Ann gasped. She hadn't meant to say it out loud. Now all the retreat members and neighbors gathered in the large great room were staring at her, expecting her to have some kind of input.

Randy glanced at Beth Ann, but when she didn't offer anything else, he continued recounting the conversation that had taken place at the property line. "This new mayor...and his sheriff...are offering us protection if we move into town and share our supplies." A hushed murmur rippled from one side of the room to the other. "Alternatively, we can stay here and pay 'taxes' in the form of food and supplies."

Brody punched one of the cabinets, like a punctuation mark, and went back to agitatedly pacing the space between the island and the kitchen. Even the wind-up mantle clock seemed to tick louder than usual.

Sean stood up. "He's given us two weeks to decide...or 'pay the consequences.'" Sean shook his head slowly. "This man is trouble...big trouble. I get the feeling he is used to getting his way, no matter what. Am I right, Beth Ann?"

All eyes turned back to Beth Ann, who was trying to recede farther into the corner than humanly possible. "Ye-es," she finally managed to stammer. Everyone waited, so she continued. "I heard somewhere that he was high up in business or government or something. And he's very rich."

"*Was* rich," Brody murmured. He stopped pacing and leaned forward on the island, bracing his weight on clenched fists and listening intently.

Self-conscious, Beth Ann glanced down and said softly, "He used to come into the restaurant where I worked…. He always gave me the creeps."

The room was quiet for nearly a minute, except for the incessant ticking of the irritated clock. Then Randy's voice broke the silence, in a tone that made a cloud of dread descend over the entire house. "There's one more thing," he said. Beth Ann noticed Sean and Brody move closer to Randy, their faces terrifyingly stony. Randy shifted his weight and cleared his throat. "They offered Rachel a place to live in town and we assume she accepted it, since she wasn't home when we went to get her for the meeting."

The stunned silence was followed by an eruption. Rose was on her feet, denying that Rachel would have willingly gone with Mr. Andrews' men and demanding that they get her back. Other retreat members and neighbors echoed their agreement, while Caleb tried to calm his distraught wife. Sean and Randy agreed with Rose that Rachel would not have gone willingly, but at the same time argued that they didn't have any options for finding her, which didn't sit well.

Brody cut in to put the focus back on Mayor Andrews. "There is no doubt that this Mr. Andrews intends to take our supplies. He was sizing us up, that's all." Based on his experience as an Army Ranger in Afghanistan, he explained that a man with food can easily control an entire town of starving people. It doesn't matter where he gets the food or who is killed in the process. "I'm betting that most townsfolk would take up arms for him just to keep their children's bellies full.

They may be unaware of what he is doing or where he is getting the food. Hungry people aren't going to ask a lot of questions when they are eating. My impression of him is that he's no one to take lightly."

The banter continued and Brody stated matter-of-factly that the only way out of this one was to kill Mayor Andrews, the head of the snake. After another deadly silence, the discussion heated up quickly. Emily gestured to Cheyenne, the oldest of all the children, to take the other kids downstairs to play.

Clearly most of those gathered were opposed to killing anyone, yet the retreat leaders urged them to consider that this man wouldn't just take a percentage of their food and guns and supplies: he would keep coming back until it was all gone. Helping people in need and sharing with the hungry is a Biblical concept, yes, but arguably not at the cost of the very lives of their own family members. Giving their food to help the town would give them only a few weeks at best to live. And since Andrews had taken the guns off the townspeople, he would surely take theirs. It would be a death sentence.

Beth Ann watched the volley of heated opinions in horror. There didn't seem to be any way out. She wouldn't be safe here; she wouldn't be safe anywhere. Travis' face suddenly flashed in front of her, taunting and leering. Subconsciously, she glanced at Brody for safe haven, and was startled to see him staring intently at her. Quickly, she looked away.

Someone was asking about defending the retreat and fighting the intruders off, but the answer was that eventually Andrews' force would overtake them. "I believe we need to do something soon," Sean pressed. "If I were to guess, the only reason he gave us two whole weeks was for his benefit, not ours. He knows we aren't going to change our minds. He needs time to recruit more foot soldiers. If we wait too long, I fear we will be outnumbered far worse than we are now."

Beth Ann noticed that the people in the room began to back down, losing their steam for the fight. But Rose's entire body was rigid with anger, and her eyes red and puffy.

Brody jumped in. "The problem is that we are going in blind. We don't know anything about the town, where this guy lives, or the proficiency of their security. We have to develop some sort of a plan." He recommended doing recon missions to figure out a way to take Andrews out of the picture, reasoning that the retreat would have a better chance of defeating the Deputies if they were leaderless, if they even attacked at all. "How often does Mr. Andrews give his little speeches? Is there any repetition to them, like every Sunday?"

Once again the room fell quiet, and the ticking silence was stifling. Beth Ann felt Christopher nudge her arm and she jumped. "Huh?" All eyes were looking in her direction, and she realized Brody's questions had been directed at her. "Oh...not really, maybe every week or two. It usually revolves around someone breaking the law or disciplinary measures, and reports from Team Leaders. They just ring the church bell to signal a meeting."

"Does he hold them at the same spot?" Brody continued to probe.

Beth Ann's heart beat rapidly. "Yes, usually in the town square," she answered. Why did she feel so panicky about answering a few questions? Probably because Brody still had that intent look in his eye, like he was plotting.

Since they couldn't predict when a meeting would take place, it was too risky to put a sniper in place in town. Randy asked Beth Ann where Andrews lived, and she informed him that no one knew; he drove in and out of town each day in an old pickup truck. Brody was getting frustrated; it could take weeks for scouts to figure out where Andrews lived, and intercepting the Deputy patrols was out of the question. Members of the group continued to throw out possible options, all of which were shot down.

Beth Ann's whole body burned like it was on fire...on the inside. Somehow, she knew what was coming. She watched Brody cross the room, coming toward her as if in slow motion. The closer he got, the more imposing he looked, even though he wasn't a tall man. He loomed over her, then crouched slowly to her eye level. She drew her knees up, hugging them tightly and pressing her back harder into the corner.

Gently, Brody began. "Beth Ann, would you be willing to go back to town and try to—"

"NO!" Christopher shouted, jumping out of his seat and stepping in between the two, causing Brody to stand up in defense. Tanya reached across her husband's empty chair to put her hand protectively on Beth Ann's knee. Christopher stood nose to nose with Brody. "No way is she going back there. They could kill her!" His voice shook.

Suddenly, out of nowhere, or maybe it was from Somewhere, Beth Ann felt a strange calm sensation flood through her body. In her mind she knew she was crazy, but in her heart she knew she had to do this…. She had to help the people who had saved her life and taken her in as one of their own. She had to face her fear of the dark and the Darkness, with God's help. It was time to do the right thing, no matter how hard, to help protect the retreat. What if she was brought here, with her connection to the town, at this exact time, for this very purpose?

She stood and gently moved her brother aside. "If this is the only way…I will go," she said softly but resolutely, looking into Brody's eyes for strength. There she found not only strength, but compassion and respect…and genuine care.

"No!" Christopher shouted angrily, glaring at Brody. "I will not allow it. You don't know what you're asking of her!"

Brody lowered his gaze. "Yes…I do," he said in nearly a whisper.

Beth Ann's face burned with shame and she squeezed her eyes shut. So, he knew. Someone had told him. She wondered how many other people in the room knew. The only ones she had told about the rapes were Christopher, Tanya and Maria.

Christopher started to shift his weight and Beth Ann feared that he would lash out against Brody. She gently enveloped his right hand with both of hers and Christopher's body instantly went limp. He spun around and gathered her into his arms, squeezing the breath out of her. She felt a tear splash the side of her neck and roll down to her t-shirt collar.

As if from a great distance, Beth Ann heard Randy's voice. "Brody, I think that should be a last resort." Sean's voice agreed. Beth Ann had forgotten for a moment that there were other people in the room.

Brody crossed the room then to join Sean and Randy. "I don't know that we have any other options here. We are *at* our last resort." He pointed at Beth Ann. "She is the only person that can enter the town without raising suspicions. We just need to come up with a good backstory in case someone challenges where she's been."

Beth Ann felt the tension building again in Christopher's body as he slowly released her from his grip. He strode to the middle of the room and faced the people–his neighbors and friends–gathered there. "This is a bad idea!" he implored, seeking direct eye contact with anyone not already looking down. He turned to Sean and pleaded, "You have no right to ask her to do this!"

Sean looked away and shifted his weight. Everyone waited. Rose buried her face into Caleb's shoulder. Finally, Sean spoke. "Let's meet again in two days. Everyone spend this time in prayer or contemplation or whatever it is you do. We'll come back together and we want more ideas, people! If we are going to ask this young lady to risk her life, then I want to know that every other possible bridge to get there has been burned." Sean turned his gaze back to Christopher, an acknowledgement that it was the best he could offer.

Christopher's response was the door slamming shut behind him in the otherwise silent room.

The next two days went by in a blur for Beth Ann. She did all the usual things: working in the garden, running drills, and helping with Molly, but she also spent most of that time in her own head. One minute she would feel brave and confident in her decision to go back to town, and the next minute she would feel certifiably insane. Her brother pleaded with her to stay. Even Rose, who wanted so much to find Rachel, approached Beth Ann in the garden and told her she didn't want another young woman to be in jeopardy by going through with this plan.

Finally, she swallowed her pride and approached Brody for help thinking the plan through and avoiding risks. Brody asked more questions about the town and Mr. Andrews, and they worked out the steps she would take getting back to Meghan's apartment building. They even prayed together. Beth Ann felt awkward at first, but then she felt empowered. She was certain that this was her calling.

The follow-up meeting at the Retreat was short. A few more ideas were raised, but in the end Beth Ann calmly stood and said she was ready to go. Christopher stormed out of the meeting...again, and Beth Ann knew he felt helpless. She excused herself to pack and spend the rest of the afternoon with her brother. Sean, Damian, Andrew and Brody would come for her by midnight.

Gary sat with his back against the charred stone wall, trying to bite off a chunk of old venison jerky and hoping that it didn't tear his teeth out in the process. Sunlight poured in through the partially collapsed ceiling, more evidence of a devastating fire. He was hiding out in a campground near the river that had obviously seen its last days during the winter. The structures were destroyed, except for the shell of this little square single-room structure that was the only one built from stone. It may have been the camp office. Human remains still lay where they had fallen; enough bodies to lead Gary to believe that multiple families had congregated here to try to survive the chaos after the power outage. They were either attacked, or they had turned on each other when they started running out of food.

He looked with wonder at the other faces in the "room." Joe and Mad Max were there, Zachary the pizza store owner, and four other men that Gary had met the previous week...on the day they had pulled him out of the river. He was still in shock and amazement that these freedom fighters had saved his life.

He leaned his head against the wall and closed his eyes, thinking back to the day he thought he was going to join Linda in heaven. After the mysterious ambush that had come out of nowhere, he had been pulled out of the river by two strangers who were wearing bandanas around their faces so that only their eyes showed. They had held him on the ground at gunpoint until a third man showed up, wearing the same strange gunslinger disguise.

"Are you Mr. Lewis?" the man had asked sternly, towering over him.

"Wha...at? N...n...no," Gary had answered through chattering teeth. The shock and the cold water made him shiver uncontrollably, lying on the riverbank.

"Do you know him?" the man had yelled like a drill sergeant...and there was something vaguely familiar about his voice.

Even in his fuzzy state of mind, Gary had suddenly realized the connection with the password code that Joe had given him on the little slip of paper. He must have answered the questions correctly because the men whisked him away to their hideout in the campground and patched up the nick in his arm from the bullet. He was amazed to discover that the ringleader with the "drill sergeant" voice was none other than Max. Several other men had defected from Andrews' rule and were hiding in the campground, too. But another young Security Team member, Dillon, and one of Branson's older officers, Roy, came and went as they were able, bringing news from town. Max and the men involved in the underground resistance movement were finalizing a plan to overthrow Mr. Andrews. And now Gary had been dragged into it.

"How did you know the ambush was coming? I remember seeing you charge at me before any shots rang out." Gary's voice broke the silence as he addressed Joe. He hadn't seen the Security Team member since Joe had kicked him into the river, until he showed up a few minutes ago, just in time for their meager meal.

Joe grinned. "I've been waiting for you to ask. You're a lucky man, Gary Howard, or else the Big Guy is looking out for you," he said, pointing upward. The other men continued to eat but watched and listened attentively. Joe grew somber as he continued.

"When Max and I were assigned to the Hunting Team's mission, we were given three directives. First, make sure you guys were doing your job and doing it thoroughly so Andrews could 'tax' anyone left alive in the area. Second, scope out any raider hideouts and protect the Team and the mission from them. And third, take you out."

"What? *Me*?" Gary asked, astonished.

"Yes, *you*," Joe emphasized. "We were supposed to stage an 'accident.' Apparently Mr. Andrews really, really doesn't like you. Or rather, I think he feels threatened by you because you had the guts to not play by his rules. But the longer it took us to get back to Tionesta, the more Max and I were convinced that Andrews would get impatient and deploy other deputies to get the job done. We were trying to figure out a way to get you out of the picture and still have a convincing story to tell the other Team members. That's why I gave you the password, in case we got separated. But the morning you told us about the green fabric the farmer had found, we knew it was too late. The 'Plan B' Security Team members had caught up to us. The best we could do was try to keep you from being killed."

Gary shook his head in disbelief and let out a low whistle.

Joe turned his head to spit out a grisly chunk and then continued. "I suspected that we were being followed, and I knew time was short. When I saw you on the ridge above that deep stream, I knew it was the perfect setup. I wanted it to look like I was taking you down, but I didn't expect anyone to start shooting! It just confirmed our suspicions," Joe said, glancing at Max, who nodded. Joe yanked another piece of the spicy dried meat off with his teeth, and turned his gaze back to Gary. "After I got you out of harm's way, I managed to put one of the guys down, and the other two ran off." He looked down and studied his calloused hands intently. "We were right. He was Security. A Tionestan—one of our own. But he was willing to kill you, so…," his voice trailed off and he cleared his throat. "I didn't have any choice," he finished with a shrug.

Max stood up, signaling that the break was over. As the rest of the men got to their feet and brushed off, Max finished the story. "Joe hustled Alex, Chuck and Bob back to town and believe you me, he had to run to keep up with those three. They were scared out of their minds. Andrews called a town meeting and made a big theatrical announcement about two Security Team members and a Hunting Team member being tragically killed by violent raiders, but privately he was irate that the group had returned without bodies and took it out on Sheriff Branson. So Joe has come here today to collect our bodies." Max lifted one eyebrow and Gary saw a twinkle in his eye.

Gary looked at Joe who shook his head once in the affirmative. Then something Max had said suddenly sank in. "Wait...they made an announcement in town? Oh, no. Beth Ann thinks I'm dead. Joe, we have to get a message to her! She's not safe! I should have gone back already. Jeez! I've been sitting around here like a prisoner! I have to go...." Gary was out of his mind. He put his hat on and started for the gaping door hanging askew on one hinge that marked the building's entrance.

Joe stepped in front of him. "Gary—hold up! You can't go anywhere! You will be shot on sight. Do you understand the words I'm saying?" Joe latched onto Gary's shoulders to stop him from pushing past. "Let's focus on getting Andrews out of the picture; that is the best way you can help Beth Ann."

"Bedtime story's over, men," Max interrupted. "You all understand the urgency here. Joe hasn't returned to town, there are bodies missing, and Andrews is unnaturally paranoid and suspicious on a GOOD day. Let's review the plan one more time and get some shuteye. We roll out at sundown."

Meghan arrived at her third-floor apartment just before dark, beating the curfew by mere minutes. Her day had been rough, not just because of the mud and the cranky patients and the constant fear of contagion since the clinic had run out of gloves and sanitizer last month. And not just because she hadn't heard from Kristen or Beth

Ann and couldn't find out anything about their whereabouts. But because she had buried a four-year-old girl who had been stung by a bee. The reaction had happened fast, but if they only had an epi-pen they might have been able to save her. The mother's grief haunted Meghan.

She dropped her bag with a thud on the floor inside the door and shed her badge, hanging it on the doorknob. More than anything, she wished she could go to the refrigerator and find some sweetened iced tea and a good snack. With a sigh, she turned toward the bedroom to change out of her scrubs. As she passed the small bookshelf laden with nursing books, devotionals, school yearbooks and novels, she froze.

"Wait a minute…," she said out loud to the dark, empty room. She ran her fingers along the book spines. The library might have books on local medicinal plants, Native American or Amish cures, old wives' tale remedies, or something. Anything would help. Meghan felt fifty pounds lighter as she strode into her room. Why hadn't someone thought of that already? She would talk with Mr. Thorpe first thing tomorrow and visit the library as soon as he would let her.

Pulling the covers back, and wishing once again for a way to wash the sheets, Meghan heard the apartment door squeak open and click shut. She was used to Dillon coming and going at odd times; his schedule changed almost daily. As she pulled the sheet up over her legs, she heard a light rap on her door. Surprised, she traipsed to the door and opened it to find Dillon waiting to talk.

"Hey, Meghan. Sorry to get you out of bed. I just wanted to let you know that I…um…will probably be gone all night," he said.

"Uh, okay," Meghan said, her eyebrows lifting. He had not gone out of his way to tell her this before.

Dillon adjusted his sash like he was stalling for time. He finally looked back up at her. "Andrews and Branson are acting strange, doubling all the guards tonight and saying that some large gang is going to attack. I don't know what's going on with that, so keep the door locked," he said, motioning toward the apartment's entrance, "and don't let anyone in, you hear?"

Meghan nodded, her eyes wide. Dillon's speech was clipped, like he was nervous. Not his usual languid self. He turned to leave and then came back to where she still stood in the gap of the partially opened bedroom door.

"There's a good chance that tonight will be Mr. Andrews' last night to play 'Dictator.' If you want something to pray about, start with that."

Dillon fled the apartment then, turning the lock on the door handle before closing it behind him. Meghan stood in the bedroom doorway for a long time, wondering what just happened.

Chapter 27

"Something's not right," Joe whispered to Gary. Max, on the other side of Gary, continued to peer through his night vision binoculars, the only set the raggle-taggle group had. The three men were lying face down beneath a heavy row of overgrown evergreen shrubs bordering the rear side of the municipal building. Dillon and two other men were surveying the northern side, and the final two men were on the southern side. The plan was simple: get into the building without getting caught, hide in the office, and wait for Andrews and his men to arrive in the morning. Then, shoot the fake mayor when he walks in the door along with anyone who defends him, sparing the young Charlie to help them find Andrews' secret hideout and food source. Step two was to find the sheriff and see if he would be willing to play by new rules. Getting out wasn't discussed in the plan–this was all or nothing. If it failed and anyone survived, they would certainly be hanged by Andrews.

Gary turned his head to look quizzically at Max, then back to Joe. Neither man offered an explanation of what "wasn't right," so he waited. He shivered...partly from being nervous, and partly from being wet.

Roy Hollenbaugh, a life-long boatman and an Allegheny River Patrol officer in his "old" life before the electricity went out, had been assigned by Sheriff Branson to be in charge of river security. But he was one of the Old Guard, secretly sympathetic to the cause of the resistance and an advocate for Mr. Andrews' removal from power. His role was key in Max's plan.

Once the light had faded from the sky, Roy had started extending his route just slightly up river to a wrinkle in the bank. The men were waiting for him there after sneaking a harrowing two miles along the river's edge from the campground to the rendezvous spot behind PennDot's facility with its dead machinery lined up like dinosaur skeletons. From this point, Roy had smuggled Max, Joe, Gary, and the other men, one at a time, under a tarp in his boat to the bridge. The bridge was heavily guarded above, but as Roy slowly passed underneath, he was out of their sightline. The man under the tarp had roughly four seconds to heave himself onto the top of the concrete pier before Roy came out under the opposite side of the bridge. With the water level higher since the Kinzua dam wasn't functioning and from the recent rain, the men were actually able to reach the top of the girders and climb up into steel cross beams beneath the deck. From there, they shimmied carefully and slowly to the eastern end of the bridge and waited under the road for the rest of the men.

The whole process took over two hours and Gary's nerves were shot by the time they were all together. At one point, they had a scare when a man suddenly appeared, but it turned out to be the Deputy Dillon, abandoning his post to help them.

Huddled in the tight crease where the slope of the bank met the bottom of the deck, Max had informed them all that Roy had passed on critical information, which Dillon affirmed was true. Apparently, Andrews and Branson had ordered double manpower at all the security checkpoints due to intel that a violent survivalist gang was planning an attack. The men had only hesitated for a minute. This was their only chance to get into the municipal building. They were out of food and had come too far to turn back. With a simple appreciative head nod, Max had signaled to move out.

One by one, led by Max, each man had slipped into the black water and made his way northbound following the shoreline, just far enough for the darkness to conceal them from the bridge security as they climbed up the bank into the foliage. Using any cover they could find between homes and landscape, they had silently made their way to their places at the city building three blocks from the river. That was at least thirty minutes ago.

Max put down the binoculars. "If Andrews doubled all the watches, why is there only one man guarding the armory?" he whispered in a way that meant he was thinking it through, not asking for an answer. Joe and Gary waited. Max picked up the binoculars and watched a little longer. "And we haven't seen the patrolling night watchman yet," he continued. From their time as Security Team members, Joe and Max both knew that in addition to three guards at the storage entrance for the extra guns and ammunition, there was supposed to be a minimum of two patrolling guards on the lot twenty-four hours a day. As of yet, they had not seen any foot patrols.

Joe finally offered, "Everyone must have been pulled to the perimeter."

"It doesn't make any sense…," Max muttered to himself, putting down the binoculars. "We'll wait a little longer. We technically have till dawn."

Gary was tired…and wet…and cold. He rested his forehead on his hands, wondering if he had survived the end of the world only to die from hypothermia. Although the May days had been warm, the temperature still dropped at night. How he longed to be in his own bed, in his own house…. Suddenly he had a thought that brought instant warmth from endorphins—and hope—being released throughout his body. "Hey!" he whispered to Max and Joe. "I'm going to find Beth Ann!" Gary started to push backward with his forearms.

Max grabbed his wrist. "No! You need to wait till tomorrow when it's safe. She's asleep now anyway."

In a low voice, calmer than he felt, Gary said, "She thinks I'm dead, Max. There's nothing I can do here; you have enough men. I need to make sure she's okay."

Max was quiet for a minute; then he let go of Gary's wrist. "Remember, if any of the security officers or deputies see you, they *will* shoot!"

"I understand. I'll be careful. But I can't just sit here! I have to go," Gary said. Max knew he meant it. He handed Gary the night vision binoculars. "Here. You'll need these more than we will."

Gary took them hesitantly, then nodded his thanks.

Joe spoke up then. "When you get there, stay there and don't let anyone see you! I know where you live. We'll come for you once Andrews is out of the picture and it's safe."

Gary nodded once more, looked each man in the eye to convey all his unspoken gratitude for their character and conviction in saving his life, and silently faded away into the night.

Meghan didn't sleep well. Anxiety crept into her dreams and she woke often, praying each time until she drifted back to sleep. At one point, she was at the golf course, where the town's dead were being taken. The sweet little girl with the bee sting was there, and behind her body was a pile of other bodies–faceless and misshapen. Meghan was digging, digging as fast as she could to get those bodies buried so she didn't have to see them any longer. But the faster and harder she tried, the more stifling the dirt became, pressing in around her like *she* was the one in the grave. Finally the dirt rose over her mouth and in a panic she tried to scream, awakening herself.

There, inches above her, was the face of Darkness. He wore a ski mask, but the dark squinty eyes and skinny braid were hard to disguise. His hand was clamped tightly over her mouth.

"Where is she?" he growled.

Meghan shook her head as much as she could against the pressure of his hand. Her eyes open wide and her heartbeat pounding in her ears, she tried to say "I don't know!," but it came out as a high-pitched three-syllable garble from her throat.

"Don't act all innocent with me, missy! Where is she?" He pressed his knee hard between her thighs and squeezed his free hand around her throat, leaning his weight into her.

She shook her head harder and tried to push him off, but she wasn't strong enough. White flashes of light clouding her vision told her that she would lose consciousness in a matter of seconds. She tried to bite his hand. He hauled back and slugged her left temple, and she screamed.

"I have a message for you to give your little friend, since you 'don't know' anything..." the man said with a sickening grin while he gagged her and then proceeded to tie her up.

The assault only took minutes, by standard clock time. But Meghan knew she would take this suffering with her into eternity, re-living this night every time she closed her eyes. It would have been better, in her mind, if he had killed her.

When Gary finally arrived at his house around 2:00 a.m., he was surprised to see no sign of Beth Ann or her dog, Romeo. Upstairs, he could definitely tell there had been a struggle–chairs tipped over, a lamp broken on the floor. He snuck next door to the Dalton's and let himself in. No sign of her there, either. Back at his house, frantic now, Gary made sure the blinds were all pulled down. Then he lit a lantern, which wasn't safe, but he had to look for a note or some clue to where Beth Ann might be. What he found was blood...enough to know that Beth Ann was in serious trouble.

With renewed passion to have Mr. Andrews taken out of the equation, Gary set his jaw. He had been wrong–there *was* something he could do. He had to get back to the municipal building and do his part.

It was going on 3:00 a.m. or even later, Beth Ann guessed, when they reached their destination: the point at the edge of the forest that she would leave her new friends behind and go forward alone. She took a deep breath and closed her eyes. A warm hand wrapped around hers and she looked up to see Brody standing inches away. He took her into his arms and held her close. She hadn't realized how much she wanted to be near this man until that very moment. For some reason, his touch didn't repulse her and she wanted to let her heart go, to melt into him. She thought she would never be comfortable with a man's touch after Travis ruined her, but this surprise was...healing. Why couldn't she just stay here now—in his arms—while the end of the world went on around them?

"Excuse me, ya big hog," Sean said to Brody, cutting in. Beth Ann wiped the tears from the corners of her eyes as she smiled and gave hugs to him, Damian and Andrew in turn.

"Don't forget to scream real loud if somebody catches you sneaking into the apartment, loud enough for us to hear you," Damian instructed. "We'll wait here for a while to make sure you get in safely."

With one last glance at Brody and one hand on the grip of the little revolver in her dark hoodie pocket, Beth Ann lunged out of the woods and carefully made her way through a sleepy neighborhood only three streets away from Meghan's apartment. She thought of her brother who had tearfully given her his sweatshirt at the last minute, making her promise to return it. Beth Ann lifted her chin a little; she aimed to keep that promise.

It took some time to cross the three blocks because she was trying to be quiet and because her mind kept playing tricks on her. She thought she saw a movement out of the corner of her eye and she snapped her head around. She thought she heard a twig break behind her and she spun to look. She thought she heard voices, she thought she saw tiny lights flashing. Finally, ahead she saw the dark outline of the small, square three-story apartment building. Her poor heart pounded loud enough that she could hear it. In a few more yards she would be safe….

Without warning she was hit on the head from behind. In slow motion she saw the street draw nearer and nearer. *Why was the street floating?* she wondered. Then her body hit the ground and pain shot through her entire body at once. As she gulped for air and the warm blackness closed in around her, she heard a faraway deep, unfamiliar voice chuckle and say, "Someone is going to be very happy to see you!"

Gary had almost reached the municipal building when shots rang out. He gasped in surprise and ducked behind a parked car. Pulling up his rifle, he peered around the front bumper. It was too dark to see what was going on, but the sound had definitely come from the direction of the municipal building.

Moving from the car to a shed, then to a large tree trunk, Gary tried to get closer to where he had left Max and Joe. He was fully aware of the increased danger now. Not only would every neighbor in a two-block radius be looking out their windows, but in the dark his own friends may mistake him for the enemy. They weren't expecting him to come back. From behind the tree he could just make out the line of shrubs he had lain under only two hours earlier. But he couldn't tell if Max and Joe were still there.

Suddenly he remembered the night vision binoculars. Fumbling to untangle the strap around his neck, he silently chided himself for taking them from Max, who needed them right now. Just as he raised them to his eyes, the sound of running feet came from somewhere behind him. The tree would only cover him from one direction; he had to hide. Frantically, he dove head-first for the shrubs, praying that the men behind him didn't have night vision and that his own buddies wouldn't shoot him.

With the prickly needles grabbing at his clothing and woody branches scraping his skin, Gary scrambled onto his side and drew the binoculars up to his eyes. Scanning frantically, he found Max and

Joe still lying in wait, a few yards north of him. Turning his attention back to the building, he saw a man lying still on the ground outside the armory door, which stood wide open. The feet he had heard behind him belonged to two men. They ran past the hedge row, across the small rear lawn, past the motionless body, and through the open door. Gary took three deep breaths to calm his racing heart and watched.

It was deathly quiet for several minutes. He thought he heard voices at one point, but he couldn't be sure. Suddenly, four men came running out of the armory carrying large boxes and multiple guns slung across their backs that jostled noisily as they ran. Two of them wore the Deputy sash. *Were they robbing Mr. Andrews?* Gary wondered. Max was right; something strange was going on. The men ran around the corner and along the south side of the building, where Gary lost sight of them.

Just as he was trying to decide what to do, he heard Max and Joe go crackling out of the evergreen. Joe ran to check on the man lying on the ground, but Max ran to to the corner of the building, his weapon leading the way. Nearby a diesel engine roar to life and it sounded extraordinarily loud in the quiet of night.

Gary jumped as the gunfire picked up again and the vehicle pealed out. Low-crawling southward, he tried to stay concealed under the shrub branches. Every joint in his body ached and he could feel his strength draining away in the physically and emotionally exhausting long night, but he pushed himself forward. He had to get far enough around the edge of the building to see what was going on.

Just as Gary lifted up the binoculars, gunfire erupted from very nearby on his left, possibly from Dillon and Roger, followed by return fire from the direction of the street. The blinding flash made him drop the goggles and scurry through the shrub to the other side. On his feet, but crouched over, he ran to the northern corner of the hedgerow, still unsure if the shots had been aimed at him.

Finding a decent sized tree to stand behind, Gary could finally survey the scene with the night vision. Max was still at the southeast corner of the building. He spoke to the glowing green shape beside him, Joe most likely, and pointed to the far end of the building. Joe took off running to where the three other friendlies were supposed to be waiting at the northern side, but they were gone. With the binoculars, Gary watched Joe kick the tire of a parked car and punch the air a couple of times. Then Joe knelt, checked his gun and his spare mags in his vest, and headed with a determined stride for the side door into the building.

The gunfire had ceased and all was quiet. Gary wanted to help Joe, but he didn't know how to approach him without getting shot. He bent down to find a couple stones to toss at the wall to get Joe's attention. Just as he stood, a man came creeping around the corner from the front of the building in time to see Joe picking the side door lock.

"Joe!" Gary shouted the warning as he slung his shotgun into position, but not before the kill shots rang out. His hunting rifle was no match to the weapon the deputy had, but as he watched Joe slowly slide down the door jam and slump onto the ground, Gary felt a deep anger rise into his chest.

Crack! *That's for Linda*, Gary thought, as he stepped out from behind the tree and took a shot. Crack! *And Beth Ann.* Crack! *Now Joe.* One of the bullets grazed the man's shoulder and, surprisingly, instead of returning fire, the Deputy turned and ran. Then all was quiet. Too quiet.

Gary jogged to Joe and checked for a heartbeat. Although he was still warm, Joe's pulse was still. His remaining years of life had escaped through the multiple holes in his chest. Gary's hand shook as he gently closed the young man's eyes.

Gary carefully moved on, looking around as he went. The armory guard, Max, Dillon and Roger were all dead, lying awkwardly where they had fallen. Knowing that he couldn't complete the mission alone, and that he had very little time before the deputy he shot came back with reinforcements, Gary dragged each body with great effort to the front lawn. In the process, he found one more body by the road–another Deputy. Six men, gone long before they should have been, lined up side by side on the gentle slope leading up to the municipal building entrance, would wait for the dawn in hopes that the town would wake up and take action against the senselessness.

Stumbling the three blocks back to the bridge, Gary was torn between going back to his house to see if Beth Ann would turn up or fleeing town to the relative safety of the campground. Knowing deep down that there was little chance of Beth Ann simply "showing up," he opted to find Roy and hitch a ride north.

Brody, Sean and Andrew had waited about thirty quiet minutes and were ready to head back to the retreat when the sound of gunfire took them by surprise. Instantly Brody coiled and tried to bolt. Sean and Andrew jumped into action and held him back.

"Hold up!" Sean said as he clutched Brody's arm.

Brody stopped, knowing the guys were right.

"Sounds farther away, like the center of town maybe," Andrew said. Sean and Brody nodded in the dark.

Whatever it was only lasted a short time. Then they heard the faraway, foreign sound of a diesel engine starting up. The men looked at each other, baffled.

"What the heck is going on out there?" Brody questioned the air in frustration.

A few more bursts of distant gunfire could be heard, but the vehicle grew louder as it drew closer, obviously taking the road out of town. More gunfire at the checkpoint, followed by three distinct rifle shots in town. Then a deep quiet settled over the area; even their breathing sounded loud. They waited a few more minutes, but hearing no screams or distress from Beth Ann, they turned toward home and hustled to beat the dawn.

Beth Ann awoke gradually, like wading through a thick stupor. It might have been the intense pounding in her head that woke her, or it could have been the roar of a truck engine being pushed to its climbing limits, or perhaps the way her aching body bounced on the hard, corrugated surface. She tried to reach up to feel her head, but her hands were tied together. That's the moment she really, fully awoke. She opened her eyes wide. Even in the dark she could tell there was a rough cloth covering her face...her whole head, in fact. The claustrophobia, the flashbacks of being lost in the dark as a child, the memory of being hit on the head trying to get to Meghan's apartment, her brother, the retreat, Brody—it all came back to her at once. She started to hyperventilate. Who had her? Where were they taking her? Did anyone know she was gone? Over the noise and the fear, Beth Ann thought she heard crying. Was it her own, or was she not alone? Mercifully, the darkness claimed her again. The answers would have to wait.

Chapter 28

Beth Ann literally stumbled down a full flight of steps. Her hands were still tied, and the sack was still over her head, smothering every breath. Travis prodded her from behind; she would know that voice anywhere. The soft crying followed a little distance behind her, so at least that little mystery was solved; someone else had been kidnapped, too. Overwhelming fear mingled with a strange calm in each shiver.

Travis yanked her to a stop and she gasped as a pain shot through her head from the sudden movement. She heard the sound of a heavy door opening and three seconds later was accosted by the most revolting smell...ever. Her throat constricted against the mixture of urine, feces, vomit and body odor. Travis didn't give her time to wonder where she was. He pushed her into the room and knocked her down onto a mattress that must have been on the floor, it was such a long drop down from standing. It would have been useless to struggle; she could not run or see to escape even if she could. She heard chains rattling and felt Travis wrap one around her waist tightly.

"Stop! What are you doing? Let me go!" the crying voice shouted, shaking and panicky. Beth Ann noted that she sounded young, probably a teenager, and her stomach roiled.

The slap that followed seemed extraordinarily loud, but not as loud as the resulting scream.

"Shut up!" Mr. Andrews growled through gritted teeth.

With a sudden surge of anger, Beth Ann swung her knees up hard to try and knock Travis off of her, but it had the opposite effect. He leaned closer, ripped the burlap bag off her head and brought his face to hers.

"Did you miss me?" he asked in his gravelly voice. Beth Ann narrowed her eyes at him but didn't give him the satisfaction of an answer. She could hear the young girl's muffled crying continuing in the background as Mr. Andrews chained her.

Just as Travis shifted his weight to get into a better position, Andrews spoke up sternly. "Travis! Get your brain out of your pants for five minutes. We have work to do. Let's go."

Travis scowled. "I'll be back!" he promised. As he stood, Beth Ann quickly took in her surroundings. Mr. Andrews stood in the doorway with a lantern of some sort, the only light in the room. The space was fairly large, longer than her living and dining rooms together at home. Spread around the room were several beds and a couple more mattresses on the floor like hers. Sheets were strung here and there, perhaps as partitions; but in the dim lantern light, they looked like limp, haggard ghosts. With horror she realized there were women chained to each bed. Some were completely naked and uncovered. There was something that looked like a table, and some other odd shapes, set back into the shadows at the far end.

As Travis and Mr. Andrews exited, the door slammed shut behind them, leaving the women in total darkness. Beth Ann heard keys jingling and the lock mechanism engaged. As the anxiety built up quickly and threatened to overwhelm her, the "Hell Hole" came to mind. It was a ride at an amusement park she had frequented as a child with her family. She had ridden it only once and decided she didn't like it. But that was just a stupid thrill ride. This...this was a *real* hell hole. How long would she survive living in total blackness, just waiting every second of the day and night for the attackers to come?

"Help! Help me!" the young girl screamed suddenly, the chains rattling and straining.

"Shhh, save your energy, honey," came a scratchy voice from the blackness. "No one will ever hear you, except the bad guys. So you want to stop screaming, okay?"

The screaming stopped, but the whimpers continued and the nose sniffled.

"What's your name?"

"Abby. Abigail Fugh. Two guys broke into my house last night and...and just took me!"

"Abby?" the voice whispered.

"Wh-where am I?" the teenager asked, her voice still shaking.

But the raspy voice continued, murmuring over and over, "Abby? Oh, no! No! Dear God...."

"Where am I?" she repeated, louder.

After a pause, the woman's voice came through the darkness with maniacal fervor. "In a nightmare! A nightmare at Mr. Andrews' house!"

"You mean the nice Mayor?" the girl asked. She sniffed twice more.

"Oh, he's not nice, Abby. He's a monster! Don't you remember? He told me I was coming to work a good job here, managing his food. Bastard!"

The bitterness in the woman's voice now sounded more familiar to Beth Ann as she listened to the conversation. "Kristen?" she interjected.

"Kristen?" Abby echoed.

It was quiet for several long seconds. "Who wants to know?"

"Beth Ann," she responded.

The voice started to cry softly, almost imperceptibly. "Oh…Oh, my God! Beth Ann…Abby…." Kristen's defenses were pierced and she sobbed into her pillow.

Beth Ann let her friend cry while her heart broke. How much more suffering could they take? Finally, she had to ask. "Kristen, what happened? What…what is this place?"

Kristen was quiet for so long that Beth Ann thought she had fallen asleep. No one else in the room made a peep, not even Abby. Then she spoke in a voice just above a whisper. "They brought me here in Mr. Andrews' truck, made me wear a burlap sack over my head." She stopped and Beth Ann waited. "When I first got here, they kept me locked in a bedroom. One of the guys brought me some water each day to wash with, and nice lotions…and food." She paused again. "But I was a prisoner. Any time of the day or night I could get…a visitor…." Beth Ann could tell Kristen had hesitated and changed what she was going to say. "At first I justified it for the food and nice place to live, but then…I…I couldn't take it anymore. I tried to escape." Kristen's voice wavered, then came back stronger, with venom. "But they caught me."

Beth Ann had no idea what to say to her friend. Meanwhile, strangely, still no one else had said a word. She could feel the trembling, burning panic coming back with a vengeance. Maybe if she kept talking, it would help. "How many women are trapped down here, besides you, me and Abby?"

"I don't know—we don't talk." Kristen said in monotone. "A woman claiming to be Sheriff Branson's girlfriend, but she's in bad shape. A couple of teens, maybe, and another lady they brought a few days ago, but she hasn't spoken a single word."

"Rachel?" Beth Ann said softly to herself, hoping she was dead wrong.

"I told you, I don't know her name!" Kristen snapped.

"Rachel? I hope to God you're not in this room!" Beth Ann said just loud enough to make sure that all the women could hear her. "But if you are, please listen up. It's me, Beth Ann. Brody and Sean and Damian and the rest of the guys are going to rescue us! They are already working on a plan!" She didn't have the heart to explain that she was part of the plan and she had botched it.

"Just...shut up, Beth Ann!" Kristen said after a long pause. Nobody named "Rachel" had responded. "There ain't no way out of this one. I'm sorry. Abby, I'm so sorry, honey." The springs of the bed complained as Kristen tried to shift her position. "It's best if you just try to sleep as much as possible...and pray for death," she mumbled. It was the last thing Beth Ann would hear her friend say in that dungeon.

Abby's little voice broke into Beth Ann's anxiety. "Is it true? That someone is going to rescue us? I...I wanna go home. And I want Kristen to come back to our house. We miss her!"

"Yes, I know that people are looking for us...good people. If you know how to pray, this would be a good time. It sure wouldn't hurt," Beth Ann responded. She shivered uncontrollably, not knowing if it was the damp cold of the basement or uncontainable fear. It was fitting that the room was pitch black. Now she had actually become a part of the darkness. Finally, the exhaustion of being awake all night caught up with her and she fell asleep.

The clanging of metal against metal woke Beth Ann up with a start and a gasp. As the key turned in the lock, Beth Ann could sense the sudden tension in the room and her heart pounded wildly. *So this is what it's like: every time the door opens, we wonder who they're coming for*, Beth Ann thought.

In walked Mr. Andrews with the lantern. His tall shape was even more imposing from her mattress on the floor. The self-appointed mayor sauntered to Beth Ann's mattress and crouched slowly. "It's time you answered a few questions, Miss Dalton," he said in his syrupy voice. "Let's start with where you've been for the last week or so."

Beth Ann prayed for courage and wisdom, then responded with the backstory she had practiced with Brody. "I have no family left in town and I wanted to see my only brother. When I got to his place, they were dead–my brother, sister-in-law and baby niece. Their house had been raided. There was no food." Her voice broke, but she forced herself to finish. "I stayed long enough to bury them and...then I came back."

"Uh huh," Andrews said as he stood and started to pace slowly, the small pool of light following his feet. "But you didn't tell anyone where you were going?"

"No! I...I didn't want to get anyone in trouble!"

Mr. Andrews nodded slowly while he took a few more steps. "You didn't see anyone else on your little excursion? Neighbors? Friends?"

Beth Ann could tell he was fishing for something, and she tried to keep her voice from shaking. "Well, they have an elderly neighbor couple. I did see them, but they couldn't help me. They're starving and distrustful...like everyone else." She paused and tried to sound less defensive. "I don't like you or what you stand for, but you do have food and you've kept us safe. And my home is in town. So I came back. I'll keep working on the Garden Team and do my part." She swallowed hard. "I'm sorry, Mr. Andrews." Hopefully that would do the trick.

Andrews stopped pacing and chuckled softly. "No, I don't think you are. But you will be." He stood at the side of her mattress. The lantern light hurt her eyes, but she could make out his military-style boots. "I'll give you one more chance to tell me the truth...."

"I AM telling the truth!" Beth Ann shouted.

The boot met its mark before she saw it coming. She let out an anguished cry as she curled into a fetal position, arms wrapped around her stomach, choking on the bile that rose into her throat.

Andrews bent over her. "LIAR!" he bellowed and she flinched. His hot, foul breath lingered around them. Then he crouched down and stroked her hair. She recoiled from his touch, still coughing. In a soft, gentle tone, he said, "You see, Beth Ann, YOU led us right to your brother and all his rebellious militia friends."

Beth Ann squeezed her eyes shut tighter. *No! God, please no!* her spirit cried.

"Yes. That's right. Their deaths will be on you! You should be grateful that you won't be alive to see them fall. Tomorrow you will be hanged as an example of what we do to spies." He stood and let that sink in. Then he shook his head. "I almost feel bad, you know? You had a lot of potential. All you had to do was play along. That's all."

Beth Ann tried to push down the stabbing guilt and gasped out the words she'd been longing to say. "Your days are numbered, Andrews."

He laughed, the maniacal sound reverberating off all the walls. "Oh! You must mean that little mutiny we had last night down at the courthouse. Yes, that took me by surprise, truly! I was trying to stage my own little attack and they interrupted me. It failed–sorry–but it worked in my favor. Now I have six bodies to blame on you and your friends! Oh, and this nice little lady, too," he said, gesturing with the lantern toward Abby's bed. Beth Ann caught a glimpse of the girl's eyes wide open in fear, her hands clamped over her mouth.

"What?" The word came out like a croak as she looked up at Andrews.

"Oh, that's right...you missed the town meeting! This morning I was forced to call the Tionestans together and tell them that a large group of looters has settled a few miles away. During the night they attacked us, infiltrated the town, raided the armory, and took a teenage girl. The whole town is outraged! Every able bodied man and woman is to report to the square tomorrow to take up arms and rid ourselves of this fearsome foe. Of course, after they watch the rebel's spy hang."

"But...you can't do that! It's not true!" Beth Ann cried out, the pitch of her voice high as her throat constricted.

The Mayor growled and brought his fist down on the side of her head. "Look who's talking about TRUTH!" He stood suddenly with a huff. "Alright. I'm tired. Let's wrap this up," Mr. Andrews said, clasping his hands together in a loud clap that made Beth Ann jump. "How many are there?"

With the searing heat in her cheek, the blinding explosions of light in her eye, and the ringing in her ear, she wasn't sure she'd heard him. "How many what?" A hoarse whisper was the best she could do.

"People! How many people are in on that militia camp you were hiding at?"

"I don't know what you're talking about!" Beth Ann shouted. Then she broke down crying, wondering what it would feel like to die while her friends and neighbors watched, believing she was a traitor. No trial, no representation, no way to tell her side of the story.

"What a useless...," Andrews began. He stood watching her for what seemed like a long time. "We're not done here–I'll be back. And maybe I'll send Travis down for a little visit when he's done with his shift on night watch."

The light left with Andrews, and the bolt locked in the darkness. Not a sound came from any of the other women in the room. She was alone yet again. Beth Ann retreated into herself, embracing the dark and hoping to simply dissolve into it.

Chapter 29

The diesel engine roared to life, sending a jolt through Beth Ann's limp body. After the long night, she vaguely remembered being dragged up the steps at dawn and being stuffed onto the floor of the truck's cab behind the front seats. They didn't bother to put the sack over her head, she noticed with indifference as her nose flared from the stench of the filthy carpet. Travis had climbed behind the wheel and Andrews took the passenger seat. The truck rolled out of the barn and stopped a little distance away; she heard two men climb into the bed of the truck.

Fully awake now, she was aware that every joint in her body ached. The bruises on her face and body burned while her head throbbed. *Maybe hanging will be a relief*, she thought. Living was becoming too hard, too painful...and, honestly, a little pointless. She was ready to leave this world behind.

While the truck bounced its way down the side of Baker Hill, Beth Ann thought of the diverse group of people she had met at the retreat, how they had formed a brave community and worked together to survive. Brody's face with the boyish grin took shape in her mind and she almost smiled, thinking back to how he had frightened her at first...and teased her about her little shovel. She thought of her parents and her neighbors Gary and Linda, and almost felt happy that she would see them in heaven in a short time; she breathed a grateful prayer that she had made things right with God.

Her only regret was leaving her brother and his family. She could imagine that her brother would feel responsible for her death and she would have no way to tell him that it's okay, that he cannot take the blame for her choices or for the evil that's in the world. She wouldn't even get to say good-bye.

Beth Ann winced as the truck hit a pothole and the nausea returned, but she let her mind continue to wander. The reflection was cathartic. She was different now, less than six months after the lights went out and her world had turned upside down. The attack on America had brought her to a crossroads in her cushy, self-centered life, forcing her to make difficult choices. There were many more ways to die now than to live, but choosing to overcome was the first step. The second step was learning some survival skills from people like Gary and Sean. Losing her parents, being forced to be independent, seeing death around her every day–these things had built strength on the inside and outside. They had developed her faith journey, built character, and turned her into a young woman, ready to know her own mind and be responsible for her own actions. Ironically, those actions were the cause of her impending death, but hey–there never were guarantees in this life.

Suddenly, Beth Ann smashed into the back of the front seats as the truck screeched to a stop. She bit her lip to keep from crying out in pain, tasting the salty blood where a split from the night before re-opened.

"What the...?" Mr. Andrews started to say, but his words were cut off by gunfire–a lot of gunfire, punctuated by a steady "boom" every couple seconds. It seemed to come from every direction, and she could hear return fire coming from the bed of the truck just behind where she lay.

Beth Ann flinched and tried to curl up, but there wasn't enough room on the floor to maneuver, and her hands and feet were tied. Was it too much to hope that either the resistance or the guys from the retreat were coming to rescue her? Or would she just be transferred from bad guys to worse guys?

Mr. Andrews yelled, "GO! GO! Get us out of here!" while firing his pistol out the passenger window. Shell casings landed on her leg, searing hot through the denim.

The truck roared and lurched forward but didn't get very far. After it rolled to a final stop, it shuddered once and died. A loud hissing sound drowned out Andrews' and Travis' confused banter, followed by the smell of smoke. Was the truck on fire? Beth Ann's skin crawled in panic and she strained against the ropes.

When the hissing stopped, Travis and Andrews were quiet, listening to a man shouting from a distance. From where she lay inside the cab, she couldn't make out his words clearly. It sounded like the attackers just wanted the truck and their guns. If they were being robbed, then it wasn't her knight in shining armor come to rescue her. As the faint hope drained out of her, she realized that in the "damsel in distress" scenario, people always focused on the prince and the romantic rescue, essentially ignoring the deadly, horrific situation the princess was in or how she was coping with the stress.

"What'll we do, Boss?" Travis asked quietly.

"Shut up! I'm thinking," Mr. Andrews snapped.

"Mike and Charlie are getting out of the truck! They're surrendering!" The pitch of Travis' voice had risen slightly.

Mr. Andrews didn't say anything at first, but then he replied calmly, "Just play along, Travis, and try not to get killed. Let me do the talking."

The voice from the hillside shouted for the Driver to step out, and with a low growl Travis opened his door and "played along." Beth Ann heard his gun hit the bed of the truck with a *clunk*.

Mr. Andrews' head appeared above the seat back, startling her. "Stay put, missy," he hissed. She closed her eyes. *As if I could run away,* she thought. *At least hanging would be faster than dying from dehydration and exposure.* "If you make so much as a peep, I will make you suffer until you beg me to kill you!" She felt a blanket being thrown over her.

Andrews threw open the door with enthusiasm and stepped out. "Hello, Gentlemen!" she heard him shout, and she could tell he was flashing his best political grin. With both cab doors left wide open, she could hear a little more of what was going on outside, although slightly muffled because of the blanket. "You are to be congratulated on a well-coordinated ambush!" His voice faded as he moved away from the truck. She made out enough of his speech to know that Andrews was trying to recruit the attackers for his security team, offering them a nice house to live in, food, better guns, and even gold. After a long, quiet pause, with only an oblivious robin chortling to welcome the new day, Mr. Andrews sweetened the deal by offering to share his ladies with them.

Beth Ann suddenly felt sick to her stomach. Was it possible for someone to be born without a moral compass? Or did he lose it somewhere along life's way? She started to cough and pressed her mouth into the carpet to prevent anyone from hearing her—especially Andrews, who would assume she did it on purpose. The acid burned her parched throat, and the pressure from coughing made a sharp pain shoot across her ribcage. Her lips were chapped, and the blood had dried to a thick crust on her lower lip.

When she finally got herself under control, she could hear a man shouting at Mr. Andrews to get on his knees beside the other men and face the river. A new, frightening thought came to Beth Ann at that moment: What if the hoodlums jumped in the truck and took off, not knowing she was in there? Just as she was trying to decide if it was better to take her chances with Andrews or the attackers, she heard a rustling sound very close by. She held her breath and remained still while someone rummaged through the front seats, the floor under the seats, and even the glove compartment. She heard the passenger side of the split bench seat pull forward, and then a hand gripped her ankle like a vice.

She gasped and flinched reflexively, which she immediately regretted as the blanket was pulled off in one swift motion. Shifting to face her attacker, she heard herself beg, "Please!" Her voice was so raspy that she wondered if he could understand her. The man was silhouetted with the bright rising sun behind him, but she could plainly see the gun in his hand.

"Beth Ann?"

She wondered if she was hallucinating. She squinted her eyes. "Brody?" Did she even dare to hope...?

"Oh, thank God!" the man said as he backed out of the truck. She heard him holler: "Darren! Get down here on the double! You too, Luke!"

Could it be? Darren...the doctor from the retreat? But she didn't know any "Luke," so maybe it was just a coincidence. The man crawled partway into the back seat area and began cutting the ropes off her feet and hands.

"Hold on, Beth Ann. We're gonna get you out of here," he said gently.

She shook her head, trying to clear the fog in her brain. "Brody? Is it really you?" Relief washed over her, making her tremble, and she squeezed her eyes shut tightly to hold back the sudden tears.

"It's me. Me and Damian. You're safe now. Here," Brody said as he reached a strong arm behind her neck and gently helped her to a seated position. With Damian on one side and Brody on the other, they carefully and slowly eased her out of the truck. As Brody lifted her into his arms, she cried out in pain. He carried her to the side of the road and gently laid her down. Damian had spread the blanket from the back of the truck over the dewy grass so she wouldn't get chilled. But she continued to tremble.

Beth Ann gazed up at the circle of faces above her, and she felt like Dorothy waking up from her dream in *The Wizard of Oz*. There was Brody and Damian, then Sean, and finally Darren the Doctor joined them. "I had a dream," she said with effort, her voice shaking at the same rate as her body, "that I went to visit my brother and you were there, and you, and you. You were soldiers and scared me half to death! But the doctor was nice," she croaked with a half-smile. She still wasn't sure if this was happening or if she was seriously delusional and still riding in the back of the truck. But she decided to go with it and enjoy it while it lasted.

The men chuckled and left to give Darren and Beth Ann a little privacy. The doctor did a simple, perfunctory examination, made her drink some water with a funny taste, and asked a lot of embarrassing questions. Meanwhile, Beth Ann could hear commotion in the background. Andrews had discovered who had "attacked" him and what they really came for...and he was furious. Once the men were searched for weapons, zip-tied and lying face down on the road, Sean sauntered in her direction. He clapped Brody on the shoulder as he passed by.

Sean knelt down beside Beth Ann. He held her gaze briefly, then looked away, his grief evident in his eyes. "I'm so sorry, Beth Ann," he finally mustered.

She reached up a small hand and placed it on his large, weathered fingers. "I knew the risks.... I'll be okay." She forced a smile and waited for him to look at her and return it. A movement to her right made her turn her head to see Brody a short distance away, arms crossed and jaw clenched tightly. She gave him a reassuring smile, too, but he just shifted his gaze to the river that ran parallel to the road.

Sean helped to ease her into a sitting position, and then he and Brody joined the other men to make a plan. Damian, Andrew, Randy and Caleb were all there, in addition to a man she didn't recognize whom they called "Luke." Within a couple short minutes the huddle broke and each man hustled to his designated task. Darren and Beth Ann watched as Andrew stood guard over the Mayor and his henchmen. Luke jogged down the road to where spike strips had been placed–to keep the truck from backing up–and started spreading leaves over them. Caleb, Randy and Brody ran off into the woods, emerging with cables and a pulley system to move a large tree that stretched across the road.

"Ohhh! That's why we stopped…," Beth Ann said aloud, but to herself.

Darren smiled compassionately at her as he unwrapped an MRE. "Those guys were pretty determined to find you...and Mr. Andrews. We've been out here all night, setting up the ambush and waiting for the truck to come rolling by."

Beth Ann took the food and slowly shook her head in wonder. It was still hard to believe she was safe.

Sean had pulled a tarp out of the truck bed and cut some seat belt webbing out of the cab. He dropped the items on the ground near Beth Ann and then ran off into the treeline. He came back dragging two thin branches, longer than he was tall, and started assembling something that looked like a cross between a stretcher and a wheelbarrow, but without wheels.

"What are you making?" Beth Ann asked when the curiosity got the better of her.

"Mode of transportation, Native American style! Doc here doesn't want you walking, and we need to get moving quick before people realize Andrews hasn't shown up in town and come looking for him," Sean explained as his hands kept moving at a fast pace.

She wasn't sure how a couple of sticks were going to "transport" her, but she let it go. "So...how did you find me?"

Sean's answer came in little bursts of breath as he hurried to finish the strange contraption. "Luke...that guy over there...showed up at the retreat yesterday with his family." He stood and stepped to the other side. "Long story short, we pieced together his story." Breath. "Found out that...the night we took you back to Tionesta, ...Andrews had raided the town's armory, ...killed some of his own deputies, ...terrorized some of the town folk...and blamed it on us." He added some cross braces while continuing. "He called a town meeting to rally people against us...and today they are supposed to attack the retreat."

Beth Ann nodded. Andrews had told her as much.

Sean stopped and looked at her. "Luke told us Andrews had caught a spy who would be hung today. Is...was that you?"

Beth Ann nodded. "I never made it to the apartment, Sean. Someone knocked me out from behind and I woke up in the truck."

Sean rubbed his hand through his hair and looked away. But neither one of them could change the past. He knelt in front of her. "There's one more thing. Luke said two of Andrews' men took his teenage daughter, so he knew Andrews was lying when he blamed it on us. Because of him we knew where to set up the ambush."

"Abby? Is her name Abby?" Beth Ann asked as she tried to stand, a surge of energy coming from panic. Here she was, all happy and comfortable while Kristen and other ladies were dying in a pit. "I know where she is! A terrible, horrible place! And there's more...chained up...we have to—" She couldn't seem to put a whole thought together in a cohesive sentence. The violent trembling had returned.

"Whoa, there!" Sean almost fell backward at her sudden movement, and Darren leapt into action. The two men gently eased her back to the ground. "Yes, we know! And we're on our way there now."

"No! No, you don't know….! You couldn't know…. O, God!" Beth Ann buried her face into her drawn up knees and sobbed while her ribs screamed at her. Everything she had been holding in for the last twenty-eight hours now came out at once.

Sean wrapped his large hands around hers in a comforting gesture. "Shhh. It's over, Beth Ann. It's over," he crooned. "I promise."

"She's still in shock, Sean," the doctor said. "We need to get her home."

Sean nodded. "I know, I know. And the longer we stay here, the more danger we're in. Go ahead and get her settled into the travois while I help the guys wrap this up."

The men pulled everything useful out of the truck—including the gasoline and a day's ration of food for a couple hundred people—and pushed the truck into the river. It was beyond repair. They stashed the food with the extra weapons and gear in a hollow and covered it with brush and leaves to be picked up later. They cleaned the debris and puddles of fluid from the truck off the road with leaves and river water, topped off their magazines, and hooked up the travois to Mike, Travis, and Charlie with the seatbelts. Mr. Andrews was tethered around his neck and given to Luke, like an animal on a leash.

Sean gave the signal to roll out. Reclined awkwardly on the travois, Beth Ann hugged her brother's sweatshirt like a life preserver. They were headed back to the hell hole. If anything happened and the rescue failed.... Beth Ann closed her eyes. She couldn't bear the thought. Time to pray some more.

Kneeling at the river's edge, Gary leaned forward to fill a bucket with the cool water flowing down the Allegheny. It was a beautiful morning, a promise of summer on its way. But the uncertainty of his future weighed heavily on his mind. After the failed assassination attempt, the resistance leaders were dead. He had managed to escape to the campground up river and by mid-day Zachary had stumbled into the camp, bringing news of Mr. Andrews' town meeting.

Gary was livid to find out that rather than the people rallying for the cause of the six Tionestan bodies and holding leadership accountable, they bought into Andrews' lies that some rebel group had attacked them. The Mayor and Sheriff had obviously staged the whole thing; Gary had witnessed it! Now there was going to be a hanging and Andrews was assembling an army. What a danger it was when people blindly followed a tale-spinner like Mr. Andrews. They had forfeited all their power to one man. But they were partly to blame, since they had no provisions to survive without him.

The remaining two men from the resistance party had not been seen or heard from. The chlorine tablets for purifying water were almost gone, the food stash had already been finished off before the attack, and their ammunition was limited to what was loaded in their guns. Gary began to think that he and Beth Ann should have taken the boat and headed down river after Linda died. He had played it safe...and look how it turned out.

As he pulled the bucket toward him, a barrage of gunfire shredded the morning calm. The surprise knocked him from his crouched position onto his back. The shots came from across the river and a good distance north, but still he was in an exposed position at the water's edge. Gary scrambled up the bank to the stone cabin ruins. Zachary was there, wide-eyed and stiffly standing against the tallest remaining wall, rifle gripped in both hands.

The battle didn't last long, but the quiet that followed it was almost worse: the wondering and not knowing. Had Andrews organized the town army so quickly? Or was it the band of looters Andrews had warned them about, taking over yet another defenseless farm?

Gary handed Zachary the canteen. "All right. It's just you and me. No more sitting around wondering what's next. It's time to come up with Plan B."

Chapter 30

The journey to Mr. Andrews' mountain mansion was grueling—mostly uphill—and took a couple of hours at their slow pace. High overhead, the sun beamed its joy in the form of summer-like heat. The motley convoy stopped a couple of times for directions, which Andrews and his men were reluctant to give. But Sean's military-trained interrogation skills, combined with a couple of nasty sock gags, persuaded all the information they needed to come forth.

When they finally arrived and Dr. Darren had helped Beth Ann out of the travois, she gazed at the beautiful cabin-like home with wonder. She had never seen it from the outside. It looked like a magazine cover. It certainly didn't look like it had a secret hell hole; no one would ever suspect.

With only one guard inside, it didn't take long for them to get in. Charlie, Andrews' youngest henchman, was giving information freely at this point. In awe Beth Ann gazed at the beautiful furnishings and modern layout. How could such an evil man live in such a nice place? Of course, it was messy, with a bunch of bachelors living there. Randy, Andrew and Caleb went up to the loft to keep watch while Sean, Brody, the now five prisoners with the house guard added in, Luke, Darren, Damian, and Beth Ann made their way downstairs.

Beth Ann stopped Luke as he tried to elbow his way to the front of the pack. "I met your daughter...well, kind of. Abby, right?"

The man nodded and shifted his weight. Sudden, fresh moisture in his eyes reflected the glow from her flashlight.

"I...I just wanted to let you know that she's okay. Scared, but okay." Beth Ann reached out to squeeze the man's wrist in reassurance.

He didn't say anything, but abruptly turned and trotted to catch up to the group. His body was rigid with coiled energy, ready to strike at anyone who stood in the way of finding his daughter.

When they entered the dark, wide hallway with doors on both sides, Beth Ann shuddered and her stomach churned violently. She wanted to turn and run. Darren, who hadn't left her side since she was pulled out of Andrews' truck, took hold of her elbow and pulled her closer to him protectively. When they reached the correct door, Sean made the prisoners sit with their backs against the wall while he tried the numerous keys until he found the right one. The padlock popped open, but Sean hesitated.

Suddenly, Luke burst past Sean and ran headlong into the room.

"Wait!" Brody yelled, making everyone jump. But Luke didn't stop.

Beth Ann held her breath, her heart pounding loudly. Brody and Sean followed Luke into the room. The putrid smell assaulted everyone in the hall as they waited. A muffled commotion of footsteps and sheets rustling and weak gasps was followed by the heart-wrenching sobs of a full-grown man. Darren sprang forward then and entered the room. Beth Ann heard obscenities come out of his mouth that she wouldn't have guessed the old doctor would know. Sean came back out into the hall, gasping for air.

"What's going on in there?" Damian demanded.

Sean's response didn't come in the form of words. He reached down and grabbed the young Charlie by the scruff of his neck, forcing him to his feet, and tossed him into the room. The house guard, Richard, was next. Beth Ann heard one of the men vomiting.

The keys rattled and she heard Sean demand, "Get them out of those freakin' chains!" More soft crying from several women could be heard now.

Beth Ann leaned against the wall for strength and covered her face with her hands until she got her emotions under control. *Breathe...slowly, deeply...breathe.* It was really true: they were all being rescued. Sean appeared in the doorway, asking Damian to bring the prisoners in and ordering Beth Ann to stay out. However, knowing that the women would be terrified to see Mr. Andrews and Travis in the room, she defied Sean's order.

"I just came from here, so don't you try and stop me!" she said, pushing ahead of Damian. If nothing else, she could be the only non-male presence and comfort in the room.

Felicia was crying like a little girl, sitting on the first bed inside the door. Beth Ann sat down and took the girl into her arms, rocking her back and forth. By the light of various flashlights and a lantern, the scene in front of her was ghastly. As much as she didn't want to watch, she couldn't tear her eyes away. Brody was cutting down the sheets and covering the women, six in all. Richard and Charlie were unlocking their chains. Darren was hovering over one of the women, acting frustrated and helpless. Luke was stroking Abby's hair with her head pressed tightly to his chest.

Damian, Mike, Travis and Andrews stood quietly just inside the door, but Beth Ann refused to look at them. She would never feel safe in their presence...ever. She dropped her head to rest it against Felicia's, so she didn't see Luke suddenly stand up. She didn't know that he headed straight for Mr. Andrews, didn't notice that he pulled the .357 revolver out of his belt. Didn't see him aim at Andrews' head, or see Sean and Damian lunge for the gun. Didn't witness Andrews pulling Travis in front of him as a human shield.

The gunshot reverberated in the room, the explosion so loud that Beth Ann thought her eardrums had burst. She screamed, along with most of the people in the room. While her ears continued to ring painfully, Beth Ann watched as Damian wrestled the gun from

Luke, who glared with hatred at the still-standing Andrews, spattered with Travis' blood. Sean sent Damian with Mr. Andrews out of the room and down the hall to check the other locked rooms. Luke, with shoulders sagging from disappointment, went back to his daughter.

And Travis.... Beth Ann finally worked up the nerve to look at Travis. A single hole in his forehead told the whole story of his form sprawled awkwardly across the floor. His eyes were open, bringing just as much terror to Beth Ann's heart in death as in life. A dark pool of liquid under his head gradually grew larger as his lifeblood drained out. She closed her eyes and heaved a sigh as she tightened her grip on Felicia. That man might show up in her nightmares for years to come, but he would never touch her—or any other woman—again.

After a brief discussion about their options for getting back to town, Sean and Brody agreed that their safest choice was to stay at the cabin in a defensible position and wait for the town to come to them, in hopes that they could negotiate without any more loss of life. In the meantime, the women needed to be moved to nice bedrooms upstairs, where the doctor could evaluate each one.

Beth Ann stood first and helped Felicia navigate around Travis' body and into the hall. Luke helped Abby, who was perking up well and getting some color back in her face. Although frightened and upset, she had not yet been assaulted, to her father's great relief. Brody helped Kristen, who was weak but able to walk on her own. The remaining three ladies had to be carried, which Sean delegated to Mike, Charlie and Richard. Although they had not directly hurt the women, they had not stopped Andrews and Travis and therefore, in Sean's eyes, a good portion of the blame fell on them.

Darren followed close on the heels of Mike, who was carrying Rachel, Butch's widow. Since the moment he had found her in the putrid room, the doctor had vacillated between anger and sorrow. He had knelt beside her bed, quiet tears tracing the paths of the wrinkles of his face; he had paced and ranted; he had pounded his fists and stomped his feet; he had talked softly to her. But she had not opened her eyes or said a single word to acknowledge his presence.

Mike gently laid her on a bed in the first room and Beth Ann handed Felicia over to Kristen as the rest of the group continued down the hall. Beth Ann followed Darren into the beautiful bedroom. The afternoon sun streaming in the window was a welcome contrast to the dank conditions they had come from.

"I thought, maybe, it would be good," Beth Ann started timidly, addressing Darren, "for me to help with your examinations. I mean, not help exactly, but be a female presence, you know...maybe help them feel more comfortable than just being alone with you. Even though you're a doctor...." Beth Ann didn't want to insult Darren, but she suspected these women may have a few trust issues with men. She just didn't know how to say it.

Darren tilted his head and stared at Beth Ann with a blank look. Then his eyebrows lifted and he said softly, "Oh, certainly. That's a fine idea, if you're feeling up to it." He scrutinized her with his doctor eyes.

"Yes. You've already examined me, and I...I want to help," she responded, letting her gaze shift to Rachel's still form, curled into a ball with her back to them. She looked back at Darren. "May I?"

He nodded and set his bag on a nearby small desk to begin organizing his tools. Beth Ann walked around the bed and knelt so that she was facing Rachel. When she gently took Rachel's hand in hers, Rachel flinched.

"Rachel? It's me, Beth Ann." No response. "You don't have to be afraid anymore. Your friends are here...; they came for us." Still Rachel didn't move. "Travis is dead, Rachel. And Mr. Andrews...well, he's not in charge anymore." Beth Ann looked up as Darren stepped to the other side of the bed with a clipboard and blood pressure cuff, the obligatory stethoscope hanging from his neck. She patted Rachel's hand. "Dr. Sorenson is going to check you over now, okay? You remember Darren, who moved in with your neighbor Peter?" Still no response. Beth Ann gave Darren a shrug. "I'm going to be right here while he examines you, okay?" She tried to pull her hand away so she could stand up, but Rachel gripped it tightly—her first sign of understanding. Beth Ann smiled as tears sprang to her eyes. She placed her other hand over Rachel's and held on for the entire exam, which Darren did his best to keep as quick and non-invasive as possible. After making some notes, the doctor packed up his bag to head to the next room.

Beth Ann smoothed Rachel's hair. "I'm going to help Darren with the rest of the girls, okay? You rest now. I'll be back with something for you to eat in a little while."

Rachel's lips started to move. Beth Ann leaned closer, clearly hearing the whispered "Thank you," the first words she had ever heard Rachel speak. Overcome, Beth Ann leaned forward and gently kissed Rachel's forehead. A single tear emerged from Rachel's closed lashes, trailing across the bridge of her nose and dropping onto the pillow. The long healing journey had begun.

Beth Ann's joy over Rachel's response was short-lived. Being present for the following five examinations was grueling and emotionally draining for her, to the extent that when they were finished, Darren forced her to lie down and sleep. She complied, but within the hour she had a second wind and was determined to do something productive.

After checking on her "patients," including the doctor who was sound asleep in a wingback chair, she made her way tentatively downstairs. The place was still foreign to her, and it represented the worst days of her life. Her body felt rigid, expecting something scary at every corner as if it was a haunted-themed house. Brody approached her as she reached the bottom of the stairs and took her elbow, leading her to a leather chair by a large, unlit stone fireplace.

"Hey, you're awake." He sat in the chair opposite hers, but stayed perched stiffly on the front edge of the cushion. His eyes were full of concern, his forehead drawn into a deep "v" between his eyebrows.

She smiled and nodded. She knew she was awake; he didn't have to tell her. "Yeah. The nap helped." Tucking a stray piece of hair behind her ear, she averted her eyes, realizing how terrible she must look. She longed to wash her face and run a brush through her hair...maybe some concealer for the bruises. It made her think that maybe the women upstairs would feel better if they had a little personal grooming....

Brody leaned forward, placing his elbows on his knees. "Listen, Beth Ann. I—"

"Please!" she interrupted, shaking her head adamantly. She leaned forward in her chair and held out both hands toward him. "Please, don't. I...I just want to look forward, not back. By God's grace you found us. And I am not going to question His plan...any part of it." The warmth and strength in Brody's hands gave her courage as she held his gaze. "But...well, thank you," she finished lamely.

The chiseled features on his face gave no indication of emotion, yet Beth Ann knew that a wrestling match was taking place in his head. Finally, he swallowed hard. "No. We should thank God," he said quietly.

Keenly aware that Abby sat on a couch nearby, Beth Ann pulled her hands from Brody's grasp and stood. "Since the doctor is asleep and can't holler at me," she said with a twinkle in her eye, "I thought I could make us...everyone...something to eat."

Brody stood, too. "Yeah, sure. That'd be good. Luke, Randy and I are going on watch duty in the tower soon. Let's go find something to heat up."

Beth Ann grabbed his wrist and stopped him. "Wait...watch duty?"

Brody nodded. "We knew someone would show up. After all, Mr. Andrews sent out the battle cry and didn't show up for the battle. And nobody in town got to eat today. It was just a matter of time."

Beth Ann's eyes grew large and she glanced at the massive front door to the left of the kitchen. "You mean, people are out there, right now, with guns?" Now she noticed Randy and Luke with their guns, positioned beside windows on separate sides of the large great room. And the house was deadly quiet.

Brody grimaced and stole a quick glance at the young Abby. "Yes, but we're working on a plan for negotiation. Don't worry. Just...stay inside, okay?" He tried to chuckle at his little joke, but it came out in an awkward sputter. He cleared his throat.

She nodded and sighed. So much for thinking she was safe. She wrapped her arms around her tender ribs and closed her eyes. "I just want to go home," she said quietly. Then she looked at Brody. "This nightmare has to end...for all of us."

He gently wrapped his arms around her, aware of her injuries, but he didn't say anything to reassure her. Too soon he pulled away. "I need to get back. Randy's waiting for me."

Abby shifted on the couch. "You wanna help me heat up something to eat, Abby?" Beth Ann asked. The young girl looked to her dad across the room, who nodded. She stood and followed Brody and Beth Ann to the kitchen.

Randy craned his neck to see the trio coming his way. He met them at the island. "It's not exactly a fully stocked kitchen. Brody, cover my window and I'll run down to the store room real quick. Then we can work on our fallback plan."

"Bring up some brothy soup, if you can find it," Beth Ann requested.

Randy stopped and looked at her with a funny expression, like he was hungrier than "soup."

"For the patients," she said, gesturing to the second level. Visibly relieved, he hurried on his way.

By the time Sean, Caleb and Andrew came down from watch, it was early evening. Their replacements had eaten hearty canned lasagna at their posts and worked out several possible negotiation scenarios and a fallback plan through the tunnel to the barn. The women upstairs had been fed as much soup as they could put down.

Damian was given a bowl of lasagna to eat while the prisoners he was guarding watched him. When Sean, Caleb and Andrew had finished off the lasagna and practically licked the large #10-size can clean, Sean went upstairs to get a report from Darren.

Mere minutes later, Sean came bounding down the steps with Darren close behind. Beth Ann, at one end of the island reviewing the fallback plan with Abby, watched Sean carefully. Something had just changed. In fact, her skin tingled–the whole atmosphere in the room had instantly transformed from tense to expectant, although no one else seemed to notice.

Sean plopped casually down into a chair at the table next to Andrew. "You'll never believe who one of the girls is," he said and then waited for someone to prompt him. Caleb glanced up from cleaning his weapon.

"Who?" Andrew asked.

Sean clasped his hands behind his head, taking full credit for the discovery. "None other than Sheriff Branson's girlfriend."

"What the heck was she doing down there?" Caleb asked, incredulous. "Does Sheriff Branson know?"

Beth Ann wondered what that had to do with getting out of their dangerous situation. She slumped down into her high-backed stool as the conversation between Sean, Caleb, Andrew and Darren continued. Would this ever end?

"Com'on, Abby," Beth Ann said. "Let's go see who's awake upstairs. I'd like to give them a chance to wash up a little. I found a bunch of different lotions in one of the drawers in the first bedroom. They'll like that. And we can brush their hair and help them find some clothes."

Darren nodded his approval as they walked past the table on the way to the stairs, then abruptly stood and followed them. He had been arguing with Sean about letting Sheriff Branson in to see his patient Sarah against her wishes. Apparently he gave up and decided to return to the place that *he* was in charge, upstairs.

Rachel and Sarah wanted to be left alone, but the rest of the girls were glad to get cleaned up and dressed. Most were quietly appreciative, but Kristen was still cynical about their situation. As Beth Ann sat with her friend, the sky flamed and gradually went out. With a feeling of despair, Beth Ann realized that she would be spending another night in this awful house.

It had not been dark long when she heard heavy footsteps running up the stairs. Frightened, she jumped up and closed the door, locking it from the inside. Standing in the dark, with her back against the door and her heart pounding in her chest, she could hear Kristen's rapid, shallow breathing mixing with her own. After several long, quiet minutes, Beth Ann mustered up the courage to sneak down the hall. There was a man in Sarah's room!

She raced down the steps to find Sean and straight into the kitchen where she froze in terror. There was Sean, surrounded by a bunch of Mr. Andrews' Security Team, green sashes and guns and all. They all turned to look at her, and she started to back away. How could this be happening? The panic squeezed her throat as she tried to decide if she could reach the front door before getting caught or shot. She couldn't stay here a minute longer.

Sean leaped forward and caught her arm. "Wait!" He chuckled. "Hold up, there, Beth Ann! It's okay."

Beth Ann shot a glance at the group of men behind him and looked back up at Sean. "But there's a man...in Sarah's room!" she whispered harshly. She flung an arm in the direction of the stairway.

Sean gently took ahold of her shoulders and bent his head to look her straight in the eye. "I know. It's Sheriff Branson, Sarah's boyfriend. He's not going to hurt her. The deputies have seen enough evidence to convince them that Andrews should go on trial. It's over, Beth Ann. We're all going into town tomorrow morning."

Beth Ann looked from face to face, her mouth gaping open. The standoff was over? She let herself down slowly onto the nearest chair and covered her face with her hands. Relief flooded over her, and her heart lifted. God had made a way out of this. She was going home.

Epilogue

White, billowy clouds moved lazily across the sky, creating welcome pockets of shade in between searing blasts of the sun's rays. It was the day before Memorial Day and summer was announcing its official arrival. Beth Ann and Brody sat side by side on the front steps of the Lutheran church. Not counting the short funeral service earlier in the week, Pastor Dan had held a non-denominational Sunday service there for the first time in months. But the building had emptied quickly and now only served as a backdrop to their conversation.

"Are you sure?" Brody asked for the third time.

"Yes!" Beth Ann replied, giggling. It felt good to smile again. "I want to stay in town, in my own house, tending my little garden. I need this, Brody. I need to stand on my own two feet, at least for a while. And don't forget, Rachel is living with me now, and my neighbor Gary is miraculously back from the dead, so I won't be alone." How could she explain why this was so important to her? She reached over to pick a bright yellow dandelion, rolling its stem between her thumb and index finger. "All my life I've relied on someone to take care of me, only thinking of myself and what I wanted. But that's changed...*I've* changed. I want to work hard and to give back. It's very...satisfying and adult-y." She looked sideways at him.

He nodded. "There's plenty of hard work at your brother's farm...."

She pushed him away playfully. "Brody! You're not making this very easy!"

"Good!" he said, nudging her gently with his shoulder. He knew that her body was still healing.

They sat in silence for a few minutes. Brody shifted on the step so that he could face her and took her hand in his. "I respect your decision. So...." He paused.

"So...what?" Beth Ann prompted with her eyes narrowed, suspicious and curious at the same time.

"So...what's a guy gotta do to get the chance to see you once in a while?" he finished.

She dropped her head, suddenly feeling shy. "Just stop by, I guess. You know where to find me." She lifted her eyes back to his. "I'd like that, Sheriff Brody."

"No, ma'am!" He shook his head with conviction. "A week is long enough! My sheriff job ended an hour ago with the election, thank goodness. You can call me anything but that! Well, almost anything...."

A week earlier, on the day that the hay wagon loaded with seven women, three prisoners, Sheriff Branson with seven Deputies, and Sean's crew had rolled into town, the church bell had summoned a town meeting. Twelve random jurors had been chosen from the Tionestans who gathered. Many testimonies had been given, and Andrews had been found guilty of murder, rape and child abuse, among other things. He was hanged that afternoon. Charlie and Mike had been found guilty of kidnapping, looting and overlooking Mr. Andrews' atrocities. They were banished from town and thrown over the bridge into the swollen Allegheny River. Sheriff Branson was found liable for aiding Mr. Andrews and for failing to serve and protect the people of Tionesta. He was banished from town and given the opportunity to take his girlfriend away to her family's farm up north, whenever she was well enough to travel. Brody had been appointed Interim Sheriff, and Pastor Dan and four other people had been assigned as Interim Town Council. The Tionestans were given one week for anyone to campaign who wanted a position in leadership, and today after church service the elections were held with a high voter turnout.

Brody stood and helped Beth Ann up, the little boyish grin on his face again. "We need to go. Darren's over there wearing a path in the grass. He's ready to get home. And we have to let Sean know that he's been elected Mayor!"

Beth Ann lifted her eyebrows. "And...how do you think he's going to take the news?"

"I think we're going to be holding another election real soon!"

They laughed comfortably together as they stalled. Finally, Beth Ann spoke. "Well, I need to get back to the Clinic. Meghan is still having a difficult time, missing Dillon and dealing with her...attack. She's really passionate about caring for the women we rescued and has taken complete charge of them. I told her I would come by and give her a break this afternoon."

Suddenly, Brody stepped in close and cupped her chin gently, bringing his lips to hers. It wasn't fireworks, but rather a deep, bittersweet blend of sorrow and joy, death and life, loss and gain. They said their good-byes and she watched his strong, wide back walk away from her as he met Darren and headed for the retreat.

Beth Ann turned toward the Clinic and sighed with contentment, breathing a prayer of thanksgiving. Even when she had felt like she was alone, she wasn't. The journey was treacherous and dark, but the destination was worth it.

Afterward
By Jonathan Hollerman

If you haven't read *Equipping Modern Patriots: A Story of Survival*, you have no way of knowing that the events in *Alone* are kicked off by an EMP attack on the United States. I don't specify who actually attacks us, as every nuclear nation in the world could easily drive a single nuclear warhead into the Gulf of Mexico on a container ship and take down our electric grid. When it detonates high in the atmosphere over our country, it interacts with the ionosphere to create a series of electromagnetic pulses that reach from coast to coast. Essentially, it fries nearly every device containing modern electronics and microchips, including our massive high voltage transformers. Because our country is serviced by only a handful of electric grids, a chain reaction would be catastrophic.

Here's the thing: This is not a fairy tale. This book, although a fictitious story, is based on a VERY likely scenario that is VERY likely to happen in our lifetime. We know that our electric grid has not been hardened against electromagnetic pulses, and we know that the US has enemies with the technology to pull off an EMP attack.

But an EMP is only one possible scenario for taking out America's electric grid. A direct hit by a large solar flare, which scientists say we are long overdue for, could also overload our fragile grid. A cyber attack may be even more likely, and more imminent. Other realistic threats include pandemic, financial collapse and nuclear or biological warfare. When you add these possibilities up, you get a fairly high percentage of probability that the US will face a national emergency at some point in our near future.

In a grid-down scenario, the government will NOT be able to help you. *Ready.gov* recommends that every household in America have at least three days' worth of food, water, medical, and other supplies stored away in case of an emergency. This is their way of acknowledging that they will not be able to help you right away in any emergency. Think of the horrific looting, pillaging, rapes, and murders following Hurricane Katrina, after only two days without food and water in a relatively small, localized area. What do you think the government will be capable of when the vast majority of the country is paralyzed...for months or even years?

In Hollywood movies, the military often comes to the rescue with food and helps the local police keep order. The truth is that the police, firefighters, US military, and the National Guard will not be able to come to your aid if we lose the electric grid. Ninety-nine percent of the US military is wholly reliant on the civilian electric grid per DOD documents I have on my website. That report is very specific that US forces will not be able to respond to social unrest. You are on your own.

I strongly recommend planning ahead and taking precautions to ensure your family is fed should a collapse scenario come to pass. Do you carry homeowners insurance, car insurance, fire insurance, flood insurance, medical insurance, and life insurance to protect from potential calamity? Do you have a savings account or "rainy day fund" in case you lose your job or face an unexpected financial hardship? Why is putting some extra food and water in your basement to keep your family alive in an emergency considered so irrational?

The fact is, the reason people look down on "preppers" is that they don't see the threat or want to believe it. There is plenty of evidence and reliable information available, but most have never seen it. The people, places, and media sources that most people surround themselves with dictate *what* information is shared and how they *think* and *feel* about the various issues facing our country. If you don't know someone who's into preparedness, your opinions on "preppers" are probably formed by how the craziest extremists are featured in the news and entertainment industry.

Every single client I have ever worked with has been an absolute, down to earth, normal and sane individual. So let's be honest. People's opinions and worries are controlled by a media that TELLS YOU exactly what you should and shouldn't care about. Don't believe me? I can prove it with a single question. Has gun crime been on the rise over the last 20 years or has it decreased? What is absolutely astonishing is that 56% of respondents to the Pew Research study think gun crime is on the rise, while 26% think it has stayed the same, and only 12% think it decreased. The truth: the gun homicide rate has dropped 50% in the last twenty years! Over 82% of people were absolutely wrong in their understanding of gun crime in America! Why? The media and academia have an anti-gun agenda which they have been pushing hard for a long time. It's not like gun violence had dropped a few percentage points over the last twenty years; gun murders were literally cut in half in 20 years and yet nearly 60% of people think it's going up!

The point I'm making doesn't have anything to do with guns, gun control, or gun crime. The point is that the media and academia are capable of completely brainwashing a large percentage of the American population into believing things that are untrue and easily debunked by spending two minutes on Google! Look it up yourself. The gun crime data I just cited comes from a Pew Research study from 2013 titled, "Gun Homicide Rate Down 49% Since 1993 Peak; Public Unaware."

Let's take another example: Cecil the Lion, killed by a hunter in Africa in July 2015. Now it's important to realize that hundreds of lions have been legally killed every year in Africa by trophy hunters and very few people have cared. The media whipped up the entire US population into a frenzy with 24-hours-a-day coverage for a week straight. People organized marches, organizations raised hundreds of thousands of dollars to protect lions, Twitter and Facebook were filled with emotional memes and memorial photos, and the hunter who shot Cecil had to go into hiding with his family, losing his livelihood after receiving numerous credible death threats.

What happened next? Nothing. The next media story came out and suddenly no one cared about the lions in Africa anymore. Everyone was then concerned about terrorism, or the plight of transgenderism, mass shootings, or something some politician said. Don't miss this: The craziest part of the story is that by February 2016, Africa was literally getting ready to kill over 200 lions in a single wildlife reserve because the population of lions had grown completely out of control, not to mention that the reserve was severely suffering from lack of funds. The locals call it "The Cecil Effect."

Preparedness and the risks of societal collapse are nowhere on the list of narratives the news media outlets regularly plug. On November 20, 2014, Admiral Rogers, Commander of US Cyber Command, testified before the Congressional Intelligence Committee that America's critical infrastructure (including the electric grid) is completely vulnerable to attack by multiple enemy nations and groups who currently have the knowledge and the ability to literally "flip the switch" on our electric grid **at any time**. You can watch his testimony on *CSPAN.org*. It will blow your mind that you've never heard of this or the fact that the media didn't feel it was important enough information to tell the American people. Do you know what the major media story was on November 20, 2014? The Supreme

Court affirming same-sex marriages in South Carolina. You have the man in charge of US Cyber Command warning Congress about an **imminent** cyber attack against the US that would result in millions of Americans dying, and the media is more concerned about who is marrying whom in South Carolina.

Frank Gaffney, the President of the Center for Security Policy, had this to say about America losing the electric grid for an extended period of time after an EMP attack: "Within a year of that attack, 9 out of 10 Americans would be dead, because we can't support a population of the present size in urban centers and the like without electricity." Seriously–think of ten people you are close to and try to imagine nine of them dying of starvation or being murdered over the course of a single year.

It is *up to you* to do your own research on these various threats to our way of life because no one else is going to tell you about them. If you need a place to start, I link dozens of supporting documents and videos on my website, *GridDownConsulting.com*.

Please do not be one of the 95% of people unprepared when that day comes: starving, sick, and huddled in the corner of your house wondering when the government is coming to save you. You will discover that no help is on the way, with deadly consequences for you and your family. However, before you make a hasty leap and buy into some monthly long-term food scam thinking you are covered, please educate yourself on what it will really take to make it through a long-term SHTF (S**t Hits The Fan) scenario. It's a lot more than storing up some food in your basement.

So, if you absolutely knew that there was a very real possibility that hard times would come in your lifetime, wouldn't you prepare for them? If you knew that a flood was coming, would you head to higher ground or would you put your faith and trust in our government to come and rescue you? If you heard a tornado off in the distance, would you take cover or continue whatever you were doing? Think of prepping as "Survival Insurance."

My main desire would be that my books help you understand the threat of a SHTF scenario and convince you that putting together a "survival insurance plan" for you and your family is the responsible thing to do. I am not suggesting that you need to drain your savings account, but you could make it part of your monthly budget. Start by getting a couple items each month. If you look at the amount of money you spend on other insurances throughout the year, "Survival Insurance" will be considerably cheaper.

Good luck in your preps and God bless.

Works by Jonathan Hollerman

Equipping Modern Patriots: A Story of Survival (2013)

Equipping Modern Patriots: The Aftermath (2015)

Survival Theory: A Preparedness Guide (2016)

Survival Bug Out: A Guide to Gear and Strategy (DVD)

Contact Mr. Hollerman to find out more about various threats facing our nation and to receive custom preparedness advice at www.GridDownConsulting.com

About the Author

Christina Hollerman has a Master of Education degree, yet she has worn many different professional hats and volunteer tiaras over the last four decades. Her favorites are WIFE and MOTHER.

Ms. Hollerman edited the first two E.M.P. novels by Jonathan Hollerman, former US Air Force S.E.R.E. (Survival, Evasion, Resistance, and Escape) Instructor and Amazon Top-Ten Bestselling Author on preparedness. In the process, she fell in love with educating through story. A voracious reader and a writer since her fairy stories of childhood, she lives and works in western Pennsylvania, where she is active in her church and community, the local playhouse, and two schools.

Ms. Hollerman is delighted to announce that the story in Tionesta will continue with Meghan, to correspond with Jonathan Hollerman's second and third novels in the series. What happens with Brody and Beth Ann? Who is the new Mayor? How does the town recover? Why does the military suddenly show up in nearby Warren? You will definitely want to watch for the sequel.

She'd love to hear from you!
Contact Ms. Hollerman at CMHollerman@gmail.com.